THE CONSTANT SOLDIER

WILLIAM RYAN

The Constant Soldier

First published 2016 by Mantle
This edition published 2023 by Crazy Horse Publishing
ISBN 979-8-409-47757-8
Copyright © William Ryan, 2016, 2022

For Yvonne

The Constant Soldier

The Constant Soldier

1

BRANDT FELT his mother's arms close round him – as if he were still a child. Her embrace was soft. Her breath, cool against his forehead. He could even smell her – milk and warm bread. How he'd ended up back here, in her arms, he didn't know.

He opened his eyes, expecting to see hers looking down at him, her cheeks swelled by her smile, her lips full and rose red – but instead found a stretcher pulled taut by the outline of a man's body, its mottled canvas less than an arm's length above him. The stretcher jerked from side to side as they moved along a rough part of the road. Close by he could hear someone swearing repeatedly, their voice shrill, and, even over the sound of the vehicle's loud engine, he could make out the rumble and thud of artillery shells pursuing them.

It didn't matter though. He knew she was still nearby, cradling him, her skin warm against his. The sunshine turning her hair golden.

All he had to do to see her was shut his eyes.

§

The first time he woke properly, he hoped that he was still dreaming. The waking reality he found himself in wasn't much to his liking. The world he'd visited in his unconscious state was far preferable.

He knew he was awake because the borders of his world were no longer flexible, something he'd become accustomed to. Instead, now, the edges and surfaces that surrounded him were rigid. He was lying down. His body ached – every centimetre of it. A dull, roaring pain. His head was covered with something wrapped tight around his face. A bandage, he thought.

He was on a train, by the sound of it, the wheels revolving to a languid rhythm, each length of track causing a small jolt that swayed the carriage slightly. The movement was soothing.

He opened his eyes, his vision bordered by the white fabric wound around his head. Above him, a canvas stretcher. He remembered grey canvas above him from some time in the past – when, he couldn't say. But not from before whatever had happened to him. This was similar but a different colour – a faded white, smudged and worn. A splash of brown dots that looked like blood. Old blood.

His?

Someone was talking to themselves nearby, a conversation with someone else in which they spoke both parts.

'I won't do it. I won't.'

'You will. You have to.'

'I don't want to. I can't.'

'You have no choice.'

'But why?'

'Why? Such a stupid question. Don't be a child. It's not why but how. How you are going to do it. And that's been decided. All you have to do is follow your orders. To the letter.'

'But I can't. I couldn't.'

'You already have. You just have to do it again. For your comrades. For yourself. For your country.'

The voice was coming from above him, he thought. He wanted to lean out and look up at the person, but he couldn't. Even blinking his eyes was hard. He shut them, suddenly too tired to hold them open any longer.

He would have slept, gone back to the other world. But the dull ache that had held his body tight turned to pain. Extreme pain.

§

He was thirsty. He had been thirsty for a long time, he thought.

'Water.'

His voice – cracked and weak – sounded remote from him. He was still on the train, that was clear – he remembered the antiseptic smell of it. The train was stationary now. It was dark in the carriage and it was hot. Footsteps approached. A young woman, a nurse. Her eyes appeared to glow, despite the lack of light, and her lips were a luminous pink. They glistened.

'What is it?' she whispered, as if, should someone overhear them, they would be in danger. He said nothing.

'What do you want?' she said.

Maybe the Russians were close by.

'Water,' he said, as quietly as he could.

'Water?'

'Yes.'

'All right. I'll get some.'

He watched her leave – wishing she would step more lightly on the wooden floor. She was making too much noise. Didn't she know what would happen if the Russians heard her?

§

Brandt was in a cafe, waiting. On the table in front of him stood a cup of coffee. Its aroma was so rich he could taste it on his tongue. The conversations around him in the long room sounded distorted – as though they were coming to him along a tunnel. The colour of the walls, the carpet, even the lips and eyes of the cafe's customers – all were impossibly vibrant. Perhaps his nervousness had, in some way, altered his perception of his surroundings. Or perhaps it was his mind playing tricks. In this version of the truth he knew the time was five minutes to four. It was Tuesday. And she would arrive at any moment.

The vividness of the cafe, as he recalled it in the dream, did not extend to the two men at the corner table, watching him. They were monochrome shadows around which the cafe gleamed. They were not a part of his memory. He would see them only later but already, even now, he felt the sadness of their presence. In some part of this recollection, even now, he was aware of them having followed him across the city. He was aware of what happened next being his fault. The knowledge made the coffee taste bitter.

In this moment – before the afterwards – it was important that he should be relaxed, that he shouldn't draw attention to himself – or to her. What they were doing was dangerous and others had been arrested already. People he knew. People she knew. Gone now. He looked down at his hand, seeing his fingers tremble as he reached once again for the cup. It was white with a gold rim – the china sparkling in the summer sunlight that flowed through the window and warmed the crisp tablecloth. His nervousness caused it to clink against the saucer, the noise like a drumstick quietly tapping on a cymbal – a jazz rhythm. He breathed deeply, lifting the cup to his mouth, forcing it against his lips, startled by its heat on his tongue.

He was conscious that the dream would end soon. That the ending would be difficult. He already felt the hollowness inside, the guilt at the consequences of his own stupidity. He had known the risks but he'd thought only of her and he'd hurried. He should have slowed, taken his time, doubled back on himself. Then he might have seen the monochrome men.

But before the end – now – she came through to the room he sat in, not seeing anyone else but him. Not seeing the shadow men sitting in their corner, also waiting for her. He rose to kiss her cheek, the startling softness of her hand in his. Neither she, nor he, saw the two men stand. He smiled at her and she smiled back – not noticing the men walking towards them.

Then the men were there, beside them – a thick hand taking Brandt's elbow as the sweat on his neck turned to ice. Squeezing it. Twisting it. He saw her eyes widen in the instant before she was turned towards the wall by the bristle-necked fellow, his shoulders filling his too-tight suit. He remembered the man's yellow eyes and yellow teeth as he snarled something into her ear. Brandt had brought them to where she was like dogs on a lead. He felt the wall hard against his cheek, his captor's breath hot on his neck. It was one minute to four. She'd been early.

The pain woke him. He was grateful for it.

The train had stopped and somewhere, up above them, the drone of aircraft engines filled the night sky.

He could almost remember her smile, before it was wiped away.

It must be the morphine, lowering his resistance. He had managed not to think about her for months now.

§

Brandt could now move his head and was able to examine his surroundings. He was on a hospital train, its length filled with injured men on stretchers, racked in rows on either side of the central aisle. He must have been wounded as well. And that was good news, wasn't it? He was alive. He was no longer at the Front.

He wondered how he'd got here. How long he'd been here. He asked the young nurse when she passed by.

'You were wounded. We're taking you home. You're going to be fine, don't worry.'

She smiled as if she were giving him a gift – anticipating his gratitude.

'Home?'

'Yes,' she said, her smile patient. 'Home.'

He could hear another of the wounded calling for her and caught her glance shift towards the voice, reading in it her decision that the other man could wait.

'Haven't you a mother and father? A place you come from?'

'I do.'

He was as surprised as she was by the tears that filled his eyes. He wanted to explain – about his mother cradling him. About the woman in the cafe. About what had happened to them. About the last five years. Where to begin, though? It was all so complicated. He opened his mouth to speak, but it was too late. She had turned to go to the other man.

When she'd left, he tried to remember what she looked like – whether she'd been the same nurse as the night before. It was difficult – his memory felt liquid. Where there should be something solid – such as a fact, an image or a sensation – there was, instead, a less substantial version of what he sought. The past and present versions of the nurse, if she was the same woman, seemed to merge and then disintegrate whenever he tried to fix them.

Could it be that she was also the woman in the cafe? Her smile was similar. She had the same suppressed radiance. But the woman in the cafe had been eaten up by the yellow-eyed man. Although so had he, hadn't he?

He closed his eyes and heard dogs howling and the crackle of blazing thatch. Another memory – a burning village somewhere to the east that they'd passed through two years earlier.

They'd begun shooting the dogs in the end, the soldiers who were there before them. They'd said it was a kindness, seeing as the villagers were dead already.

§

Another memory, from not long after they had met.

Their hands were wrapped tight inside each other's. They were strolling around a circular pond. As they walked their shoulders touched, as if by accident – but there was nothing accidental about it. He'd found it hard to breathe, he remembered that. It was warm – July, he thought. They hadn't slept at all the night before and he'd wondered, if they let each other go, whether they might just tumble to the ground. Looking back at it, they'd known then how it must end.

'I love you,' he'd said. It was a statement of fact. He hadn't meant to say it out loud. He looked at her, wondering what she might say. He'd had to lean towards her, his cheek touching her cheek, to hear her response.

'I know.'

She carried her own light with her that day – a glow that made each detail of her shimmer even though the sky was overcast. It tore the breath from his lungs when he looked at her. It emptied his mind so that the simplest task was made complex. Each time he was near her he wanted to wrap his arms around her – not to hold her but to protect her. When he was close enough to catch her scent it made him feel drunk.

He smiled at her and, even then, tried to hold the moment within himself – to fix it just as it was. He'd known the memory would be precious in the times to come. And it was just the two of them for that instant. All that surrounded them – the Gestapo, the police, the brutality and the fear – was somewhere else.

Later, in the east, when everything was white and grey and death was never further away than the next moment, he'd tried to bring that morning back to life. But the joy had gone from it. In his memory they'd become mourners, following their own cortège. The war had changed him by then. He'd become a pale, frayed version of himself and the hardness he had accumulated along the way had distorted even the past. She was gone. And he was to blame. And what was the point in thinking about it?

But, still, he had been that other person once. It was something to hold on to, painful as it was.

The man above him died during the night. Quietly, without fuss. He wondered, in his lucid moments, if he was dying also. Then he reminded himself that he'd been dying since the moment he'd been born. That was how life worked. Once you remembered that, everything became easier.

§

He had no idea how long they had been on the train, or where they were. Time was something that had ceased to be tangible. Sometimes it was dark and sometimes it was light. Sometimes the sun was in the sky, sometimes the moon. There was no pattern to it. The orderlies placed his stretcher beside a window and sometimes the nurse opened it a crack, allowing in a freezing current of air that cut like a scalpel through the fug that filled the carriage – the fetid mixture of disinfectant and bodily stench.

The train now travelled through snow-heavy forests and glassy tunnels, across ice-arced bridges and along frozen rivers. It passed white fields that stretched as far as the eye could see, for days on end. At one stage it slowly picked its way through a bombed-out train station – the buildings still smouldering. The snow had melted in blackened circles around them. The smell reminded him of where he'd come from – burned flesh and charred wood. There was no order to the scenery they had passed – he had no idea when or where each image belonged. He hoped they were going west – away from the Front.

He didn't see many people – but that didn't surprise him. There were fewer of them these days. The war had taken so many.

Another moment from the past. A meeting in the apartment of a man he didn't know – possibly a lecturer from the university, although it was not discussed. Someone had asked Brandt to come. A friend. Someone who had known how he felt about the Nazis. The man in the apartment had given them new names. He had been insistent that they must never use their real ones. They must never ask any other member of the group anything about themselves and they must never reveal anything either. It would be better this way. The less they knew about each other, the better.

The man in the apartment took the name Willi. Brandt's new name had been Oskar. The blonde girl, his own age, was Judith. Oskar and Judith. They had been paired together. They would leave the leaflets in public places, where ordinary people might find them and know there were people who still resisted. No one would suspect a young couple.

Not with the swastika pins they would wear in their lapels.

§

The nurse said they were going to a hospital near Hamburg. All the other hospitals were full. Each morning the sun rose behind them and each evening it set ahead of them. And that was good. He'd had enough of the east.

Sometimes they had to wait while other trains passed – going towards where they'd come from. He saw boys looking at the train with round eyes, their uniforms still stiff with newness – their faces framed by windows grey with ice and fog. They were so young. Someone had told him they were calling up sixteen-year-olds now, and these must be some of them. Their pink cheeks had never seen a razor, of that he was sure.

The older men, the pale ones who had been to the Front before, paid no attention to the hospital train – they concentrated on their cigarettes or just looked away. He didn't mind – he would have done the same.

§

Another moment from the past, whenever that had been. A bench outside Willi's apartment building, Brandt sitting beside her. They were early and Willi hadn't put the watering can out onto his balcony yet – the signal that it was safe to come up. It had been a warm afternoon. They decided to enjoy the sun while they waited.

The city was quiet. The only sound he remembered was the rumble of a cart's wheels along the cobbled street and the clip-clop of the horse's lethargic hooves. They didn't hear the door open onto the balcony. They never saw the men drag him out. The first they knew that anything was wrong was Willi's body hitting the pavement – a wet thud. By the time they'd stood up he was nothing more than a crumpled pile of clothing. A widening pool of blood surrounding him. Someone screamed. People ran towards the body. Brandt looked up and saw the two men arguing on Willi's balcony.

Without a word they walked away, her trembling hand holding on to his elbow. By the time they reached the corner, he was almost carrying her. There was a queue outside a cinema and they joined it. A Zarah Leander movie – they'd been planning to go and see it anyway.

In the darkness, they held each other close and after a while they calmed down. Zarah Leander's silver face filled the screen, singing:

I will never regret what I did
and what happened from love

Judith turned to him and brought his ear close to her mouth.

'Take me home.'

And later, while they lay in her bed, holding on to each other in case they might lose one another in its narrow space, she told him her secret.

§

On the last day, not long before the train arrived at a yard filled with ambulances and efficient women, they saw another train – a long line of snow-roofed cattle trucks, halted in a siding to allow them to pass slowly by. The stationary wagons had no windows, only small slits high in their wooden sides from which steam rose into the frozen air. The slits were blocked by rusted iron bars, garlanded with barbed wire. From some of them – not all – thin, blood-streaked hands ignored the wire to reach out, as if looking for something their owners couldn't see. The hands moved like weeds in a turgid sea, slowly, back and forth. And even over the sound of their own train's rolling wheels he could hear the music of the people inside – a groaning dissonance.

On top of one of the cars a guard stood, his rifle slung over his shoulder, his chin buried into a fur-lined coat. He was smoking a cigarette that poked out from his upturned collar, its glowing tip bright against the white of the sky behind him.

At first he didn't seem aware of the train as it slowly passed. But then he looked across, squinting against the flat sun – examining it. His chin coming out of its hiding place so that Brandt could see the kindly eyes and a plump lower lip.

Somehow, they caught each other's eye.

The guard looked across the small space between them and smiled. His teeth were broken and yellow. His eyes glittered. He appeared to be on the point of laughing merrily. The guard's smile grew even wider and then he inclined his head towards the truck beneath him, as if inviting Brandt to look for himself.

Then he winked.

And then he was gone.

2

IT WASN'T CERTAIN how Brandt had been injured. No one else from his unit had been on the train and no one knew anything about him. This wasn't so unusual, it seemed – no one was certain what was happening at the Front these days. That disappointed him. He'd hoped someone had known – that there had been some point to it all.

He'd no memory of the Soviet attack – the one which the other men from the train remembered so clearly. He remembered only that they had been in retreat for months but that they had held the Russians, more or less, at the Dnieper. They'd been hoping for a quiet Christmas – a chance to make sense of things, to dig in deeper. To make themselves a little more comfortable. But the Ivans had only been gathering their strength. He must have been blown up in the early stages of the new offensive – by a shell or a bomb or a rocket. Or maybe all three. Certainly, the doctors spent enough time picking shrapnel out of him, taking him apart, putting him back together. For weeks he lay on his back, seeing the frozen steppe he'd left behind in the cracked white ceiling above him. And, when the morphine took its hold – seeing other things as well.

The months came and went. Easter passed by and, slowly, he became a little more solid – in his own mind at least. He was alive.

He knew he was lucky. The rest of the battalion had been surrounded near Korsun. Some of them must have got out – some always did. But he heard nothing from anyone. Perhaps they had just been swallowed up by the winter snow.

Perhaps he was the last of them.

§

When he was sufficiently recovered to sit outside, and it was warm enough, the nurses found a uniform for him. It wasn't new but he didn't mind that it probably belonged to a dead man – he was long past being squeamish about such things. They ordered duplicates of his combat badges and his medals and a nurse with a permanent frown was kind enough to sew the badges on so that everyone could see he'd done his duty.

An older, one-armed man came and spoke to the patients about his career as a bootmaker, and how having one arm was in many ways an advantage. He spoke with his head bowed, looking at the floor in front of him. They listened politely, understanding his reluctance to meet their gaze.

§

Another time a priest came to visit and sat with Brandt in the gardens, speaking to him about God's infinite wisdom and how his sacrifice might have been for a greater purpose. Brandt let him talk. When, eventually, the priest ran out of words, he turned to him and asked the question that had been in his mind for some time.

'Father, I used to be a soldier – and now I can't be any more. You could say one life has ended and another has begun. How should I live this new life of mine, do you think?'

The priest looked at him in surprise, as if the answer were obvious. As if that was what he had been talking about for the last however long it was.

'Why, in Christ, of course.'

'As a good man, you mean? I should resist evil, then? In all its forms?'

The priest looked uncertain, turning to see if they could be overheard. He opened his mouth to speak, then thought better of it.

'There's no need to say anything, Father. I think I understand.'

The priest didn't stay long after that.

§

Brandt wrote to his father. His father was a medical man, so he spared him none of the details. His father had been a surgeon in the first war so there was little chance of him being shocked by the injuries themselves. Obviously, no one liked such things to happen to their own son, but Brandt was alive, more or less. His father would take comfort from that.

§

The act of writing home brought to mind the pressing dilemma of what to do when he was discharged. The army no longer needed him, they only wanted healthy flesh for the graves to the east, and hammering nails into leather for the rest of his life didn't appeal. He considered picking up the student life that had ended so abruptly – but the thought of returning to Vienna and the university brought with it so many memories and emotions that he soon discarded the idea. There was nothing for him in Vienna. He thought about going somewhere else – a different university – but he was too old now. Not so much in years – twenty-five was still young enough – but in other ways.

If the truth were told, he hadn't much enthusiasm for the life that faced him. Most of the time, the mere thought of another day's existence had him swallowing bile.

Even if he could find a job, he wasn't sure he had the physical or mental strength to move to somewhere he didn't know. Not least because the American and British had bombed the larger German cities to rubble and were now moving on to the smaller ones. The closer the Allies advanced the worse it would become. They'd be bombing hamlets by the time the war ended. Aside from the danger, the destruction meant that finding a place to live would be almost impossible – so many houses had been bombed out that people were camping in the parks in some places, or sleeping in air-raid shelters. In his condition, he needed a roof over his head. And then there was the food problem, the soldiers who knew better told him. The ration wasn't enough and in the cities it was hard to supplement it from other sources if you didn't have connections – and he didn't. Even if he did, it was clear his soldier's pension wouldn't go far.

And then, after all that, there was the likelihood of more bombing.

It wasn't that he was afraid of dying. He was afraid of the pain that might go with another injury, but to a large extent he was reconciled to his mortality. He'd been living in expectation of death for so long he wondered whether, now that he was safe, a part of him missed the fear. Dying, in his experience, was easy enough. And after you were gone, few people cared that much. Not past the first week or so, anyway. They just carried on with their own existence. With his injuries, the likelihood was his future would be difficult – at best, bearable. But it would be, as he'd said to the priest, a new life – something different. He would make the best of it – live virtuously, if such a thing were still possible in a world like this.

He would make amends.

§

So he decided to go back to the village. It was the place where everything had begun, after all.

3

ANOTHER TRAIN JOURNEY. This one to the south-eastern reaches of the Reichsgau of Upper Silesia – to home.

The first train, when it arrived, was full. Brandt's heart sank when he saw the passengers' bodies pressed flat against the windows and the flushed faces of those already crammed into the carriage. He wasn't sure if he was strong enough to push his way on. Nor whether he had the endurance to stand for the six hours this stage of the journey would take. But when the passengers saw him – with his empty sleeve and his still raw, torn, patched-together face – a seat was found for him. It was done quietly, without fuss – and without reference to him.

The strange thing about the whole business was that no one looked at him and no one spoke to him. What discussion could there have been, anyway? You fought, you were broken and now you have returned. So what? At least he got a seat out of it. And when the guard forced her way through, looking for tickets, it turned out he needn't have bought one. Not that he had. The army had been kind enough to send him home, at least.

§

He must have fallen asleep at some point. There wasn't much air in the carriage, it was warm and the rhythm of the train had lulled him. He remembered how his head had become heavy and his eyes had closed of their own accord.

He hadn't dreamed about the woman from the cafe for months – not since they'd stopped giving him morphine, and possibly even before that. Yet here she was, sitting opposite him – in the same train, except it was now empty but for the two of them. She wore a tweed skirt, beneath which her legs were crossed. He could see the shape of her ankle above her shoe, remembered his lips kissing her there

– just there. Remembered how she'd laughed and twisted, claiming she was ticklish there – just there.

He raised his eyes to meet hers. Grey, amused. Her lips, fuller than he remembered, were shaped by a small, secret smile – as if she knew something that he did not. She tilted her head backwards, an appraising angle – her nose raised as if to sniff him out.

He opened his mouth to speak to her – to ask where she had been, what had happened to her. To tell her that there was still a part of him that—. She raised a long finger to her lips to stop his words.

She looked out of the window, at the countryside they passed through. It was different now, he saw. There were bodies in each ploughed furrow – hundreds of naked corpses cluttering the fields.

She turned back to him, shaking her head – a tear rolling down her cheek. He could smell burning flesh.

He awoke with a start. Someone was pushing at his knee. He looked around him, disorientated by all the people who had suddenly appeared in the carriage, by the empty yellow fields the train passed through. He was shivering.

The other passengers looked at him sideways from round eyes and he wondered what he might have said.

§

Germany had seen better days, that much was clear. The cities had been flattened and what was left standing looked as though it stood out of stubbornness alone. The train stations were broken and scarred, the rubble pushed into mounds wherever there was space for it, bricks stacked in incongruously neat piles. Yet, somehow, everything was still carrying on – he couldn't imagine how. No one looked as though they'd slept and only those with Party badges as if they'd eaten recently – and even they didn't look as though it had been more than once or twice. Everyone's clothes seemed to have been handed down from a larger sibling and no one appeared to have the energy to wash any more. But still they stood and still they moved.

At least Dresden was untouched. He spent the time until the next train arrived walking through its narrow streets, overhung by teetering medieval houses and history itself. He found himself in a bar with a mug of weak beer in front of him – no charge for the returning hero – and looked around him – at the other customers, at the people who passed by in the street outside. He wondered if they knew that all of this must come to an end. It didn't seem so. The radio was still spewing out the same rubbish from behind the bar and the newspaper that had been left on the counter for the customers was nonsense from front to back. So no one had told them that the war was lost – that all they were doing in the east was delaying the end. But everyone knew, didn't they? They must know by now.

Back at the station, the train was filled with refugees – mothers and children making their way to the eastern Reichgaus, far away from the Allied bombers – and soldiers with a destination still further east. He wondered if the women knew any safety would only be temporary. The soldiers knew it. He could see it in their blank gazes and the way their mouths pinched tight around their cigarettes. The way they avoided looking at the crippled soldier they shared the carriage with.

Brandt sat back and thought about the village. He hadn't lived there for a long time – and he had changed, of course. But the village had changed as well. For a start it was German now, whereas it had been Polish when he'd left it and Austrian when he'd been born – although that was a different story. When his father had written to him, he'd dropped hints as to what kind of changes had come to pass:
The Glintzmanns have moved away.

He'd an idea what that meant – and it wasn't good news for the Glintzmanns. How many Jews had been living in the village and its surroundings before the war? Brandt could think of six families off the top of his head and he was sure there would have been more. When the peace came, there would be a settling of accounts – of that he was certain. And not just for what had been done to the Jews.

Pavel has come to work for me.

Pavel, his father's old friend, had owned one of the largest farms in the valley. His son, Hubert, had been Brandt's childhood playmate and, more than that, Hubert had been engaged to Brandt's sister before the war. But Pavel and Hubert were Polish and the valley was now part of Germany. Their land must have been given to ethnic Germans from the Balkans or further east – the Volksdeutsche. Otherwise why would Pavel Lensky have come to work for Brandt's father? And what, Brandt wondered, had become of Hubert?

The thing was, he might never have a chance to visit his home again, if he didn't go now. He'd stay for a week or two. Maybe a month. He'd make his peace with his father. He'd visit his mother's grave. He'd see people he hadn't seen for a long time – old friends, relatives.

But the Glintzmanns would be gone, of course. He wouldn't be seeing the Glintzmanns on his visit.

4

THE STATION in the town beneath the valley hadn't
changed, as far as he could see. He looked around him as
the train wheezed to a slow halt. Then made his way
through the carriage to the door. A young woman opened it
for him and passed down his suitcase. He thanked her but
she didn't smile or meet his eye. He was used to that by
now and took no offence.

He remembered the ticket office from before, with its
white wooden panelling and the list of train times displayed
in a brass frame beside its arched window. The last time
he'd been here, his father had bought the ticket to Vienna
from that same window – not knowing the train would end
up taking his son halfway across Russia.

The waiting rooms were the same and the platforms,
turned a warm yellow by the summer sun, were also as his
memory had preserved them – straight, clean and graced by
evenly distanced benches that precisely matched their twins
on the other side of the tracks. They didn't have stations
like this in Russia. Not any more, anyway.

The stationmaster blew her whistle, there was a
whooshing cloud of steam and then the engine began to
move forward, the train squealing and clanking as it
followed it.

It was hot – he put his case down for a moment and
wiped the sweat from his neck with the sleeve of his jacket.

There were differences, of course – not least the fact that
the stationmaster who stood, her flag under her arm,
watching the train disappear, was a woman. He
remembered a stout gentleman with silver buttons and a
white handlebar moustache, the tips stained yellow by
nicotine. He'd been a Pole and the woman was an ethnic
German. From Romania, he thought when she spoke to
him, offering to carry his suitcase.

'No thanks, I can manage it.'

'Are you sure?' she asked, her eyes examining his medals and badges – his empty sleeve.

He nodded. He could manage his suitcase.

'Thank you all the same.'

§

There were no longer any posters in Polish, of course. Not that there had been that many before. This area had always been largely German speaking, even before the war. A more pronounced difference was in the subject matter. Before, the posters had been full of smiling men and women, tins of food, cars and holiday destinations – bright colours and images of happiness. Now they were starker. Soldiers, bombs, aeroplanes, tanks, monstrous enemies and, of course, swastikas. Everywhere swastikas.

'Are you going far?' The stationmaster had followed him along the platform. 'I could ask someone to give you a lift, if you'd like.'

'It's all right, my father is coming. I'll wait outside for him. Thank you again.'

He was surprised his father hadn't been there to meet him off the train, but perhaps he'd been delayed. He walked out into the sunshine of a fine July afternoon, leant back against one of the columns that held up the entrance portico and pulled the packet of cigarettes from the top pocket of his tunic, manoeuvring one into his mouth. The railway woman watched him from inside the station. He watched her in return, wondering what was bothering her. He saw her coming to a decision, then walking towards him.

'Is it all right if I wait here?' he said, deciding to pre-empt her.

'There's a bench to the side. It's in the shade. You'd be happier there.'

Her voice was firm – the kind of voice you might use with a child who needed to be corrected.

He decided to say nothing in response.

After a moment she began to shake her head slowly, placing her hands on her hips. He saw her mouth tightening and it made him smile. He shook his head, equally slowly, also in the negative.

'What do you mean – shaking your head like that at me?'

'You mean the way you're shaking yours at me?'

He wondered if she'd been offended by his not allowing her to carry his bag. Or was it just his standing here? A mutilated, one-armed soldier – perhaps she thought he made the station look untidy?

'Didn't you hear what I said?' she asked, ignoring his question.

He'd had enough of her now.

'I hear you. I see your bench. But it's shaded over there and I need to be in the sun. It's good for my skin, the doctors say. They've ordered me to spend as much time as possible in the sun. Therefore the relationship between me and the sun is a military matter. And as you know – military matters take precedence over civilian concerns until the final victory is achieved.'

She looked at him for a moment, her mouth open. He was impressed as well. He hadn't spoken that many words, all at once, since he'd been injured. He lit his cigarette, closed his eyes and, leaning back against the cast-iron column, allowed the smoke to wash through him. Even through his closed eyelids, the sun was red and hot. Somewhere nearby a bonfire was burning and grass had recently been cut.

He heard the woman grunt, then listened to the sound of her footsteps making their way back into the station. He imagined her angry mouth had shrivelled in on itself. Woe betide anyone who didn't have the right ticket this afternoon.

The satisfaction didn't last long. He felt regret. He'd

promised himself, back in the hospital, to live his life in a certain way. Not like this. He thought about following her and apologizing – but decided against it. She wouldn't take it easily. He could be certain of that. It would only make things worse. No, he should just enjoy his cigarette and the warmth of the sun and forget about the whole thing. That would be best.

So he did.

§

'Paul?'

The tone was uncertain, but he recognized the voice. He opened his eyes and found his father was smaller than he remembered – his face thinner. His black hair was now grey and there was less of it, the mottled skin of his scalp visible through its thin covering. His blue eyes were still clear, though. They were also wary.

'Here I am, Father. Home from the war.'

He saw relief, tinged with a more understandable regret, which his father did his best to hide.

'Good, I'm glad of it. I'm late, of course. And today of all days. It was unavoidable. An Order Police road block. I should have left earlier.'

Brandt shook his head.

'Don't worry – I've been enjoying the sun.'

His father climbed the steps toward him, reached out and touched Brandt's arm with the tips of his fingers, gently, as if concerned he might hurt him if his touch was any heavier.

'It's good to have you back,' he said. 'Thank God you made it through. You don't look so bad, you know. Not so bad at all.'

Brandt couldn't help himself, he laughed. He knew what he looked like. There was no point in pretending otherwise.

His father said nothing in response. He leant down and picked up Brandt's suitcase, his expression grave. He took

Brandt's arm once again to guide him across the road.
'You must be tired. Come on, the buggy is over there. I
can't tell you how happy I am. Monika and Ernst and the
others are at the farm, waiting to see you. It's so good to
have you back.'

His father tried to carry on, but shook his head – unable
to.

Brandt made an effort to smile. He wasn't sure what the
smile would look like, if it would look like anything at all.
Hopefully it would appear agreeable. His father appeared
more vulnerable than before. He wanted to reassure him, to
wash away the harsh sound of his earlier laughter. They
mounted the buggy and sat side by side in silence, his
father unwinding the traces and then flicking the horses
onwards.

There were very few people on the streets as they made
their way through the town and those who were about
showed no interest in them, walking with their heads low,
focussed on the pavement in front of them. They passed the
Party offices, where blood-red flags hung loose, adorned
with spider-like swastikas. His father guided the buggy
through the market, closed today – empty boxes piled
beside empty stalls. The main square was also deserted, the
Catholic church's doors closed. He imagined people
watching them from windows. Eyes following them as the
horses made their way slowly along the road that led out of
the town in the direction of their village. He felt cold, even
though the day was warm.

The outskirts of the town had changed out of all
recognition. Factories stood where open fields had once
rolled. Steam and smoke pumped out of tall chimneys and
the clank of heavy machinery could be heard. They passed
a building site, on which thin men in threadbare uniforms
worked. They spoke to each other in English.

'British prisoners of war,' his father said, in response to

his unvoiced question.

'And them?' Brandt asked, inclining his head towards a column of shaven-headed men, their cheeks hollowed and their eyes shadowed. They wore striped pyjama uniforms. On their breasts were white strips on which were numbers and symbols. Many of them, but not all, had yellow stars. Others had green triangles, some red. Many were barefoot or wore hand-fashioned wooden clogs – some had caps – others didn't. All of them were black with sun and dirt. None of them paid any attention to Brandt and his father. Four bored-looking guards walked alongside the column, SS badges on their collars.

'There's a work camp outside the town,' his father said in a quiet voice, when they had passed. 'The prisoners are assigned to the local factories and farms.'

They passed another factory, and then crossed the river. They turned right onto the gravel road that led up to the valley. It ran alongside the river, farmland rolling away on either side of them into the distance. He could see young men working in the fields, their arms thin but muscled.

'Who are they?'

His father squinted across at them, then shrugged his shoulders.

'Not from the camp. Foreign workers or prisoners of war. They could be Poles – most were sent further east four years ago, but they've brought thousands of them back as labourers now.'

'I remember. So Pavel works for you now?'

His father nodded and spat onto the verge. As if he had a bad taste in his mouth. Brandt couldn't remember him ever having spat in the past.

'He does. It was the only way he could stay in the valley.'

'Thank you for the letters,' Brandt said, changing the subject. 'They were always welcome.'

'And yours. Not so many of them, of course. But I know how war is.'

'I'm sorry.'

'Don't be. You're taller, did you know that?'

'Am I?'

'Ten centimetres, I should think. Or perhaps I'm shorter. And your voice is very different.'

'The injuries weren't only external.' There was a pause in the conversation. Brandt wasn't surprised – in fact, he had expected things to be more awkward than they were. He looked around him, seeing how the surroundings had changed and yet also remained the same. Up ahead the road rose, as did the forested hills on either side of the river, closing in as they did so. Soon they would be shaded by the trees that overhung the road. It was just as well – the heat was making him sleepy.

'How was it?' his father asked when the pause had stretched so long that Brandt had begun to wonder if he might have to say something himself.

'How was what?'

'The last few years, of course.'

Brandt glanced across at his father, who gave him a half-smile.

'Well, I can see it wasn't good,' his father said. 'I may be older but I'm not blind. Is it as bad out there as they say?'

'It's everything they say, and then worse again.'

His father nodded, his suspicions confirmed.

'So you didn't become a believer, then? In all this?'

'A Nazi? Me? No.'

'We thought at first – when you enlisted – that you might have.'

Brandt shook his head.

'I got into some trouble and I was arrested. They gave me a choice – a camp or the Wehrmacht. It wasn't much of a choice.'

There was a long pause. Brandt remembered sitting in the back of the van on the way to the Hotel Metropole – the Gestapo Headquarters in Vienna. The last time he'd seen her. They'd sat facing each other, knee to knee. The Gestapo men had been beside them, talking about a football game they'd been to – ignoring them. He pushed the memory away from him but not before he wished, as always, that he'd leant forward and kissed her, one last time.

'It must have seemed strange,' he said.

'It did. We found out what had happened later on, of course – some of it, anyway. We were proud.'

Brandt felt the temptation to laugh once again, but suppressed it. The idea that his father should be proud of him seemed odd. He took a deep breath.

'It was childish stuff, really,' Brandt said. 'Posters and leaflets. We were students. Naive. We didn't last long before they caught us. I couldn't write and tell you anything, of course. My post was monitored. I had a black mark against my name.'

'We guessed as much.'

Another long pause before his father continued.

'You hear stories about the east and then you see what happens close to home. All the Jews have gone from the village. Every single one of them. And from everywhere around as well. The work camp in the town is bad enough but there's a much bigger camp – further down the river. Everyone knows what goes on there, even if no one speaks of it. And this is Germany, for now at least. It must be even worse out there.'

'It's bad everywhere.'

There was another lengthy silence. He hadn't known there were camps this close to the village, but there seemed to be camps wherever there were Germans. The thought made him sick.

When the silence became oppressive, Brandt took a cigarette from his pocket and lit it. He offered the packet to his father.

'Here, these aren't too bad.'

His father took one, running its length under his nose as though it were a fine cigar.

'I might save it for my pipe. Have you many cigarettes with you?'

His father tried to sound offhand, but he didn't quite convince. Yet another humiliation of the war – to want things so badly that it became necessary to embarrass yourself to obtain them.

'A couple of hundred – I got as many as I could before I left the hospital. Go on, smoke it, you might not get the chance later. That's what we used to say at the Front. Are they hard to come by here?'

'Very hard. There's the black market, but it isn't worth the risk. If I was a member of the Party, then it might be possible, but I'm not and there's Monika to think of. I've got a black mark against my name as well, you know. And they like to make examples of people from time to time, even though they know everyone does it.'

'What kind of black mark?'

'I don't practise any more. When the Jews were still here – well, some of them had been my patients for years. I couldn't just abandon them.'

'They stopped you practising?'

'The mayor advised me to concentrate on the farm. You'll remember him – Weber the baker. He was in the Party from the start – before you even left, I think. Back before the war.'

Brandt remembered Weber. A thick-armed, thick-chested man with unnaturally round eyes and corn-blonde hair. A weak man in a strong body.

'I think he meant well – in fact, I think he intervened on my behalf. He was involved in evicting the Poles but at least he was from around here. He did his best for those he knew – he's turned a blind eye to Pavel for all this time. The Jews we can't speak about – and he was in that up to his neck – but there are far worse than him.'

'All of them are gone?'

'The Jews? All of them. He organized it. He knew where they lived. He led the operation personally.'

'I see,' Brandt said. He felt a shiver run through him and rolled his shoulder to shake it off – but the disquiet stayed with him. He closed his eyes for a moment, the sunshine seeming too bright for his dark thoughts.

'It was Weber who told me about Vienna. About your arrest. At the time, I was frightened for you but it explained some things. At least you did something. I wish I had done more.'

'You did. That's why we both have our black marks.'

His father nodded.

'Maybe I did a very small thing. Not enough.'

Brandt couldn't help but nod. It was the right thing to think – it was what he thought. He'd been given another life, after all. It was tempting to think there might be a reason for it.

'I'm sorry I couldn't come before,' Brandt said. 'I wasn't allowed to for the first three years. Local passes only – two days at most. And by then we were fighting in Russia. After that, whenever my turn came round – and it didn't much – something came up to get in the way of it. They gave the married men priority, naturally – particularly the ones with children. And then there were the Party members, of course. I nearly made it once but then a man in my platoon lost his wife in an air raid. Two children in hospital, so he got my place. And then it was last year and we were surrounded for a week and had to fight our way

out, and after that, well, it was more difficult. I'm sorry.'
His father shook his head in disagreement.

'Your mother understood. She knew you'd have come if
you could.'

Brandt nodded, conscious that he hadn't told the entire
truth. He wondered if his father could tell.

'Things are very different,' his father said. 'Not for the
better. Many people have left. We live in a German village
now, you see. There's no room for non-Germans. And even
the Germans have been thinned out. Just women, children
and old men like me.'

Brandt was glad when another silence developed
between them – not entirely a comfortable one perhaps, but
one that didn't need filling. It was such a peaceful scene –
the perfume of the flowers that lined the verges filled the
air around them. He wanted just to exist for a moment or
two. To let some of the emotion he felt fall away. Perhaps
he was successful in his aim, or perhaps the warmth of the
sun and the rhythmic sway of the buggy combined to have
their effect, but he soon found himself struggling to keep
his eyes open.

Whether he drifted off or not, he couldn't be sure, but he
must have come close. What alerted him, abruptly, was the
change in temperature. He found that he was fully awake,
looking around him for something not quite right. They
were inside the trees now, following the winding road that
ran along the steeply sloped side of the valley. It was
narrow here, and the drop to the river below was almost
vertical. The only noise was the sound of the horse's
hooves and the turning of the buggy's wheels. Brandt found
himself squinting upwards, looking for something or
someone in the dark shadows of the wooded slope to their
right. He had the strong sensation that they were being
watched.

'They don't bother anyone during the day, don't worry,'

his father said.

'Who?'

'Partisans, bandits, people trying to survive. They hide out in the forest around here. The Order Police used to sweep for them – but there aren't enough Order Police left for that now.'

'Partisans? Here?'

'Most certainly here.'

Brandt lit a cigarette and handed another to his father. He stopped scanning the forest. If they were there, there wasn't anything he could do about it. When he finished half the cigarette he stubbed the butt out on his heel, putting it in his pocket.

'For your pipe,' he said when he saw his father looking across at him.

'Thank you.'

They sat, once again silent, listening to the horse's heavy tread. The road levelled off as it turned gently to the left, the trees thinning where the valley widened. Soon they would be able to see the church's spire.

5

SEVERAL HUNDRED years previously, a bridge had been built ahead of them, where the river was calmed by a wide bend in its course. Not long after the bridge had been built, a church had followed and, as the valley here was broad and fertile, a village had grown around it, building by building. Fields had been cleared on the gentle slopes that rose and farm buildings scattered on both sides of the river – right up to the tree line.

The bridge's arches still marched across the river's width but the dam – built further up the valley where it narrowed once again – now carried most of the traffic that would otherwise have come this way. The church's spire still dominated the village's few streets and alleyways and, as they approached, its bell rang out twice, as if in greeting. There were some new houses on the outskirts and some of the older buildings had been re-roofed and spruced up while others had tumbled still further into disrepair. It was even sleepier than Brandt remembered it.

The road took them along the main street, where the butcher's and the bakery still stood, past the police station and the small village hall, then through the church square to the higher valley beyond. The only people they passed were two youngsters in brown shirts and shorts, talking underneath the square's oak tree. The red scarves at their necks marked them out as Hitler Youth. Apart from the boys, who paid them no attention, they saw no one.

'It seems empty without—' Brandt began, but his father interrupted him by raising a hand – nodding in greeting to an older man approaching them along the valley road. It was neatly done. Brandt didn't recognize the man but he returned Brandt's gaze intently, his grey eyes bright in a face dark from the summer sun. They strayed to Brandt's empty sleeve before turning their attention to Brandt's father, nodding in response to his raised hand.

When they were alone on the road that led away from the village, his father finally spoke.

'That was Brunner. A Volksdeutsch from the Ukraine. A Party member.'

Brandt understood.

'I don't come into the village much these days,' his father continued, as if Brunner might be the explanation. 'Monika goes instead, mostly. It's good for her to get out away from the farm – even to here.'

His father was waiting for him to ask a question.

'What happened to Hubert?'

His father sighed.

'He was here for a while – I took him on, of course. He could have stayed and been safe – at least safer than he would have been anywhere else – but then one day he was gone. I didn't ask where he went because it's better that way. But not too far away, I don't think. Perhaps Monika doesn't stay here just to keep me company.' Brandt wondered about his sister, spending her youth in the valley – isolated, by virtue of being German, from much of the terror and loss that surrounded her. Her staying seemed a sensible choice to him. But as for Hubert?

Brandt thought back to the watchers in the forest and wondered if Hubert had been one of them.

The road turned once again, climbing as the valley closed in, trees coming down the slope to run alongside it, so that the buggy travelled in their shade. To their right, far below, he could see the remnants of the old road, built before the dam and made redundant by it. Ahead of them, the dam itself spread across the narrow gap, its buttresses, containing the turbines, spewing water down into a pool from where the new river flowed. The old river, when it had been in the mood, had regularly burst its banks further down its course, inundating the town and flooding the plain. The dam had tamed it, and widened the lake that had always run along the centre of the valley to form a reservoir. Now the dam's turbines powered the factories in the town from which they had just come.

On this side of the dam, the eastern side, men were working with spades and picks, digging out wide and deep trenches on either side of the road that led across the barrier's length. They piled the earth that they were excavating onto the higher side, the water side, creating large banks in front of which the deep ditches ran – ten metres or so in width. Tank traps.

The dam was being fortified. Tumbles of barbed wire ran across the approaches and behind the tank traps. Higher so it would dominate the approaches to the dam, Brandt could see a bunker being built into the side of the slope and, on either side of the road, a zig-zag trench. Someone, somewhere, was expecting the Russians to roll into this valley in the near future. He glanced across at his father, who shrugged his shoulders.

'After all that's happened over the last few years, a price will have to be paid.'

Brandt thought about replying – but what could he say? After all, even if none of this had been their fault – even if they'd done their best – it had been done in their name. And, of course, in Brandt's case, he'd fought in the east – and no one who had fought in Russia could wash their hands of what had happened there.

The dam behind them, the road ran alongside the reservoir, wide and twinkling blue in the sunlight. He considered asking his father to stop for a moment. Perhaps he could cool his feet in its water. But he remembered Monika waiting at home for him and quashed the thought.

There were more young men working in the fields here – some of them wearing worn-out military uniforms. Some were French and British but he heard other accents and languages as well. He saw no Russian prisoners of war but they must be here somewhere. They couldn't all have been murdered.

They turned off the main road, towards the farm. So strong was the sense of home now that it was as if he recognized each rock, each tree and each fence post. He saw thin, dark men in prison pyjamas cutting hay, a guard watching over them – his rifle at the ready. His father answered his unvoiced question.

'There's another work camp at the far end of the valley, to serve the mine. Most of them work in the mine, of course, but some are sent out to the fields if the farmer pays them enough. Not to our farm, I can promise you that.'

The buggy's traces were wrapped around the older man's fists, and when he said the word 'them', he pointed towards a new building, one that Brandt didn't remember, that stood up from the road ahead. It was long and low, more than fifty metres from one end to the other, its wooden walls still crisp with new whitewash. The grassy slope that led down to the road in front of the building was carefully tended – if it weren't for the high barbed-wire fence and deep protective ditch that surrounded it, you might have thought the place was a hotel. Before the war, there had been a military fortification in the same spot, built by the Polish army to defend the dam from the Germans. At first he couldn't see it, but it was still there, partially obscured by a manicured hedge – useless now that the threat was coming from the opposite direction. In front of the hut, on a tall whitewashed pole, an SS flag flew.

'What are they doing here?'

Brandt looked at the building with fresh eyes. Its rustic decoration, the terrace that ran the entire length of the side of the building that overlooked the reservoir, the wooden-tiled roof – all seemed now to have a more sinister aspect to them. And then there was the wire. And the guardhouse.

'It's a rest hut,' his father answered.

But Brandt wasn't listening – he was watching a woman walk down the slope of the hut's lawn, a rake held in her hands. She was thin, painfully so, and the grubby pyjamas she wore were several sizes too large for her, the black vertical stripes like prison bars she could carry around with her. Above her left breast a thin strip of white fabric had been sewn then marked with a hand-drawn red triangle and a number. The woman's hair was little more than fuzz but it might have been blonde, originally. It was too short to be able to tell for certain.

'It's best not to look too closely. They don't take kindly to it.'

An SS man sat on a low wall, further up the hill, his rifle beside him and the top buttons of his tunic undone. He was more interested in the view than Brandt and his father – or indeed the women who were working in the garden. There were six women in total, two with a red triangle on their prison pyjamas, two with a dark blue triangle and two with a yellow star. He had no idea what the triangles indicated, but he knew what the yellow star meant.

The strange thing was that the woman he'd noticed first was familiar to him for some reason.

'What did you say this place was?' Brandt asked, keeping his voice low.

'It's for the SS.'

His father didn't look at him or the building, instead keeping his eyes on the road ahead.

'You said it was a rest hut.'

'I told you there was a place near here. A camp.'

'I see,' Brandt said, and found himself turning to spit. It landed black and wet on the pale dust of the road. He looked back up towards the hut, and found that something about his action had caught her attention.

Their eyes met for an instant but the brief glance felt like a slap. It was as though the world had closed in around him and, for an instant, he was at one end of a tunnel and she at the other. Brandt found that his fingers were digging into the wooden bench. He could feel splinters cutting in under his nails.

He must have made a noise because his father looked over to him, concerned.

'Are you all right?'

'I'm fine,' he said, struggling to find the breath to speak. 'Sometimes there's pain.'

'I'll look at you when we get home. Do you want to stop for a moment?'

The lane that led to their farm was only a few hundred metres further along. He risked a glance over towards the woman but she had turned away. Brandt shook his head.

'No. Let's carry on.'

He was conscious that his words had been growled rather than spoken. It couldn't be her. If it was – wouldn't she be wearing a yellow star?

He took one last look up at the hut. She was raking the grass now, her back to the road. There was something about the way she held herself, even after all these years that removed all doubt.

'Paul?'

'Yes?'

'What are you going to do, now that you're back here?'

Brandt swallowed.

'I plan to make amends,' he said. 'For all of my sins.'

6

BRANDT'S UNCLE ERNST, his mother's brother, helped him down from the buggy when they reached the farm. Ernst was older than he remembered – his round face thinner, as was his hair. There was a welcoming committee. His aunt Ursula, Ernst's wife, pushed forward a small girl and a boy of around six.

'Who are you?' he asked them, looking for fear in their eyes and finding none.

'These are Horst's children – Eva and Johann.'

Brandt tried to remember. Someone must have written to him about them, surely. Horst was Ernst and Ursula's son – the last he'd heard, he'd been stationed in France.

'It's nice to meet you,' he said, and extended his hand. The boy took it but the girl hid in her grandmother's skirt. He didn't blame her – and anyway it was more out of shyness than fright.

'How is Horst?' he asked, and as soon as the words were out of his mouth, knew the answer.

'Horst was killed in Yugoslavia,' his father said in a quiet voice. 'In March of last year. I sent you a letter.'

'I'm sorry,' he said. 'Sometimes the post didn't get through. If I'd have known, I would have written.'

Ernst smiled reassuringly and the children didn't seem to have noticed. Their mother died in childbirth with the girl so Horst's death had made them orphans. All they had in the world were their grandparents. He felt tears itch at the corners of his eyes. He reached out to ruffle the boy's hair.

'Your father was a fine man,' Brandt said. 'A hero.'

'And here is Monika,' someone said, but by now his legs were slowly giving way. He reached for something to support his weight and felt strong hands take his arm.

'I'm sorry,' he said and saw their concerned faces as if through a fog. He did his best to smile. Monika was there, he was sure of it. At one stage he thought he saw his mother, but that was when he was being helped upstairs and the house was swirling around him and he was so cold that his body shivered at the touch of their warm hands.

He could hear someone – it sounded like him – repeating Judith's name. The exhaustion went deep inside him, to the very marrow of his bones – but even that couldn't account for the tears that ran down his frozen cheeks.

§

Perhaps his father looked in on him during the next day, he couldn't be sure, but if he did, he didn't wake him. And so, as it turned out, he slept for nearly a day and a half, managing to ignore the sunlight slipping through the shutters, the sounds from the yard beneath his window and the dull pain of his own battered body.

§

When he eventually awoke Brandt made his way, barefoot, down the wooden stairs, worn dark by hundreds of years of other feet making the same short journey. His father sat at the kitchen table, a newspaper open in front of him, its wartime paper yellow in the light from the window.

Sleep and the strangeness of his surroundings, familiar and yet unfamiliar, had left Brandt disoriented.

'What time is it?'

'It's the morning still, just past eight o'clock. A day later than you think perhaps.'

'I slept for that long?'

'You were tired and you're not fully recovered from your injuries – sleep is good medicine. And cheap.'

His place was set on the long table. The place he'd always sat at when he was a boy – beside his father and across from his mother. There was bread, butter, cheese and jam – a jug of creamy milk. A feast.

'Is this your work?'

'Monika's,' his father said, stuffing his pipe with

cigarette tobacco.

'Is she here?'

'It's good to have you back, Paul.'

He turned to see a woman he barely recognized, standing in the doorway. The Monika he remembered had been nineteen years old when he left, bookish and pale. This Monika was older, tanned, with bobbed brown hair. Her smile was open and if she noticed his injuries, she gave no sign of it.

'Monika?'

She laughed and stepped forward to embrace him.

'We've both changed a little bit.'

He couldn't remember the last time anyone had held him. He found that his face was hot.

'You'd better sit down,' she said, smiling at him once again. He was pleased to see that her teeth weren't quite straight.

'I think I'd better,' he said, and did as he was told.

§

Another two days passed before Brandt put on an old pair of trousers, for which he needed a belt, and a jacket that, in contrast, was too narrow for him now. He hadn't worn civilian clothes, not once, since he'd left Vienna for the training barracks. He put on his military boots – heavier than he remembered – and made his way down the stairs and out into the yard. He listened – no one was about. It wasn't that he didn't want to see anyone – he just didn't want them to stop him. They would only say he wasn't strong enough to go outside but he couldn't wait any longer.

His path, each step of which he'd gone over in his mind a hundred times, led him past the SS hut. He walked slowly, not because he was tired, but because he wanted to be consistent. He didn't know if one of the guards might be watching him as he approached, and he wanted to take his time when he reached the hut, so a constant pace made sense.

When he reached the fenced garden, she was nowhere to be seen. It was all right, he decided, he would be patient. If nothing else, he had time. Perhaps he would see her on the way back.

The walk up from the reservoir was harder. He stopped more than once to gather his strength, sitting at the side of the road, watching the workers in the fields and listening to the hum of insects around him. Before the war, there would have been the sound of farm machinery from somewhere in the valley – but not now, when there was barely petrol enough to keep the tanks moving. He stopped for a moment once again outside the hut. He glanced around to see if she was there, but saw no one, then turned to look across the water towards the forested upper slopes of the other side of the valley. It was a view you might put on a picture postcard – he could understand why they'd chosen this place.

He fell into the habit of going for a walk in the morning and in the evening, and each time his path led him past the hut. He was careful, he hoped. He didn't stare. But he paid attention whenever his gaze found its way up to the hillside on which the hut sat – and he took note of what he saw.

The main building, whitewashed with a pitched roof, was surrounded by a long wooden terrace, which ran round the three sides that were visible from the road. Often he saw officers sitting in deckchairs taking the sun, or sitting in the shade provided by two cream awnings that were rolled down when the sun was stronger than usual. There were window boxes bursting with bright flowers. The building had been carefully modelled to look like some pre-war holiday camp.

But it was not a normal place. He doubted that many passing vacationers would mistake it for a welcoming spot to rest their head for the night, even if the SS flag hadn't flown above it.

It was surrounded by two high barbed-wire fences, one inside the other, and the gate, up a steep lane from the main road, was protected by a double-height concrete pillbox which, along with a smaller wooden one on the other side of the hut, covered the fences as well. Because of the hut's raised position, there was not a centimetre of the enclosed perimeter that was not within sight of one of the guard towers. And when Brandt looked closer at the hut, he noticed how thick the oak window shutters were, backed with iron sheeting that had been decorated with scrolling – and rifle slits.

The hut also had a presence, which he found disconcerting. Even when no one was visible, as he passed, he had the feeling that he was being watched from within – or perhaps by the building itself. There was something in that – the place made the back of his neck feel cold, even with the sun doing its best to warm it.

Of course, the person he really wanted to see was the woman with the red triangle.

What if it was her? What if it wasn't? If it was her, he'd have to do something. He had no choice.

And then it occurred to him that even if it wasn't her – he should do something. He had a debt that needed to be repaid.

There were wrongs he needed to right.

7

'BE CAREFUL when you pass that place,' his father said
to him one evening, his voice low. 'I saw you today,
looking up at it. They could shoot you – just for that.'

Brandt nodded – it was the simplest thing to do. It wasn't
a discussion he wanted to let run on.

'I didn't realize – I'll be more careful, don't worry.'

His father held Brandt's eyes for a moment longer than
was comfortable. As if he had a question that he would like
to have answered but was not quite ready to ask.

Monika leaned forward, reaching a hand across the table
towards him.

'You have to understand – there are no restraints on the
SS here. They can do whatever they want. It's best to avoid
the place as much as possible.'

Brandt had to admit they had a point. There was no sense
in getting shot for no good reason. But he might have a
solution.

After they'd eaten, Brandt went to his bedroom and took
his uniform from the wardrobe. He considered the insignia
of his former rank, the badges and medal ribbons he'd been
awarded for his service. He no longer wanted anything to
do with what the tunic represented – but even the SS would
think twice before shooting someone wearing it.

The next day he wore it on his morning walk, taking the
roundabout route that went above and behind the hut before
coming down to it along the narrow lane that ran past its
main gate. It was only when he was walking in the forest's
cool shade that he remembered it wasn't only the SS he
needed to be worried about. He looked around him, at the
shadows and the brush that ran close to the path. For all he
knew, up here where few people lived or visited, there
might be a partisan tracking his progress through the sights
of his rifle at this very moment. He could be dead before he

heard the shot fired. He would keep to the lower, more travelled roads, he decided, when next going out for a walk dressed as a soldier.

As it turned out, the only person he met was Pavel with a wagonload of hay from one of the higher meadows. They hadn't spoken since he'd returned, which wasn't surprising, given, Brandt remembered, he was still enlisted in the army of the oppressors who had taken his farm and forced his son from the valley. Pavel looked through him as though he wasn't there and Brandt shrugged. What was there to be said? That he was sorry? Saying sorry meant little without action to back it up.

In the evening, Brandt went out again, although this time he decided to take the road that led towards the dam, directly past the hut. It was busy at this time of day – with farmers returning from their fields and workers returning from their work. He was passed by a line of British prisoners, making their way to the POW camp near the town from the farms where they worked during the day. He caught their sideways glances as they noticed his tunic and his missing arm. He wondered if they thought themselves lucky to be here and not fighting in France, where such things could happen to a man.

Brandt had forty-one cigarettes remaining from those he'd brought home and he'd decided to give the last forty to his father for his pipe – he'd left them on his desk with a note. Now he took the remaining one – the last one – from his pocket. He wouldn't light it just yet – he'd let it hang from his mouth and inhale the tobacco's aroma for a minute or two. Then he'd light it. And when it was finished, well, perhaps the village shop would have some next week.

He didn't see the two men until he was right beside them. They were standing in the shadow of a tree – and he was, as usual, looking into the hut's garden for a sign of the woman. The first he knew of their presence was when the mayor called out to him.

'Paul Brandt? How are you?'

Weber the baker had done well for himself – despite the heat he wore a wide-lapelled grey suit with a Party badge in its buttonhole. The suit looked as if it had been made for him. He also looked plumper than before, his round cheeks rounded still further by his smile. Beside him stood an SS officer, shirtsleeves rolled up above the elbow and a forage cap tilted forward so that it touched his left eyebrow. He was tall, slim, late forties – a pale face despite the summer weather. The men were physical opposites – long and thin, short and round.

'I'm well, thank you, Mayor Weber. I hope the same is true for you.' Brandt was conscious of the cigarette in the corner of his mouth. He removed it. 'Excuse me. My last one. I was contemplating it.'

The mayor's smile widened and Brandt couldn't help but feel that the fact he was down to his last cigarette pleased the man.

'I was looking for you, as it happens, Paul. But let me introduce you to Obersturmführer Neumann. He commands the SS rest hut here.'

Weber pointed over his shoulder towards the hut. Brandt found himself stiffening to attention. It was natural. He had been a civilian for only a matter of days, after all, and Neumann was an officer.

'Obersturmführer.'

'Paul here is the local hero, Obersturmführer Neumann. He fought on the Eastern Front, you know. Before . . .'

'Well, let's just say that some of me is still there,' Brandt said, and felt the stretching of scar tissue that came with his smile these days. He decided it would be as well if this Neumann fellow had a good impression of him.

'I can see you served the Fatherland well,' Neumann said. At first Brandt thought he was talking about his arm, but then he saw he was looking at the combat badges and the medal ribbons.

'The Tank Destruction Badge in Silver,' Weber said, as proudly as if he'd been awarded it himself, 'A real tank-killer, our Paul. The Iron Cross first class, the Infantry Assault Badge in Silver. And what else?'

'The Wound Badge in Gold. Probably not necessary – the empty sleeve tells its own story.'

Neumann got the joke, even if it passed Weber by. Brandt decided to light the cigarette – he might as well.

'Do you mind?' he asked Neumann, who nodded – reaching inside his pocket for his own cigarettes.

Weber's forehead was lined with a sincere frown.

'It's inspiring for the people, to have a real hero amongst them.'

'I'll take your word for it.'

'Everyone knows all about you, Paul – we kept them informed. The Party, that is. Which is why I was looking for you, as it happens. I have responsibility for the Hitler Youth in the village. Their heart is in the right place, of course, but they need to be prepared. For when their time comes. The right man could teach them a lot.'

Brandt nodded, as if Weber's suggestion was an attractive proposition. He tried not to think of the smooth-chinned boys he'd seen on the train heading east. He didn't want to have any part in sending more young men to die in a lost war.

'I'm still recuperating, Herr Weber. And even if I weren't, I might not be the best advertisement for a soldier's life.'

Weber smiled warmly, reaching forward to put his hand on Brandt's shoulder. The man's touch irritated Brandt.

'If it were up to me, Paul, I'd say: *Absolutely. If anyone has done enough – it's Paul Brandt.* But I must ask you to give still more in the struggle towards our final victory. If

you can walk up and down this road several times a day –
and I've seen you do it – then you can talk to a group of
youngsters once or twice a week, I'm sure. Of course, I
should be clear that your loyalty isn't in question, and nor
is your father's – it's just that at this stage of the struggle,
the Party has to ask for a little more from everyone.'

Brandt raised an eyebrow at the mention of his father. If
it wasn't a threat, then it was a strange thing to say.

'So what do you think, Paul?'

Brandt considered the proposal, but not for long. There
was no choice – that had been made clear.

'When you put it like that – I am, of course, happy to
give still more towards the final victory, Herr Weber,' he
said, then gave what he hoped was a good impression of a
smile. 'Which piece of me do you think you'll want this
time?'

There was a moment's silence, during which Weber
turned to Neumann, his face distorted by indecision,
somewhere between a smile and a scowl, turning to relief
when the SS man began to laugh. It wasn't a joyous laugh
but then it wasn't a joyous joke. Weber joined in, his eyes
gleaming with moisture. He laughed a little too hard, in
Brandt's opinion – as if he might not have understood the
humour. Neumann had, of course. Brandt had hoped he
would.

'That's good,' Weber said at last, drying his eyes with a
knuckle.

'I was looking for something to do, as it happens. To
pass the time,' Brandt said. 'Does the position come with a
cigarette ration?'

'A cigarette ration?' The mayor's features rearranged
themselves to assume an expression of disappointment –
even if Brandt suspected the disappointment was going to
be felt by Brandt rather than the mayor. 'It's only a couple
of evenings a week – but I can see what might be done.'

'My last one,' Brandt reminded him, holding up the stub that was left of it. The tip was close to his fingers, hot enough to hurt. He inhaled one final time, the burn scouring the back of his throat, and threw it away. All good things must come to an end, even things that weren't so good.

Brandt saw the SS man glance across at the mayor and had the impression that a silent question was being asked. Weber shrugged in response. For a moment Brandt considered stooping to pick up the butt in case he'd broken some rule or other.

'You said you were looking for something to do – a job perhaps?' Neumann asked.

'I might be.'

'It's only that Neumann needs someone up at the rest hut,' the mayor said, pushing his jacket back behind his hips, slipping his thumbs into his belt.

'A steward, of sorts. We were just discussing it. Not with you in mind, of course.'

'A steward?' Brandt asked, looking up at the hut and not quite believing his ears.

Neumann reached into his tunic pocket and withdrew a silver cigarette case. It gleamed.

'It's a simple enough role, Brandt. Your job would be to make things run smoothly. The physical work is already taken care of. We've had SS men as orderlies up until now – but they have been transferred to more active roles.'

By which, Brandt decided, he meant that the orderlies were up to their ankles in their own shit in some foxhole at the Front.

'By whom?' Brandt asked. 'Is the physical work done, that is.'

'By prisoners. Female prisoners.'

Neumann offered the cigarette case to him. Brandt took one and the mayor's hand appeared between them, its fingers curled around a lighter.

'I am still building up my strength. I wasn't being misleading on that.'

'I understand. You could start off a few afternoons a week – an evening here and there. There's a shortage of available men around here, of course, and a woman wouldn't be suitable. If you were interested, we would be patient. You could take on as much work as you were able, until you recover your health.'

Brandt looked through the trees at the nearest guard tower.

'You say it's a rest hut and you say a woman wouldn't be suitable. If you don't mind my asking – what kind of rest activities are on offer?'

Neumann's easy smile tightened momentarily before it relaxed again.

'It's not a brothel, if that's what you mean. It's just a place where officers come for a day or two, sometimes longer if they're recovering from injuries. They talk, they sing, they do nothing. Whatever suits them, they do. They can swim in the reservoir, go walking – it's a rest from the stresses of the war. Much needed, for some of them. They drink. Sometimes a lot. A woman might make them feel restrained.'

Unless she was a female prisoner, of course.

'Walking?' Brandt said, aloud. 'In the forest?'

Neumann smiled.

'Not so much these days. The partisans are more active than they were.'

'It would be good for you, Paul.' The mayor nodded in the direction of the hut. 'It's a very pleasant atmosphere. And it could be combined with your Hitler Youth duties, I should think.'

'Of course,' Neumann said, nodding. 'I would see to it that you were available when you were needed. It's light work – I'm sure you could manage it. But, if not, then we wouldn't hold you to the commitment. Well, are you interested?'

'And the pay?'

'We'll talk about it. More than you received from the army, anyway. Oh – and cigarettes, of course. The hut is well provided for. I'll make sure you receive a sensible ration. Generous, even. There will be other benefits, along the same lines. We aren't skinflints.'

Brandt contemplated the cigarette Neumann had already given him. It wasn't bad. A nice smoke.

'Is there a pension?'

The mayor looked as if he'd swallowed something unpleasant and Brandt thought, for a moment, that he might have gone too far. But Neumann was made of sterner stuff.

'If you see out the first twelve months, we'll talk.'

His tone was dry as dust – but Brandt couldn't help but laugh. In twelve months' time they would all most probably be dead, or in a Russian gulag. Neumann smiled – they understood each other.

He wasn't sure how he was going to explain taking the job to his father, but he wasn't going to sell his soul for a packet of cigarettes just yet. He'd wanted to get close to the woman and this was the opportunity he'd been looking for.

'When do I start?'

8

NEUMANN watched Brandt leave, his tunic loose around
his shoulders, one sleeve folded up to the elbow. There was
no reason to feel proud, but he did feel a little pleased with
himself. Of course, giving the man the job had been no
more than his duty as a decent German. He was sure that
behind Brandt's scarred face he was the same decent sort
he'd always been. Perhaps not exactly the same – these
things changed a man – but similar in many ways, at least.

The mayor interrupted Neumann's thoughts with a
cough. Neumann waited. He knew this cough. The mayor
was preparing to ask something of him. He wondered what
it would be this time.

'He's not a bad fellow, Brandt,' the mayor said. 'His
humour may be a little different than we're used to here –
but he is only just back from the Front. It was the same in
the first war. We always had that black humour. It's
understandable, I suppose.'

Neumann examined the mayor. It was clear he was
regretting his endorsement of the cripple. There was a
sheen of sweat on his brow and his mouth looked unsteady,
uncertain whether to smile or scowl. The man was nervous.
He needn't be, for once.

'He's a soldier who has given his all for his country. I'm
certain he'll fill the role more than adequately. If not, he
will be let go. It needn't concern you. I won't hold you
responsible, if that's what you're concerned about.'

The mayor relaxed, and his mouth risked a crooked
smile.

'I'm pleased to hear you say it. That you're sure about
him.'

Neumann didn't necessarily want to smile, but the man
needed reassurance. It would be unkind not to.

'Was there anything else we needed to discuss?'

Brandt had arrived in the middle of a conversation about the local farms' need for labour to bring in their crops. Weber wanted additional workers from the camp – an extension to the arrangement they'd already reached. Neumann didn't think it would be a problem but there would have to be something in exchange.

'You'll do what you can for us?'

'I'll talk to the Commandant. There is a possibility – I can't say any more than that. There will be some logistical problems.'

'If it's a question of payment.'

'I understand – you are happy to pay the organization.'

'We'll pay whoever we have to – just to make it clear. I could mention a figure.'

As bribes went, it wasn't too bad an effort and the Commandant wasn't averse to such things. Not averse at all. But Neumann didn't deal with bribes – Schlosser did.

'I'll let the Commandant know. I'm sure Obersturmführer Schlosser will be in touch.'

'We are in real need – if you could suggest anything that might sway the Commandant's mind in our favour.'

What was he going to offer now? The farmers' womenfolk, perhaps? Their firstborn children?

'It's not always easy to obtain dairy products, for example – we could help with those. There will be other things our people can provide to the hut and to the camp as well. Over and above what we contribute already. All the Commandant has to do is ask. We have to get the harvest in, you see. Soon. We need the manpower. Urgently.'

'Schlosser will call you this evening, Herr Weber. I feel certain the response from the Commandant will be positive. Particularly in light of your previous generosity.'

Weber's smile was like a small boy's – joyful almost. He said his farewells, made the customary salutes and protestations of loyalty to the leader to whom they must all

be loyal and then marched off down the lane, shoulders
widening as his confidence returned. Neumann knew how
the scheme worked – the farmers paid the mayor, the
mayor paid Schlosser and Schlosser made sure the
Commandant was taken care of. If there was enough money
involved some of it might even be sent to Berlin. Everyone
would be happy – except the prisoners, of course.

Neumann's fingers went to the twin silver shapes on his
collar. They were smooth to the touch. The source of his
authority. If it weren't for the runes, of course, Weber
wouldn't fear him. But they worked as a disguise as much
as anything. A way for the world to perceive the wearer and
one that was often quite different from the truth. The fact
was Neumann felt more and more, with each day that
passed, like an impostor. There was more similarity
between him and Brandt than the mayor knew.

There was a rustle in the bushes behind him. The sound
of a body thrusting itself through the low-lying vegetation,
brittle leaves crunching under a paw. He held out his hand
and Wolf came to him, his wet nose pushing at his
fingertips.

'Good boy.'

The dog sensed his mood and pushed once again – he
looked down at the hooded almond eyes, intense with
devotion, the tongue pink against the white teeth.

'Come on, then. We'll go to the reservoir.'

The dog understood him, he thought. Understood when
each step, however brisk and efficient Neumann might
force it to be, felt like it forced its way through sand.

§

Brandt found that he was whistling. It wasn't a cheery tune
or even recognizable as a particular piece of music. His lips
were no longer full enough or soft enough for that and he
was out of practice. Whistling wasn't something he'd done
for a very long time. A passerby might think he was

pleased with himself, but he wasn't. After all, tomorrow morning he would be going to work for the SS and he would also find out for certain whether the woman was who he thought she was. Tomorrow was likely to be a difficult day. Yet, all the same, here he was, whistling.

He wondered why.

9

IT WAS QUIET in the bunker. The walls were a metre thick and made from reinforced concrete and, beyond the walls – beside them and above them – was half a hillside of earth. The solitary door was steel and so heavy it had wheels to bear its weight – which, no matter how much oil was used to smooth their turning, squealed when it was opened.

Some sounds did reach them, however – the firing slits hadn't been fully sealed when the Germans had decided the bunker could be as easily used to keep people in as it could to keep them out. And there was a tiny barred window in the door. So they listened, even in their sleep, to the faint echoes of the world outside. And whatever they heard they did their best to decipher. After all, one word could mean the difference between life and death to existences as precariously balanced as theirs.

There were only six of them left now: the two German women, Joanna the Pole, and the two Jewish sisters – Lena and Rachel.

And her.

Six of them living in what had been the sleeping quarters for twenty Polish soldiers sometime before the war and three times as many again when the building crew had been quartered here during the hut's construction. They should consider themselves lucky, to have so much space. But the winter was coming and they would feel the cold with only a few thin bodies to warm it.

Six women were all that were needed to serve the hut now and they would have to make do with five soon. Lena was close to the end. They all knew it. Lena didn't, but then Lena was past the point of knowing anything very much.

The women occupied the corner of the room beside the door where they'd pushed the last two good bunks together.

Most of the bunks on which the building crew had slept in had now been reduced to skeletal outlines, the wooden bases taken by the guards for firewood, leaving only the metal frames. They slept across the two intact bunks like a row of tinned fish. Even in the summer, the bunker was cool at night and, sleeping close, they shared their warmth. In the winter, they would have to huddle closer still. It had been so cold some nights the last winter, they'd been afraid they wouldn't wake at all.

Now they stood, just inside the door, listening to the guards – two guards – approaching along the path from the hut, their heels sounding heavy on the stone path. Another sound – the soft patter of a guard dog walking beside them. And when they came to a halt outside, the swish of its tail against a leather boot. They listened. They made a picture in their minds. They studied the picture for any change to the routine.

Now the guards would wait outside, talking in Ukrainian about this and that, until Peichl came – the German Scharführer. If they were lucky, it wouldn't be the NCO but the officer – Neumann.

Once either Peichl or Neumann arrived, and not before, the guards would open the door and line them up outside. If it was Peichl, he would insist on the line being absolutely straight before he would even consider counting them. It was, of course, impossible to ensure that none of them had tunnelled through the concrete walls overnight if the line was crooked. If it was Neumann, he would look them over for an instant, say, 'Very good,' and send them about their business. If it was Neumann, she would be happy.

Peichl was different. He must have been an insignificant person before the war – ordered hither and thither by his superiors, smiling and bowing as he went, while underneath he'd raged. And then the war had come and he had found himself in a place where rage and stupidity were cherished values and he was the one who gave the orders. She imagined he lulled himself to sleep each night thinking about the power he held over them and what he could do with it. There had been twelve of them in the spring.

She stopped herself. Anger had a way of showing. She must appear compliant and uncomplaining. She must be invisible. She found herself involuntarily smiling, as if to perfect the necessary ingratiation. She felt her chapped lips crack as she did so, surprised by the effort it involved, at how the muscles in her cheeks resisted the attempt. Anyway, to smile would be unusual – and she mustn't do anything unusual. But what if one of them made a joke or passed a pleasant comment? It happened sometimes. As a political prisoner, as a German, at least in their eyes, she was different from Joanna and the Jewish women. Obersturmführer Neumann, for example, would sometimes speak politely to her, even attempt a conversation. She wasn't trusted the way Katerina and Gertrud were, of course – the Bible students – but she was in a different category, an Aryan category. The wrong category, as it happened. She looked across at Lena, at the small yellow star beside her prisoner number. She shook herself. She must never think about that. She must hide it even from herself.

She looked at the others. The hazy light from the small window in the door softened their gaunt features. Gertrud and Katerina stood closest, their hands clasped and their mouths moving as they prayed. Gertrud's white hair was pulled back tightly. Her eyes were downcast but she knew they were the clearest, palest blue. She looked like someone's grandmother. As she was, or had been. Gertrud had been in the camps nearly as long as she had, and yet her face was unmarked by the experience. Gertrud would come through all of this – she was sure of it.

She caught Rachel's gaze – her face drawn and pale. She

knew she was asking for her help. But there was nothing anyone could do for Lena now. They'd done what they could. It was possible to help another person here in the hut – it was possible to help out with another prisoner's work, and they were hungry but they weren't starving. But Lena was too far gone now. Lena – her face grey, her eyes lifeless – only stood because Rachel held her. She found herself shaking her head. She looked away.

She understood love. She understood why Rachel held her. She understood why she would hold her until it was no longer possible to. But she also understood that soon Lena would fall and she would not get up again. She had been ill for months and the Germans hadn't treated her and so she had steadily declined. There had been nothing that any of them could do about it – not even Rachel.

If Lena could just keep going for a little longer, all this would come to an end. She could be free. She could die in her own bed, of old age – happy to go, most likely. Perhaps there was still a chance for her. She glanced across at the young woman. Lena hadn't the strength to hold her head up straight.

There was a pause in the conversation outside. The guards shuffled their feet to attention. Heavy boots stamped down the wooden steps of the hut. The owner walked with the bow-legged gait of a cavalryman – you could hear the shape of his legs in his ungainly march. She felt her breath shorten.

Peichl.

'Open it up,' Peichl called as he approached. He was annoyed. With who or what, it was impossible to say. She filled her lungs with air and let it slowly out. There was nothing to be done except to calm herself. She mustn't show fear.

The key scraped into the lock and she recognized Evanko from the grunt of effort he made as he turned it.

Evanko was one of the older guards – in his mid thirties – a worried frown, perpetually in place – not as dangerous as the others. She had to squint her eyes against the brightness of the morning. Then they were moving, quickly as they could, their clogs clipping over the concrete as they filed out to stand in the expected line. She listened to Lena coming along behind her. She was moving, she still had a chance.

Peichl looked them over while Adamik – barely out of his teens and pretty as a girl – went through the list. He called out their numbers, waited for their answer, checked the number on the front of their blouses – ticking them off in the log book. Lena's voice was faint but she answered. Maybe, just maybe, she would last one more day.

The last name was called. All present. No tunnellers. Peichl took the register from the guard and read it through, as if memorizing each name.

'Prisoner Müller,' he said, eventually.

Katerina, the younger of the two Bible students, stepped forward. She had square shoulders, a frame that had once carried more weight. The camps had aged her but she was still strong. Peichl smiled.

'Did you sleep well, Prisoner?'

'No, Scharführer.'

His smile broadened.

'Why not? Do you think we should provide you with a feather bed? Would you like more blankets? Crisp white sheets, perhaps.'

Katerina didn't answer. The Bible students had a leeway with the SS that no one else had. They could renounce their opposition to the war at any time and walk away from the camp – or so the SS said. The fact that they didn't gave them a power of sorts. And they were needed. They could be trusted not to kill them when they cooked their food. They followed the Lord's Commandments even if no one else did.

'You're here to be punished, aren't you? It shouldn't be comfortable, should it?'

'It isn't my place to decide such matters, Scharführer.'

She found her hands had clenched into fists, anticipating Peichl's reaction. But he said nothing, only smiled more broadly. The smile didn't reach his eyes, however.

'That's correct, Prisoner – it is good that you know your place. Now that your God has forsaken you.'

'I have been brought here to be punished for my faith, Scharführer. The torments I face are torments inflicted by you, not by him. If our Lord Jesus faced death on a cross for me, then I will face your punishments for him.'

Peichl's laugh was hollow, she thought. She wondered if he would stay faithful to his beliefs when they came to punish him. Of course not. He wasn't brave, she was certain of it. She knew something about courage.

'What was said last night? Amongst you prisoners.'

'Nothing, Scharführer.'

'I asked what was said. Answer me precisely. Remember you must tell me the truth.'

She kept her gaze on the gravel at her feet and waited for the answer. She felt the same terror she felt every morning. What if she had said something in her sleep?

'Nothing. The other prisoners know you ask us each morning what was said the night before and they know we cannot lie. So they say nothing. And so we hear nothing.'

'But you know things. Secret things. What secrets have you for me this morning?'

'I know the secret of Our Lord's love for each man and each woman amongst us.'

Peichl laughed. This time the amusement wasn't feigned.

'Even me?'

'Even you, Scharführer.'

'What other secrets do you know? About the other

prisoners?'

'I know no secrets. I know nothing which isn't already known to you.'

She had once thought Katerina was slow – perhaps even stupid – but she didn't think that any more.

'What secrets do I know?' Peichl asked.

'If I knew, surely they wouldn't be secrets?'

There was silence for a moment and she felt her fear form itself into a small bubble of laughter deep inside her. She squashed it immediately. Imagine if she let it out – what Peichl might do to her.

When Peichl broke the silence, his voice was soft – almost gentle.

'Do they love us, Prisoner Müller? The other prisoners? Remember, you can't lie.'

'I do not.'

'I didn't ask about you. I asked about the other prisoners.'

'They have never discussed loving you or otherwise, so I can't be sure.'

'Do they hate us, Prisoner Müller? Do you think they might hate us?'

She felt fear block her throat. She had said something once, something stupid. And she knew Katerina had overheard her.

'I do not hate you. You are one of God's children. I try to love you. I fail in that, I admit it.'

'I asked about the others.'

'I have heard no one say they hate you.'

She blinked. Katerina had lied, or close enough that there wasn't much difference.

'I don't think I believe you. I don't think your God will either.'

'You know I must tell the truth, Scharführer,' Katerina said.

There was the slightest inflection in Katerina's voice – a defiant edge to it that no one else would dare risk. A lengthy silence followed. She wanted to look at the SS man, to see if she could tell what he might be thinking. Instead she studied the silence.

'We'll see about that,' Peichl said.

The SS man walked around the women, each footstep on the loose stones in front of the bunker's entrance sounding as though it were breaking something fragile. The skin on her back wanted to crawl round to her front as he moved behind her. The muscles in her shoulders braced in anticipation of a blow. When he reappeared in front of them, she watched out of the corner of her eye as his gaze ran along the line, prisoner after prisoner, until it rested on her.

'What about you, Prisoner? Do you hate us? Look at me, Prisoner.'

She lifted her head slowly. He looked almost kindly and she felt her fear fall from her. She knew what he wanted from her. After all she'd been through – after all the countless times she'd been closer to death than anyone should be and survived – she would meet her fate now, so close to the end. She found herself looking up at the blue sky above the German's head. She wanted to float high up there, where there was nothing.

'Well, Prisoner? I'm waiting for your answer.'

When the noise came, it was not clear what made it – her first thought was some earth had dislodged from the bunker's roof. It happened sometimes. But Peichl was looking at the ground in front of him.

'What is this?' Peichl took a step forward, shaking his head. 'What is going on here?'

Lena was lying on the ground, her knees bent up almost to her chest – as if her body had collapsed downwards. Her eyes were open and she was taking quick shallow breaths.

One of her hands was on her knee, trying to gain a purchase to stand up again. Rachel reached down to help her, but it was too late. Peichl was standing over Lena now, looking down at her, his hands on his hips. He raised the toe of his boot and pushed at her shoulder. Lena fell to the side.

'Kick her,' Peichl said to Adamik.

Adamik took a step back to put his weight behind his boot. It struck Lena hard in the back, making a hollow sound – as if the woman were a drum. Lena's moan was barely audible.

'She's finished, Scharführer.'

'I can see that,' Peichl said. 'Müller and Gruber. You will bury her.'

'She's still alive, Scharführer. She should see a doctor.'

Katerina's voice was calm and she blessed her for speaking up.

'I take your point.'

He unbuttoned his holster, his hand reached in. Two steps forward. Adamik stepping backwards as Peichl advanced – the Ukrainian's mouth opening in a bored yawn. At the last moment, Lena lifted a hand towards Peichl. Too late.

After the shot, Rachel's quiet sobbing was the only sound she could hear. A raven lifted itself from its perch on the hut's peaked roof and flew slowly off towards the reservoir. Peichl looked down at the dead woman, pushing her over onto her back with the sole of his boot – her blood turning the hard, scrabbly earth red.

'Now you can bury her,' Peichl said to Katerina. The pistol was still in his hand, smoke curling around his forearm as it rose. He pointed it at Rachel. 'Stop that mewling or you'll join her in the hole.'

Rachel stopped and Katerina, for once, had the good sense to say nothing.

'Evanko, see to it.'

'Of course, Scharführer.'

Peichl gestured the other prisoners towards the house and she found herself looking at the top of Peichl's neck, just above his collar – the spot where an executioner would aim his pistol. She imagined herself holding the gun and the image was so vivid that she could even feel its weight, the texture of its grip in her hand, her finger crooking around the trigger. To press the muzzle into just that place. To observe his flinch as the gun touched his bare neck. To push. To see him shrink away from the cold metal.

'You must be Brandt,' she heard Peichl say. 'You're early.'

A man in a military tunic, its arm folded where his own should be, stood beside the entrance to the hut. His face appeared expressionless – but it was so disfigured by burning and scarring that it would be hard to tell one way or the other.

'I wasn't sure what time to come,' she heard him say.

He spoke to Peichl, but he stared at her. His gaze was so direct that she closed her eyes to avoid it, lowering her head. After a moment, gathering herself, she risked another glance. Meeting her gaze, he nodded, turned away and followed Peichl up the wooden steps.

Evanko, the older Ukrainian guard, was standing over Lena's body. She appeared even smaller in death, not much bigger than a child.

'Quick now, you see what mood he's in,' Evanko said.

She and Katerina lifted her between them. Lena was light. When they reached the fence they placed her on the ground. They knew where to take her – the uneven, rolling ground bore witness to earlier murders.

'Go and get the spades,' the guard said to Katerina, toeing the ground with his boot. 'And a pick. The ground is dry.'

The guard turned to her as Katerina walked toward the

hut.

'Take her clothes off. Bring them to the store room.'

She knelt down beside Lena and began to unfasten the buttons of the striped tunic. She wished she could remember the Hebrew prayers she'd heard at her grandfather's funeral. All she could do was treat the body with care, pulling the rough jacket gently across Lena's bone-sculpted shoulders before she lowered her back to the ground. She took the opportunity to close her eyes. Poor Lena had weighed almost nothing at the end.

She was surprised when one of her tears fell on the dead woman's pale skin. She hadn't thought she was capable of crying any more. But the body should be washed, she knew, and so she rubbed the tear along the line of a rib.

It was something, at least.

10

IT WAS ONLY WHEN the shot was fired that Brandt
noticed the prisoners. At first, he thought the dead woman
must be her – but it wasn't. He must have said something in
response when the stocky Scharführer came bustling over,
replacing his pistol in his holster, telling him he was early,
but he couldn't remember what. Instead of paying attention
to Peichl, he was looking across the yard at the woman. She
was still alive.

'Well, don't just stand there, Brandt. Come on inside.'

Peichl gestured for Brandt to follow him up the stairs just
as Judith and another prisoner lifted the dead prisoner's
corpse. They began to carry it towards the far fence.

§

Neumann showed him round the hut personally.

'Prisoner Müller and Prisoner Lang, the Bible students,
can be trusted to prepare food for the officers and men. The
others cannot.' He handed Brandt a key. 'You have control
of the cutlery and knives. Don't take risks.'

'And what is my role, Obersturmführer?'

'Your responsibility is to ensure that the officers who
visit the hut are kept content. Meals must be of good
quality, plentiful and, most importantly, on time. Their
rooms must be clean, the linen spotless. Alcohol must be
available in quantity whenever and wherever they might
look for it. We have an extensive cellar, I'll show you.'

'Do the officers drink much when they visit,
Obersturmführer?'

Neumann smiled.

'They come to relax, to forget about the Front or their
often difficult work. They want to unwind, of course.
Sometimes things can get a little raucous – but all within
the bounds of propriety. Just make sure any mess is cleaned
up before they awake. Here, you'll wear one of these. It

looks about your size.'

Neumann handed him a white mess coat.

'A white shirt, black trousers and a black tie. A simple uniform. We have a Jewess tailor who can make alterations if you need it. She's very good. Many of the officers have her make uniforms for them.'

Neumann frowned.

'We had two tailors until this morning.'

That was the only comment Neumann made on the killing of the prisoner.

In the kitchen, Neumann introduced him to Prisoner Lang and Prisoner Müller – the trusted Bible students. They nodded to him, confirmed their names and turned back to their work.

'Müller and Lang know everything and they are reliable. I'll leave you to make yourself acquainted, Brandt. Remember, you are in charge here. You must tolerate nothing except excellence.'

When Neumann left, Brandt stood for a moment in the middle of the kitchen, listening to the sound of his own breathing. Considering the situation. He hadn't thought it through properly, he realized. Now that he was here, somehow, without intending it, he had become complicit, whether he liked it or not. He was as good as a guard in the women's eyes. Still, the situation was what it was.

'My name is Brandt,' he said.

His instinct was to shake the Bible students' hands – but he knew he couldn't.

'Good morning, Herr Brandt,' they said, almost in unison.

He did his best to smile, but they had already turned away.

'What are you making for lunch?' he asked.

'Roast chicken,' the younger one said, speaking over her shoulder as she peeled potatoes.

'Good. Very good,' he said in response and felt self-disgust threatening to overwhelm him.

There were two smaller rooms at the far end of the kitchen – the scullery and the laundry. He walked towards them. The Jewish prisoner he'd seen outside on his walks was working in the laundry. She was pressing down on a linen tablecloth with a heavy iron. Uniforms and shirts hung on a rail behind her. He knocked on the doorframe to get her attention and she turned to him, her face wet with tears. For a moment, he didn't know what to say. She quickly dried her eyes, avoiding his gaze and taking a step backwards as she did so. He saw her fear. She thought he was going to punish her.

'I'm Brandt,' he said in a quiet voice. 'The new steward.'

His voice sounded uncertain, hesitant. He saw an echo of the dead girl's face in the prisoner's. Half-considered words were already leaving his mouth.

'The dead girl – were you related?'

Her surprise was clear.

'She was my sister.'

'I'm very sorry to hear it.'

Something flickered behind her wary expression – a secret thought. An unspoken comment on his sympathy. It made him even more ashamed – not only of himself but also this whole tragic business.

'What was her name?'

It was all he could think of to say.

'Glasser.'

She spoke a cultured German, he noticed, the kind that wasn't supposed to be spoken by a woman with a shaven head and hollow, sallow cheeks.

'I meant her first name.'

'Lena.'

Her voice had dropped to a whisper. His question had

unsettled her. He wanted nothing more than to be away from this room – to leave her in peace.

'I'm sorry about Lena.' It wasn't a lie. He was more sorry that there was nothing he could do. 'Take your time today. I'll send someone in to work with you, if you'd like. Some company.'

'Thank you.'

Her voice was so quiet he could barely hear her.

He walked back out into the kitchen. The Bible students didn't look at him but he knew he was the focus of their attention. Judith and the other woman were peeling vegetables in the small scullery to the laundry room's right.

It took a moment for him to gather himself. It hadn't occurred to him, outside the hut, how life must really be inside. How his appearance here must inevitably place him, in the women's eyes, alongside the likes of Peichl. He had been prepared for danger – had understood that he would be putting himself at great risk. He hadn't, however, expected this terrible guilt – this soul-scraping self-loathing. He had played a part in all this, even from a distance. He had known about the mass killings and what was happening in the camps – everyone had. And this was being done in his name. What was more, this was what he had been fighting for – whether he'd known it at the time or not. It was his responsibility – and everyone else's.

But he had a more direct reason for his guilt. He had brought the Gestapo to the meeting place where she'd been arrested. If he'd looked around – if he'd seen them – they would probably have caught him, but probably not her. She might still be free. It was her, of course. He hadn't been certain, even after he'd seen her outside, but now he was this close, he wondered how there could have been any doubt. It had been a long time and she'd changed – but then neither of them would be the way they were that day in the cafe on the Ringstrasse again. That was behind them.

She looked up as he approached – a cautious, covert assessment. There was no recognition in her glance. She didn't see Oskar in the damaged man who stood a few metres away from her, and she'd never known him as Brandt. It was good she didn't know who he was. He wasn't here to talk over old times. It was important he kept his distance, for the moment. Still.

'My name is Brandt,' he said. 'Paul Brandt. I'm the new steward.'

Her eyes reserved judgement. The woman working alongside looked up in acknowledgement. They said nothing.

'Would one of you—' he turned to the other woman. 'You perhaps – go and work in the laundry today.'

She nodded and made her way past him. He stood for a few moments, looking at Judith.

'What's your name?' he asked.

'Gruber.'

'Don't worry. I don't bite. I don't even bark much. First name?'

She lifted her eyes to meet his gaze.

'Agneta.'

'Thank you. And your colleague?'

'Joanna. She is Polish.'

'I see. May I ask – what does the red triangle signify?'

She looked down at the number on her chest, then back up.

'It means I am a political prisoner.'

She held his gaze for an instant. She showed no emotion and her tone was carefully neutral, but there was surprise, he thought, that he didn't know what the red triangle meant. He was grateful for his injuries now – it was unlikely she would be able to see anything of the turmoil he felt. That was for the best.

He gave a half smile and made his way back into the

main kitchen. He felt better now – more certain of what he was doing. Seeing her so close, her face worn and gaunt – her eyes still, despite everything, the same – had clarified things. His presence here was necessary. He owed her this and more.

It was strange he thought, as he climbed the stairs, that it was only now, after all this time and all they'd been through, that he finally knew her real name.

11

BRANDT LOOKED across the table at his father's downturned mouth, at the way his skin was pulled taut by disapproval. He shifted his attention to Monika – unnaturally pale, her eyes fixed on her plate. There were no happy smiles for Brandt tonight.

There was food arranged on the table. There were plates and cutlery. His father had said grace – in an angry growl. They should be eating. But they weren't eating. They were waiting to see who would raise the topic of Brandt's taking a job with the SS first.

They had found out during the day somehow, that was clear. Perhaps his father had seen him there or someone had told him. Brandt had been wondering how best to approach the matter, concerned that he might get off on the wrong foot and make a mess of it. At least he didn't have to worry about that any more. It already was a mess.

'I was going to tell you this evening,' he said, after considering his options – which weren't many. 'It isn't what you might think.'

No one said anything. A wisp of steam rose from the potatoes. Eventually, his father began to scratch at the stubble on his neck. A sign of irritation. Brandt could hear the rasping sound quite clearly. His father's voice, when it came, was little more than a whisper.

'What might we think? What do you think we might think?'

Brandt sighed. It was never going to have been an easy conversation.

'You might think I've gone to work for the SS for the wrong reasons.'

'What right reasons could there be?' His father's voice was rising. 'I told you about the camp, I told who those people are over there.'

'It's not just what happens at the camp. There are prisoners in that place,' Monika said, her tone more measured. 'Women prisoners.'

'I know who the SS are. I know what they have done. I know about the women prisoners.'

He reached across and pulled the bowl of potatoes closer to him. He didn't feel like eating but he needed his strength. The scrape of the bowl across the table's wooden surface sounded louder than it should. His father and sister might have stopped breathing, the silence was so profound.

'So answer me this question,' he continued. 'If you want to prevent evil, should you watch from afar and do nothing or take steps to confront it directly?'

Another silence.

'What are you talking about?' his father asked.

'I've probably had a serious head injury. Who knows what state I might be in? So if I do something stupid, there's no reason for you to be held accountable. Unless you knew something about it in advance, of course.'

He pulled a packet of cigarettes from his pocket and put them on the table.

'Just so we're clear,' he said, 'I'm not working for the SS for their damned cigarettes.'

He lifted the packet to his mouth, opening it with his teeth.

'Tell me,' he asked, turning to his father, 'when you saw me at the train station – did you recognize me?'

His father hesitated.

'The honest answer, please. I won't be offended.'

'If I hadn't known you were coming,' his father began. 'If I hadn't known something of your injuries, rather – then, no, I probably wouldn't have recognized you. If I met you in the street, that is.'

Brandt nodded, pleased.

'I thought so. Don't worry – I don't recognize myself

these last few days. I've changed. And that, believe me, is a good thing.'

12

AGNETA wondered what had happened to Brandt. He'd certainly been burnt. Even though the surgeons had done their best for him, his face reminded her of melted candle wax – the features made indistinct, the skin thin and taut across his cheekbones and around his narrow-lipped mouth. His blonde hair, which he wore short, was ravaged to the point of desolation in places, revealing scars and burns over much of his scalp. Most of his left ear was missing and, of course, his arm. It must have been an explosion, she decided. She wondered what he'd looked like before.

'Don't worry, I don't bite. I don't even bark much.'

She'd been surprised that he'd spoken to her in a polite voice. And that his lips had twisted into what she thought must be his smile. His voice sounded constrained, as though it had been altered by whatever had happened to him.

She and the other women were wary of him – the SS orderlies who he replaced had been free with their fists and curses. Who was to say he wouldn't turn out to be the same? And it was difficult to read him. Brandt could smile, more or less, and he could nod, of course, but the tiny visual clues that revealed a person's true feelings were largely absent. Who could tell if he felt anything at all? Perhaps he understood this – perhaps that was why he was so specific in his explanations of what he expected of them.

She realized that she remembered him from before he came to work in the hut. They'd been working in the garden one afternoon not long before and he'd passed on a horse and cart with an older man she knew lived nearby. She remembered Brandt had nodded to her as if he knew her. She'd thought, at the time, that his injuries had made him simple – because no one who passed the hut looked up at it, unless they were SS, of course. The old man knew this

– he'd kept his eyes fixed on the road in front of him. But Brandt examined the building without fear. If she'd seen anything in his expression, as she remembered it, she thought it might have been disgust. Perhaps that was another reason she'd been surprised when he'd shown up at the hut.

Perhaps he was a good person. His kindness to Rachel counted in his favour. It was hard to be sure, of course. You would never be able to tell from the camp Commandant's benevolent exterior that he'd sent countless souls from this world to the next. And how many SS had she come across in the camps who had seemed to be ordinary men, yet had turned out to be monsters? Brandt could be the same – his stiff features gave nothing away.

Then again, it occurred to her, the prisoners' faces were also masks. They held their emotions tight within, even amongst themselves. How could you trust anyone when betrayal might mean their life as opposed to yours?

Perhaps Brandt was also protecting himself.

13

FROM THE ROAD, the hut had the hard edges of a newly constructed building – its woodwork barely scuffed, the paint still clean. The interior, however, was very different – ancient oak panelling, polished by smoke and time, clad the walls in the entrance hall to a height of over two metres, while above the panelling pikes, swords, crossbows and muskets had been fixed to the creamy plaster in great semicircles. Even the floorboards were ancient, creaking under Brandt's weight as he walked through the hut – making it hard to move silently, if he ever needed to.

It was what Brandt imagined a Vienna gentleman's club might be like – with its time-polished armchairs and sunwashed Persian carpets. It was only the SS banners and the portraits of Hitler and Himmler that spoiled the illusion. Although a visitor would also notice, soon enough, that all the other paintings were of battles and heroic military endeavour. There were no pretty pastoral scenes or anything like that. Nothing that might weaken the officers' resolve. He could understand why the officers liked to come and visit. It all felt timeless – not quite part of the world outside. It might just be possible to forget the murder and violence here, for a day or so. Or to reinvent it, as the paintings on the wall had done, into something noble and worthwhile.

§

There were only a handful of officers in the building for the first few days. Three of them were on leave and had chosen to spend it here rather than try to make their way home across the war-ravaged rail system. The other two were recuperating from their wounds, still under the auspices of the SS hospital that formed part of the camp. All of them would be returning to the Front, sooner or later. They were easy enough to deal with. They noted Brandt's injuries and decorations, but didn't mention them. They looked older than they should, their uniforms faded and their skin roughened from years fighting in the open. They carried within them the tension of those waiting for battle.

The camp officers arrived at the weekend – a busload of them. As soon as they stepped out of it, it was obvious they were different from the men from the Front. Their uniforms were smarter for a start, tailored tunics and patent leather boots. They weren't active men, however. These men spent their time sitting at desks. They reminded him of successful businessmen – particularly when they changed out of their uniforms, as they soon did. They looked prosperous in their country tweeds, their shirtsleeves weighed down by heavy gold cufflinks – watches glittering on their wrists. Business, to judge from their jewellery, was good at the camp.

They looked like someone you might talk to on a train. Only one or two of them carried their crimes with them like dark shadows.

Later, in the laundry, when he came across a pile of their clothes waiting to be washed, he understood why they changed out of them so quickly. His nostrils caught a familiar scent and he leaned down.

Their uniforms were impregnated with the stench of burning flesh.

14

PERHAPS IT WAS the thought of returning to the camp and breathing its foul air again that caused Schmidt, a young untersturmführer, to shoot himself. It was the first Sunday morning Brandt spent in the hut and he was pouring what passed for coffee into Neumann's cup in the dining room. The officers were cheerful enough, talking amongst themselves, but the conversation stopped mid-sentence when there came the muffled pop of a pistol shot from the sleeping quarters. Neumann's dog, Wolf, got to his feet, his clever eyes anxious.

There were eight officers gathered around the table and each of them was completely still. Neumann was the first to move, reaching for his napkin and bringing it to his lips – dabbing them – then reaching down to place a calming hand on Wolf's neck.

Brandt's first thought was for Agneta. She was cleaning the washroom in the sleeping quarters, where the shot had come from. A cold chill ran down his neck. He had seen Peichl going down to the village so it couldn't have been him. Brandt checked the officers – there were eight of them. One was missing. Schmidt.

'Brandt?'

'Yes, Obersturmführer?'

'Would you go and see what that noise was?' Neumann said, his lips lifting in a tight, mirthless smile. 'Find out what has happened.'

Brandt walked across the dining room and opened the door that led to the bedrooms, closing it behind him. He stood for a moment. It was quiet. Nothing was out of place. Behind him, in the dining room, there was quiet laughter. Someone must have made one of the dark witticisms people came up with when they waited for bad news.

Brandt made his way to the washroom first. He found

Agneta, to his great relief, standing outside it. She must have been cleaning when the shot came and now stood there, waiting for whatever might happen next. She glanced up at him before looking back down to her feet. He wanted to reach out, to hold her. To tell her he would make sure she got out of this place safe and well.

'There was a shot?' he asked – and it sounded callous to him. But he couldn't say anything more.

'In there.'

She pointed at a bedroom door – Schmidt's. Brandt knocked, not expecting a response, before turning the handle. The hinges squealed as the door opened and his sense of anticipation was such that he stopped, his heartbeat thudding in his ears, then gave the door a firm push. Even before he saw the SS man he smelled the heavy, sweet scent of blood.

Schmidt lay on his bed, his feet pointing at the ceiling – pale and veined, surprisingly delicate. There was a pillow over his face.

He remembered Agneta was standing behind him.

'He's dead,' Brandt said, as much to himself as to her.

The dead man was wearing a silk dressing gown, the upper part of which he had protected from the blood with towels. He'd fixed a small label to one of its pockets with a pin. Brandt leant down to read it:

Please send this dressing gown to my mother.

Generous of him – to bequeath a memento of his suicide to the woman who'd given birth to him. There was a burned circle in the centre of the pillow that covered the young man's head and his arm hung down from the bed, a finger caught in the trigger guard of a small automatic pistol. Maybe he hadn't wanted to see the gun. Perhaps that was why he'd fired through the pillow.

Just to be certain, Brandt removed it – the cotton peeling away from Schmidt's bloody face as he did so. The dead man's eyes were closed. If it weren't for the hole in his forehead – and the blood – he might have been asleep.

Agneta had followed him in. He turned towards her, glimpsing something in her gaze before she lowered her eyes.

'You knew him?'

She looked up, surprised.

'You looked as if you knew him, that's all. Maybe from the camp?'

She lowered her gaze.

'I didn't know him, Herr Brandt,' she said in a low voice. 'It's always tragic when a life ends.'

Perhaps the irony was unintentional. Brandt doubted it. He looked at her bowed head for a moment, thinking of what she must have seen and experienced in the last few years. Of course she would have changed. So had he. It didn't alter anything.

'Go down the back stairs to the kitchen. It's best if you and the others stay away from here until I call for you.'

'Of course, Herr Brandt.'

She left. Relieved, he suspected, that he hadn't questioned her further about her fleeting look of exultation.

Brandt glanced around the SS man's bedroom. The room was small and spartan, as all the rooms were – the luxury was all at the other end of the hut. There were few personal possessions on display – no photographs, no books. A portable gramophone and a box of records. Brandt leafed through them, out of curiosity. Some classical music, some popular tunes.

Brandt opened the wardrobe – the few items of clothing had been labelled in the same way as the dressing gown. There were three parcels, small, with labels marked for his brothers: Franz, Kurt and Dietrich. He picked one up and whatever was inside it rattled. There was no one nearby and he was curious. He untied the string and unwrapped it.

Inside was a small box and inside that hundreds of small, misshapen pieces of yellow metal.

Gold fillings and gold teeth.

§

'Well?' Neumann asked, when he returned to the dining room.

'I'm afraid Untersturmführer Schmidt had an accident.'

'Fatal?'

'Yes.'

Neumann looked around at the other officers, shrugging – as if to say 'these things happen'.

'A shame,' Neumann said.

There was a long pause.

'Should we . . .' began a doctor with a razor thin moustache.

Neumann shook his head.

'We have a procedure.'

Neumann picked up a knife from the table and began to tap it gently on the rim of his coffee cup. At first Brandt thought he was making some kind of point, but it seemed Neumann was unaware of the noise the knife made.

'Thank you, Brandt. Inform Scharführer Peichl. He'll tell you what to do. Please bring any papers you find in Schmidt's room to my office – without exception. Now, gentlemen, let's resume our breakfast.'

The conversation started up before Brandt had left the room. He had been working in the hut for less than a week and there had been two deaths – but no one, except for him, appeared to think this unusual.

15

NEUMANN SAT at his desk, concentrating on breathing slowly and deeply. He needed to be still, to calm down. Despite himself, he stood up, moving to the window – looking out – seeing nothing unusual. He sat back down. He sat for long enough to breathe three times and then stood up again, pushing his chair back. He found he was rubbing the side of his head. For some reason he couldn't stop doing it. He put his hands in his pockets, bunching them into fists. They were safer there. Out of the way.

It was all that boy Schmidt's fault. Maybe Schmidt had the right idea. Perhaps it was, after all, better to shoot yourself. To get it over with. He took one of the fists out of his pocket and pushed it, knuckle first against the wall – as hard as he could. It hurt. It helped. He began to walk again. He found his hands were covering his face.

Neumann caught his reflection in the small mirror on top of one of the filing cabinets. His nose was between his fingers, which pointed upwards. He looked as though he was praying. Which in a way he was. His best chance for a solution was the Commandant. The Commandant always talked sense – he could be trusted. Their friendship was built on solid ground – it stretched back over thirty years. The Commandant would look after him. He'd tell him what to do. How to forget.

'Obersturmführer.'

He turned to find Brandt standing in the doorway. He hadn't heard him come in. He was conscious that his hands were still pressed together. He dropped them to his sides. Then clasped them behind his back.

'What is it, Brandt?' he said, trying to keep his voice level. 'Why didn't you knock?'

Brandt appeared confused by the question.

'But I did, Obersturmführer. There was no response. I

was going to leave these on your desk. Schmidt's papers, as requested.'

Brandt held out a black leather notebook towards him. Neumann made the effort to smile and saw the man relax a little. Neumann knew he needed to control his inner anxiety. He must behave absolutely normally.

'Obersturmführer?'

Neumann had almost forgotten Brandt was there.

'I'm sorry, I was distracted. What is it you have for me?'

'The young officer's papers. They include a diary – and some photographs.'

'He kept a diary?'

Neumann took it from Brandt and then glanced up to see if any information about the diary's contents could be gleaned from his expression. A fruitless exercise, given his injuries.

'Yes, Obersturmführer.'

Neumann found that he had opened the notebook, without thinking. He looked down, and his eyes were drawn to a photograph. A bearded man, his blurred face almost as blank as Brandt's – his black eyes asking no questions and offering no explanation as to why Schmidt, whose image was crisp in contrast to his victim's, was pressing a gun into the side of his head.

'My God.'

The diary tumbled to the floor and four photographs fell out, sliding across the floor as if they were alive. He stepped back from them, finding the desk behind him, and was grateful for its support. The photographs made a series. The man was dead at the end of it, with Schmidt's boot pressing onto his corpse. The hunter and his quarry. Neumann looked up to see Brandt examining him.

'He left a note – asking that his parents be sent the diary. All his clothes have labels attached to them, marking them for members of his family.'

'My God,' Neumann repeated. He didn't believe in a supreme being but there was something reassuring about saying the words aloud.

'His parents can't see these photographs,' he said, hearing the constriction in his throat. 'Burn them. Have you read the diary?'

'No.'

Neumann stooped down and opened the small black notebook at random. Four lines were enough to tell him it must also be destroyed. He looked at the note Schmidt had left for his mother. It wouldn't do either.

'Burn everything, Brandt. His clothes, his papers – the lot.'

'As you wish, Obersturmführer.'

Neumann handed the book to Brandt but he left the photographs where they lay. He wanted nothing to do with them. He walked towards the window and watched Brandt's reflection as he gathered up the pictures of the dead man. Neumann heard a low grunt as he leant forward. Of pain? Of shock? He knew he should destroy the photographs himself but already thoughts of the train were filling his head, threatening to overwhelm him. Brandt stood awkwardly to his feet.

'Thank you, Brandt.'

After he left, Neumann allowed his forehead to rest against the window. He had been conscious, for some time, that the real world was no longer quite solid and in its place something frightening made up of memories and sensation was emerging. His past was beginning to overlay his present. It was worst at night but even now, on a summer's morning, he had the strongest feeling of the presence of others in the room. He closed his eyes and listened. He could hear breathing. He wasn't certain it was his.

He knew that there was no one there, but what if one day he forgot that?

He sat down, once again, at his desk. He breathed deeply and placed his hands flat on its surface, spreading his fingers wide. He felt a tear roll down his cheek. He watched it drop onto the desk at a point almost exactly equidistant between his thumbs. He took a deep breath. Tried to stop the people he'd killed on the train forcing themselves into his consciousness.

A nose pushed against his hip – Wolf – the dog's soft eyes looking up at him. Neumann smiled down at him.

Neumann was saved, for the moment at least. He picked up the telephone.

He would have to tell the Commandant about Schmidt. He would have to ask him what should be done.

16

BRANDT TOOK the diary to the scullery at the back of the kitchen area. He wouldn't be disturbed here – at least not immediately anyway. Joanna and Agneta were upstairs, dealing with Schmidt's body. He placed the notebook on the porcelain-tiled counter and opened it.

There was no obvious claim of ownership on the exterior. Someone – Schmidt, he suspected – had cut a patch from the board on its inside cover. The hole was big enough to have contained a man's name and address.

At first the diary was an ordinary enough description of military life – nothing too remarkable. Schmidt had been stationed in Bavaria and the events he recounted were normal enough – a dance here, a commendation there. It was when his battalion formed part of the invasion of the Ukraine in 1941 that the story changed abruptly. In the beginning there had been anger and confusion. He'd feared what he was being asked to do was wrong. But soon the doubts faded. After that, pages were filled with names of villages and towns and the tallies of the dead. Twenty dead Jews here. Forty there. Sometimes only a handful – *a slow day*. And beside the numbers of Jews killed by his platoon, there was another tally – the ones he'd killed personally. Hundreds of them, when you added the numbers up. He had kept count.

The photographs brought the diary into focus. Brandt examined the images in the single electric bulb's weak glow. In this light, the greys and blacks were less harsh than in Neumann's office, almost as though a warm yellow wash had been applied.

They were from the summer of 1941, if he wasn't mistaken – you could tell from the happiness of the soldiers and the way their summer uniforms had been crusted with dust from the speed of their advance. Schmidt had been a

Scharführer then – the SS equivalent of a sergeant – his chevrons black and silver against his grey uniform. He looked young to have commanded other men.

Brandt had his own memories of that summer. He remembered the heat and the grime as they'd rolled across the empty steppe, pursuing an enemy that was learning how to fight back by losing battle after battle. It had been some kind of collective madness. They were to be the masters of a new empire and even the humblest of them held the power of death over anyone they came across. Even more so when it came to the Jews.

And it was clear the man Schmidt was about to shoot in the first of the photographs was a Jew. A prayer shawl hung over his shoulders and stiff locks of hair hung down from his black skullcap. The man did not seem frightened – his eyes were calm. Perhaps he hadn't understood what was about to happen. The soldiers who surrounded him were laughing and joking – perhaps he had hoped that they would let him go when they'd had their fun with him.

Schmidt, in particular, appeared to fizz with the excitement of it all – his face was more distinct than the others, his eyes bright in the flat sunlight that cast long shadows along the dusty road behind them. Perhaps it was their youth that bothered Brandt most. He'd seen plenty of pointless horror during his time in Russia but these men looked like children playing a game. Schmidt seemed to be seeking approval from the camera in the way a young boy might from a parent. If there was guilt, it was a child's guilt, one who knew his mischief was being tolerated just this once, even encouraged. Now that Brandt looked again, he wondered if the photographer had been the one in charge, rather than Schmidt or any of the others. Perhaps it was the officer commanding the platoon? Yes, that was it – the performance was for the camera's benefit. The young SS men's smiling faces filled the frame precisely and the image was crisp. The lighting, although natural, had been chosen carefully. The sun must have been low to the soldiers' right to have cast such long shadows. The picture must been taken just before dusk – some of the men still had dust circles around their eyes from their driving goggles. They were waiting for the photographer's decision as to what would happen next.

At first he'd thought the dead man was out of focus, but this wasn't the case. He'd turned, either voluntarily or on instruction, slightly away from the low sun so that much of his face was in shadow. He must have been very tall – even on his knees his head came up to Schmidt's collar. Had that been what had drawn their attention to him – why they'd marked him out? His height? One side of the Jew's face was swollen and there were dark splatters on his white shirt. Another detail struck Brandt now – Schmidt's hand was raised to his ear. As though he were listening for an instruction. Perhaps that was why the soldiers appeared to show no awareness of the crime they were participating in – because, after all, they were only following the orders of the man with the camera. At the precise moment of the first photograph, everything was still a joke. A man was being humiliated, yes, but this was as far as it would go. He wondered if the photograph encapsulated the moment before the photographer decided otherwise.

Maybe, without the photographer's instruction, nothing would have happened – the Jew would have lived a little longer. That didn't mean the soldiers weren't to blame. They could all have taken ten steps to the left or right and the photographer would have been left with only the Jew in front of him. But they hadn't. The photographer had told Schmidt what to do but Schmidt had pulled the trigger. The second photograph was less posed. The dead man was toppling sideways, lifeless. Schmidt was no longer looking at the camera, but at the gun in his hand – as if it had suddenly become inexplicable. The young men standing behind him were no longer uniformly elated – one had turned away, his hand to his mouth. Another was looking at the camera, his anger clearly visible. Most looked confused, as if they hadn't understood the joke's punchline. Had they really thought it would end in a different way?

In the third photograph, some of the soldiers had left. Schmidt, frowning now, had leant down – his hand touching the dead man's neck. A taller comrade with blonde hair slicked across his skull had placed a hand on Schmidt's shoulder. It wasn't clear whether he was reassuring Schmidt or congratulating him – his expression was serious, but not disapproving. This was how it had been, often as not, when these things had happened – men had encouraged each other into something and then reassured each other afterwards. But, in their hearts, they'd known the truth of the matter. No one was the same after killing. He wondered if this had been Schmidt's first murder.

The fourth photograph – the last – was different again. Now Schmidt stood in mock triumph, one foot on the dead man's chest. His smile was dazzling white. How long had passed, it was impossible to tell. A few minutes perhaps – long enough for the other soldiers to leave Schmidt on his own – with only the corpse and the photographer for company.

He heard Agneta's footsteps behind him – he recognized them, of course. Watching and listening to Agneta was almost all he did – he needed to know where she was and that she was safe. He placed the photographs back into the diary and closed it.

'Herr Brandt?'

'Agneta.'

'We're finished upstairs.' She paused. 'I've washing to do.'

'I'll get out of your way.'

Brandt turned to face her. He held the diary in both his hands like a promise. She looked at him, waiting for him to move. But, for a moment, he was transfixed. Something about the way the light caught her standing in the doorway reminded him intensely of how she had been in Vienna. He swallowed.

'I'm sorry. I was thinking of something else.'

He passed her, taking the diary into the main kitchen. The photographs burned brightly in the stove's firebox – the diary less so. He wondered what had possessed Schmidt to keep them. And then Brandt's eyes strayed to the rucksack he wore when he came to work.

Inside it now were three small packages, wrapped again – but without their labels. Aside from the gold, there was a package full of foreign currency and a package full of jewellery.

They would come in useful, he decided.

17

ON THE Wednesday of the second week working in the hut, Mayor Weber came to fetch him down to the village hall. It was a mild evening, so they walked. The news from France was bad and even worse from the east, where the Russians were tearing Army Group Centre to pieces. The mayor, loyal optimist though he was, had begun to think of the valley in strategic terms. He waved his hand as if the landscape they looked across were a map.

'The dam is the key, Brandt. The reservoir extends right the way up into the higher valley, where the slopes are higher and steeper, and easy to defend. Below the dam, there's only the village bridge between the dam and the town. There's nowhere for the Russians to easily cross if we release water from the dam.'

Brandt said nothing. He'd grown up in the valley, he knew what was where.

'If the Soviets capture the dam or the bridge intact, they'll have a crossing. Of course, we will destroy the bridge if they advance too close. But the dam is a different story. Army engineers have drawn up plans for its demolition if the worst comes to the worst – but I believe it could be held – by committed defenders. After all, if it's blown up, it might weaken our defences further up the valley. On top of which the factories in the town would no longer have electricity.'

'I see,' Brandt said.

'Also,' Weber continued, warming to his task, 'if the dam is destroyed, the flooding further down the river would extend for a great distance, making a counter-attack more difficult. It's all about tanks these days, Brandt. Our Tigers and Panthers are superior to anything they have – we let them extend themselves and then we throw them back to Siberia. That's what I think must happen.'

Brandt nodded as if everything made perfect sense.

'So you see, Brandt, our little village is a place of some significance after all. With brave leadership and iron will, we might hold the Soviets here. This might be where their attack fails. Right here.'

Weber's chin rose slightly, and Brandt wondered if the mayor saw himself as being the brave leader who would save the Reich in this meaningless place. 'Sacrifices must be made if Germany is to survive. We should be proud if fate gives us the opportunity to make them on the nation's behalf.'

'Of course,' Brandt said.

'This is why I wanted to walk with you. So that we understand the challenge that may await us.'

They had passed the dam now, and the mayor stopped, turning to look back at it. It rose twenty metres above the river beneath it.

'The destiny of the boys you speak to tonight could lie here. It's important they should be prepared for the task they may have to fulfil.'

Brandt looked at the mayor and then at the dam, thinking of all the water that was held behind it. Surely they would just blow the thing up. Surely they wouldn't use children to fight a pointless battle. If they did, he was having none of it.

'I'll do my best for them,' Brandt said.

§

Brandt found himself standing on a small stage. The boys sat cross-legged on the floor in front of him, their skin brown from the sun and their clothes dark from working in the fields – every hand was needed to bring in the harvest. They wore red and white cotton scarves at their throats, gathered together by brass rings they somehow kept bright, despite their manual work.

Brandt stood behind a long metal gun, its barrel

honeycombed, the wooden stock curved to fit a man's shoulder. In front of it ammunition belts had been stretched across the table like snake skins. He felt like a stallholder at a market.

'We are going to look at two weapons this evening. The first is the MG42 machine gun, kindly lent to us by Obersturmführer Neumann from the SS hut further up the valley. Does anyone know what the soldiers at the Front call it?'

Hands went up. He nodded to the youngest boy, a tumble of chestnut brown curls above a cherub's plump face. Fischer. He couldn't be older than twelve.

'The bone saw, Herr Brandt.'

'That's correct. Well done, Fischer.'

The cherub cheeks reddened at the praise.

'The MG42 sounds like a saw. Brrrrrp. The fire rate of twelve hundred bullets per minute makes it impossible to hear the individual shots. It is light, under twelve kilos with its bipod fitting in place – heavier with a tripod. It is good at its job but the barrel overheats quite easily. Tonight you're going to learn how to take it apart for cleaning, how to clear blockages and how to change the barrel quickly – which you will have to do repeatedly in battle. When every one of you can change a barrel in less than twenty seconds – we might think about firing it.'

They smiled like little wolves at the prospect. He had to pause for a moment – a sudden image of them all lying dead in a field distracting him. In his mind's eye, a bullet had smashed a hole where one of Fischer's cherubic cheeks had been. 'And then we have this.'

He reached down to where he'd placed the long grey tube with its cylindrical head, leaning against the table. It looked like a giant metal lollipop.

'The Panzerfaust is very simple to use. You place it on your shoulder, like this, push up the sight. Like so. Not that you really need it because tanks are large and you fire this from very close – its effective range is about thirty metres but the closer the better. And then you pull this pedal. There is almost no recoil so even a one-armed man like me can fire it. Bang.'

He paused, looking down at them – wondering if they knew how dangerous firing this weapon was. They didn't seem to.

'If all goes to plan, the tank goes up in smoke. As I said, you need to be close. It isn't really practical for use in open country. Why?'

A youth raised a hand. Grey eyes, freckles, blonde hair oiled back from the side parting.

'Müller?'

'They would see you first?'

'That's right. If they see you, they won't come close enough. Their guns have much longer ranges so they will sit there and fire them until the way is clear.'

He put the Panzerfaust down beside the machine gun, conscious that the thought of the tank had made him feel nauseous. Another hand went up. A tall youth, his face thinner than it should be – all bones and sharp edges. Black hair and dark, almost black, eyes that looked at him with an intensity Brandt didn't much care for.

'Yes. Wessel, isn't it?'

'Yes, Herr Brandt.'

'You have a question?'

'You knocked out two tanks, didn't you? For your combat badge?'

'I did.'

'With a Panzerfaust?'

'One of them.'

'What did it feel like?'

Brandt looked at the boy, into his piercing eyes, and shivered. He thought back to lying in the slit trench, waiting for the tank – the sound of it, so loud it was impossible to tell how close it was, except that it kept getting closer. Metal grinding against metal, its tracks crushing the very road beneath it. If he moved too early the tank would kill him. When he did move, the infantry would kill him. He'd made no decision he could remember, he'd only acted. The tank had appeared to his left, rolling up over the bank of earth and rubble that the company had raised as a defence. He'd aimed. He'd fired. The heat of the explosion had pushed him backwards. The shouts of the Russian soldiers. The screams of the flaming commander as he struggled from the turret. The smell of men and petrol burning. The bullets that whipped around him as he ran along the trench away from the exploding ammunition that had lifted the tank's turret and tossed it to the side.

He shrugged.

'It was terrifying.'

The boys laughed again. They thought he was joking. He could see no understanding of what a tank was – a rolling, crushing death machine. He let them finish.

'Never fire your Panzerfaust at the front armour,' he said. 'Aim at the sides or, even better, at the back. The armour is thickest at the front and it's sloped, so your charge may just bounce off it. Aside from which it's where the guns are. If you fire from the front, it will see you and it will kill you. If you're dead, you're no use to anyone.'

He paused to let his words sink in. They were attentive now.

'If you're dead, you're no use to you either. You won't achieve the things you dream of, you will never kiss the perfect girl and, most importantly, you won't be able to hit the next tank. So fire at the sides or, even better, its behind.' He paused, looking down at the upturned faces. 'And watch out for the infantry – a tank is almost never without infantry. They are there to stop people like you.

They will stop you by killing you.'

No one was laughing now.

'I need a volunteer to strip this machine gun and show us how it's done.'

No one raised their hand.

'You, Fischer. Come on. Let's see what you can do.'

As Fischer rose to his feet, Brandt glanced towards the back of the hall, where the mayor stood, his arms folded. He wondered whether he had gone too far – but no. Weber was nodding with approval, his expression grave.

Brandt wondered if the mayor was imagining a desperate battle for the dam. It wouldn't be like the paintings up at the hut if it came to that. There would be boys lying dead on the road, crushed so flat by Russian tanks that all that would be left was a wet smudge and blood-soaked scraps of a uniform. The defences would be strewn with collapsed corpses, bloodied marionettes that had lost their strings.

There would be no glory in the defeat.

18

THE LAST WEEKEND of August a party was held at the
hut for the camp officers, their families and selected guests
– well over a hundred people. It was beyond Brandt and the
women to cater for such a large gathering. The mayor
volunteered the Hitler Youth from the village to act as
waiters and the Commandant provided three fat-armed,
round-bellied SS cooks from the camp to work in the
kitchen.

'Brandt,' Neumann said on the morning of the event. 'It
is important that our guests should enjoy themselves.
Today the war must feel a thousand kilometres away. They
have been very busy this summer.'

'Of course, Herr Obersturmführer,' Brandt said,
wondering if Neumann had forgotten the numerous
wounded officers convalescing at the hut. It had been a
hard few months at the Front as well, and there was no
shortage of limping, bandaged soldiers to remind the camp
officers that the war was coming closer.

The guests began to arrive at lunchtime, those with
families nearby bringing their wives and children with
them. As it turned out, no one noticed the wounded officers
walking amongst them, like ghosts at a wedding feast. Nor
did they pay much attention to the prisoners, an even more
obvious reminder of what they were meant to be forgetting.
It wasn't long before the gardens around the hut were filled
with elegantly dressed women and well-scrubbed children
– their menfolk gathered in small groups. It was hot but the
breeze from the hills made it bearable. Meanwhile, in the
kitchen, the SS cooks glowered at Brandt whenever he
asked them to do anything. He ignored their mutterings and
low laughter. At least if they were making fun of him they
were less likely to be picking on the women.

Brandt made his way upstairs to the terrace, where

officers had gathered to talk and drink. The Commandant, his oiled hair precisely parted, was holding court at one end, surrounded by the eager smiles of younger officers. At the far end a soldier who had been wounded in the fighting in Warsaw was talking to a group of less enthusiastic camp doctors. Some of their glasses were empty so Brandt took a bottle over to them.

'Why is it taking so long? That's what I want to know,' one of the doctors was asking, his nose already pink from standing in the sun.

The soldier's head was bandaged and his face looked sallow underneath the white cloth. He appeared to be finding the conversation tiresome.

'They are determined and well led and they fight to the last man,' he said. 'Each building is its own battle.'

'We should just destroy the place, brick by brick.'

'That's what we're doing, believe me.'

'But it's been weeks now.'

'It takes longer than you'd think to flatten a whole city.'

Brandt topped up his glass with wine, noticing Neumann joining the group.

'Send them to us, we know how to deal with sub-humans,' the first doctor said.

'These sub-humans have guns,' the wounded officer said, allowing his irritation to show now. 'These ones shoot back.'

Neumann took his chance.

'Comrades, join the others down in the garden. Möller has his accordion and we're going to sing songs.'

Brandt followed his gaze. A young officer in a leather flight jacket was playing snatches of tunes to entice people to join him – his teeth white and his smile false.

'An excellent idea,' the wounded officer said, not bothering to hide his relief that he might be released from the conversation.

'Bring your glasses, gentlemen,' Neumann said. 'We don't want to leave poor Möller on his own.'

Brant didn't know if it was Neumann's insistence or Möller's launching into a cheerful version of 'Erika', but the men began to walk down the terrace steps to join the growing choir. The wounded officer even managed a terse smile.

On the heath, there blooms a little flower. And she is called – Erika!

Neumann returned to the now empty terrace, shaking his head.

'Fetch me if there is any more of that kind of talk, Brandt. We must nip it in the bud.'

'Very good, Herr Obersturmführer.'

Seeing that the officers were now otherwise engaged, Brandt took his opportunity. It was quiet on the other side of the building and he needed a cigarette. He had just managed to light it when Bobrik, one of the Ukrainian guards, joined him. Brandt offered him his packet and the Ukrainian helped himself. He made an effort to build a good relationship with the guards. It was a relationship he kept warm with vodka and other hard-to-get items from the hut's stores.

'Not joining in the celebration, Brandt?' Bobrik asked.

'I can't sing,' Brandt said. 'Not very well, anyway.'

'Nor can any of them,' Bobrik said dismissively, but not before he'd looked around in case any of the officers were close enough to overhear. Brandt smiled.

'Anyway,' Bobrik continued, 'what they're celebrating isn't something to be happy about.'

Brandt said nothing. He knew as well as anyone what a busy summer in the camp must mean.

'Did you hear the news?' Bobrik asked, lowering his voice to not much more than a whisper.

'What news?'

'Paris has fallen to the Americans.'

It wasn't that Brandt hadn't expected it – everyone knew things were going badly in France – but he was surprised by his physical reaction. It reminded him of a time he'd looked over the edge of a cliff. Vertigo.

'You're sure?' Brandt asked. 'When?'

'It was on the radio. It didn't say when it had happened.'

They shared a glance. Brandt shrugged – what could be safely said, after all?

'What are you going to do afterwards?' Bobrik asked. He made a circle with his cigarette, encompassing the hut and its surroundings. Now it was Brandt's turn to look around in case they might be overheard.

'It won't be long. Not now they're in Paris.'

He had a point. The Allies were squeezing them from both the west and the east. There was no one close – perhaps something could be risked.

'I suppose it depends on who gets here first. If it's the British and Americans, it shouldn't be too bad.'

'Maybe not for you,' Bobrik said. 'But for us, I'm not so sure.'

'Of course if it looks like it will be the Soviets . . .'

They exchanged a glance. Neither of them wanted to be captured by the Soviets.

'Have you any plans?' Brandt asked, not anticipating an honest answer.

'We'll follow orders to the end, of course,' Bobrik said, but his gaze lifted skywards, giving the lie to his words. He paused to blow out a smoke ring.

'Of course, I know others who think differently – men who know what will happen if the Russians get hold of them. It's one thing being a German. That's bad enough. But if you're from the Ukraine, you're a traitor as well.' Bobrik made the shape of a gun out of his hand and pressed its imaginary trigger, indicating the likely fate that awaited them if they fell into Soviet hands. 'So these others may not wait till the end. Of course, desertion is punishable with death, so there are risks. And then, afterwards, where will they be safe? Spain? Africa? South America, perhaps? How can they get to such a place? These men have to think these things through.'

Brandt kept quiet, waiting to hear what Bobrik might say next. Bobrik nodded, smiling as if to acknowledge Brandt was right to be cautious. It wasn't a very comfortable smile. Brandt saw the roll in the SS man's throat as he swallowed.

'I suspect they're making preparations, these men,' he said. 'They'll need civilian clothes and papers. They will need things for the journey – food and suchlike. And it would all have to be acquired without anyone . . .' Bobrik paused. 'Certainly not the officers finding out. They have money, of course. And other things of value. They just need someone they can trust. A local, perhaps?'

'Civilian clothes shouldn't be too hard to find,' Brandt said. He examined each word before he spoke it, considering how incriminating it might be and weighing the risk.

'Except that these men can't just go to the nearest clothes shop and buy such things, can they? The Ukrainian SS aren't permitted to wear civilian clothes, not like the Germans, and the locals don't like them much. Someone would inform on them within the hour. No, these men need someone to act on their behalf.'

Brandt felt his world tilting once again. It was his turn to swallow, his mouth so dry his tongue stuck to his teeth.

'I'm sure such a man could be found, if the price were right,' he said, then paused.

Bobrik nodded in agreement. He seemed relieved, as though a difficult topic had been dealt with to both parties' satisfaction.

'The timing is important, of course. Too soon brings its

own risks. Too late, though . . .'

Bobrik left the sentence hanging.

'I would say,' Brandt said. 'That these men will find their local man easily enough, and when the time comes, that a discussion can be had.'

Bobrik smiled again. He looked almost cheerful now.

'It's good to talk about such things.'

He stubbed out his cigarette and nodded over toward the guardhouse.

'I'd better get back before Peichl does his rounds.'

Bobrik paused after a few steps and turned back to him.

'You haven't been here for one of these parties, have you?'

Brandt shook his head.

'Keep your wits about you. When they get drunk, things can happen.'

Brandt watched the Ukrainian walk towards the gate. If Bobrik had looked back he would have seen him lost in thought, and perhaps might have deduced that Brandt was taking his warning to heart. In fact, Brandt was thinking about what the hell he had just got himself into and how he could take advantage of it.

19

THE WIVES AND children left not long after the sing-
song ended. The later part of the evening was ostensibly a
purely military affair, although not exclusively male. Two
busloads of female SS auxiliaries from the camp arrived
not long after the last of the families left and Brandt
wondered if they had been kept waiting further along the
valley until the coast was clear.

Certainly, once they arrived, the party took on a different
tone. The furniture was pushed back against the walls of
the entrance hall and someone put a record on the
gramophone. It helped, of course, that many of the officers
had been drinking for some time, but it wasn't long before
couples filled the impromptu dance floor. Brandt noticed
married officers who'd said farewell to their wives and
children not long before dancing cheek to cheek with
telephonists half their age.

It wasn't clear exactly when the news about Paris began
to spread but its effect was soon apparent. Many of the
officers stood like statues, lost in contemplation, moving
only to raise a glass to drink from it. When the record on
the gramophone stopped playing, no one moved to replace
it – the dance floor was empty by then – and the silence
that replaced the tinny music was disconcerting.

Brandt walked among the officers, filling their glasses.
Even the Commandant was not immune to the general
atmosphere. Brandt found him on the terrace, leaning
forward against the rail, looking out at the reservoir and the
hills on the other side of the valley, apparently lost in
contemplation.

'Some more wine, Herr Commandant?'

'Yes, thank you.'

At first he spoke as if not fully aware of Brandt's
presence, but then he turned to examine him.

'The new steward, isn't that right?'

'Yes, Herr Commandant. Brandt.'

'You're from this place?'

'My father's farm is past those trees to the left. Not far.'

'It's a lovely part of the world, this valley. I have often thought I should build myself a house here, after the war – with a terrace much like this. It's a wonderful place on a summer's evening.'

'It is beautiful at this time of year,' Brandt said, after too long a pause.

The Commandant reached out to take a paternal hold of Brandt's shoulder.

'You have suffered for the Fatherland, I can see that. Don't be downhearted at this news. The war isn't over yet. The Führer has never failed us, remember that. Happier times will come again.'

The Commandant's touch made Brandt's skin crawl. He had to fight the urge to shake off the SS man's grip.

'Herr Commandant?'

Neumann's voice came from the other end of the terrace, where the door through to the entrance hall was open. Neumann's dog advanced across the terrace towards them, his tongue lolling and his tail wagging, and Brandt took advantage of the interruption to take a step back, leaving the Commandant's hand alone in mid air. The Commandant looked at him, surprised, but was distracted by Wolf – his nose pushing at his leg. The Commandant smiled down at the dog.

'This is a fine hound. Isn't it, Brandt?'

'Herr Commandant?' Neumann repeated quietly. Brandt noticed the way he looked over his shoulder, as if he didn't want to be overheard. The Commandant sighed.

'Yes, I know, Neumann. You think I should take some action to cheer everyone up. I agree. We don't want them to hang themselves.'

Brandt followed them towards the entrance hall, watching as the Commandant clapped his hands at the officers he passed, breaking up their conversations. The Commandant's smile was wide, his teeth sharp and white.

'Come on, gentlemen, come on. We're not here to mope about. Talk, drink, sing, be merry. Anyone with a sad face will be shot. Ladies, that applies to you as well.'

The Commandant laughed as he made his threat but, even so, his words awoke the officers and the auxiliaries so suddenly that they seemed to bounce like breadcrumbs on a shaken tablecloth. They smiled. They laughed. They began to move about. The bottle Brandt was holding was empty in moments as they sought him out for refills. He went to fetch another.

All seemed well, and yet it wasn't. Despite the sudden cheeriness, he sensed malevolent eyes following him. The skin on the back of his neck felt cold. It was like walking through a room of smiling wolves. He brushed against a laughing doctor who turned around, saw who it was and leaned in close to him, still smiling. His eyes a pale grey. He whispered: 'Watch where you're going, idiot.'

The doctor took a hold of his arm, digging his fingers into the flesh. Brandt nodded his agreement, doing his best not to show his pain.

'I apologize, Herr Doktor.'

The doctor's smile didn't slip as he pushed him and Brandt stumbled back a step before he managed to regain his balance. Brandt waited to hear if his apology was accepted. He didn't want to turn his back on this man. He saw curiosity in the doctor's gaze, as if he found Brandt's lack of reaction intriguing, but it was soon replaced with contempt.

'Be more careful. Next time I won't be so gentle.'

'Thank you, Herr Doktor.'

Brandt made his way to the long table that was serving

as a bar. The incident had shaken him. Now when he looked around the room he saw it with a layer of subterfuge removed. The smiles seemed strained, the faces contorted, almost grotesque. The Commandant appeared in front of him, a thin film of sweat glittering on his forehead.

'Champagne, Brandt. We need champagne.'

'There's some in the cellar.'

'Then what are you waiting for?'

Brandt walked through the dining room, disturbing a couple just inside the door, their mouths fused and their hands pulling at each other's clothes. They didn't see him. He passed the long table, a buffet meal laid out on crisp white linen, and saw a hundred versions of the writhing couple reflected in the silverware and glass.

When he reached the bottom of the staircase he stopped for a moment, taking a deep breath to steady himself. The younger of the Bible students, Katerina, glanced over at him. One of the SS cooks looked up from the table, where they sat around a bottle of wine they had helped themselves to.

'Is the hot food ready to go upstairs?' Brandt asked.

The largest of them considered the question. The other two examined the backs of their hands, ignoring him.

'Yes,' he said.

Brandt looked at his watch. It was nearly seven o'clock but still bright outside.

'It had better be good,' he said. All three SS men looked up at him in unison, pulling back their shoulders. Brandt held up his hand and shook his head in half apology. He'd no desire for another confrontation.

'I didn't mean it that way. It's just that there's a strange mood upstairs. The news, I suppose.'

The one who had spoken turned back to his glass.

'Why wouldn't there be a strange mood?' he said, lifting it towards his mouth. 'Everyone is in the shit.'

Brandt glanced at Katerina, at her prison uniform, and thought about the men upstairs. He looked over to the scullery, where Agneta was washing glasses. The evening sun from the other side of the building reached across the room to bathe her in golden light. He could do something for them.

'You women can go to the bunker in a couple of minutes. I just need you to help me get some champagne out of the cellar. The boys from the village will bring it up.'

The women would be safer in the bunker, he decided, and he'd send the boys home early.

The SS cooks could earn their keep.

20

AGNETA COULD hear the music through the machine-gun slit, as well as laughter that grew steadily louder and more raucous. It was a warm evening and all the hut's windows and doors were open. They could hear snatches of conversation as people walked nearby. No one was asleep in the bunker – they were listening.

'I wonder why Brandt let us off early,' Katerina said. Agneta turned her head to look at her. She could just about make out Katerina's profile in the weak light. She knew Katerina didn't care about the answer. She was speaking to hear the sound of her own voice.

'He has the SS cooks and the boys from the village and most of the work was done,' Gertrud said. 'I'm sure he'll have us up early to clean the place before breakfast.'

It was true – they had been working since six o'clock in the morning and, while Brandt had given them what breaks he could, they were exhausted. Not that that usually made much difference. 'He is kind to us,' Rachel said, and Agneta could see heads nodding in agreement.

'I'm glad we're in here and not out there. With them.'

Joanna had a point. It was safer to be in the bunker. The SS would get drunk tonight.

'It's nice to listen to the music,' Rachel whispered after a minute or two of silence. 'It reminds me of before.'

No one said anything and Agneta wondered if they, like her, were thinking back to other summer evenings – before the world had turned upside down.

A man's voice came from outside.

'No one will see us. I promise.'

'Are you sure?' A woman's voice. Uncertain but not unwilling.

There was silence for a moment. Perhaps the man whispered to her.

'Quickly then,' she said, a smile in her voice.

'I adore you,' the man said. His words sounded slurred with either alcohol or lust, or perhaps both.

The women inside the bunker hardly dared breathe. Who could tell how the officer might react if he knew there were prisoners listening to his every grunt and thrust?

Thankfully, he obeyed the woman's instruction and was quick.

'I needed that,' he said, gasping for breath. 'It goes to show – there are still happy moments to be had. Even now.'

The woman laughed. They heard the sound of clothes being adjusted, then footsteps walking away.

Even now? Did he mean the end was close?

Over in the hut, someone changed the record. Zarah Leander's cheery, confident voice sang out.

Can it really be a sin?
When one only thinks of one person,
When one gives him everything,
Out of happiness?

Agneta found a tear pushing at the corner of her eye. She remembered the song and the film it was from. She remembered Oskar holding her close in the silvered darkness of the cinema, his embrace warming away the chill of her terror on the afternoon of Willi's murder. They'd been arrested a few days later.

She wondered where Oskar was. If he was even still alive.

21

IN THE WEEKS that followed the summer party, Brandt ran over his conversation with Bobrik countless times. It was clear, to his mind, that Bobrik had asked for his help and that he and the other Ukrainian guards intended to desert their posts when the time was right. They wanted food, civilian clothes and papers and they wanted him to provide them. The first two he could obtain easily enough. Civilian papers, however, would be another matter.

One afternoon when he was not required at the hut, he took a walk up into the hills above the farm – using paths and tracks that only locals knew about. He wanted to be alone amongst the trees – to let the effort of walking uphill empty his mind of anything except the ground in front of him. Once or twice he heard a rustle from the undergrowth or a breaking branch somewhere close but he didn't look round. It would almost certainly be only an animal. No one had been hunting them in recent years and they had multiplied. And if it was a person, then he was better off leaving them be and hoping that they felt the same way about him. He felt the strain in his calf muscles and his thighs and knew he would be tired that night but otherwise he found the usual chatter of thoughts had gone quiet – as he had hoped.

Perhaps if he had been more alert he would have heard Monika approach. In any event, they were only a few metres apart when they became aware of each other. They stopped simultaneously, facing each other along the narrow track. It was shaded here by overhanging branches and the ground underfoot was soft with pine needles, but sunlight still made its way in thin beams to the forest floor.

'Paul,' she said, to break the silence. She looked around her, as if confused by finding him so far above the farm.

'Out for a walk?' he asked, and didn't like the way it

sounded.

'Sometimes I come up here,' she answered, and he thought her answer was too carefully worded not to be suspicious.

'Me too,' he said. 'I like to clear the cobwebs away.'

He smiled, or did his best to, and she smiled back. 'Were you successful?'

'Yes,' he said, which was almost true.

She pushed a stray hair behind her ear then crossed her arms.

'It's quiet up here. The war seems far away.'

It was his turn to look around. He listened. The silence was almost complete. She smiled, and tilted her head sideways.

'I'm going back down if you would like to walk with me?'

He nodded his agreement.

'I would.'

'We don't have to talk,' Monika said as they turned together to retrace his steps. 'If you'd rather not, that is.'

She offered him another of her slanted smiles and placed her arm inside his.

§

Later however, when they'd returned home, Brandt found himself wondering about Hubert, Monika's former fiancé. He remembered his father's suspicion that Monika stayed in the valley because Hubert was close by. And he wondered whether Monika might have had another motive than exercise for walking so high amongst the trees.

And then another thought occurred to him.

22

BRANDT BEGAN to observe Monika. He didn't follow her, or attempt to catch her out, but he watched her when they were together, and became more conscious of her absences. It wasn't long before he became certain that she was also more aware of him – and his suspicion.

The thing was, if Hubert was hiding close by, he must have some connections with the partisans, or even be one himself. Brandt considered the peril associated with the possibility. If Monika was walking up into the hills to meet Hubert then she was in danger. If she was taking him food – and Brandt noticed how often she carried a rucksack on her walks – then she might well be shot if she was caught. Or hanged, like the couple who had sheltered a Jewish girl in the next valley. On the other hand, if Brandt was able to get the women out of the hut, then having contact with the local partisans might be helpful. More than helpful. It could be the difference between failure and success – but to say the risks that went with such contact were great would be to underestimate them.

§

Brandt sat listening to the radio in the kitchen after his father had gone to bed. British and American parachutists had been overcome by German forces in the Netherlands. The bulletin made it sound like a great victory, but to Brandt it sounded as though the Allies were advancing ever closer while he was not much further forward with his plans. His slow progress was making him anxious. If he wasn't ready to act when the time came, he would have failed Agneta twice.

Monika came in through the yard door, taking off her overcoat as she entered. He looked up, raising his hand in greeting.

'There's a plate for you in the warming oven.'

She had been out visiting a friend, or so she'd told their father, but something in the quick glance she threw his way struck him as surreptitious.

'Good, it's cold outside. The autumn is coming early this year.'

She hung up her coat and began to set herself a place at the table. He watched her – the way she moved, stiffly and avoiding looking up at him. He thought about the Western Allies approaching the Rhine and the Russians to the east. He thought about Hubert, who must surely be hiding in the hills. He thought about how quickly the days were passing – and how few of them might be left.

'Father said you went to see a friend?' Brandt posed it as a cross between a statement and a question.

'Helga Dorfmann. She lives over on the other side of the reservoir. You know them, her father owns the Red Farm.'

He knew the family and he knew the farm. The father was quite elderly, a contemporary of his father's. He watched Monika take the plate from the oven and remove the metal cover. That side of the valley, the western side, was steeper and more wooded than their side. She would have had to cross the dam and then cycle several kilometres along the road that ran along the reservoir, before climbing up a winding, poorly surfaced track. He thought about the Red Farm and its remote location.

'Have you heard from Hubert recently?' he asked.

He was surprised by the bluntness of his question. Monika showed no reaction – which in itself was all the confirmation he needed. He watched how she placed her plate on the table, carefully positioning it between her knife and fork. He noticed the small movement of her chest as she breathed. She didn't speak.

'I would never tell anyone anything about you and Hubert,' he said. 'You must know that.'

She sat down, scraping the chair along the stone floor.

He found himself looking at the top of her head. She picked up a fork but only to hold it. She was thinking how to respond, he knew. She wanted to keep her thoughts to herself until she decided what she might say. She had never rushed into anything.

'Monika,' he said, when the silence became oppressive, 'I need to explain to you about the hut.'

She lifted her gaze to meet his. Her expression was calm and her words, when she spoke, were almost maternal.

'I barely know you, Paul. You came back from the war, which I'm happy about, of course. But for all those years we had almost no contact with you. Why should I trust you?'

He found himself nodding in agreement.

'Perhaps I need to trust you first,' he said.

'Go on,' she said.

And he told her about the women. About Vienna. About Neumann and Peichl. About the perimeter fences and the guards' routines. About where the keys were kept and how the generator might be dealt with.

And all the while, she listened.

23

THE EVENINGS shortened, the weather turned colder and in October the news came that the Führer had ordered the formation of a new military formation to defend the borders of the Reich – the Volkssturm – to be made up of the very old and the very young, the final dregs of the Fatherland's manpower barrel. The village was required to provide this new military force with a platoon of fighting men and the mayor, as the local Party leader, appointed himself its commander. Brandt found himself, three days later, standing by Weber's side, looking at a room full of grandfathers and grandsons.

'Men,' the mayor began and let the word hang in the air for a while. Brandt thought the description was stretching it for half the attendees, but the boys looked pleased and that was something.

'The Führer has placed great trust in us. This is a crucial time for Germany and for National Socialism. We face our moment of destiny.'

Brandt had heard this speech, or variations of it, more than once. He knew what the mayor would finish up by asking them to do and it disgusted him. He found himself looking down at the men gathered together to listen to it. Many of them had only the red and black Volkssturm armbands to mark them out as soldiers, while others wore parts of uniforms that dated back to the first war. The mayor, however, had had Rachel at the hut run up a new uniform for him as soon as he had been confirmed in his position. Brandt suspected the meeting had been delayed until the uniform was ready. The mayor was proud of the two silver lozenges at his throat and the jacket's tailored fit.

'As a sign of our importance to local readiness we can feel honoured, comrades, that the responsibility for protecting the dam from enemy infiltrators has been passed to our unit from tomorrow.'

Brandt turned his head slightly to look at the mayor. This was news to him. The Order Police had been guarding the dam up until now. The mayor caught his covert glance and gestured towards him.

'We are fortunate to have amongst our number Paul Brandt, who, as we all know, served with great distinction on the Eastern Front. He will be squad leader under my command. With brave men like him amongst us, we can be certain we will be ready to face the enemy.'

Brandt nodded gravely. His father had been exempted by reason of his age but his uncle, Ernst, had not been so lucky. Brandt saw him smile at the announcement – a solitary friendly face amongst the older men. Brandt knew how wary they were of him. And of the boys, for that matter. Everyone knew the Hitler Youth were capable of informing on an overheard conversation. And everyone knew Brandt worked for the SS and what that must mean. He understood their closed expressions but they didn't bother him as much as he would have thought. He wasn't here to be friends with them, after all. Instead, while the mayor talked, Brandt counted the number of men and began to work out a sentry rota for the dam. Three should be enough at night, with less during the day. It was a gesture, after all – if the partisans wanted the dam they would likely take it, even if the whole platoon was dug in around it.

The mayor was coming to the end of his speech – his voice rising with each word, slapping a fist into his hand to emphasize each point.

'If we do not fail the Führer, the Führer will not fail us. Remember – we fight for our home, for our families and for our future. We cannot fail.'

The mayor stopped, waiting for applause. There was a silence and Brandt saw that the men weren't certain how to react. The mayor looked across at Brandt expectantly, as if he thought Brandt could clap with only one hand. Brandt considered his dilemma for a brief moment, then stamped his foot three times to signal an approval he certainly didn't feel.

The Hitler Youth, on cue, threw their right hands upwards in stiff-armed salute and shouted Hitler's name. The older men, many of whom had fought in the first war, were more reserved. Brandt couldn't help his wry smile, which he knew, from his shaving mirror, would look more like a grimace. Not only did they know better, the older men, but he also realized, looking along their ranks, that fewer than half of them had lived in the valley before the war. It wasn't even really their home. Why should they fight?

§

The day after the mayor's speech, American aircraft attacked a chemical factory in a nearby town, and if anyone had any doubts that the war was coming ever closer, then the rumble of the bombing echoing along the valley and the drone of high-flying aircraft removed them. Brandt wondered how the Volkssturm men were meant to fight against bombers and artillery with a few pop guns and a speech.

24

POLYA KOLANKA had pulled the engine out of her tank. It hung from a hoist above its usual resting place and now she was taking it apart piece by piece. She whistled to herself as she worked.

The battalion had been in reserve since they'd lost most of their tanks, and a quarter of the men, in the big operation around Minsk during the early summer but now the time for taking it easy was over. There was a sense of urgency to the preparations they were making these last few days. Everyone knew that another operation was in the wind.

The battalion had been reinforced, of course, with new T34s – faster, with bigger guns and an extra crew member. They could have had one if they'd wanted but she and Lapshin had decided to stick with Galechka. She'd seen them through two battles now and, as the saying went, only a fool changed his horse when crossing a river. Not that that had stopped Polya upgrading her with new extractor fans, heating, radio and anything else that she could borrow or, if necessary, acquire by other means. She was loyal to Galechka but she wasn't stupid. She knew Galechka was a lucky tank – but it wouldn't do any harm to make her luckier still.

Polya didn't concern herself much about her life before tanks. She had memories, yes, but they belonged to her childhood, which was a long time ago. Or to her time at the orphanage, at which point her childhood was over.

She only had some scattered recollections of her father. The scent of pipe tobacco on his wet woollen jumper. His prickly moustache. A kindly smile that she couldn't be sure was his. They'd come for him when she was only seven, after all. Polya had clearer memories of her mother, of her kindness, the warmth of the bed with the two of them in it. Polya didn't know what her mother had been arrested for –

it wasn't sensible to ask, even if you were a relative – and she wasn't sure it mattered. There must have been a reason. There always was. Anyway, her mother wasn't coming back and it was best to leave her in the past where she belonged. Polya was all about the future – what was the point of spending your life peering into the past when the future was bright and full of hope?

She did remember, however, how her mother had embraced her that last time – when they'd come for her. She had squeezed Polya so hard that she hadn't been able to breathe. It was only the Chekist dragging her mother away that had saved Polya from passing out. She remembered that. She remembered the hot tears on her cheek. Not her own – she'd been half-asleep and hadn't known what was happening. And she remembered her mother's big brown eyes, bulging, shining wet in the candlelight, and her saying: 'Go see Aunt Tonya. Tonya will look after you.'

And then her mother was gone – just like that – and she'd been left sitting on the stairs with her belongings all wrapped up in paper. Her mother had taken the only suitcase. A State Security seal had been placed on the door to the room they'd lived in – her and her parents – for as long as she could remember. The seal had been made of red wax and string, and it was clear poor Polya didn't live there any more.

It was clear, as she sat there, that that part of her life was over. It was two in the morning, in February, no less, when she stood up and walked out the front door of the building and left it all behind her. She made her way across Kharkiv, in the dead of night, in the snow, with her tears freezing on her cheeks, and knocked on Aunt Tonya's door.

Tonya looked after her all right – just not how her mother had thought she would. A phone call to the Militia and a trip to the orphanage was what she got from her:

'First the father, then the mother – it's you who'll be next, Polya, my girl – and it's better for all of us if you're somewhere else when they come for you.' Ten years old and her own mother's sister brushed her out of her life like dust. Well, she'd survived. And Aunt Tonya had been the one arrested in the end. The Party knows everything.

She couldn't complain about the orphanage – she'd been lucky it had taken her in at all. There were plenty of children like her who died on the streets that winter – and that summer too. Not just kids either. The peasants were starving in the countryside – and while they hadn't been fed well in the orphanage – they'd all come through it. They even sent her to school, which had been good of them, though she'd had to sit at the back of the class with the other socially tainted girls. Perhaps she had some happy memories from back then, somewhere. She couldn't recall them, and even if she could have, she wouldn't. They'd taught her to read and write and scrub floors and count and curse them to hell under her breath and then, at the age of twelve, they'd sent her to the Kharkiv Locomotive Factory to work off her debt to the State. She thanked them for that, if nothing else.

The Kharkiv Locomotive Factory no longer built railway engines by then, as it turned out, but tanks. Well, tractors too – but she'd never had anything to do with the tractors – nor with the people who worked on the tractors. She was a tank woman from the first – she'd known it from the moment she set foot inside the assembly building. Steam and metal and the noise and smell – the roof so high above you might think it was the sky, and the far end of the building so far away you could barely see it. The heat from the furnaces, the crashing assembly lines. The power of the place. It was like being inside a great, thundering, rattling machine. And while a person was just a tiny part of it – the truth was that without each of them working together the whole place would fall apart. She felt she belonged. More than that, she knew she was needed here.

The foreman, Nikolai Nikolayevich – bless the man – had taken her by the shoulder and said in that stern voice of his, even if his eyes were always gentle: 'Comrade Kolanka – welcome to the Kharkiv Locomotive Factory. You, Comrade Kolanka, will be judged on your contribution to your brigade's effectiveness – both in its work and in its political activities. I don't care what you were before, or what your mother and father did. Comrade Stalin tells us the sins of the parents shouldn't be visited on the children – and I'm not one to disagree with Comrade Stalin. So what do you say? Will you give us your all?'

She'd said nothing – she hadn't needed to. This time her tears were tears of joy and he patted her cheek and said: 'You'll do.'

She'd found a new home and never looked back – well, not too often, anyway. And for five years she *had* given her all to the Kharkiv Locomotive Factory, and when the fascists had invaded she'd been one of the few – out of thousands – who'd been chosen to go on the first train – all the way across Russia and over the Urals – to Nizhny Tagil. And she'd been the one awarded a medal for her efforts in building the new work shed so quickly that tanks were rolling out the door of it before even a month was past. And she'd been the one who'd organized the work brigade fund raising, and it had been their brigade – of all the work brigades – who were the first to buy their own tank and give it to the State. And when its driver had broken his arm – it was customary for the tank crews to work in the factory while they trained and he'd been clumsier than most – it had been Nikolai Nikolayevich, now Political Commissar for the whole of Factory Number 183, who'd had the excellent idea that she should be its driver. That no one would drive that tank as well as she would. And that, from a political perspective, nothing could inspire the workers of Factory Number 183 more so than to have one of their own driving a tank they'd built. And a girl like Polya to boot.

And he was right. Eight years hefting tank metal had made her as strong as most men – and there was nothing about the T34 that she didn't know the truth of and the trick for. And this tank was perfect – the girls in her work brigade had seen to it. There wasn't a bolt or a spring or the smallest ball bearing on their tank that hadn't been sweated over. The welding was so fine you might think it had been done by jewellers – not the rough-and-ready job they'd normally make do with. She'd seen the look on Senior Lieutenant Lapshin's face when the new tank had rolled through the doors of the Assembly Hall – shining silver, yet to be painted – with Polya Kolanka at the steering levers. She'd seen his slow smile. He'd known she was perfect – the tank, that was, of course, not her. She smiled to herself at the thought of Comrade Lapshin looking at her in such a way – it was inconceivable. He was a serious man with no time for romantic interests.

Even if she liked to think of the tank as her tank, that wasn't quite correct. All right, she'd built her and had a hand in paying for her – but that was in the past. Comrade Senior Lieutenant Lapshin was the commander and the tank did his bidding now – she was only one of the crew. Still, the tank was hers in that its well-being and its readiness were her responsibility. She was the one who made sure it kept moving and it was she who checked each tread of track, each wheel, each bearing, each cog, each welded joint – each centimetre of her. It was she who had chosen the tank's name: Galechka. Even if she hadn't told the others why.

Only Comrade Lapshin came close to giving as much attention to the tank as she did.

And the fact was that Lapshin and she – and Galechka –

were still here when plenty of others hadn't made it through the summer operation. That was why she'd spent so much time making sure Galechka's motor was in perfect running order. She knew it mattered – that it was the difference between this life and the next. And if a lot of the other drivers had been busy chasing the nurses in the nearby field hospital, that was their foolishness. A wise person did his best to stay well clear of field hospitals. Lapshin understood that. He'd been in the thick of it since the first day of the war and he made sure the other men in the crew understood it as well. Stick with us and you'll see your villages once more, he'd told Avedyev and Vitsin, the new men assigned to their tank – they'd spread the veterans across the whole battalion so they'd lost the old gunners. And Avedyev and Vitsin may have been young but they were smart enough to listen up. They would do their part – she was sure of it.

And Galechka would be ready. The only question was whether Polya herself would be. She hoped she would. She felt confident she and Galechka could give Lapshin whatever he needed when the time came. She might not be the strongest – it pained her to admit that, of course. On the other hand, it wasn't just strength that made a good driver. You had to know your tank's limitations, how it interacted with its surroundings – it was almost scientific, all the factors you had to take into account. The ground was cold now, which made things easier, of course – but if the weather became milder and the ground cut up, her skill would become more apparent. She knew how to move in the open as well, to take advantage of the contours of the land – to always keep the thick armour at the front pointed at the enemy. Lapshin knew this – he valued her. He wouldn't want anyone else driving him when they went on the offensive. And she wouldn't want anyone else in the commander's seat.

The tank was her life now. It was as much a part of her as her skin was. It was her world. The truth of it was if she strayed more than a hundred metres from her tank these days, she was lost. Even if she knew exactly where she was.

And wasn't that as strange as anything else?

25

AT THE END OF November it seemed clear they were facing a long, cold winter and Neumann asked the Commandant for a work detail of prisoners from one of the nearby satellite camps to chop wood for the hut. A gang of twenty men came each day for a week and chopped and sawed at the trees behind the hut. They worked from first thing in the morning till last thing at night. He wondered how they were able to, given just how thin they were.

When they'd left, and the stacked logs filled the open-sided shed beside the bunker, it worried him that the prisoners' efforts might turn out to be for the Russians' benefit, rather than the camp's. But when he thought it through, he decided it didn't matter, one way or the other. What was wood for, really, other than to be burned? And what were prisoners for, other than to work?

§

Neumann wrapped himself up, put on fur-lined boots to keep his feet warm and took Wolf for a walk down to the lake. It was the morning after the prisoners had finished stocking the hut with winter fuel. Wolf weaved his way along beside him, his tail wagging, his paws leaving their melting imprints in the light dusting of overnight snow. The cold air stung Neumann's cheeks. Ahead of them, the reservoir was obscured by a clinging blanket of low white fog while the fields in between were grey with frost. The valley had lost its summer sheen and he knew it was unlikely he would see it again at its best. He sighed at the melancholy thought, which caused Wolf to stop and look back at him for a moment. Neumann leant down to rub between the dog's ears.

'Thank you, Wolf.'

His breath was a wispy white in the still air when he spoke. They walked on. The church bell rang eight o'clock down in the village, then all returned to silence.

He heard the postman before he saw him – there was almost no lubricating oil to be had these days. Although the ancient black bicycle's chain would probably have squealed with each turn of the pedal in any event.

'Herr Obersturmführer,' the postman said, coming to a wheezing halt when he was close. 'I have a letter for you, if you'd like it now. Otherwise I'll take it up to the hut with the rest.'

Neumann didn't get much post these days. The postal service was struggling with the bombing and with the lack of personnel and Marguerite was very busy, of course, now that she had been forced to move – the British having flattened the Hamburg apartment building they'd lived in. At least the small town she'd moved to with the boys was not too far from the city. Although far away enough to be safe from bombs. So far at least.

'Thank you, Herr Schmidt. I'll have it now.'

He held out his hand while the postman looked inside his leather satchel. Marguerite's handwriting. Neumann slipped the letter inside the pocket of his greatcoat.

'Thank you.'

'It's a good one, I hope.'

'From my wife.'

'I'm pleased. They aren't always, these days.'

The older man got back on his bicycle and resumed cycling up the hill towards the hut and the higher farms. Neumann noticed the Volkssturm armband and found himself shaking his head. He wasn't even certain this man would make it to the top of the slope without having to get off and walk, and yet the mayor thought the old fellow should be a soldier.

When they reached the lake, Neumann threw a stick for Wolf. Then encouraged the dog to go for swim. Wolf shook the water off when he emerged, then sat down on his haunches, looking at Neumann as if he expected to be entertained and Neumann was the performance. Neumann reached into his pocket and slipped a finger under the envelope's flap, tearing it open. The letter was only two sides long, although Marguerite's handwriting was tightly packed in, its black copperplate filling up the entirety of each page. He read it through once. Then once again. He shook his head, not in disagreement, but to clear it, then read it once more. It was clear and it was precise. Not one word had been crossed out or needed alteration. She must have carefully crafted it – not wanting there to be any ambiguity as to its meaning. Wolf came towards him, his doleful gaze seeking out his master's. Neumann found his fingers wrapping themselves into the Alsatian's long fur and a part of him, he was surprised to discover, wanted to rip the handful he held away from Wolf's head, to hear the dog's howl of pain.

'Good boy,' he said. 'Let's go back home.'

They had almost reached the hut when they came across Brandt.

'Herr Obersturmführer?' Brandt asked, but what the question was he didn't say.

'Yes, Brandt?'

'You look a little pale. Are you all right?'

'I'm fine, thank you. Better for the walk.'

Brandt hesitated, as if there was something on his mind.

'Spit it out, whatever it is.'

'It's the prisoners, Herr Obersturmführer. I found some Soviet padded coats in the store. I don't know where they came from – war booty of some sort, I suppose – but I was wondering, now that the weather has turned cold, if you would permit them to be given to the prisoners?'

'Why?'

'Why not, Herr Obersturmführer? No one else is using them and we'll get more work out of them if they stay healthy over the winter.'

Neumann shook his head – Brandt really didn't understand a single thing about this place. And yet. Neumann was not cold-hearted. He had not forgotten how to be kind. He was still a human being. Marguerite was wrong about those things.

'Tell Peichl I have ordered you to give the jackets to the women. Otherwise he'll only come to me complaining. Is that all?'

Brandt looked surprised, but pleased at the same time. He saluted him. A proper military salute. Neumann experienced a flash of pleasure and wasn't quite sure why.

'Thank you, Herr Obersturmführer.'

Neumann nodded and carried on his way feeling, once again, numb.

26

BRANDT WAS unfolding a linen tablecloth in the dining room – his right hand, accustomed to the task, moved in an efficient pattern as he spread it across the table. A whole man could just fling it open, of course, it would be the work of a moment. But Brandt would get the job done all the same. Most of the officers were still in bed. Outside, the early morning light was flat and grey. A December morning – the summer seemed very far away.

Jäger, a grey-eyed tanker who didn't seem to need sleep, had taken a seat beside the fireplace and watched him. For some reason, Jäger had taken a liking to him. When the shouting started outside there was a moment where they exchanged a glance.

'What's happening?' Jäger said, his expression more interested than concerned.

Brandt was already on the other side of the room, wiping the mist from the window pane to see outside, looking for the women prisoners. The women stood in a line, snow shovels in their hands, being addressed by Peichl. Brandt counted them – all still there – but Peichl's voice was rising in pitch. His pistol was out of his holster.

'Will he shoot one of them?'

Jäger stood beside him, trembling fingers fumbling with his cigarette case.

'I don't know.'

Brandt's sense of helplessness was absolute but, to Brandt's relief, Peichl holstered his pistol, waving the women with his other hand towards the snow-covered driveway.

'At least he's stopped shouting.'

Brandt didn't reply. He exhaled slowly, his breath re-forming the mist on the glass in front of him. He could feel his blood fizzing with rage.

Jäger handed him one of his cigarettes, and Brandt took it instinctively, without acknowledging the gesture. He found its presence between his fingers comforting, then remembered his manners.

'Thank you.'

He reached into his pocket, offering the flame from his lighter to Jäger first. When he inhaled, he held the smoke in his lungs for several seconds before releasing it.

'Why do you work here, Brandt?'

The danger came out of nowhere.

'I don't understand the question.'

Brandt was pleased with how calm his voice sounded in the circumstances. He had been off guard for an instant and look what had happened.

'You're a decorated soldier, Brandt. Surely you can't be reduced to working for these people.'

Brandt allowed himself the luxury of formulating a real answer – of explaining why the hut was exactly the place a man like him should be working. Instead he smiled.

'The village isn't that big a place, Herr Hauptsturmführer, and there aren't so many jobs a one-armed man is capable of. I'm fortunate to be able to assist the war effort in this small way.'

Brandt turned to face Jäger. A serving SS officer with a knight's cross around his neck could afford to say whatever he liked about the hut and the SS. Brandt could not.

'You think this work helps the war effort?' Jäger asked, pointing his cigarette case at the women who pushed and scraped at the icy driveway.

'If I do this, a fitter man can work as a farmer, or fight at the Front. I do what I can – so that another can do more. That makes sense, doesn't it?'

Brandt returned to the tablecloth, lining up the folds just so, then holding them fast at each corner with metal clips. Jäger was silent. When Brandt had finished placing the last of the clips, he stood up and examined his work. The table was perfect, the linen white, the creases precisely aligned. Even the camp doctors couldn't complain about it. It made him want to slash it with a knife.

'Very pretty.'

'Thank you, Herr Hauptsturmführer.'

Jäger had sat back down in his armchair, placed his hands flat on his knees and was watching them intently. They still shook.

'Do you care about them, I wonder? The women? Is that the reason?'

Brandt turned back to the cabinet, taking his time reaching for the next glass. He wanted to consider his response carefully. He wanted to be certain his face showed no trace of his fear.

'As human beings, I mean. Do you care about them as human beings?'

Brandt could feel a vein pulsing in his forehead and wondered if it were visible. It was best not to answer the question – he couldn't be sure his voice would achieve the correct tone. But Jäger, as it turned out, wasn't waiting for Brandt's response. He stood to his feet, walked to the window and looked out at the snow-covered lawn. His profile was a fine one – a wide chin, long forehead and an aquiline nose. Brandt wondered whether the SS man was conscious of the fact. His skin must once have been smooth but years in the outdoors – the Russian winters and the Russian summers – had changed it, causing premature lining around the eyes that made him look older than he was and roughening and tightening the skin across his cheekbones. And then there was that long purple scar that ran down the side of his face until it disappeared under his collar. He'd told him what had caused it, but Brandt didn't pay much attention to talk about wounds and scars and other injuries. He didn't care about such things.

'You must have a reason for being here, Brandt – that's all I can think. It's the only possible explanation.' Jäger's voice was low and intimate, as if he were inviting Brandt to unburden himself. 'Otherwise your being here doesn't make sense.'

Brandt's chuckle wasn't entirely forced. He felt strangely light-headed.

'You think it doesn't make sense that I should perform this small duty to the Fatherland?' Brandt said. 'Don't let anyone in the SS hear you say such a thing.'

Jäger's smile was really nothing more than a thinning of his lips.

'I hear myself and I absolve myself. Anyway, you know as well as I do this whole thing ends in flames.'

'You think so?'

'I've been sure of it since 'forty-one.'

Brandt had placed the cutlery box on the table and was opening its lid when he stopped, interested despite himself.

'How so?'

'We were in the Ukraine. You know the kind of business. The Soviets had dug themselves in along a river and had decided to stay there. We, of course, had decided they shouldn't. I was sent to the adjoining infantry regiment to coordinate the details of our attack. Their commander and I went to look over the ground. On the way, we passed a field full of dead Soviets. A large field. Someone had decided they weren't taking prisoners that day. Hundreds of men. Perhaps thousands. Some weren't old enough to be called men, some didn't even have uniforms. Some, and I'm not lying about this, didn't even have shirts. They must have rounded them up from the local factory. Heavy calibre machine guns at close range. I'm sure you saw such things – I don't need to tell you about the sheer mess, the blood, crows picking at the corpses. Not a scene for the film reels.'

Brandt remembered the smell. And the silence.

'There were so many prisoners,' he found himself saying. As if a few less could have made no difference.

'The infantry Oberst turned and said: "We're shooting our own men when we do this. I wish they'd realize it."'

'We thought we were unstoppable.'

'Well, we had to fight like hell to break through when we attacked the next morning. The Russians fought to the last – and we'd made them do it. It wasn't their officers or their love of Stalin did it. And we were the ones who trained them to show us no mercy when it was our turn to lose. That was the Oberst's point.'

Brandt sighed.

'I prefer not to think about the war these days.' 'Why not?'

'I'm a civilian now, Herr Hauptsturmführer and I work here. I don't listen, I don't see, and when I do think, I'd prefer to think about some film actress. It makes my life easier.'

Jäger's snort was either laughter or contempt – Brandt didn't much care either way.

'What did you do before?'

'Before the army?'

'Yes. Before that. Before this.'

'I was a student.'

Jäger snorted again.

'I should have known. What did you study?'

Brandt placed the fork he was positioning on the table and looked at it for a moment. He'd had enough of Jäger's constant questioning. Each time he opened his mouth he walked on dangerous ground. He considered how to change the course of the conversation.

'Why are you so interested in me, Herr Hauptsturmführer? I don't understand your curiosity – why you seem so determined to draw me out.'

Jäger reached into his coat pocket, his fingers seeming to catch on the fabric as he did so. He managed to extract his cigarette case once again, scuffed and dented as a soldier's belongings often were. He clicked it open and offered the contents to Brandt. It shook as he held it – the SS man unable to keep it still.

'No thank you, Herr Hauptsturmführer. I'm grateful.'

'It wasn't good, the last one?'

'I'm not permitted to smoke while I'm working. I shouldn't have accepted it.'

'I outrank Peichl and Neumann. I order you to smoke. If they quibble, I'll have them shot. You think I wouldn't?'

Brandt found himself smiling, despite himself.

'In which case, thanks.'

Brandt took one and then, when Jäger reached in his pocket, held out his lighter to the SS man's cigarette.

'Thank you,' Jäger said.

'For what?'

'For lighting my cigarette. For saving me the embarrassment. My shaking hands.'

'I noticed nothing, Herr Hauptsturmführer.'

'Good for you. What do you think? Nice tobacco?'

'Not bad.'

'Turkish. A friend had them sent them to me. From Berlin.'

'A kind friend.'

'A dead friend.'

'I'm sorry to hear it.'

'So was I. An air raid. She was a nice girl. Too good for me.'

Jäger shook his head slowly, then turned his attention back to Brandt.

'Why didn't they make you an officer? When did you enlist?'

'Nineteen thirty-eight.'

'Before the war, then?'

'Yes.'

'And when were you wounded?'

'Last October.'

'That long? A university man? And they didn't bump you up?'

Brandt sighed. To hell with it, if the mayor knew about Vienna then it was certain Neumann knew as well. Jäger wouldn't be telling anyone anything they didn't know already.

'There was a restriction. I got into some trouble. Joining the army was the solution. Not that I wanted to become an officer – but it wasn't a possibility.'

Jäger considered this for a moment, allowing his finger to run down his facial scar.

'It must have been political trouble. Which university?'

'Vienna.'

'Nineteen thirty-eight? Ah. I can imagine. A Red, were you?'

'No. Well, not what I would call a Red. There was some resistance when the German troops marched in. Not much. I was caught up in what there was.'

'But no arrest – no punishment.'

'I was given a choice.'

'And you chose the army.'

'It seemed a sensible decision at the time.'

'You're not so sure in hindsight? You surprise me. These female prisoners outside with the red triangles – they're here for political offences. That could have been you.'

Brandt inhaled a lungful of tobacco smoke and savoured the way the nicotine crept its way to the furthest tips of the extremities he had left. He thought about Agneta pushing snow from the driveway. It could indeed have been him. It probably should have been him.

'May I ask you a question Herr Hauptsturmführer?

Seeing as we are being so open?'

'Of course, we can speak freely. No one else is here.'

'Why did you join the SS?'

Jäger turned and gave him a lopsided version of his thin-lipped smile. He appeared embarrassed.

'The Führer spoke to my soul with his sanity and logic.'

'And now?'

'Now I am not quite in my right mind – it's probably the concussion. I'm not alone. The morale at the Front is not what it was. We fight because there's nothing else to be done.'

'What do you think?' Brandt inclined his head to the east.

'It's a mess. When they attack it will be like last summer, and the summer before – only worse. And they won't wait for the summer.'

Brandt nodded. Jäger blew a smoke ring.

'I'm going straight back to the Front. The doctors have to approve it this time. I'm physically fit enough – a little bit of pain perhaps, and if I have to hold my hand to keep it steady, that's all right. There'll be plenty of Russians to aim at.'

'Don't you have leave coming? Because of the wound?'

'Leave? I've nowhere to go, Brandt. An air raid. On Berlin. I thought I mentioned it.'

As he spoke, Jäger turned away from Brandt so that it was impossible to see the SS man's facial expression. Brandt wondered if he was trying to hide it from him. Jäger stamped his feet twice, as if shaking snow off his boots – and then left the room. The door swung shut behind him.

Brandt looked at it for a moment, running back over the conversation – extracting what information there was to be had from it – evaluating his own words for any risk they might have placed him in and considering whether the Hauptsturmführer was a danger – or something else. Then he heard the front door open and Peichl's footsteps coming through the entrance hall. With one deft movement, he removed the glowing tip from the SS man's excellent cigarette by knocking it against the heel of his boot, then stamping on it to extinguish it. He pinched the tip of what was left and placed it in his pocket.

It was too good to waste.

27

IT WAS Christmas Day, for most people, but for the SS it was Julfest – an ancient Germanic celebration. The Bible students had prepared a hunter's stew, in keeping with the proposed shoot the following day. There were no geese to be had.

'Not bad. Not bad at all. Is this your work, Gertrud?'

'We have no nutmeg,' Gertrud said, lowering her gaze as if embarrassed. 'It should have nutmeg.'

'I'm sure the officers will understand. The British blockade is hardly your fault.'

He knew the reason the Bible students prepared the food was nothing to do with their culinary abilities – rather because their literal belief in the Bible's precepts meant they wouldn't poison anyone. Still, they took pride in their work.

'Herr Brandt?'

The pretty telephonist was standing in the middle of the kitchen. She appeared unsure where to look. Her gaze wandered the room, looking everywhere except at him. He was surprised that she hadn't become used to his physical appearance by now. Perhaps she thought it was contagious.

'Fräulein Beck? How can I help you?'

'Obersturmführer Neumann would like to see you.'

As usual it was only her mouth that spoke to him.

'Of course.'

He turned to Gertrud and Katerina.

'I'll be back in a few minutes, continue as you propose.'

The women's heads were bowed but of course they were listening. The prisoners were always alert.

He followed the auxiliary up to the floor above, allowing himself to examine the way the bottom half of her body moved underneath the thin grey military skirt. There was nothing else to look at, after all. After a step or two she clasped her hands behind her back, as if by chance, managing to block his view. How had she known?

'He's in his office,' she said, when they reached the floor above. Her hands now rested in front of her, between them. 'He's waiting for you.'

She was looking at him intently now, he noticed. Her cheeks were redder than usual.

'What does he want to see me about?' he asked, at least partially to break the silence.

'I don't know.'

For a moment, he thought that was all she'd say, but it wasn't.

'Perhaps it's about our evacuation?'

She pushed at a wisp of hair that had slipped down to curl around her chin. He, meanwhile, did his best to appear calm.

'Our evacuation?' he asked.

'The local Party have prepared a plan for the evacuation of civilians – I heard the Obersturmführer discussing it with the mayor. And last week they finally began to decommission the camp. So if the camp is going, and there's a plan for the civilians, then there must be a plan for us too. Don't you think?' Her voice tailed off. 'As a precaution, of course. Like a fire exercise.'

She held his gaze for a moment and he saw she was concerned about his reaction so he nodded his agreement with her suggestion, not trusting himself to speak. When she continued, it was in a softer, more plaintive tone, one more inviting of a shared confidence. She did not look in his direction, but there was no one else there.

'Perhaps it is something you might have discussed with the Obersturmführer? Or would like to? Just an exercise, of course – as I said. But how we would leave? Where would we go? When?'

'You're sure about the camp?'

She nodded, a swift nervous smile.

'And it's already begun?' He kept his voice neutral and low. The camp officers had been discussing an evacuation for some time – that it must happen soon, that they were waiting for authorization from Berlin. The authorization must have come.

'Some of the . . .' she hesitated, before continuing, 'the installations – are being deconstructed. And the officers are drawing up plans for removing the prisoners.' His question must have shown in his eyes. 'To other camps, I believe. Further back.'

'I see.'

'Will you ask him?'

'Yes,' he said, considering each word as he spoke. 'And if you could keep me informed about any developments at the camp? It would make sense to make each other aware of anything we hear.'

'I will,' she said – and they were in agreement. He took a deep breath.

'I have some advice, Fräulein Beck. Even if there are no orders, don't wait until the last moment – you and Fräulein Werth. If the Soviets come this way, stay ahead of them. Hide if they are close. Don't fall into their hands.'

She looked surprised and he found his mouth had opened once again. Was there no end to his stupidity?

'It's best to be prepared for all eventualities. Both of you. I have some experience of this – from the Front. And, whatever you do, don't fall into their hands in uniform.'

She said nothing for a few moments and he watched a tear form in the corner of her eye, grow large and then roll swiftly down the side of her nose until she stopped it with the tip of a long finger. She wiped it away.

'I'm sure it won't come to that,' he said.

She nodded and, to his surprise, smiled. A pretty, cheerful smile.

'Thank you, Herr Brandt.'
She had always had a cheerful disposition.

28

NEUMANN SAT at his desk. He'd arranged his papers and his pen, ready to start his work. But he found himself staring at them, without the slightest inclination to begin. He should be preparing for the Commandant's visit. He would, as always, have questions. But there had been more bombing last night. They had mentioned Hamburg. Marguerite was near there. And the boys. Their town was small – barely twenty thousand people – but they were bombing towns not much larger now.

The thought of Marguerite and the boys saddened him. He had heard nothing from her since her letter. Nor from the boys either. And now it was Christmas.

There was a knock at the door, quiet. Two more knocks, quiet but firmer. You could tell a lot from a person's knock. It was something that could be studied. This one wasn't going away unanswered.

'Come in, Brandt.'

Brandt slipped around the door. He was an interesting fellow, full of a false obsequiousness. Neumann almost admired the deception. No doubt he felt superior to them. But at least Neumann was here because he had been ordered to be here – even if the Commandant had been behind the orders. Brandt had been bought for a cigarette ration. He had no reason to feel superior to anyone.

'Sit down.'

'Thank you, Herr Obersturmführer,' Brandt took the chair in front of the desk.

'All is well? In the kitchen?'

'I think so. When will the officers arrive?'

'Hopefully at three. I'll suggest a walk down to the reservoir when they arrive, if the weather isn't too cold. To stretch their legs before it gets dark. Then they can change for dinner.'

'And in the morning?'

'They'll be up early for the shoot.'

'In which case I'll need the prisoners early as well.'

'I'll tell Peichl.'

Neumann looked up at Brandt, at his missing arm. He wondered.

'Do you think you could manage a camera, Brandt? The Commandant would like someone to take photographs of the dinner. Something to remember the evening by.'

Neumann thought he saw the glimmer of a smile draw at the man's raw mask. He should pull him into line. So what if the Commandant wished to remember this evening in later years. Yes, everything would no doubt be different but it was his right to do as he pleased in this place until things changed. In their world, for the moment, the Commandant was supreme. All fortune and misfortune was in his power.

On the other hand, of course, Brandt might have a point. This place and these times would be best forgotten, if that was possible.

'If it's an easy enough camera to handle, I can do it.'

'It's a Leica. I'll set the exposure for you. Just get close and press the button. You wind the film forward with your thumb, I'll show you. It's easy enough.'

'Then I'm at the Commandant's service, Herr Obersturmführer.'

'Good. And the tree?'

'It's ready.'

Neumann nodded his satisfaction. A thought occurred to him.

'Before, I mean, when you were younger.' Neumann found himself nodding towards where the man's missing arm should be. Exactly the kind of thing he'd wanted to avoid.

He gathered himself.

'Did you shoot, is my question. Animals, birds, that sort

of thing. The Commandant has asked for this hunt and the mayor has helped arrange it. It's not something I know anything about. Will it be a success?'

'I should think so. The mayor knows his business. All you have to do is stand in a long line and shoot anything that comes your way. A bit like at the Front.'

Neumann wondered if the man was mocking him. There was no hint of it – but it was hard to tell.

'Let's hope the animals don't shoot back,' Neumann said, and Brandt's thin mouth turned upwards.

'Speaking of the mayor, Herr Obersturmführer, I understand he is making preparations for an evacuation of the civilian population – purely as a precaution, of course.'

'And you're wondering if we should do the same?'

Brandt nodded. Neumann considered rebuking him, but decided it was too much effort. 'We have no orders yet – perhaps this evening. When the Commandant comes. I intend to ask him.'

'Thank you, Herr Obersturmführer.'

When Brandt had left, Neumann got up from his chair and walked to the window, looking down across the frozen reservoir and then over to the hills on the other side. In the reflection he thought he could see a shape behind him, just beside the door – the blurry outline of a man.

He paid it no attention. If he jumped every time he thought he saw a ghost in this place, he'd be worn out by breakfast.

29

THE OFFICERS from the camp were late and there had been yet another power cut. The third already that day. Brandt lit a candle and started his final check with the bedrooms at the far end of the building, the end closest to the village.

There wasn't much to be checked. The rooms were small and bare – designed for brief stays rather than permanent occupation. Jäger had been here for six weeks now, but he was an exception and he should be going tomorrow if the doctors who were coming for the dinner approved his return to active duty. The narrow beds had been made up with several blankets and the linen was clean and freshly ironed. Each room looked like a mirror of any one of the others – all very disciplined, all very regular.

Next, he checked the washroom with its row of sinks and the toilet cubicles – all appeared spotless. He would like to be absolutely certain but the flickering candlelight prevented this. There would be consequences if the expected standards weren't met. Not for him but for the women prisoners. The doctors, in particular, had a horror of dirt.

He walked through into the dining room. It was warmer here, a fire had been lit and the orange glow from its flames swirled across the ceiling. The long table filled the room and each place had been set. Twenty-four would sit down to dinner. Silver cutlery twinkled golden and the glass sparkled in the firelight. The windows that lined one side of the dining room, overlooking the yard, glittered.

If he was concerned about anything, it was about the candles. Antique silver candlesticks lined the centre of the table like soldiers on parade. He wouldn't light them yet. Already a candle was worth two packets of cigarettes. Candles, cigarettes and matches were as good as money when the world turned upside down. Perhaps they would be worth as much as a human life soon. He wouldn't waste them.

The Yule tree – as Neumann insisted it be called – stood in the entrance hall. It looked like a Christmas tree to Brandt. He found Neumann standing in front of it, a candle in his hand, contemplating the silver swastika that had been placed at its top with a look of puzzled concentration. He was wearing his dress uniform, a golden braid hanging down from his left shoulder epaulette. The braid and his polished black boots reflected back what light there was. He looked tired.

'If only we could have found a goose.'

Brandt wondered if Neumann expected him to go out and try to find one, in the dark, on Christmas Eve.

'The stew is good, Herr Obersturmführer. The mayor tried everything. There are no geese to be had.'

'I know. And we are soldiers, not children. Still – for the time of year – a goose would have been more appropriate.'

Neumann looked at his watch and then walked to the window. It was pitch black outside. He looked out as if hoping to see the officers arriving. The only sound was the crackling of the burning logs in the fireplace.

'We should light the candles.'

Brandt found himself frowning. All those candles burning down, just for one man.

'The candles, Herr Obersturmführer?'

'The tree should be lit when they walk through the door – it will set the tone for the evening. It will put them in a better mood.'

'An excellent suggestion, Herr Obersturmführer.'

'It wasn't a suggestion, Brandt.'

Brandt found his teeth had clenched, top against bottom.

'I will light them,' Neumann said. 'You will take photographs. I want to have this memory for my children. I want them to know I wasn't always a . . .' He paused as though searching for the correct word. 'A soldier. That there were quieter times. That I thought about them. Especially tonight.'

Neumann turned to face Brandt once again.

'The camera is on the table. You must hold it very still – rest it on something perhaps. In this light, if you move, even slightly, the image will be blurred and the moment will be lost.'

'I'll make sure I hold it steady.'

Brandt listened to himself speaking, conscious the words had revealed some of his anger. Neumann didn't notice.

Brandt positioned the camera on the back of an armchair and squinted through the viewfinder. Neumann looked small beside the enormous tree – it was nearly twice his height. Brandt had had to find the tallest of the Ukrainians and a step ladder to place the swastika and the higher candles.

Neumann stooped to light the long taper in his hand from the fireplace.

'Can you make out my face?'

'Not clearly.'

'Am I in shadow?'

'Yes.'

Only his oiled hair, his boots and his gold braid reflected any light.

'I'll light some of the candles.'

There were twenty-four on the tree. Neumann addressed them one by one, and soon the SS officer's face was a half-moon against the dark behind him. Click, whirr. Click, whirr. With each photograph the image of Neumann in the viewfinder became more distinct.

'Doesn't it look magnificent?'

Neumann stood back to examine his handiwork. 'Very elegant,' Jäger said. 'Just like a Christmas tree.'

Brandt hadn't heard Jäger come in but here he was – in black tanker uniform with silver runes at his collar and a chest and neck filled with ribbons and crosses. His sardonic smile was in full working order.

'A Yule tree, Herr Hauptsturmführer,' Neumann corrected him.

'Of course. A Christmas tree. As you say.'

Jäger stepped closer to it, passing a hand over the flame of a candle. Slowly.

'So, when do our comrades arrive from elsewhere?'

'In half an hour. For certain this time.'

'Excellent,' Jäger said. 'The Last Supper will finally take place.'

Neumann frowned.

'What's the matter, Neumann? It was at Christmas, wasn't it? The Last Supper? Brandt, you went to university?'

Jäger's gaze shifted between Brandt and Neumann – but ended up with Brandt.

'It was Easter, Herr Hauptsturmführer,' Brandt said. 'The Thursday before Easter.'

'I see. My mistake. It's only that I'm hungry, Neumann,' Jäger said, giving the Obersturmführer a pleasant smile. 'I feel like I've been waiting for a very long time for this supper, you see.'

30

BY THE TIME the officers sat down to dinner, some of them were already quite drunk. It wasn't an exclusively male affair – five SS women from the camp had been invited as well as the two telephone girls from the hut. The guests were arranged along the length of the table so that the officers would have a woman close enough to talk to. It didn't make them behave any better. Brandt and the two white-jacketed SS clerks from the camp were kept busy filling up glasses.

The mood wasn't cheerful. There was a shadow behind the polite smiles and forced laughter, and as the first course progressed the conversation began to reduce in volume to a muted mutter, with some withdrawing from it altogether. Even the two clerks seemed more like undertakers offering condolences than waiters serving a meal.

Only the Commandant, plump and self-assured, his round face made luminous by the candlelight, was enjoying himself. He was sitting in the middle of the long table with his officers arranged either side of him – Neumann to his right, looking concerned as he contemplated the glum expressions of his guests. The talk, by now, had fallen away to the occasional whispered request for a glass to be filled or a salt cellar to be passed. Brandt watched as Neumann leant over to whisper in the Commandant's ear, and saw the Commandant nod, rising to his feet and clinking the glass in front of him with a knife. The clinking was unnecessary. All eyes were already on him. But the Commandant, benevolent as his gaze might be, was making some sort of point.

When he stopped, there was almost perfect silence. Only the hiss and occasional pop from the fireplace disturbed it. The Commandant stood back from the table, his posture straightening, his shoulders filling out, his eyes narrowing.

He allowed his sharp gaze to move along the table – nodding to each in turn. Only when his gaze had traversed the entire company did he begin to speak in a conversational tone – quiet enough that those seated at the far end felt compelled to lean forward.

'Comrades, there is sadness in our hearts this evening. The Führer has marked this day on the Fatherland's calendar as one on which our nation should remember our many comrades who have fallen in the great struggle for a final, decisive victory. Let us take a few moments to think about them, the many who have made that ultimate sacrifice. Let us acknowledge their ghostly presence amongst us this evening. Let us remember them.'

The Commandant bowed his head.

'And let us stand to honour them.'

The chairs scraped back on the wooden floor as his guests stood and followed the Commandant's example, bowing their heads. It was some time before the Commandant broke the silence.

'And let us drink to them.'

They raised their glasses. When the glasses were back on the table, the Commandant stuck his thumbs in his belt and drummed his fingers on his stomach.

'Our comrades were happy to die for their country – and their homeland. Tonight we should celebrate their achievements and also celebrate our own. We can be proud of what we have done – fiercely proud. So let us cast off our cares for this one evening. Let's enjoy ourselves, friends. Let's celebrate the happy life our comrades led – and salute the glory of their deaths.'

Brandt felt his anger corroding his stomach. What had these men and women achieved, after all? The deaths of countless fellow humans was nothing to be proud of. It was something to be disgusted by. However, the Commandant's words had a different effect on the gathering. The thought of their dead comrades seemed to lift their spirits, rather than oppress them. They were cheerful now.

And soon after that, they were jolly.

31

NEUMANN looked around the table. The dessert had come and gone – the coffee, such as it was, had been drunk, and things had gone well – considering the slow start to the evening. It was late now and many of the guests had gone to their rooms – including all of the women. He didn't blame them. The remaining officers were drunk and, the majority of them, boorish. One of them had been sick in the entrance hall, and the white-jacketed SS waiters from the camp were nowhere to be seen.

There were eleven men still at the table, although one of the doctors – Heller – was slumped on top of it, snoring, using his crossed arms as a pillow. Ten, then. They had moved so that they sat together in the middle of the table, close to the Commandant. Neumann knew he was drunk, but he was behaving as an officer should behave. He was certain of it. The others laughed and swore, slapped each other's backs and beat the table with their fists. Only he and Heller weren't behaving like buffoons. He looked at Heller – the doctor's face was pale and saliva had darkened the grey sleeve beneath his half-open mouth but his lips were shaped by a cupid's smile.

Neumann understood it was almost the point of these evenings – that they needed to behave disgustingly, these men. Not all of them, of course – some had gone to bed precisely to avoid this part of the evening. Everyone had drunk heroically, even the women, but now was the dangerous time. The ones that were left, like him, sought oblivion or a means to vent their self-disgust.

With luck, there would be no violence – although he could feel the hunger for it running through the room like something electric. For half an hour, even he'd wanted to pick up one of the candlesticks and brain that smug rascal Beltz from the accounts department. Why had he sat the fool across from him? Always stroking his plump stomach or rubbing his thick fingers over his close-shaven, fat-padded scalp – Beltz had an unnaturally moist mouth and eyes that filled with tears when he laughed. He was laughing now. His teeth yellow against his purple lips – his tongue a quivering pink snake's head. He would like to rip that snake's head out. That might shut him up.

'Can I help you, Neumann?'

Neumann could only imagine what expression his face must have held. He mustered a smile.

'I was wondering what you were laughing at, dear Beltz.'

'Just something Jäger said.'

Neumann turned his attention to Jäger. The tanker wore a crooked smile. His weary grey eyes twinkled like cracked beads in the candlelight.

'What did he say?' Neumann asked, holding Jäger's gaze.

Beltz thought about it for a moment.

'I can't remember.'

Beltz couldn't help himself. He laughed again, dabbing at his eyes with a corner of the tablecloth as he wheezed for breath.

'I'm thought to be very witty, in my own way.' Jäger's smile looked as if it had been painted on. 'I think it was something about death. Something humorous. Death is a very amusing subject, don't you think?'

'I've spoken enough about death,' Neumann said, conscious that the edges of his vision had begun to swirl. 'I'd prefer to talk about women. Or the hunt tomorrow. The last film you saw, perhaps. Or music.'

A twitch of Jäger's thin lips.

'What is your favourite piece of music, Neumann?'

Neumann looked away, a thick belch forcing itself into his mouth. The black-jacketed tanker seemed to be a great distance away even though he could reach out with his arm and touch him. What had he asked? Ah yes. He remembered now. He would play along.

'I don't remember the tune's name. Da, da, da. Something like that. Uplifting. A dance of some sort. Classical. Do you know it?'

'I think I do,' Beltz said, putting his hands over his ears as if that might help him hear it. The fool.

'Don't be confused by his version, Beltz,' Jäger said. 'It goes quite differently.'

Beltz looked troubled, as though considering whether he should be offended or not, and when Jäger began to laugh, it didn't help matters. Now Neumann felt sorry for Beltz. He wanted to take the round little accountant into his arms and reassure him. What a rat Jäger was – to make fun of such a fine fellow.

The Commandant was sitting to Neumann's left and Neumann watched his superior's hand inch across the table. The Commandant placed it on top of Neumann's. As if in slow motion, Neumann saw the Commandant's kindly blue eyes approach until they were only a few centimetres in front of his own. If they came any closer their noses would touch.

'Neumann? You're white as a ghost – white as a sheet of paper.'

His superior's breath smelled like rotting flesh.

'I do feel a little unwell.'

'Don't give in to it, old friend. The night is still young.'

'We should sing songs.' Jäger's voice was slurred. He appeared surprised by his own suggestion. The Commandant turned towards the tanker and Neumann took the opportunity to lean back and breathe in sweeter air, reaching as he did so for the glass of brandy on the table in front of him. The movement almost unbalanced him. There were howls of amusement from the other end of the table –

but not because of him, he didn't think.

'Songs you say, Jäger?' The Commandant was enthusiastic. Neumann, on the other hand, was wary. 'What song should we begin with?'

'"It Was an Edelweiss"?' Jäger suggested. 'I like that song.'

'Do you know all the words?'

'Of course. Holla-hidi hollala, hollahi diho.'

'That's not singing.' His voice sounded strange to Neumann – like a poor recording, played too slowly. 'It's yodelling.'

It transpired that *yodelling* was a sticky word, one that clung to the teeth. Care had to be taken that the word didn't trip up on itself.

'It's part of the song,' Jäger said, slipping slowly under the table. 'It's part of the chorus.'

One moment Jäger was all there, brow crinkled by concentration. Then there was a bit less of him, his frown now one of irritation. Then his elbows gave way and he disappeared altogether.

'Where's Jäger gone?' the Commandant asked.

Jäger's voice came from beneath the table.

'Just a moment, I dropped something.'

'Let us know if you find it.' The Commandant beamed as if he'd made the finest of jokes. Beltz's head rolled back, his mouth like a cannon's muzzle ready to fire. When Beltz finally let his laugh out he beat his hands on his chest as if his heart might be in danger of stopping. Neumann wished it would.

'I found what I was looking for,' Jäger's voice sounded amused. Neumann took a grip on the table and leant down to see what it might be. He found Jäger sitting cross-legged, bent forward, a small black pistol in his hand. Pointed at Neumann. The tanker's finger was on the trigger, a smile on his face.

'I know what we should do,' Jäger said. 'We should play Russian roulette.'

'With an automatic?'

'Maybe you're right. Too easy. I was going to take the first turn, of course. But you're right – no point in shooting yourself if there are others happy to do it for you.'

Jäger put the gun back in his pocket, then turned to pull himself back onto his chair.

'What's he up to down there?'

The Commandant's expression was quizzical – his voice gentle.

Neumann felt more sober now. Jäger who had regained his seat and lifted a finger to his lips as if to say, 'Our little secret.'

'Excuse me, comrades,' Neumann said, standing to his feet. 'I need to relieve myself. Too much drink. I'll be back, don't worry.' Nobody was listening to him and his words were so quiet, they wouldn't have heard him if they had been. It was just as well. He needed to hold on to the table with both hands to stand upright. He felt precarious. When he felt more secure, he leant down to whisper in the Commandant's ear.

'Herr Sturmbannführer?'

'No ranks, Friedrich. Not between us, anyway. What is it?'

'Can we speak? Not now, but tomorrow? About the situation?'

The Commandant's mouth pursed but he gave a single sharp nod.

'Tomorrow. At the shoot. We'll take a walk.'

'Thank you.'

The Commandant looked up at him – his eyes golden in the firelight. His mouth relaxed into a sympathetic smile. He took Neumann's elbow and squeezed it.

'Go to bed. Don't worry about this warrior band – I'll

keep them in check. Get a good night's rest. This evening has been a great success, thanks to you.'

Neumann didn't trust himself to speak. He nodded and somehow, with a tottering momentum, walked to the far end of the table. There he steadied himself on one of the chairs. Breathed deeply. None of the officers was looking at him. It was as though he were invisible. At least until Brandt stepped forward, the camera in his hand. He heard the click as the steward took his photograph.

Neumann leaned forward and took Brandt's arm.

'No more pictures. That's enough,' he said, as calmly as he could.

'As you wish, Herr Obersturmführer.'

'Go home.'

'Of course, Herr Obersturmführer. And the women prisoners? In the kitchen?'

'Do I look as though I care what happens to them?'

'No, Herr Obersturmführer.'

Neumann saw the sullen anger in Brandt's eyes and considered, for a moment, dealing with it. But the evening was going well. And his eyes were heavy. He let it go, satisfying himself with a hard push to the steward's shoulder as he passed him.

32

NEUMANN LEANT his head against the wall as the urinal
swayed in front of him. Or perhaps it was him who was
swaying. He was tired, that was his problem – it wasn't the
drink. Had he even drunk anything? Yes. He remembered.
Quite a lot.

All the same, he'd been tired for nearly two years now
and that must take its toll. He'd been tired since the
Commandant had plucked him from the desk job in Kiev
and told him there were opportunities for a man like him in
the new German provinces that had been taken from the
Poles. Kiev was dangerous and unpleasant and only a fool
would have stayed there rather than return to Germany,
where, even in a newly acquired province, it would be safer
and more comfortable. Of course, his childhood friend
hadn't told him the work he was offering. Of course,
Neumann should have guessed. Neumann was aware of the
Commandant's involvement with the camps and, by then,
everyone knew what went on in them. But he'd been
greedy for advancement, of course, and, at the time, he'd
thought anywhere must be better than Kiev. All he'd
wanted was to be closer to his family, to climb another rung
on the ladder – to be somewhere safe. He hadn't planned to
become a murderer, he didn't think. It had just turned out
that way.

Neumann sighed as he fumbled with his buttons. They
were more difficult to do up than they had been to undo.

He wasn't quite sure when he'd first become aware of
his presence. Not immediately. About six months after the
train, he thought – although Neumann hadn't looked for
him before then. Perhaps he'd been there all along. He had
been easy to overlook – a suggestion of a shadow at dusk, a
movement out of the corner of his eye in a place where
everything should be still. It was intangible except that,

once he became aware of it, Neumann had known, almost immediately, who the presence must be.

He'd been picking up the old man's scent all day – a musty mixture of stale sweat and mothballs. He didn't remember it from the train, but he supposed it must come from there. What other reason could there be for it? It was growing stronger. He'd noticed it when he'd been lighting the candles – the piney tang of the tree couldn't smother it. It had been there when the guests had arrived and he'd smelled it all through the meal. And now the odour of fear and age was so pronounced that he was certain the old man was standing right behind him. Neumann took a deep breath and turned.

There was nothing to see – only the flickering candlelight sending strange shadows across the wall. Was he losing his mind? Neumann knew the old man must be nothing more than a twist of his imagination. And yet, perhaps soon, he might forget the difference between reality and unreality. The two would merge.

Of course, it was also logical that, if the old man came from within his own mind, then there was a simple way to put an end to him. But Neumann wasn't ready to take that step. Not just yet.

33

BRANDT descended the stairs to the kitchen, still feeling the grip of Neumann's fingers on his shoulder. He wanted to wash himself – to cleanse his skin of the contact. He also wanted to take back his stupid petulance. He could only hope Neumann wouldn't remember the conversation in the morning.

In the kitchen, the Bible students stood beside the counter, as if waiting for inspection. The others had been sent to the bunker earlier.

'The Obersturmführer says you can go to bed.'

Gertrud, the older one, closed her eyes as if a prayer had been granted. Katerina held his gaze. Neither of them moved. Katerina's tone was patient.

'Someone has to unlock the bunker.'

'Of course. I'll get one of the guards.'

Outside, the pale moon lit the snow and made the shadows of trees, fences and even guard towers crisp. The air was sharp, it stung his eyes it was so cold. He could see Bobrik in the tower by the gate, his face orange – he must have had the stove's door open, trying to keep himself warm.

'Bobrik?' he called up to him, his voice breaking the silence of the night.

Bobrik's shadow appeared above him, leaning over the parapet.

'Brandt? Are you going home?'

'In a few minutes. But the women need to be taken back to the bunker first.'

'Wait a moment.'

There was a delay and the sound of Bobrik's iron-nailed boots walking across the tower's concrete floor.

'Here.' The keys dropped into the snow beside him. 'It's the big round one.'

Brandt looked down at the keys then up at the guard

tower.

'Bobrik?' he said, and heard the anger in his voice. 'I'm not a guard. This isn't my work.'

'I can't leave the gate. Peichl would have my skin. It's just letting them in. You can manage that.'

Brandt cursed as he bent down. Bobrik was still leaning out over the parapet – watching him – and Brandt felt a scowl pulling at his taut, frosted skin. He was certain he heard Bobrik's chuckle as he walked back towards the kitchen, the cold keys heavy in his hand.

'Come on,' he said, opening the door. 'There is no one else to take you.'

Katerina walked towards him, her eyes on the floor in front of her. Gertrud followed, also avoiding his gaze. The women said nothing.

They walked along the concrete path that ran along the side of the hut, hearing the revelry above them. The concrete was icy underfoot and Brandt saw Gertrud reach for Katerina's arm when her clogs slipped. And here he was, walking behind them, the key to their prison in his hand.

The sound of their footsteps changed when they turned towards the bunker – the gravel on the path was frozen together and it crunched apart under their weight. The noise from the dining room receded and the silence of the valley took its place. Above them countless stars were scattered across the sky – the snow-shrouded trees shining in their silver glow. The women stopped beside the heavy metal door, standing aside while he inserted the key. He needed all his strength to turn it and, when the door was unlocked, he had to lean his whole body on it until momentum took over and it swung, squealing, open.

'It's only this once,' he said as they entered. 'I'm not one of them.'

'Who are you, then?'

The voice wasn't much more than a whisper. He wasn't even certain anyone had said anything, it was so quiet. Agneta.

He swallowed his bitter retort, pushed the door closed and turned the key in the lock. He felt desperate, cornered like a rat. He had betrayed her once again.

As he walked back towards the hut his frustration grew until it solidified into a need. A need to take some action. A willingness to risk all.

34

POLYA KOLANKA lay in her new uniform, her new quilted jacket over it, wearing her new winter boots which were keeping her feet snug and warm. She had taken the best spot, over the tank's transmission – still warm from the night's march – and now snow was covering the tarpaulin under which she lay like a second blanket. Life wasn't too bad. She'd savour this warmth for as long as she had it, the clothes for as long as they were clean and free from lice and engine oil. She'd enjoy the weight of the bellyful of food until she needed to eat again.

Best of all, no one was shooting at them – they'd reached the position undetected. She listened to Avdeyev the machine gunner and Vitsin the loader digging the tank in, their spades sounding brittle on the cold earth. Polya would have to get up in an hour and take her turn, of course, but at least their spot in the forest was relatively free from roots. Artemeyev's lot hadn't been so lucky – she could hear them swearing as they chopped their way down, centimetre by centimetre. They'd been told to do the job properly, that they'd be here for a while. And the Germans were close – so the deeper the hole, the safer they'd be.

She was tired. Her shoulders ached from pushing and pulling at the steering levers on the march, although she'd never admit it to the others or use it as an excuse to get out of the digging. She might be a woman but she wanted no special treatment. Anyway, Avdeyev and Vitsin had broken through the frosted crust now – so her part would be easier. By the time they finished they'd have shifted tens of tonnes of soil – but the tank would be safe unless a German shell landed straight on top of them. And when they'd covered it with branches and brush only the crows would know they were here – and by the morning, the crows would have forgotten where. As it should be.

It was worth the effort, the German artillery would pound them if they knew the battalion was here. And she hated artillery.

She was pleased that all their hard work making sure Galechka was ready for the coming battle had paid off. They'd had no trouble on the march here, while some of the skirt-chasers who'd spent their time running round after the field hospital nurses had broken down and been pushed off the road. And when the battalion had made its way through the forest, tank by tank so as not to let the Fritzes know what they were up to, Galechka had slipped through the trees like a ghost. They were only a few hundred metres away from the trenches – close enough to hear rifle fire – but some people, like that fellow in the third company, didn't understand the operational necessities of being quiet. Crushing a motorbike? What a piece of work that was. The Germans must have been asleep not to have heard it.

'Well done, Polina Ivanovna – not bad for a girl,' Lapshin had said to her when they'd arrived. She knew he'd been teasing her, that he'd expected nothing less. Little Polya had done it again. She'd been glad he'd been up behind her in the commander's seat, unable to see how her face had glowed with pride. She liked, as well, that he used her given name and patronymic – it was respectful. Although, she thought, calling her Little Polya, as everyone else did, would be quite acceptable also. She lay on top of the tank, feeling the heat from the engine against her back – and decided it was best not to think too much about Comrade Lapshin. It was distracting. Yet here he was coming towards the tank, picking his way across the snow. She knew the sound of his walk. She listened for it when he wasn't there.

She heard him climb up the side of the tank and slip under the tarpaulin alongside her.

'Comrade Lieutenant?'

'Ah, home sweet home. How long till our turn to dig?'

'An hour. I kept the watch.'

'Time enough for a nap, then.'

'All went well?'

'With the meeting? Well, enough. Your driving was picked out by the battalion commander for special praise – "If Little Polya can drive her tank like a man – everyone can." Don't expect kind looks from the third company – they were singled out for criticism.'

In the darkness Polya grinned hard enough to split her face.

'And now?'

'We wait. No more stripping engines, Polya. It could be at any moment. Turn her over, grease her up, keep her warm but nothing more than that. Now, if you'll excuse me – an hour's sleep is an hour's sleep.'

There it was, just like that. Comrade Lapshin had called her Polya. She smiled, turned on her side, and shut her own eyes.

As Comrade Lapshin said, an hour's sleep was an hour's sleep.

35

IT WAS STILL dark the next morning when Brandt opened the hut's front door. He hadn't had much sleep and he felt anxiety like a physical weight. He'd tossed and turned in bed and eventually got up, going downstairs to sit in the armchair and have a smoke – at which point his eyes had promptly closed. He awoke feeling tired and stiff, the key to the bunker, which he'd removed from the bunch, still clutched in his fist. What had he been thinking – taking it?

Brandt turned on the light switch and, miracle of miracles, light resulted. He checked his watch, just past five o'clock, and looked around the entrance hall – the must of stale cigarettes and spilled wine clung to the air. And something else. He found the vomit under a carefully placed armchair. The Christmas tree had been pushed sideways at some stage so that it now leaned crookedly against the wall. He tugged it upright. At least someone had snuffed out the candles. He wrapped his fingers around the key in his pocket. He'd say it came off by accident when they asked him. It didn't make sense, of course. But he could think of no better excuse.

Adamik brought the women in at six. Brandt knew he must have used a spare key to open the bunker, so the guards knew the other one was missing. Brandt waited for the question, but Adamik barely even looked at Brandt – just took the cup of hot milk Brandt had made for him. Brandt felt the cold sweat sticking his vest to his skin. Perhaps it was a trick. He felt the key's shape in his pocket like a weight dragging him into his grave.

The officers began appearing for breakfast around seven. They were dressed for the shoot, in winter jackets and woollen jumpers. Most of them looked as though they'd rather be in bed. At least they had nothing to complain about – the dining table was once again covered in a clean, crisp cloth and the smell of fresh bread and soup had replaced the other, more unpleasant odours.

Downstairs, in the kitchen, he began to prepare the meat for the evening meal. He waited. Maybe they were waiting for him to take it to the guardhouse. Perhaps holding on to the key was the worst thing he could do. He pressed the mutton onto the spiked carving board and began to trim away the fat. He tried to focus completely, for a moment, on the blade and the cutting. On days like this, his missing forearm hurt him – and not just where the material of his jacket rubbed against his still-raw stump. Each of his lost knuckles ached, even though they were long gone.

He wondered if perhaps his fingers *were* still there, in another version of this world, attached to a version of him that hadn't been to war. A different world from this one, where the camp had never been built and the valley was as it always had been. Where he had finished his studies and never had to kill a man. One where he hadn't taken the damned key.

His thoughts were interrupted by the sound of footsteps descending the staircase that led to the hut's upper level – the wood creaking under their weight. Someone was coming now – looking for him.

'Brandt?' Peichl's voice came down. 'Are you there?'

'I'm here,' Brandt said, forcing the words through the fear that filled his throat.

'And?'

The key pressed against his thigh, cold through the fabric of his pocket.

'At your service, Herr Scharführer.'

Three more steps, the boots and belt appearing. Then four more. Then the final three. Peichl's black belt cut into the taut fabric of his uniform like a tourniquet. Brandt reminded himself to breathe.

'What's wrong with you, Brandt? You seem out of sorts.'

Peichl made his way over to him, standing so close that Brandt could smell the onions and stale schnapps on his breath. The SS man, not being an officer, had taken his entertainment in the village the night before. Brandt wondered if he might still be drunk.

'I wasn't aware I was out of sorts, Herr Scharführer. I thought I was just the same as every other day.'

Peichl laughed, walking over to the cast-iron cooking stove. He lifted his buttocks one after the other onto the round metal rail that ran along its length.

'Bobrik said you locked the prisoners up last night.'

Brandt kept his eyes on the meat. He didn't dare look up.

'There was no one else. I wanted to go home. It was late.'

'Did you tuck them in?'

'I don't understand.'

'You think I don't notice your little kindnesses to them, Brandt?'

Brandt said nothing. Even if he'd wanted to, he wasn't certain his mouth could form the words he required.

'I imagine you were an awkward soldier, Brandt,' Peichl said. 'Even when you were all in one piece.'

Brandt turned and picked up the knife once again, sliding the blade along and down into the flesh. Adrenaline made him clumsy.

'I was awkward enough, I suppose, Herr Scharführer. But awkward soldiers are often good at fighting – they have their own minds, you see.'

Brandt heard the inference in his words as soon as they were spoken. He turned and saw that Peichl had heard it as well. 'You think I wouldn't be much use when it comes to fighting the Russians, do you, Brandt? You think I don't have my own mind?'

With slow menace Peichl lifted himself away from the stove.

'I could have a couple of the Ukrainians take you for a walk in the wood. Perhaps I should take you myself. Then we'd see how brave you really are, for all your talk.'

Brandt held the knife in his hand loosely. A lunge and a twist. Pull it out, slash, slash. Lunge again. He could be in the forest before anyone was the wiser. He could leave this place behind him. All he saw, for an instant, was Peichl and the place beneath his ribcage where he'd stick him. Peichl stopped, his eyes narrowing. And then there was a noise. A plate being placed, very carefully, on a hard surface. Agneta washing dishes in the small pantry. The sound calmed him. He had forgotten why he was here. He remembered now. He swallowed, allowing some of the tension to flow out of him.

Peichl hadn't mentioned the key. And that was important. Because if he was going to, he would have by now. Brandt gave Peichl his best attempt at an ingratiating smile, holding his hand out wide – pointing the knife away from the SS man. He didn't place it on the counter, however, that would be stupid.

'Who would supervise your kitchen for you then, Herr Scharführer? Who would look after the officers from the camp? Who would make sure you and your men had sandwiches and soup at the end of the shoot? And a flask of something to take with you this morning?' Brandt pointed with the knife to the army water bottle on the counter, which he had filled with brandy. 'I didn't mean to cause any offence.'

Peichl's eyes narrowed, as if looking for another insult. Brandt was conscious that the only sounds came from upstairs, where the mood of the officers' breakfast had begun to lighten. Laughter. Brandt kept his gaze fixed on Peichl's, then leant his head forward infinitesimally. A gesture of subjugation to Peichl's will. There was a long, tense pause. But the gesture seemed to satisfy Peichl. He grunted.

'We can always find someone else from the village, Brandt. You aren't irreplaceable. Not at all.' Peichl lifted the water bottle, unscrewed the camp and sniffed. 'This is the good French stuff?'

'Armagnac. The best we have.'

Brandt leant his head forward another fraction, lowering his eyes.

'Make sure the soup is hot, Brandt. It will be cold up in the forest.'

Peichl screwed the cap back on and nodded, allowing his gaze to wander around the kitchen, before turning his attention back to Brandt.

'Be careful, cripple. I'm not a man to be crossed.'

Brandt looked after Peichl as he made his way back upstairs. And began to breathe once more. He was surprised by how much he'd wanted to put the knife into him – even at the Front he'd never felt anything like it. He shivered.

He needed to talk to Bobrik. He needed to understand why no one knew about the missing key.

36

AGNETA WATCHED the confrontation from her place in the scullery and waited for it to boil over. Peichl had killed people with his own hands. She'd seen him do it. And Brandt looked frail compared to the solidity of the SS man.

Yet Brandt stood his ground.

She watched the way he held the knife. She saw how he turned the blade so that its edge was uppermost – a small movement, easily missed. For a moment, she thought he might use it. Fillet the fat SS man right in front of them. And felt cold fear. Everything she did to stay out of sight, to keep out of harm's way – yet something like this could happen in an instant, leaving her hanging by the slenderest of threads. But Brandt had got away with it.

Now she felt anger – and exhaustion. She was tired of being – constantly, always – caught in the moment before her own death.

She considered Brandt. He was an enigma to her, almost as much as she suspected he was to Peichl. Behind his frozen face he could be anyone. But the question that bothered her most was why he was here in the hut. It didn't make sense.

'Agneta, do you have a moment?'

She turned to find him standing beside her. His lack of eyebrows making his gaze seem unnaturally intense. She nodded. He shut the door to the kitchen behind him. They were alone. No one could overhear them if they spoke quietly.

'I need to speak to you,' he began. 'If you'll permit me?'

His politeness annoyed her – as if she had a choice in the matter. Aside from which she knew how seductive it could be, this apparent kindness. Already she could feel it soften her. She needed all the strength she could gather and yet this man was weakening her. And this only moments after he'd put all their lives at risk.

'Of course, Herr Brandt – as you wish.'

She would talk to him, if she must.

'The Obersturmführer is anxious. All of them are anxious – it's because of the Russians, because of the way things are going. You saw how Peichl was just then – they must be given no excuses, do you understand? You must all take special care.'

Of course she knew. Was the man an idiot? She took special care with every breath and every movement she made. It was Brandt who needed to take more care, not her.

'I always take special care, Herr Brandt.'

'I know. I'm reminding you, that is all. I want you to remind the others as well. They look up to you. The cutlery must glow, the linen must dazzle, the glass must shimmer. Do you understand me? I'm not saying this for my sake, I'd break every last glass in this place if it were left to me.'

His eyes squinted slightly – he wanted her to take him seriously. He needn't worry about that. She took everything seriously. She took his stupidity most seriously of all.

'Of course, Herr Brandt.'

He looked around him, checking whether the walls might be listening. He reached for her hand. Instinctively she pulled it out of his grasp and took a step back. She couldn't help the horror she felt. It must have shown in her face because his thin lips curled into what he presented to the world as a smile.

'That was clumsy. I meant to say, I am not like them. Even if I turned the key last night. Please understand that.'

She said nothing. His smile remained constant and patient. Eventually he shrugged, as if agreeing with something she'd said.

'What I wanted to say,' he began and then stopped. He coughed. 'I wanted to tell you – and the others – not to be afraid. Do you understand? If you are careful, if you are patient, if we all work together – there will come a happier time.'

She was speechless. What did he mean? That there would come a happier time? And what did he mean by saying 'we'?

'Just be careful,' Brandt said. 'And patient.'

Despite herself she responded with a nod. She immediately regretted it.

She should give no encouragement to his madness.

37

THE BUS WHEEZED as it climbed the road towards the
higher valley. Behind them came a covered truck with
Brandt and his Volkssturm boys – and the picnic. The small
convoy had crossed the dam and now the frozen reservoir
lay below them to their left. The road was barely more than
a track, and icy with it. Occasionally the tyres would slip
and the bus slide sideways before the driver corrected it.
The officers shouted out in pretend fear, and then laughed.
Neumann did his best to smile, but the truth was the
prospect of tumbling down into the valley terrified him.

The problem was the bus. It was an old school bus and
its engine wasn't powerful enough for an incline like this.
Painting it field grey didn't make it a military vehicle. They
hadn't even changed the seats. The officers, swaddled in
tweed and felt, their rifles wedged between their knees,
swelled out into the central aisle, rubbing shoulders with
the officers on the other side of the bus. With each bump
and turn in the road, they leaned and swayed as one.

Despite the cramped conditions and their hangovers, they
were in a good mood – there was a burble of anticipation
despite the struggling motor and the steep slope. Each slide
and slip, each twist that took them closer to the precipice,
made them more cheerful still.

It helped that they'd left the SS women back at the hut –
the officers were more relaxed as a result. It was cold in the
bus and their breath had fogged the windows. Beltz drew a
penis on the misted glass. Neumann doubted he'd have
done it if an auxiliary had been sitting beside him, rolling
blonde hair around a pretty finger. None of the others
would have laughed along with Beltz if there had been
women with them. The Commandant passed him a small
flask. He drank from it. Better than leaving it to the
Russians, after all. It burned as it made its way down but it

warmed him. The Commandant took it back, sipping in turn. He gasped, his smile fleshy and wide, and took a grip on Neumann's knee.

'Well, what have you arranged for us?'

He spoke not only to him but also to Weber, who sat beside Neumann, his fat thighs taking up more than his fair share of the seat.

'It's a driven shoot, Herr Commandant,' Weber said.

'I know that much.'

Neumann smiled at Weber's downcast reaction.

'There is plenty of game in the woods up by the Red Farm, where we're going; I've seen it myself,' Weber said. 'The shooting should be excellent.'

'I'm pleased to hear it, Weber.' The Commandant turned to the other occupants of the bus, raising his voice. 'Hopefully our celebrations from last night will not affect our aim.'

The officers, even the grey ones – the ones with the swampy eyes who didn't laugh when the bus slid – even they smiled.

'Where did you get beaters from?' Jäger asked. He looked the palest of all – his cheeks seeming to have shrunk in on themselves overnight.

Neumann paused, considering how to answer. It was an awkward question but not deliberately so, he didn't think. Jäger looked more curious than mischievous.

'The Commandant was able to assist,' Neumann said.

He'd have preferred to appear offhand, not to draw attention to his words. The hesitation had been a mistake and, sure enough, Jäger noticed. He might still be half drunk, but his brain was working efficiently enough. It took him a moment or two, but he reached the correct conclusion.

'Prisoners? From the camp? It will be nice for them to get out for a walk in the fresh air. How lucky they must feel.'

Beltz's laugh was like a dog's bark but it stopped when the others looked away, discomfited. The mood on the bus had turned sour. Jäger looked around him, no longer appearing quite so bleary-eyed. In fact his blunder appeared to have revived him. The oldest of the doctors, a man in his late fifties, closed his eyes, his lips moving without words. Neumann wondered if he was praying.

'I apologize, gentlemen,' Jäger said, louder than was necessary. 'I didn't mean to offend your sensibilities.'

The irony was pitch perfect. Neumann had to admire it. He had to say something, of course. It was his duty to ensure the officers enjoyed themselves this morning. But before he had a chance, the Commandant leaned forward, taking Jäger's shoulder in his hand.

'Perhaps we should sing a song, what do you think, Jäger?' The Commandant made the suggestion sound like a threat. 'You were so keen to sing for us last night.'

Neumann knew the Commandant well enough to realize how annoyed he was. But Jäger wasn't intimidated – he shook his head regretfully.

'I apologize, Herr Sturmbannführer. I've forgotten all the words to all the songs I ever knew. I must have drunk too much last night.'

'You could just hum, Jäger. That would be sufficient. Hum for us, why don't you?'

It was enough to make one or two of the officers chuckle – but the Commandant wasn't intending to amuse.

Jäger smiled. And began to hum.

38

WHEN THEY arrived at their destination, Weber drew a diagram in the snow with his shooting stick. He explained how the valley's ridge split here, forming a natural funnel. The beaters, and their guards, would push whatever game there was along it to where the officers waited, strung out in a line some fifty metres from the edge of the forest.

Neumann was surprised by the anticipation he felt, once he made his way to his assigned position. Wolf stood behind him – his pink tongue lolling, his eyes sparkling in the morning sun. If Neumann shot well, then the dog would eat meat today. At first there was nothing but the snow-smoothed silence. Then Neumann heard the beaters coming, felt his heart quicken as he pushed the safety catch on his rifle to the off position. He slid his gloved finger inside the trigger guard and breathed out slowly, calming himself. The air was cold – his cheeks were smarting. When he breathed back in, he felt its sharpness in his chest.

He looked to his right and saw Beltz's eagerness; to his left, the Commandant had taken a wide stance, the butt of his weapon tucked under his armpit, ready to flick it up and fire.

They'd been friends since childhood – they'd even fought in the same regiment during the last war – and something in the Commandant's watchful anticipation reminded Neumann of the younger man. After their discharge, the Commandant had been the one who'd done well – at least until the crash in 'twenty-nine. And even when his business had failed, he'd landed on his feet with the Nazis – and then the SS. Neumann hadn't joined the Party until much later, and only after the Commandant had explained to him the importance of being on the winning side in the new Germany. It had even been the Commandant who'd pulled the strings that landed him a commission in the SS.

It wasn't that Neumann had opposed the Nazis. It had been clear that the country needed strong leadership and the Führer had certainly offered that. It was just that, back then, he'd had other matters on his mind. After all, his position had not been so bad – a pretty wife and two young children – the thought of whom caused a constriction in his throat – and a job in the local bank when many had none. He'd kept his head down, avoided the violent demonstrations, kept his opinions to himself. But it had been clear that things were changing, that the Nazis were the new power in the land, that the democrats, the liberals, socialists and communists – and most particularly the Jews – would be dealt with harshly. And then the Commandant had told him they were looking for fellows just like him – well, he didn't want to be left behind, did he?

How it had got from that to this wasn't so strange. There had been a momentum – everyone was rolled up in it and it bore you on. Everyone – well, a lot of people – had thought the Jews were responsible for the failure of the last war, for the crash, for every little wrong they'd ever suffered. One thing had led to another. No one wanted to be the one who stood out – the one to say things were going too far. It had been quite the opposite, in fact. People had said they weren't going far enough. But mostly, no one had ever imagined it would come to this. Until it had, of course.

There was a cracking of branches in front of him and a fox sprang out of the undergrowth like a rusty bullet, a dark blur against the snow. He aimed and fired. Missed – fired again. He'd been holding the rifle loosely for the first shot and the recoil hurt his shoulder. It woke him up. The second shot caught the fox in the chest and flung it backwards into a still mound of fur.

'Bravo!' The Commandant shouted and there were other congratulations, from his left and right. Wolf loped forward to collect the dead animal, dragging it back towards him, a trail of blood behind. The first kill was his but he felt no pride in it. There had been no skill or thought. The truth of the matter was he wasn't sure he'd wanted to kill the creature. If it had made it past him to freedom he wouldn't have minded.

All along the line rifles were firing now – not continuously, but there was a kind of rhythm to it all the same. There was a cheer as a huge boar burst out onto the snowy field, and aimed for the gap in the line between the Commandant and the next officer. The Commandant swung his rifle in time with the boar's run and fired once, killing it instantly. It slid to a halt nose first – carried by its momentum.

Further up the line a deer came bounding through the brush and there was more cheering as blood exploded from its head. Soon, animal corpses littered the expanse in front of the line of shooters, the snow turning pink around them. The chatter and cheering decreased as the opportunities came more frequently. Then, in a long pause where each man concentrated on the area in front of him, rifle held at the ready, there came the sound of gunfire from inside the forest – three shots in rapid succession. Further along the line a deer broke cover but no one fired. It bounded through the line, its eyes white with fear.

It had sounded like a pistol. The Commandant looked across at him. Neumann lowered his rifle and shrugged – uncertain. He listened. All along the line others did the same. But there was only silence. Even the beaters were no longer making any noise.

'It must have been one of the guards,' Beltz said to no one in particular. Perhaps to himself.

One of the beaters trying to escape? Or just moving too slowly. It was the most likely explanation. But, just in case, he held his rifle close to his shoulder and scanned the tree line for movement.

The shouting from inside the forest, unmistakably men telling other men to do things they didn't want to, came as a relief. A hare, perhaps startled by the sound, tumbled out onto the snow, running left, then right.

'Nothing to worry about,' the Commandant called out, turning so that the officers further down the line could hear him. Saying which, he raised his rifle to his shoulder and fired at the hare, missing it. On either side, the shooting started afresh. The hare, terrified, bounded between Neumann and the Commandant and Neumann watched as the Commandant's rifle followed it until it was pointed directly at him – when he fired. The bullet cracked past Neumann – so close he could have sworn he felt the heat of it on his cheek. The Commandant pointed his rifle upwards immediately – a look of shock on his face, quickly replaced by an apologetic smile. No one else had noticed the incident.

'It got away, blast it,' the Commandant called over to him. Neumann found himself smiling, feeling the adrenaline surge through him. It wasn't fear as such – he'd almost enjoyed the experience. In fact, it amused him – the thought that his old friend might have shot him. A final gift from the Commandant – on Christmas Day.

'Better luck next time,' he said. And the Commandant smiled back at him, appreciating the double meaning.

Neumann was pleased. He hadn't made a fuss about the incident. He had shown he was a man of courage.

It was surprising to Neumann how much game there was but eventually, despite the plenty, the animals that broke from the brush became fewer, and further between. The firing decreased in intensity and the shouts and crashing of the beaters came closer and closer. The end of the shoot approached. It had gone off well – despite his having nearly been shot by the Commandant. Neumann permitted himself some satisfaction. It was fleeting, though – ended by a final spate of firing and a high-pitched wail of pain that paused only when the wounded man drew breath.

What had happened wasn't entirely clear – there was shrill laughter and some confusion at the other end of the line. Neumann thought he recognized the laughter as belonging to Weber – the mayor. Then there were two more shots and more laughter – although this time it sounded almost hysterical. Already the Commandant was marching along the line towards the commotion, shouting at people to stop firing. Neumann ran after him, cursing as he did so. He could see what had happened now – a bundle of striped rags lay on the snow, a few metres in from the trees. A dead prisoner. Twenty metres further along another prisoner squirmed in agony, another dead man lying beside him. The fools had shot at the beaters. No one looked up as they approached the officers who had gathered around the nearest corpse. The dead man's mouth hung open in a broken-toothed, black-tongued yawn. He stared up at the clouded sky – unseeing. A bullet had hit him in the chest.

'Who is responsible for this?' the Commandant demanded.

'It was an accident.' The older doctor from the bus looked to be in shock – his face was white as the snow itself. 'I thought he was a deer.'

'Since when do deer wear stripes?'

The doctor had the good sense to say nothing. The other officers looked away, except for Jäger, who poked at the dead man with his rifle.

'Maybe he thought he was a zebra?' Jäger suggested.

'You think this is amusing, Hauptsturmführer Jäger?' the Commandant shouted. 'Something to laugh about?'

'I never laugh at death, Herr Commandant. I think it's a very serious matter.'

'It is a serious matter, Jäger. So wipe that smile off your

face.'

The Commandant turned back to the doctor, pointing to the wounded prisoner – furious now.

'And him? Is he your work too?'

He'd been shot twice, once in the leg and once in the stomach. His eyes were a bright blue in a dark face that was all bones and little flesh, its gauntness accentuated by his beard. The bullet in his leg had hit an artery, that much was evident. Blood pumped from the man's thigh out on to the snow, forming a smoking red puddle. The dying man stared around him at the circle of officers., In contrast to them, healthy and hearty in their hunting tweeds, the prisoner was so thin it seemed that only his taut skin held his bones together. He appeared surprised by their interest in him.

'It was me,' the mayor said, looking almost as abject as the doctor. 'I thought that we were meant to. That it was part of the shoot.'

'You thought you were meant to shoot the beaters?' The Commandant's amazement was real.

'They're prisoners, Herr Commandant. From the mining camp. The others were doing it. I thought I was entering into the spirit of things.'

Weber looked as if he might cry. Why should today be different from any other day? Just because it was Christmas or Julfest or whatever he should call it? Why should there be no killing today?

More prisoners came through the trees and stood, confused by the dead animals strewn across the field, before being drawn by the dying man's moaning. They wore wooden clogs – their feet wrapped in frozen rags, their hair stiff and clumped. Those who had any. They were tanned by filth, their grimy striped jackets hanging from thin shoulders like oversized ponchos. They were so exhausted that their open eyes were sightless, as if the small amount of energy it might take to focus them was too

much. They were drawn in closer and closer by the dying
man's screams. The Commandant pointed them out to the
officers.

'Get rid of them,' he said. 'And someone deal with this
mess. Where are the guards?
Neumann?' Neumann stood to attention.

'Herr Commandant, there are sandwiches and
refreshments back at the bus. Please, allow me to deal with
this matter.'

The Commandant was as angry as Neumann had ever
seen him but, after a moment's hesitation, he nodded.

'Yes, yes. We'll put this matter behind us. Have these,'
the Commandant pointed to the prisoners, 'bring the game
over to the vehicles – let's see what we've achieved here.
Come on, gentlemen – let's do as Obersturmführer
Neumann has suggested. I certainly could do with a drink.'

The prisoners moved aside for the officers, the two
groups each choosing to ignore the other. The doctor and
the mayor stayed back.

'Is there anything we can do?' the mayor asked. The
doctor nodded his agreement with the question.

'You're a doctor, aren't you?' Neumann said.

The doctor glanced down at the wounded man and
shrugged his shoulders.

'There's nothing to be done for him. Take my word for
it.'

'Nothing?'

'Not in his condition. With those wounds? And anyway
– what do we do with him then?'

The prisoner looked up at the doctor, his eyes wide. He
appeared offended. Or perhaps he didn't understand.

'Here's Peichl,' the mayor said, relieved. 'Peichl will
deal with things.'

The Scharführer approached, a cigarette hanging from
the side of his mouth.

'Trouble, Herr Obersturmführer?' Peichl said, looking at the dead beaters and their injured comrade. The other guards followed him out of the trees, faces wrapped in scarves, thick overcoats dusted with snow. Some were from the mining camp and some from the hut. Peichl nodded towards the prisoners and the guards began to organize them into lines. Their shouting was tired – the swing of their rifles slow. Quick enough to make contact all the same.

'An accident,' Neumann said.

Peichl shrugged, examining the wounded man.

'I've just shot one myself, Herr Obersturmführer. Not an accident, of course.' He peered down at the dead man.

'The Commandant is unhappy about the incident. Today was meant to be a break from this.'

Neumann found the toe of his boot was pushing at the prisoner's thigh. It was unintentional – he'd merely meant to indicate what he was talking about. He looked down and found himself staring into the dying man's eyes.

'What are your orders, Herr Obersturmführer?'

It took an effort to break the prisoner's empty gaze.

'See what can be done for this one and get rid of the prisoners we've managed not to shoot.'

'Get rid?'

'Not that. Get them organized, then back to the mining camp.'

Peichl looked over at the emaciated prisoners. 'You don't want us to march them back the whole way, do you, Herr Obersturmführer? Not the men from the hut, at least. Surely the camp guards can look after them.'

Neumann looked down at the dead prisoner. He could tell from the yellow star on the grimy strip of fabric which category he was.

'They didn't come in a truck?'

'The mining camp's trucks have been reallocated. They

haven't even got a handcart these days.'

Neumann saw the resentment in Peichl's half-concealed scowl. He didn't care.

'See you get them there and see it's done properly. No more accidents. I hold you responsible.'

Peichl hesitated just before he gave his salute. Neumann smiled. It gave him pleasure to irritate the Scharführer from time to time.

Peichl said nothing. Neumann turned back to the mayor.

'An unfortunate incident, Herr Weber – but one we can forget about, I think.'

The mayor's attention was elsewhere, on something that was happening behind him. There was a gunshot, very close, accompanied by the unmistakable thud of a bullet driving its way into flesh. The dying man's moaning came to an abrupt end. Neumann turned to find Peichl replacing his pistol into its holster. He shrugged.

'I put him out of his misery. Herr Doktor Bayer said he was on the way out.'

Neumann looked down at the dead man – his empty gaze stared back at him. It wasn't that he'd thought he could save him – he'd known he couldn't be saved. It was that he'd wanted at least a part of this mess to be fixed. And now, of course, it had been – just not in the way he'd wanted.

'See that these three are buried,' he said to Peichl. 'Find some shovels and do it properly. And the one you shot in the forest as well. And get the dead animals over to the bus. If one of those prisoners – just one – doesn't make it back to the mining camp I'll have you transferred to the Front before the day is out. I promise you that, Peichl. Quick now.'

Peichl saluted properly this time and set about organizing the prisoners and guards. Wolf, who had disappeared off somewhere, now reappeared at Neumann's side, his mouth smeared with blood. He hoped it was an animal's.

Neumann looked at the men gathered around the bus – no one looked over. A pistol shot, a dead man – for other people this might be a moment of significance. For the officers from the camp it was nothing compared with a sandwich and a tot of schnapps.

He looked again. There was one exception – Brandt stared across the snow at him. It was impossible to make out his expression from this distance. Perhaps he felt outraged. He should have picked a different place to work if he was. It was too late for him to sit in judgement now – not since he'd taken their cigarettes, their wages and whatever he'd pilfered from the kitchens. He was as much a part of this as any of them. He could spare them his crocodile tears.

And, now that he looked again, there were other exceptions – the Hitler Youth that the mayor had provided to help serve food and drinks to the officers. Three youngsters with ears and eyes too big for their thin faces, who looked past him to where the dead bodies lay. How old were they? Thirteen or fourteen – one of them even younger perhaps. No longer children, soldiers now. They'd been enlisted into the Volkssturm in October and now, only a few weeks later, here they were watching prisoners being killed for fun.

Neumann pulled his scarf tighter around his face, surprised by his sudden nausea. The last thing he needed was to fall ill. And there was ice in this wind – more bad weather was coming, no doubt. And it would be January soon.

January was always the bitterest of months.

39

BRANDT WAS shivering. He had to lean back against the bus to stay upright. He was cold, that was true, but he'd been much, much colder before. He wasn't sick, he didn't think – not physically. Nor was he frightened – the murder of the beaters had brought with it no sense of personal danger, for him at least. Certainly nothing like what he had experienced at the Front. This uncontrollable trembling – almost like spasming – was caused by something else.

He should be overseeing the passing out of soup and sandwiches to the officers – making sure their glasses were topped up with schnapps and brandy when needed. Simple tasks, but they would require a steadier hand than he currently could lay claim to and, if he had to face the officers at this very moment, there was a risk the fury that raged through his entire body might reveal itself in some way. He needed to calm himself.

'Fischer?'

The young boy turned to him. Moist round eyes and a tight, pale-lipped mouth. Not so cheerful now, it would seem. He wanted to offer him some comfort – but what could he say? That the dead men had deserved it?

'I need to warm up. I've a cold coming on. Can you manage without me for a few minutes?'

Fischer looked to his empty sleeve and nodded his agreement, managing a smile for him.

'Of course. Would you like me to find you a blanket?'

'I know where they are. I'll be five minutes. But come and fetch me if you need me.'

Once he was sitting in the back of the bus, swaddled in thick wool, the tremors that had taken control of his body began to fade. It had been like a sudden fever. One moment he'd been perfectly normal and then his body hadn't been quite his own. Even now he felt nauseous.

He was clear-headed enough to realize the moment which had triggered the reaction. It wasn't when the prisoners had been shot. He'd almost been expecting something like that to happen, he realized now. And when the Commandant had reprimanded Jäger so publicly, it had been reassuring in a strange way. Even amongst these men there were rules about death, and perhaps it helped that he heard some, a tiny portion, of his outrage spoken out loud – even if it was by the Commandant.

No, what had set it off had been when Peichl had shot the wounded man. He'd seen, even from a distance, the look that had passed between the Scharführer and the doctor when Neumann turned away. Peichl had pulled his pistol out, pointed it at the wounded man, glanced over at the doctor – who'd shrugged as if to say: 'What are you waiting for?'

And Peichl had fired. As simple as that.

But it wasn't even this moment that had caused him the most disquiet – he'd seen people shot in such a way before. There were no prisoners taken at Stalingrad – or few enough. It was the setting. The contented, chortling officers gathered around the soup urns and the fact that not one of them so much as turned – not even the Commandant, who had been so angry only moments before. There had been a mess, it had been tidied up. It would have been impolite for any of them to acknowledge that the cleaning up had involved another murder. It was curious, he thought, that the anger he felt was mostly with himself – and at his own powerlessness.

Even now, sitting in the relative warmth, calmer – he could hear them talking about the shots they'd made and the shots they'd missed – the ripe cheeriness in their voices and their self-satisfaction. They'd forgotten the dead men, if they'd ever even been especially aware of them, of course. He felt that peculiar pressure just above his Adam's apple, the tang of bile in his mouth that told him he was a momentary lapse of will away from spewing up his breakfast. He concentrated on breathing. Slowly. Nothing else until he felt his self-control returning.

He reminded himself why he was here. He cleared his mind of doubt.

When he was ready, Brandt pulled himself to his feet, letting the blankets fall down behind him. One of the officers could pick them up, fold them – make them into something orderly. Tidy up the mess in the same way they'd tidied up the wounded beater. He would go back out into the snow and smile – joke even, if necessary, with the officers. He was not completely powerless – there were things that he could achieve in the face of this bitter evil. A great good might be within his grasp. But the time for patience was over – it was time to take risks. And to find out where things stood.

He found Bobrik standing beside the dead animals and guided him away from the other guards, walking until there was no prospect of them being overheard. Bobrik was smiling, as if amused.

'Why did you take the key?' asked the Ukrainian.

'It was an accident.'

'Was it? I covered for you anyway.'

Brandt took a moment to think the situation through. Bobrik didn't care about the key.

'Why didn't you report it?'

'Because you're going to help us, aren't you? The time is coming soon. The papers that we asked for. Have you found someone?'

'I might have. I need photographs.'

'That can be arranged. What do they want in exchange?'

Brandt leaned forward and whispered in Bobrik's ear. When he'd finished, he stood back and waited for his reaction. He had rolled the dice.

He watched the smile slip off the Ukrainian's face like snow off a roof. There was no outrage, however. He could see concern, of course, but that was only natural. Bobrik coughed, scratched his ear and coughed again. But he didn't say no.

Instead he leaned his head forward to hear more.

40

NEUMANN WASN'T certain how long had passed since the killings. An hour? Ten minutes? Neumann had drunk one too many schnapps – possibly even more than that. He wasn't the only one, of course, but now the Commandant was coming towards him, his good mood apparently restored. Neumann cursed his foolishness and smiled a greeting – hoping it would be sufficient.

'Neumann,' the Commandant said, indicating with a twitch of his chin the spot where the dead men had lain before they'd been removed. 'Thank you for dealing with that matter.'

'I only did my duty, Herr Sturmbannführer.'

'We're on our own now, Friedrich. You should address me as Klaus.'

'Thank you . . .' Neumann hesitated – he didn't entirely trust his tongue. 'Klaus.'

Not so bad. He risked another smile.

'Last night you wanted to ask me something,' the Commandant said. 'Can I guess what it was?'

Neumann decided it was safe to say nothing, and so didn't.

'You wanted to know what happens when the Russians come. Am I correct?'

'Then they are coming?' Neumann risked.

'Our intelligence anticipates an attack is imminent – no more than two to three weeks away. Our current offensive in the Ardennes is intended to drive the Americans and British back into the sea. We must hope that success in the west will allow us to return to the offensive in the east. But we must be realistic – we are no longer as strong as we were in nineteen forty-one.'

'And if we aren't successful?'

'Then we must contemplate defeat. Reichsführer

Himmler has ordered contingency plans to be put into operation. At last. Where possible, we will move prisoners capable of work further west so that they may still contribute to the war effort. Those not capable of productive work will be dealt with in a different way. This war is coming to an end. Therefore we must contemplate our future.'

The thudding in Neumann's ears was so loud that it was hard for him to hear what the Commandant was saying.

'What kind of future should we expect?' he asked, realizing as soon as he'd asked it that it was a stupid question.

The Commandant smiled. A thin smile.

'The most important thing is not to be captured by the Russians. You worked in the east, so you know why. Germany isn't finished, Friedrich – we will rise again. Sooner or later the Americans and British will fight the Russians and then they'll need a strong Germany as an ally. And a strong Germany will need men like us. We must survive for just this reason. It's our duty, even. Otherwise all of this will have been in vain.'

'I never wanted to be part of it.'

The words were out before he'd thought what they might be. He shook his head, both to disagree with them and to shake some sobriety back into his thinking.

'I didn't mean,' he began, but the Commandant held up his hand to stop him. The gesture was gentle, his frown compassionate. He reached out and took Neumann's arm, turning him away from where the officers had gathered to watch the animals they'd killed being laid in two rows, grouped by species.

'Some of us were better suited to the work we undertook than others. That's why I assigned you here, to the hut, where you perform a useful – no – a vital role. The relaxations that you've arranged have been essential to the

well-being of our comrades. After the incident on the train
– which would have been a terrible event for anyone –
having you work in the camp would have been a waste of a
talented officer.'

Neumann sensed the world around him shifting shape,
even as he listened to the Commandant's words. The musty
scent he associated with the old man from the train filled
his nose, even his mouth. He kept his eyes fixed on the
snow in front of them, watching his boots as they pressed
into the crisp surface. Step, step, step. He knew if he looked
around for the old man from the train he'd see him.

'I wasn't prepared – I hadn't fully understood,' he said.

'That train was worse than anything we saw in the last
war.' The Commandant's voice was smooth and reassuring.
'Most of us who have been involved in these duties have
had comrades around us to support us, to share the burden
with – to encourage us even. We haven't been on our own.
I lodged an official complaint about the transportation
officer. His men failed to prevent tools being smuggled on
board the train – the same tools used to break out of the
wagons. Then he assigned you, an inexperienced officer, in
these matters at least, to command a half-strength guard of
recruits. And, worst of all – given the circumstances – he
sent the train by the slowest possible route. And the
prisoners were completely the wrong sort – too many
young men. It was incredible you weren't all murdered.
That you managed to achieve what you did was
extraordinary in the circumstances. That he put you and
your men in such a situation – it makes my blood boil to
this day.'

Neumann had no pity for himself, or his men. After all,
they had been the ones doing the murdering. The old man
had no pity for him either. Had he spoken to him, back
then? He couldn't remember.

'We ran out of bullets. We had to . . .'

'. . . use bayonets and rifle butts. I know. Horrific. Medieval. But all in the past now.' The Commandant squeezed his elbow. 'I feel responsibility for what happened – that I put you in harm's way. But you've been happy here, haven't you? I've done my best to make it up to you.'

Neumann glanced across at the Commandant, momentarily bewildered. It was such a complex question.

'There's no need to say a word. It was the least I could do. I've made some contingency plans, and I've taken the liberty of including you in them. I've orders to another posting near Nordhausen when we've finished up here and you will come with me. Well, what do you think? Nordhausen is a pleasant spot. We'll find you somewhere to live. A nice house, perhaps. You can go to Hamburg – talk it through with Marguerite. I'm sure she'll see sense. She can bring the boys to Nordhausen and things will be back to normal.'

Neumann didn't think things would ever be normal again between Marguerite and him. He was far past any kind of normality now, he understood that.

'What about the hut?' he asked. 'The prisoners?'

They turned and walked back towards the bus and the Commandant nodded towards where the guards were standing.

'They aren't your concern – Peichl will take responsibility for them. As for the hut, you must ensure nothing is left behind that might be used against us. Clear the place out of any paperwork, photographs, everything. No trace of our presence must remain.'

The last of the dead animals had been brought across. The officers were in good spirits, although their voices sounded unnaturally loud – as if they were trying to talk over another conversation.

'Look, Friedrich. See how content our comrades are?

Even in the current situation? Your work here has been of great importance. Without you, I don't know if we'd have been able to carry on.'

Neumann found his teeth had clenched tight, his hair was standing up on his scalp.

'That can't be true.'

'Don't be so humble. Reichsführer Himmler himself has spoken often about the stress our people face – diversion from their duties was essential and you provided it. You were the glue that held us together.'

The conversation appeared to be taking place between the Commandant and some other person Neumann had never met, talking about things which he'd never understood. And all around him were the ghosts of dead prisoners – he wondered if the dead beaters had joined them already. Could it really be true? That without the hut, the killing machine would have ceased to operate?

Of course not. But even so – he'd had a part in its smooth operation. He had to accept that, standing here, he was just as culpable as when he'd been standing on the train.

'We should have a photograph taken,' the Commandant said. 'Did you bring your camera?'

'Yes,' he managed to say, even though the Commandant's voice came from a great distance. 'Brandt knows how to use it.'

'Excellent.'

The Commandant called the officers together and arranged them in a long line, much as the guards had arranged the beaters earlier. He waved the mayor in, but when Jäger held back, the Commandant didn't press him. The officers stood behind the rows of torn wildlife, still leaking blood onto the white snow, their hands clasped around the barrels of their rifles, almost as though they were in prayer – their expressions grave.

Brandt faced them – the Leica in his hand, the weak, misty sun behind the steward as it should be. It seemed to Neumann that everything and everyone was somehow imprecise. The world was blurred – the soft light washing its colours out. He wasn't even sure that he was real himself. He'd stabbed the old man twice in the stomach with a forty-centimetre bayonet. He hadn't even been trying to escape from the train when Neumann had come across him. But, by then, Neumann was killing everyone. There was no thought in it – just a determination to clear up a mess.

'Isn't the photograph missing something?' Jäger stood to Brandt's side, observing them. His voice had a bitter edge to it that boded trouble. Neumann didn't care. It was hard enough to open his mouth to breathe, let alone speak.

'We have our guns,' said Beltz, still cheery.

'Not them – but what about the dead beaters? Shouldn't they be part of the tally?'

Neumann felt very tired. Someone close by him sighed. He could hear another person walk away.

'Ignore Hauptsturmführer Jäger,' the Commandant said, just when Neumann had become certain he would say nothing. 'I will explain to him later how German officers should behave.'

Jäger's response was a harsh laugh and, from the other side of the bus, it was joined by more innocent children's laughter. The Hitler Youth who had come to help serve the officers.

It seemed very out of place.

41

BRANDT SAT in one of the armchairs in the sitting room at the farm. They had been positioned beside the low window that overlooked the valley by his mother, many years before – one for her and one for his father. The view took in most of the reservoir – from the dam at the northern end to where it disappeared from sight amongst the higher southern slopes. Even in the daylight, it was hard to make out where the reservoir ended and the land began, now that snow had fallen on its frozen surface. Immediately beneath the window, the white fields and farms of their neighbours fell away towards the road that ran along the reservoir's edge while, to his left, from where he was sitting, Brandt could see the lights of the SS hut. He thought about Agneta sleeping in the freezing bunker, ice on the walls. He prayed she dreamed of happier times and that in her dreams the sun shone and its heat warmed her shoulders.

He sighed and turned his attention to the other side of the valley. The Red Farm stood over there, in the darkness, close to the tree line that marked the end of the higher fields – where the shoot had taken place earlier in the day. The memory was still raw. He closed his eyes and ran his hand over his stubbled scalp, then pinched the bridge of his nose, feeling his taut skin stretch at its scars as he did so. He recognized the sound of his father's footsteps coming down the staircase. He heard him cross the sitting room – the matching armchair, alongside his, sighing as it took his weight. Brandt didn't need to open his eyes to know that he was already aware of the killings. He heard him reach for his pipe where it stood on the windowsill, then fill it with tobacco. He listened as his father opened the door of the small iron stove that warmed the room, heard him tear a page out of the ancient medical magazine that stood waiting beside it. He would roll the page into a taper now and use the flame from it to light his pipe.

Perhaps his father wouldn't say anything – perhaps they'd sit there until the last of the light disappeared. They might even be able to convince each other that it was a companionable silence. He opened his eyes and glanced across. He could see the distress in his father's downturned mouth. Maybe it would simply pass – like the muscled, dark clouds that had moved across the sky before the last of the sun had disappeared.

Perhaps it was just as well that his mother was no longer alive. His memory of her was fragmented and, he suspected, unreliable. Occasionally, something he saw or heard would bring with it a vivid image of her. He'd be able to see each crease that formed around her eyes when she smiled, the dimples that had dented her round cheeks. The green and blue flecks in her wolf-grey eyes. He would have liked to have seen her one last time before she'd passed on. To have a fresher memory. To be able to recall the soft warmth of her hand small in his. To remember what they spoke about. She would have understood what he was doing with the SS. He would have been able to explain it to her.

His father cleared his throat. 'I heard they shot three prisoners in the woods today, over near the Red Farm,' he said. 'I heard you were there. Were you?'

'I was – I saw it.'

His father nodded.

'I heard Weber shot one of them – a Jewish prisoner.'

His father gave a hacking cough, as if to get something foul out of his throat.

'He thought it was part of the sport,' Brandt said, hearing the anger in his voice – at the banal, half-hearted evil Weber represented, at himself for being a part of it.

'He boasted about it in the village,' his father said. 'Ernst heard him. He came to tell me.'

'How is Ernst?'

Brandt listened to himself. Did he think he could avoid the conversation by asking about his uncle's health?

'He's well enough.'

His father tapped the bowl of his pipe empty into the ashtray beside him, reaching for his pouch to refill it.

'I didn't think Weber was capable of something like this.'

'I think it was a misunderstanding, not that I want to defend him.'

'He shot a man for sport, how could that have been a misunderstanding?' his father said.

Brandt considered this. The problem – the terrible reflection of the times they lived in – was that Weber probably hadn't even thought before he'd fired.

'Others were shooting and he shot as well. He didn't know it was wrong.'

'Explain that. Explain how he could not know it is wrong to kill a human being.'

Brandt could hear the anger in his father's voice but he was tired of all this. He was tired of his own anger as well. The anger was no longer useful to him.

'He's not exceptional – you must see how brutalized people have become. We have forgotten what's right and what's wrong. In the army you don't think for yourself – you are directed by your superiors and the will and cohesion of the group in which you fight. Personal feelings of morality, right and wrong, pity, compassion – they all fall away. When everyone else is doing something, you end up doing it too – without thinking about it. Sometimes terrible things. It's the same here. With the Party. With the farmers who use prisoners as workers. It's almost as if . . .'

Brandt stopped speaking. He realized he was talking about himself, not Weber. He looked across at his father. It was nearly dark outside now – it was difficult to make out his expression in what was left of the light. When his father spoke, he appeared to choose his words carefully.

'I know something of war. From the last one.'

'You were a doctor, Father. You saved men's lives. I took them away.'

There was a silence between them. Brandt knew it wouldn't last.

'What did you do? Out there – in the east? You did something, didn't you?'

His father's voice was little more than a whisper.

The glowing tip of Brandt's cigarette now provided the only light in the room – just enough to remind him of his surroundings and to be grateful that he was sitting here in comfort and not up to his neck in snow in some trench overlooking the Vistula, his face frozen stiff as wood, cold piercing each pore. The Wound Badge in Gold hadn't felt like much compensation when they'd pinned it on his chest – but sitting here, being warmed by an iron stove, in a comfortable chair and with an SS cigarette in his hand – well, he might not have both arms but he'd see the morning.

'I asked a question.'

'Do you really want to know the answer?'

'Of course not. But that isn't the point.'

Brandt found his fingers had clenched tight enough that his nails were digging into his palm. He must ask Monika to cut them for him.

'If you're asking about the Jews, I have nothing to confess. I saw things, of course. I took no part. I made my unhappiness clear by my silence, as did others. No one forced the matter. But I know some of the men in our unit went to the place where the Jews were being shot, and watched, and perhaps joined in. And I know that amongst themselves they shared around the photographs they had taken. Perhaps I should have said more, done something.

But back then I was an ordinary private – with a political background that would have meant trouble for me. I kept quiet. I should have said something. I should have done something. Whatever the consequences.'

'Thank God you weren't involved in that. And what could you have done?'

'Something,' Brandt said. 'But perhaps it's not too late.'

'Is the reason you're working for them worth it?' his father asked, indicating with a nod the direction in which the hut lay, further along the valley. 'Are you certain?'

'It's worthwhile. Believe me.'

His father said nothing in response, only turned towards him in the darkness, his head inclining forward as if he was expecting more – but Brandt allowed the conversation to lapse. The electricity was rationed now, and even when it was scheduled to be on, it often wasn't, so they looked out across a dark valley. There were, however, two sources of light – the small power station attached to the dam was lit and, through the trees, the glow from the hut, where a generator kept the perimeter illuminated.

'Father?'

'Yes.'

'The Russians only stopped in the summer because they needed to regroup – not because of anything we were able to do. When the time comes – when they attack – when it's a choice between staying and leaving, you must leave. Everything we did to the Russians will be done in return now.'

42

THE NEW YEAR was approaching but no one in the valley felt much like celebrating it. The change from one year to the next was a time to take stock and to look forward, but Brandt had the sense that people wanted the calendar to stop still at the end of nineteen forty-four, for the future to remain unknown and for the past to remain hidden. But that was impossible – the days marched on. Their fate, whatever it was to be, advanced a little closer.

The mood in the village had been grim in the week that followed the Red Farm shoot – it was an unwelcome reminder of how close the mining camp was and how many had some connection with it. Then a man was hanged in the town at the bottom of the valley for saying the war was lost, alongside two partisans and a black-market profiteer, and that had made things even worse. His father had sighed and said things must be getting really bad if they were hanging the black marketeers.

At night in the dark village – the blackouts were even more frequent now – the lightless houses were anything but silent. From behind the closed wooden shutters there came the sounds of hammering and sawing and urgent conversation. The smallest noise carried clearly in the still air. Bags were being packed, harness repaired, horses reshod and cabins built on carts to give protection on a long winter journey.

The fear wasn't limited to the Germans of the valley. The foreign workers and prisoners of war who worked for its farms and businesses all shared in the sense of foreboding. No one felt confident about the future. They lived in limbo, with a sense that each time the clock ticked it brought this halfway life one second closer to its end. The grim sense of an imminent conclusion seemed to reach up into the very sky itself – grey clouds moved towards the western hills slowly and relentlessly.

And it was cold – bitterly and utterly cold.

Brandt was busy. There were things that needed to be done – done urgently – and it didn't help that the Volkssturm had been placed on higher alert. They now had to mount a guard on the valley road as well as the village bridge. Some of the men slept in the village hall rather than go home to their farms, only to turn round in the morning and come back again. Prisoners from the mining camp were brought down the valley to dig more defences. They left four of their number buried in one of the trenches they dug.

Two ancient machine guns with Czech markings arrived at the village hall with a supply of ammunition that looked even older. And then Wehrmacht engineers appeared and filled the corridor that ran inside the dam from one side to the other with crates of explosive.

The regional Party boss must have been concerned about morale because, two days before the New Year, all the local Volkssturm units were summoned to a rally in the town at the bottom of the valley. If anyone had asked Brandt he could have told them not to show the newsreel – but no one did. Brandt and the rest of the Volkssturm marched down from the village and sat in their allocated seats, numb with cold from the journey and then with shock, as black and white atrocities flickered across the screen. The narrator explained in detail what the Soviets had done to the population of the small East Prussian village – no horror was left undocumented, no image was too graphic.

But the thing was, Nemmersdorf wasn't so different from their village – the dead could have been their people; the houses, their houses. Brandt looked along the row and saw the emptiness and resignation in the older men's pale faces. Afterwards some young fellow, younger than Brandt, anyway, wearing round glasses and a swastika armband over his leather coat, his dark hair slicked back, took to the stage. He spoke about wonder weapons and the necessity for faith in the all-seeing wisdom of the Führer. He told them the current situation was a test of the German people's will, but that they would emerge triumphant. There was no applause when the speech finished.

The snow whirled down around them as they marched back up the valley. He exchanged a glance with Uncle Ernst on several occasions – they didn't need words. And then, when they were nearly back at the village and the blizzard was at its worst, a figure appeared, almost right beside them. No one else noticed the man. His face was obscured by the brim of his trilby, pulled low, and a scarf – but, for an instant, his eyes met Brandt's and they recognized each other.

It was Hubert.

43

THE FOOTSTEPS came as no surprise to Brandt. Monika had an instinct for when he couldn't sleep.

'I'm here,' he called out – although he was sure she already knew. Her bare feet sounded soft on the wooden floorboards.

She put a hand on the back of the armchair that faced him, leaning her weight on it and looking across the valley. She was barely visible in the dark.

'Have you been awake for long?' she asked.

'Not too long.'

He opened the pack of cigarettes on his lap, extracted one and leant forward to place it into her fingers, then took another and placed it in his mouth. The match was like a tiny explosion in the dark. She leant down to it – the flame washing her face with orange and yellow and turning her blue eyes black.

'Worried about something?'

He shrugged.

'Perhaps.'

'The hut?'

Brandt was pleased. She had raised the very topic he had wanted to discuss but hadn't known how to.

'Yes.'

Silence fell between them. He knew she was waiting for him to explain but he was in no rush. He had time. When their cigarettes were nearly finished, he took out two more. He weighed his options.

'The women,' he said, his voice sounding higher than usual. He paused and began again. 'The prisoners, I mean. I told you about them before but I didn't tell you that I knew one of them – a long time ago. Before she ended up in the hut. In Vienna. We were arrested at the same time.'

Another silence fell between them. Monika would be

analysing the new information, if he knew her.

'This woman you knew before – were you in love with her?'

A good question. You could rely on Monika to be direct. He thought back to that summer when they'd lived from breath to breath. Their relationship, in retrospect, seemed dreamlike – a wisp of a thing.

'I didn't get the chance to find out for certain, but I think so.'

'What happened?'

'As I said, we were arrested. I had to join the army – or be sent to a camp. I chose the army. I had no idea what had happened to her and there was no way of finding out. I couldn't send a letter. There was no one I could trust to ask. I hoped she'd been treated leniently. As I was. Then I saw her here – at the hut.'

'By chance?'

'Completely.' He could see Monika's head shaking from side to side in the darkness. Disbelief? Amusement? Terror, even? 'At first I wasn't certain, but it is her. She doesn't remember me. Or recognize me, anyway. I've changed, of course.'

The tip of Monika's cigarette glowed red.

'Do you love her now?'

A good question. How could he be sure?

'Does it matter? Even if I'd never known her at all, it's clear what I should do.'

'But you did love her – and still do.'

'Yes. I think so. Listen, Monika, when the Russians attack it's likely there will be little resistance. It will be chaos. If I can keep them alive until then, five prisoners will be the last thing on anyone's mind. If I get them out – I don't think anyone will look for them.'

'You can get them out, then.'

Brandt noticed it was a statement rather than a question.

He picked up the key that sat on the table in front of them and handed it to her.

'The key to the bunker where they are kept.'

She held it up, examining it in the faint light from her cigarette.

'I also know how to turn off the electric fence, if that's necessary – but it might not be. And I know how to kill someone, if that's required. I have food for them. I have a place to hide them.'

The tip of her cigarette glowed red once again.

'Maybe they will be safer where they are. When the Russians arrive, they'll be well looked after. Escaping might be more dangerous that staying.'

'If they stay, they will most likely die. The SS want the camp forgotten. They've already erased other camps, further east – nothing left but empty fields. They plan to do the same with the camps here – it's already started. The camp is being decommissioned, the sub-camps wound down.'

Monika considered this.

'How long before you have to act?'

'Not long.'

She stood, walking behind him, leaning down on the back of his chair. He felt her shift her weight and then her hand was on his shoulder. The touch was gentle and it made him blink back tears. He was so tired and the warmth of her hand made him remember it.

'Unless I have to move sooner, I want to wait until the Russians attack.'

'What if the army can hold the Russians – push them back, even?'

'They won't. They're building defences near Breslau. We're two hundred kilometres closer to the Front here. The army knows the Russians are unstoppable – we've known for the last two years. It's why the Volkssturm was formed.

It's why the Gauleiter has sent the mayor plans for a civilian evacuation. It's why the SS are covering their tracks.'

'Why are you telling me all this?'

'I saw Hubert.' There was no physical reaction. Her hand still rested on his shoulder and there was no alteration to its gentle pressure. She must already know. Which must mean she had a way of contacting him, surely?

'I need civilian papers. For the guards. If I can provide the guards with papers, then they might just help me with the women. Do you think Hubert might be able to assist with something like that?'

Monika tousled what there was of his hair and then walked to the window. She yawned, stretching her arms wide behind her back. The gesture was almost as intimate as her touch.

'You seem certain I know how to get in contact with him.'

'I need his help.'

He heard her quiet laugh.

'You have it all planned out. If you saw him, you must know he shouldn't be here, that if he were caught he would be shot. That most likely he is with the partisans in the hills. And then there's you – working for the SS and training the Volkssturm. Surely he would think it was a trap. Wouldn't you?'

'I know it's a lot to ask.'

Monika let her breath out in a sigh.

'Remember when we were children, how easy it was between us? Who could have thought that it would come to this?'

Monika's voice sounded hollow, as if she were drained. He found he had no words that came to mind. It seemed as strange to him as it must to her. And yet, here they were.

'I'm going back to my bed,' she said, bending down to

stub the cigarette out in the ashtray placed on the low table between his mother's chair and his father's. He could smell her – a mixture of the cigarette and a warmer, sleepy odour that must be her own.

'If you did see Hubert, I'm grateful you told no one except me, and I'm sure he is too. In the meantime, what you're doing at the hut is brave, if insane. I wish you success. More than that, I can't say yet. But, who knows. I may be able to tell you something soon.'

He listened to her make her way to the back of the house, the floorboards creaking as she moved. Then the soft sound of her bedroom door closing. Outside, the clouds in the night sky had grown darker. The dawn that must eventually come now seemed uncertain.

44

THEY'D BEEN LIVING underneath Galechka for a week now. They'd found an empty house nearby with floorboards and a door that no one had been keeping an eye on so they'd dug the trench deeper, laid the tarpaulin on the ground beneath and used the floorboards and the door for walls. Galechka provided the roof. A small diesel stove hung from the tank's belly – keeping them warm and Galechka's engine from freezing. There was plenty of food – tinned meat from America and even chocolate, while the cooks brought hot food round twice a day in a jeep. They were happy enough. They played cards for twigs, listened to the radio and the occasional artillery shell passing overhead, polished the bullets and shells and turned over the tank's engine from time to time. They waited.

Around them the forest was busy. There were thirty-two tanks in the battalion – all of them gone to ground the same as Galechka, dug in so only their turrets showed. It wasn't only their battalion, however. There were Siberians, Cossacks, Ukrainians, Mongolians, Kazakhs, Georgians, Armenians and even Poles in the forest, each with a tank to call home. Every tree covered its own tank, as far as Polya could see. And each tank covered its crew. And each tank formation had infantry to go with it, and engineers were carving out new roads each day. More soldiers were arriving constantly. Who knew how many men, and women, were in the woods? Who knew how far the Front extended? Perhaps it was like this all the way to the sea in the north – and maybe even down to the southern sea as well.

It felt as though they were all tiny drops of water in a great ocean wave that was slowly growing in size – as though they were a part of something – something that grew larger with every passing hour. She was afraid of the battle to come, of course. Who wouldn't be? But when you looked around the forest and saw the thousands of soldiers, tanks and pieces of artillery – well, what did one girl matter amongst so many?

The heavy curtain that served as their little bunker's entrance – another item liberated from the abandoned house – was pushed aside and Lapshin looked in. Behind him she could see the early morning sun lighting the snow that bowed down the branches of the trees. The glare was startling and she shielded her eyes.

'Don't let the heat out.'

She thought she saw Lapshin smile. It was difficult to be certain with the sun behind him.

'Come on, Little Polya,' he whispered. 'Let's go for a walk.'

She thought, afterwards, that she should have been less enthusiastic. Maybe she could have yawned, or looked at her German watch. Instead she got to her feet so quickly she nearly split her head open on Galechka's belly.

'Where are we going?' she asked when they had been walking for a little while. They were following a corrugated track that was slippery with ice. It was quiet, considering there were so many nearby. Every now and then she'd see the outline of a tank's turret or the barrel of a cannon pointing out of a bush but she saw no humans. The soldiers were under orders to keep movement to a minimum during the daylight.

'To look at the Front,' Lapshin said. 'To see what we're getting ourselves into.'

They walked until the trees began to thin, when Lapshin put his hand on her arm to bring her to a halt. Ahead she could see open country.

'Let's take our time. There's no point in taking unnecessary risks.'

They moved slowly, from tree to tree – almost stumbling

into three staff officers who were doing the same as them –
looking across the river at the enemy hills. In front of the
forest, about fifty metres beyond where the trees ended,
were their own trenches. A ruined bridge stood in between,
the turgid river swirling around its broken spans. It looked
as though it might freeze before long.

'How do we get across?' she whispered.

Lapshin pointed to the north.

'We're already on their side of the river further over – a
few kilometres upstream. We'll break out from there. In the
meantime – here – our infantry will go over in rubber boats.
We'll have bridges across before they know what hit them.'

Polya didn't like pontoon bridges. They had a habit of
coming apart when hit by enemy shells or bombs. And
tanks didn't float. She strained her eyes looking for the
Germans.

'Where are their trenches?'

'The snow is hiding them but they're just down from the
ridge.'

There was an explosion on the far hill – snow and earth
flung into the air, leaving a black scar in the snow behind it.
Then another further along the hill's slope. They watched
and waited and, sure enough, less than a minute later, there
was the shriek of shells flying high overhead as the
Germans returned the favour.

'It's New Year's Eve, the artillery are exchanging
pleasantries.'

45

THE HUT WAS quiet now. The officers from the camp hadn't returned since the shoot, and no injured men had arrived in the fortnight since. Jäger was still with them – but he was the only one now. It was just as well – Brandt was busy. Neumann had ordered him to make an inventory of the hut's supplies and contents and then store the listed items in boxes for removal. There had been no more talk about the evacuation – but they were preparing for it. The question that preoccupied Brandt was when it would take place.

'Is it two weeks already, Brandt?'

Jäger was standing in his usual spot, at the window in the dining room, looking out at the women prisoners clearing the snow and ice from the paths. The tremble in the tanker's hands wasn't so apparent now but the doctors from the camp hospital hadn't passed him fit for the Front as yet. He smoked cigarette after cigarette – the hut still had plenty of them, at least. He played gramophone records that no one listened to except him – and which annoyed the telephonists, who reminded him that the record player was only to be used at the weekends and in the evenings. Jäger didn't care and, as he outranked everyone, there wasn't much that could be done about it.

'Since when, Herr Hauptsturmführer?'

'Since the shoot.'

'It's the tenth of January.'

'Is it? More than two weeks then. Nearly two months since I first arrived. It's quiet, isn't it? Even those people from the camp would be a welcome change.'

'Obersturmführer Neumann says they are very busy.'

'I'm sure they are.'

Jäger ran a finger down the window's glass.

'The Commandant has been punishing me.'

'How so, Herr Hauptsturmführer?'

'He was annoyed with me after the shoot. I don't know why – I wasn't the one who shot the prisoners.'

'You think you annoyed him? The Commandant?' Brandt said, half wanting to laugh at the SS man.

Jäger managed a smile.

'Well, perhaps I was at fault. But I said to him – you can get rid of me whenever you want – just have the doctors pass me fit and pack me off to the Front. But he took a different approach. He's been making me wait.'

So desperate for an honourable death – and thwarted by the Commandant, of all people. It was hard not to see some irony in it. Jäger scowled.

'That's enough, Brandt. I don't find it quite as amusing as you do. God help me, if we had that shoot again, I'd put a bullet through him. By mistake, of course. I'd say I thought he was a Jew.'

Brandt looked around him. He didn't think they could be overheard – but all the same.

'I should go.'

Jäger held up a hand to stop him.

'I apologize. I went too far. Stay a moment.'

Jäger looked at him with such a soft expression – one that didn't seem to fit his angular face – that Brandt felt obliged to nod his agreement.

'We've lived through strange times, Brandt, don't you think? Future generations, if there are any, will look back at us and scratch their heads.' He lit another cigarette, his eyes narrowing against the match's burn. 'That will be long after we have achieved the final victory, of course. Which I'm confident will be achieved in the next week or so.'

'I'm relieved to hear it.'

Jäger's laugh was more of a series of coughs.

'Take my word on it. I have it from the highest authority. Goebbels himself was on the radio last night. Apparently we have the Allies just where we want them.'

Brandt glanced once again towards the doors at either end of the room. Jäger shrugged and pointed his cigarette at the women working outside.

'They must be very dangerous, those prisoners. Two SS men for five starved women.'

Brandt looked up at him.

'It gives them something to do.'

'What do you mean?'

'The guards. They're here to protect the hut and its guests – in case the partisans come calling. But in the absence of guests, they guard the prisoners. And the prisoners sweep the snow because there isn't much else for them to do either, now that our only guest is you.'

Jäger nodded.

'Do you ever wonder what those Ukrainians must be thinking, Brandt? What must be going through their heads?' He touched the SS runes on his collar. 'This uniform won't do me any favours if I am captured – but the Ukrainians? The Ivans have something special planned for the Ukrainians. We're fascist murderers – they shoot us, they move on. The Ukrainians are fascist murderers *and* traitors to the Motherland. The question is, though – what would you do if you were in their position if you knew that? Would you just wait around for the axe to fall?'

Brandt decided it was best to say nothing.

'The Ukraine is back in Soviet hands,' Jäger went on. 'So what do they do now? Do they lay down their lives for Germany? Or do they make a run for it?'

'Where to?'

He hadn't meant to ask the question out loud – not that Jäger appeared to hear him. His eyes were fixed on the guards.

'I think they run. We haven't treated them well, let's be clear about that. We lied to them and used them – and, if

our charming comrades from the camp are to be believed,
made them perform the worst of our crimes. They owe us
nothing, except perhaps a bullet in the back. If they run
now, they might make it to safety. There will be millions of
people trying to make their way home when this war ends.
It will be chaos. They might have a chance. They'll need to
move quickly, though.'

'Why?'

'Because soon they'll be sent to the Front, and there's
nothing good waiting for them there.'

Brandt looked around once again.

'Why do you think that?'

'The camp is being shut down and the men stationed
there are being transferred to combat units. The Reich
needs more blood to spill, you see. That was the final
gathering – our little Julfest dinner.'

It all fell into place. The sense of an ending at the dinner
– the times he'd heard officers wish each other luck for the
year ahead. They hadn't been talking about their work at
the camp. Even the telephonists knew – that was clear.
Only he had been in the dark. He looked out at the women
prisoners; they'd nearly finished their work – they would
be coming inside soon.

'And the prisoners? What happens to them?'

The women had on the Soviet quilted jackets he'd
persuaded Neumann to allow them to wear. They were
several sizes too big for them. They looked like children in
hand-me-down clothes.

'Why go to the effort of destroying the camp and leave
witnesses?'

It made sense. Of course it did.

'So what will you do, Brandt?'

'I don't think anyone will want me at the Front, if that's
what you mean.'

Jäger smiled.

'That wasn't what I meant, although you'd probably be more use than the likes of Peichl.'

The Scharführer was walking up the lane from the main gate. As he approached he began to shout at the women, pointing out snow they had missed, shoving Joanna roughly towards one pile that hadn't been pushed far enough to the side for his liking.

'What do you mean?' Brandt said, his attention on Peichl.

'What are you going to do about them, Brandt? The women outside. The ones we're looking at?'

Brandt found he had no breath in his lungs – not enough to voice a denial, in any event.

'A doctor will come to see me the day after tomorrow, Brandt. Neumann has just confirmed it. I will soon be gone. If I go in two days then my suspicion is that this place will be shut down soon afterwards. I want to know, before I go, what you intend to do about the women.'

'The women?' Brandt said. 'What should I do about the women?'

'That is the question. Are you frightened?'

'I don't understand.'

'Now. By this conversation. I'm an intellectually curious man. I want to know what your emotional state is at this precise moment. Do me the favour of answering truthfully – and I might do one for you in return.'

Brandt thought he saw a flicker of amusement – a warmth behind Jäger's eyes. He looked inside himself and found, to his surprise, that he felt nothing. Not fear, anyway. Regret perhaps, and even that wasn't for himself.

'I think, Herr Hauptsturmführer, that if you were to tell Obersturmführer Neumann of your suspicions, whatever they might be, then I should feel fear. But I don't feel anything much these days.'

Jäger nodded, his thoughts unreadable. Brandt waited.

Eventually, the SS man smiled.

'I've left you a small gift in the washroom. Look in the third cubicle from the door – in the cistern. Just in case you might need it. This place is already living on borrowed time. Keep an eye on the Ukrainians, Brandt. I'm not sure they're going to keep playing by the rules. That could work for you, or against you.'

Brandt wasn't sure what to say.

'Don't look so glum – your heart still beats, Brandt. And so do theirs. For the moment.'

Jäger had turned his attention to the scene outside and something in his voice warned Brandt to follow his example. Peichl had taken off his belt, the buckle shone as it whirled through the air. Blood leapt from Agneta's cheek. Brandt turned to leave – to make his way outside – to put a stop to it. But Jäger held him back.

'Not you, Brandt. Not this time. Another small favour I'll do for you. And myself perhaps.'

46

AT FIRST Peichl had been merely exasperated – disappointed with the standard of their work, more than anything. But the women knew Peichl and they knew how his irritation could quickly turn into something much more dangerous. They could smell, even here – outside in the cold – the alcohol on him. And they could hear, in his slurred words and his disjointed sentences, that he was still drunk from the night before. And they knew – he was famous for it, their Scharführer Peichl – what he could do with just his fists, should he choose to. So they hurried to do his bidding. They kept their eyes low, tried to make themselves invisible – rounding their shoulders, bending their knees, shrinking themselves. Wishing they could disappear into the ground itself. Praying that they wouldn't.

The women hurried to remedy the failings Peichl spotted – even when they couldn't see what it was he'd found fault with. They swept at the snow with their brushes and chipped at the ice with their spades. But they were nervous and their movements were imprecise. Their wooden clogs slipped and slid, giving them no purchase. Their terror became self-fulfilling in some way. Whatever caused it, his rage, when it began, was like an engine that progressed from a sputtering start – a series of irregular barks – then wound itself up to a snarling, constant scream.

He kicked them, he pushed them, he punched them. Then his belt was off. Agneta felt the first blow on her shoulder, the next on her cheek. She hurried to do what he asked of her, startled by the red drops that scattered on the snow beneath her.

'Don't bleed there, Prisoner. Did I tell you to bleed there?'

Peichl kicked her thigh – all of his weight behind it. In a moment of clarity Agneta saw one of the Ukrainian guards

– the blonde youth with the angel's face – gazing at her. She was trying not to fall – her leg was buckling – and Peichl was kicking at her again, holding her by her hair. The Ukrainian stood beside the path, his rifle slung over his shoulder. His expression didn't change when Peichl began to punch her. He showed no reaction when Peichl's knuckles cracked against her skull, the pain so sharp she couldn't see for an instant.

The Ukrainian could have been watching someone swinging their legs on a fence for all the interest he showed.

If she fell, she would die – she was certain of it. Peichl would kick her with his heavy boots until she was dead. She wouldn't fall. She felt her own anger warming her chest. She wouldn't end like this. Peichl took a fistful of her hair in his hand once again, twisting her so he could shout in her face, pulling her back from the abyss.

'What have you got to say, Prisoner?'

She had to focus, move past the pain.

'I apologize, Herr Scharführer. I will fix it. I will fix it immediately.'

He shoved her away from him and she staggered, pushing her brush down hard at the ground for balance. She stopped, then ran past him, swerving out of his reach, and began sweeping. It didn't matter what she swept, she just had to be busy, keep her head down, keep out of his way. Joanna was beside her. Long, hard, quick strokes. Harder than they could manage for more than a few seconds. She concentrated on the ground in front of her, ignoring her pain, leaning her cheek against her jacket so that the blood would be soaked up by it and not fall to the ground.

Now it was Rachel who was taking the worst of Peichl's fury. 'Do you think I'm stupid, Jew? You think you can pull the wool over my eyes, do you? You think you can leave this lane in a disgusting mess? You think I will stand for it? You foolish Jew. You idiot Jew.'

Peichl pushed the girl and she slipped, spilling down to the ground. He kicked her, lifting her with the force of it – sending her rolling away. Her head flopped as she came to a halt and Agneta thought she might be dead. Peichl threw his belt down at Rachel, then picked up her broom and, turning towards them, he swung it back and – the sharp sound of wood hitting bone – he'd hit her arm. Agneta gasped. But she must not cry, she must not fall.

'Well?' Peichl hit out at Joanna, then turned towards the Bible students. 'Well?'

Agneta saw Rachel move, her body twisting on the snow. She was trying to stand. Good girl. Don't give in.

'Where is your God now?'

Crack – he'd hit someone else.

'Where is he? Tell me. Where is he?'

Agneta risked a look – Katerina and Gertrud had fallen to their knees and held their clasped hands to their chests. Rivulets of blood ran down Katerina's face. They were praying.

'Do you think your God is listening?'

Crack.

'Do you think he's going to save you from me? I'm going to see what kind of mush is inside your skulls that you believe in such nonsense.'

Footsteps were approaching from the hut. Whoever it was walked purposefully. Peichl stopped talking, turning, standing to attention.

'Herr – Haupt – sturm – führer.'

Peichl spoke in bursts. Out of breath.

'Scharführer Peichl. Your morning exercise?'

'Disciplining prisoners. Herr Hauptsturmführer. They've become. Lazy. They think we've become. Soft.'

'Well, carry on, then. But when you've finished, come and talk to me. I need to explain how things work in a tank battalion. It will be different from what you're used to – you'll have to be prepared for that. But a man of your abilities and toughness – I think you'll manage.'

Rachel got to her feet, nearly unbalancing, then came over beside them, picking up the broom Peichl had now discarded – joining in the work. More red droplets scattering on the snow-encrusted gravel, her brushstrokes mixing them in until the ground turned a pale pink.

Peichl was silent. Sensing his attention was elsewhere, Agneta slowed her pace. They all did. They had to keep their strength.

'I'm sorry, Herr Hauptsturmführer,' Peichl said. 'I don't understand.'

'We're leaving tomorrow, Peichl. The battalion needs machine gunners. It's an easy job – you just keep the gun loaded and fire it. Plenty of targets, believe me. It's not the best seat in the tank, of course – hard to get out if we burn – but we all must do our duty.'

'I still don't understand, Herr Hauptsturmführer. Machine gunners?'

'Did Obersturmführer Neumann not speak to you? No? He's told you nothing? But it's all arranged – your transfer has come through. And my health has been spoken for. We leave the day after tomorrow.'

'Transfer? Tomorrow?'

Peichl sounded confused – his words were slurred.

'Have you been drinking, Peichl?' Jäger's voice was low, Agneta saw his boots take three steps forward until they were directly in front of Peichl's, who took two small steps back before coming back to attention.

'Last night, Herr Hauptsturmführer. In the village. Not this morning.'

'You stink of it, Peichl. You know what would happen if you were under my command – if we were near the enemy and I found you like this?'

'Yes, Herr Hauptsturmführer.'

'You do? You think you know my mind?'

'I only meant to say—' Peichl began.

'I would have you shot, Peichl. Pop. Just like that.'

Footsteps approached.

'Good morning, Herr Hauptsturmführer.'

'Good morning, Neumann. I've just been telling Peichl here what I would do if I found him drunk and we were close to the enemy. I think it's important he understands. Here at the hut, of course, some flexibility can be allowed. I understand that. There is no criticism of you involved. But at the Front . . .'

'Peichl?' Neumann said after a pause. He stepped closer now. 'Have you been drinking? On duty?'

The women stopped sweeping – they leant on their tools, they watched the SS men's feet as Neumann circled the Scharführer. They imagined him looking at Peichl closely – nodding to himself.

'Go to your quarters, Peichl. I'll deal with you later.'

Peichl hesitated.

'I said go.'

Peichl turned to leave.

'At the run, Scharführer.'

Peichl ran. His legs were too short for it – they seemed to move quicker than he did.

'And you two – get these prisoners back to work.'

Agneta and the others needed no encouragement. They bent their back to it, thanking their gods. A miracle had come to pass.

47

'I WISH YOU *would* send him with me.'

'Herr Hauptsturmführer,' Neumann began, trying to control his anger.

'I know. I apologize. I was bored – I thought I'd have a little fun.'

'The Scharführer was carrying out duties assigned to him under the authority of the Commandant,' Neumann said, but Jäger merely shrugged his shoulders.

'I shouldn't have interfered – I accept it. But you saw how he ran. Like a fat waddling baby. You aren't made of stone, Neumann. You must have been tempted to smile. I wanted to roar with laughter.'

Neumann couldn't acknowledge the fact – but the image of Peichl running toward the hut was as clear to him now as when he'd seen it. He needed to be stern, however.

'I ask you to remember that the doctor's visit is still within the Commandant's discretion,' Neumann said, managing to keep his tone even.

'I understand. And I'll be gone before the hour is out when he signs me off, believe me.'

'As for Peichl,' Neumann said.

'I'll explain to him that you intervened on his behalf,' Jäger said. 'I'll tell him he won't be seeing the inside of a Tiger just yet.'

'I was thinking of an apology, Herr Hauptsturmführer.'

Jäger's eyes seemed to glitter with hidden amusement.

'I don't think that would be a good idea, Neumann. If he knows I've made fun of him, he'll be ashamed – but if he thinks you made representations on his behalf? Think how grateful he will be. How much easier to manage.'

Neumann considered his position. He couldn't order Jäger to apologize – and, of course, Jäger had a point.

'Look, Neumann,' Jäger continued. 'I was foolish and

I've made life awkward for you. But look at the man – do you really want to have Peichl thinking you were involved in his public humiliation? In front of the prisoners?'

Jäger's smile reminded Neumann of a gambler who had played a winning card. Neumann rose to his feet, resolving to put the unpleasant incident behind him. After a moment, Jäger did the same. He shook Neumann's hand as gently as if it belonged to a woman.

'If you reconsider?' Jäger said, almost whispering.

'About Peichl's transfer? I'd see the Scharführer was well looked after.'

Neumann swallowed the scowl he felt pushing at his lips.

'Thank you, Herr Hauptsturmführer. I'll bear your offer in mind.'

'Please do.'

When Jäger had left, Neumann let his scowl loose. He wanted to kick something. That comment Jäger had made outside – about how here there could be flexibility but 'at the Front' things were different – did he think Neumann was a coward? He'd fought at Verdun in the first war. He'd seen entire regiments ground into the mud. What had Jäger done that compared with that? Had he even been weaned when Neumann had been crawling through corpses? He kicked the desk. It felt good. He kicked it again.

He'd have that idiot Peichl's hide for this, though. He'd make the Scharführer pay. It was that fool's fault he'd been put in this intolerable position.

Outside, in the drawing room, he heard the sound of someone putting a record on the gramophone and, after a short pause, its music wound its serpentine way into his office.

The piece was familiar, although he couldn't place it at first. It was calming. He took a deep breath and let it out slowly. He sat down. Of its own accord, his head began to sway from side to side to the music's rhythm. There was something comforting about the half-memories it invoked. He needed to be calm. Jäger would be gone tomorrow. He would never see him again. He would just empty his mind and fill it with the music.

Almost immediately, Neumann felt better. The music brought memories with it. The hot stillness of his father's house on a summer's afternoon – the image as clear to him now as though it had taken place not ten minutes before. That must have been where he'd heard this piece, at home, all those years ago. He'd been reading a newspaper in his father's drawing room, his knees bare. Before the last war, then – long before it. When was the last time he'd worn short trousers? He couldn't remember – yet the image was so clear.

Another memory. A game of cards being played, he was sure of it, and a withered bouquet of sepia-toned roses forgotten on a sideboard, the corrupted scent of the dead flowers filling his nostrils even now. And what was that? Yes, his sister Clara's laughter – coming from the garden, he was sure – in the old house – in happier times. He was wearing a light cotton shirt, crisp against his skin. It was hot. That summer before the war – the warmth of it. Not this war, the one before. Thirty years ago but it seemed as if it were only yesterday. Who could forget how perfect that summer had been? Back then, when all was well with the world.

He prayed that Clara was safe – he'd had no word from her. And the bombing was every night, every day now. The thought of his sister reminded him of his sons – and Marguerite. Familiar numb emptiness filled him but the music, at least, was something.

He stood up and walked to the door, opening it wide to hear the music better. He wanted to make sure the music was real. Not another trick of his mind. It was an old recording, the poor quality of the sound dating it. A violin solo swaggered above the orchestra's accompaniment – a real virtuoso performance. It was uplifting, truly uplifting. He was certain he'd listened to every record in the hut's collection a hundred times – but this was new to him. A mystery.

'Herr Obersturmführer, someone is playing a record again, in the middle of the day.'

One of the auxiliaries had leaned out of their cubicle. The unattractive one. The switchboard was closer to the gramophone than his office – and it was something the telephone girls disliked. They said the music playing in the background made it sound like they worked in a hotel. Which, in a way, they did – even if for the last two weeks all they'd done was sit reading romantic novels and worrying about the Ivans. The good news was she could hear the record too. It wasn't only in his mind.

'I'll turn it off. I don't know who put it on.'

It must have been Jäger.

'The tune,' he continued, relieved that there was an earthly source for it, 'I can't put a name to it. It's familiar, though. Do you know it?'

'I'm afraid not, Herr Obersturmführer.'

His question irritated him for some reason. The music was no longer quite so pleasing. It was the same tune as before but something about it itched at him now. It was to do with that soaring violin, he was sure of it. Some moment in his past that it brought to mind – an unpleasant association this one, although he couldn't quite think what. The memories from before, the ones recalled by the piece's opening chords, they'd been more agreeable – the smell of tobacco smoke, the flowers and the stillness of the drawing room – Clara's happy laughter. But whatever recollection the music was bringing back now was not so welcome – he'd the gnawing sense of having failed at something – of having performed an act unworthy of himself. A feeling of guilt.

More guilt? Could that even be possible?

He was in the dining room now. Brandt was counting the silver, writing notes as he did so. The room was magnificent.

'Hauptsturmführer Jäger will be leaving the day after tomorrow, Brandt.'

He was surprised by the harsh tone in his voice, and attempted to soften it with a half-smile. Brandt turned towards him, his melted mouth slightly open – his marred face livid and twisted. Neumann couldn't help but feel distaste. He hoped it didn't show.

'Shall I find something special in the cellar, Herr Obersturmführer?'

Neumann thought about holding the dusty neck of a bottle in his hand, raising it high – then bringing it down hard onto Jäger's head. The thought cheered him.

'Why not?'

'I'll see to it.'

'What is this music, Brandt?' Neumann was surprised to hear how anxious and angry his voice sounded. He prided himself on his even nature with subordinates, despite everything, but today he knew he was more fractious than usual. Jäger's fault. He must control himself. He forced a calm smile, and shrugged.

'It was playing when I came up from the kitchen, Herr Obersturmführer.'

Neumann walked through to the sitting room where the gramophone stood. He lifted the needle from the record – causing a squeal as it cut into the surface.

'I was listening to that, Neumann.'

Jäger's voice came from the depths of an armchair.

'The hut's rules forbid it, Herr Hauptsturmführer. Until five, anyway. The rules are approved by the Commandant. You could call him, if you wanted to?'

Jäger said nothing and Neumann felt a flush of something like triumph. That had shut him up. He lifted the record from the turntable. He looked at the label. He couldn't quite believe what he was reading.

'Where did this record come from, Herr Hauptsturmführer?'

'I don't know, Herr Obersturmführer. Has it not always been here?'

Neumann considered Jäger for a moment, aware of a pulsing vein in his forehead. Was it possible? Was this another shift in his reality? Were his ghosts now capable of this? Or was this Jäger making fun of him.

'Brandt,' he called, his voice remaining calm, he was pleased to discover, even if his mind was screaming.

'Read this label,' Neumann said to Brandt when he came in. Brandt took the record from him, and the remains of his eyebrows raised in surprise. Thank God. It was happening in the real world, this scene of theirs. The record existed.

'This is no record of ours, is it, Brandt?'

'I'd be surprised, Herr Obersturmführer.'

Jäger stood to his feet and walked over, taking the record from Brandt.

'I think you have some explaining to do here, Neumann,' he said. 'You can't be permitting banned composers in a place like this. I doubt the Commandant would approve.'

Neumann reached out to snatch the record back from him, barely resisting the temptation to stamp it underfoot. Damn the man. Playing that Jew, Mendelssohn, in this place of all places.

'Schmidt,' Brandt said. 'He had some records – I put them in with ours. That must be where it came from.'

Neumann examined Brandt, then looked down at the broken record. Could it really be the case? A camp officer listening to Jewish music? The man had shot himself, of course. It was possible. He swallowed.

'Go through them. Make sure there are no other unpleasant surprises.'

'Of course, Herr Obersturmführer.'

The sooner Jäger was gone, the better.

48

SHE'D MISS the place, Polya thought, as they tore their shelter apart. It had been pleasant, living in their makeshift home. They'd been like a family for these last few days – a happy family. It made her eyes smart just thinking of it. They'd almost forgotten about the operation that was coming. Then, twenty minutes earlier, Lapshin had come back and reminded them that they were soldiers and that their fate would be decided in the morning.

It shouldn't have come as any surprise. All day long staff officers had been driving back and forth in their American jeeps, couriers slipping and sliding on their motorbikes – and Lapshin had been as jumpy as she could remember. He'd gone over every centimetre of the tank with her. He'd made them check the ammunition two or three times until he was satisfied that each bullet, each shell, was perfect. He'd checked the radios, the tracks, the guns – everything.

'We don't want anything jamming, Polya. When I press the trigger, I want to see dead Germans. Not a live one pointing a Panzerfaust at me.'

And now he'd woken them – telling them the attack was in a few hours. And so they'd shaken themselves down, and set about getting ready to move off. No one spoke much. It was always like that before a big operation. You were nervous, of course you were, but that wasn't something they were going to talk about. Anyway, they'd a good commander and they all knew their jobs. Most importantly, they had a lucky tank – one that had been through much more than most. With God's will, they'd see the end of the next day. Maybe even the war.

When they were ready, the commander of the battalion, Raskov, called all the crews to a nearby clearing. They found him standing beside a cut-down oil drum in which a fire burned, staring at the burning rags it contained. They waited for the last of the tank crews to arrive.

Finally, she saw Raskov check his watch then raise his eyes to look around at the circle of men, and one woman, that surrounded him. He checked his watch again – his lips narrowing as he did so. A couple of hundred flame-lit soldiers surrounded him, so silent you could hear them breathing, and it was as if the battalion had stepped down from the wall of a church. Noble, serious men. And her. Raskov looked directly at her and she felt her stomach turn with fear, not of him but at the words he was about to speak. His eyes were coal black in the night's shadow and his mouth a slash in his marble-still skin, stained red by the fire's glow.

'Well, men,' he began. 'And Polya, of course.'

She smiled at that – or tried to. No one laughed, and she was grateful to them.

'War has not made us tender.'

For a moment she wondered if that was all he had to say. She could have told everyone that herself and been back sleeping under Galechka's warmth. Then Raskov coughed, cleared his throat. It was difficult to be certain in the flickering light but it seemed he felt he'd started on the wrong foot.

'War has made us hard,' the major said after a moment – in a quieter voice now that carried all the more clearly for it. He raised an arm and pointed behind him. Towards the enemy.

'Soon you won't be able to hear me. There are thousands of guns behind us – they're lined up wheel to wheel. Then there are the Katyushas, ready to send countless rockets down on to the enemy's heads. In front of us, there are the infantry – packed into our trenches tighter than matches in a box – and in the woods behind them there are boats. When the guns start they will begin to move, they will cross the river under the cover of the bombardment and when the guns stop, they will take the forward enemy trenches. There is no question of that.'

He looked around him once more. The battalion waited to hear what their part was to be in all of this.

'Once the first line of the enemy defences is secured, the guns will crush the second line. The infantry will go forward again. They will take the second line. We wait. But we won't wait long. Our engineers will already be building bridges linking us to the other side. And attacks from the salient further up the river will have broken through and made any attempt to prevent us crossing impossible. And when we cross and take our place in the general attack, we won't stop until we are in Germany itself.'

The battalion leaned forward like hounds scenting their quarry.

'Remember, Comrades, when we face the Germans, that we represent the Court of the Soviet People's justice. The people have judged the enemy's crimes and have bestowed on us the honour of carrying out the people's sentence. We will be fearless. We will be resolute. We will be merciless.'

Polya felt that they'd become one single entity, she and the others. Somewhere to the right, in the distance, men cheered – and she realized that all along the line, commanders were speaking to their soldiers just like this. She remembered that the battalion was but a handful among millions. Polya found that tears were once again itching at the corners of her eyes and she hoped no one was close enough to see. 'Remember the dead, Comrades, remember the innocent citizens murdered by the aggressor. Remember we were a peaceful nation attacked by the fascist beast without provocation or warning. Remember what, under Comrade Stalin's leadership, we have withstood. The enemy knows we are coming and they tremble. And they are right to tremble. We will not halt until we reach Berlin.'

And then the artillery started to fire and the noise of it drowned out any reaction that might have been possible to such a speech. Polya looked at her watch – it was as visible in the orange glow of the shells exploding to the west as if it were daylight.

It was five exactly. The twelfth of January. The year of Our Lord 1945.

And when they went back to the tanks, the way made easier by the burning sky, she saw the slogan on Galechka's turret that they'd decided on, its black lettering clear on her white turret in the orange light:

To Berlin!

§

Far off to the west, Brandt felt the guns' vibrations. His tiredness, momentarily, was forgotten and adrenaline flowed through him. And fear.

The dice were rolling and he had no idea how they might land.

49

NEUMANN HAD been asleep and now he was awake.
He lay there, wondering what had disturbed him. The
curtains were pulled tight and the room dark as a sealed
coffin. Nothing appeared to be out of the ordinary but he
held himself still, not breathing – listening. There was a
faint noise, one that in an ordinary time and place no one
would pay any attention to – more of a tremor than a
rumble, really. It wasn't coming from inside the building,
or even from its immediate surroundings. It might be
indistinct, this sound – and yet it was persistent. There was
always the possibility that it might be far-off thunder, but
thunder didn't roll for minutes on end.

At first, he thought it odd that the noise had woken him –
but then he realized he'd been listening for it, without being
aware of the fact, for months now. And not only him. He
could hear the enlisted men moving around on the floor
below, making their way to the dormitory's windows. Their
muffled voices sounded calm enough, but they were
fatalists, the Ukrainians . . .

He felt for the bedside lamp, but there was no electricity
– just a metallic click when he turned the switch. That
meant nothing. He pushed the blankets down and got out of
bed, feeling the cold of the floorboards against his bare
feet, and walked across to the window. He pulled the
curtains open, hoping he was mistaken – that the persistent
rolling rumble from the east was indeed, after all, only far-
off thunder. Behind him, on the floor, he heard Wolf. The
hound was coming to push against his leg, sensing his
unease.

Neumann stood there for a moment, looking across the
valley at the sky above the forest and thinking how
beautiful it was. He touched the fingers of his left hand to
the glass and found that the chill surface was trembling – as

if it were alive. And that vibration, he knew, most likely represented the destruction of thousands of men. Even here, at this distance from the Front, the building was shaking with the terror of the thing. And yet he couldn't help but admire the way the colours swirled and shifted on the clouds.

The Ukrainians were silent in the downstairs dormitory and he imagined them standing, just as he was standing, looking out at the troubled sky, wondering what the Russians would have in store for them when they came. He didn't doubt it would be death – but what was death but a change? He yawned. He was tired. So very tired. He reached down and rubbed Wolf behind his ears.

His eyes were already closing as he walked back across the room – back to the bed whose sheets, he hoped, would still be warm with his own body's heat. Then he stopped.

He was no longer alone.

The old man moved from side to side as he prayed – his hands folded tight across his chest. He was the barest of outlines, but he was there, he was sure of it. But he couldn't be there. He must be dreaming. It was a trick of the mind.

He felt no fear, he was pleased to discover. He thought that must be because there was nothing to be done. He felt regret that it had been him, not someone else, who had been on that damned train. And what did it matter anyway – he'd done what he had and now he was faced with the consequence – a silent, weaving spirit in the corner of his bedroom. This could end only one way now.

Wolf pushed against his leg, his wet nose trying to reassure him, and Neumann ran his hand through the dog's thick winter pelt. There wouldn't be room for Wolf in the Commandant's car. Should he set him free? Or should he shoot him?

After a while, he felt his eyes begin to close once again, and so he lay down and pulled the blankets around his head.

If the old man wanted to stay, he was welcome to.

50

THE WORLD had changed.

They lay, as always, close together in the bunker – their bodies battered from Peichl's assault. Agneta traced the cut on her cheek, the crusted blood rough under her finger. They were alive – they could easily not be.

'The Lord protected us,' Gertrud had said when they'd finally been alone in the bunker. Katerina had agreed.

'Did you see his face?' Joanna whispered. 'When he told him to pack his bags for the Front?'

No one answered and it had been impossible, in the dark, to know what they might be thinking – but she savoured the memory.

'If only he really were going,' Rachel said.

They'd been afraid when Brandt had told them that Peichl wasn't leaving. They'd thought he'd come after them, given they'd witnessed his humiliation – but he'd barely acknowledged their existence. It was as if he had been hollowed out by the experience. She wondered if it would last.

It wasn't only him. She'd seen the Ukrainians talking. Bobrik, their leader, had been in conversation with one or other of them throughout the day – their faces narrow, their features pinched. She noticed the way their eyes slid towards the eastern hills repeatedly as they spoke. Had they had news of their own? She lay there awake, thinking through the permutations. She would observe everyone carefully in the morning – especially Peichl.

It wasn't clear when she first heard the low rumble – not that it mattered. They had been asleep and now they were awake. They listened, each separately, each of them, no doubt, wondering if it could be what they'd been praying for.

'Do you hear it?'

Rachel's voice, quiet as a mouse's whisper. There was no need for anyone to answer.

'Is it them?'

Again no need to answer. It had to be. Far away to the east, the Red Army's guns – thousands of them, tens of thousands perhaps – were firing shell after shell after shell. She'd been waiting for these guns for years now, and now here they were. She could feel them – even from this distance. The earth itself was absorbing their power and sending it to her.

'It's them,' Agneta said, and regretted it. She should have stayed silent. They were all the same, she was sure of it. Each of them wondering what the Russians advancing might mean for them and hoping it would lead to an end to the hell they lived in. But that was no excuse. She couldn't be careless now.

'God forgive the men who die tonight,' Katerina said.

Agneta wanted to reply – to say something less Christian in sentiment – but she restrained herself. She'd made one mistake, she wouldn't make two. She must be invisible until the end, whatever the end was. She must not speak, she must not be seen – she must not be heard. When people looked at her, they must see through her. She must not even think about the Russians, in case her thoughts might be revealed in some minuscule twitch of a muscle. She watched the SS for infinitesimal clues as to what they might be thinking. Perhaps they watched her that carefully as well.

To die now – to not see the end of all this – that would be the cruellest thing.

51

IT HAD SNOWED – heavily – in the last hour or so, and some of it still clung to the glass. The snow had softened everything – made it seem rounder, smoother. He remembered that snow made even the camp seem beautiful. Or, at least, cleaner.

Neumann stood at a window, once again. He couldn't hear the guns but when he put his fingertip to the window pane he could still feel them. Perhaps they were German guns now. Perhaps the counter-attack had started.

He made his way over to the row of sinks, putting his hand on a tap's cold metal and listening to it squeal as he turned it. The noise made him anxious. He wanted silence. He wanted to preserve the calm he had woken up with.

Why wasn't there any water?

There was a creak and a bang from the pipes and then he could hear the water coming. Thank God. That would be all they needed – to have no water. There was a trickle and then it burst out of the tap in a red-brown belch. Another belch, then it ran more smoothly. It ran a murky dark red at first, before flowing clear. Rust in the pipes, he hoped, rather than another trick played by his mind.

He examined himself in the mirror. He looked exhausted – even though he'd slept well enough, despite everything. He always hoped to see his old face, the one from before. But that face, full-cheeked, with its hearty inner glow, was gone. Nowadays his skin hung from his bones like slum washing – grey and shapeless, tired and worn. His eyes had faded to an ersatz approximation of the blue they once were and, as usual, seemed not to like the look of him much, sliding away from him as if they wanted to avoid their own gaze.

Oh well.

He raised both hands to his face and slapped his cheeks,

feeling his skin cling to his fingers as he did so, clammy despite the cold. The skin swung slightly beneath the blows – but didn't redden. What a mess he was. He rubbed his face, hard, so that the pain might bring him back to some kind of sense of himself.

He heard steps approaching along the corridor outside and then knocking on one of the bedroom doors – his, most likely. He looked at his watch. Peichl. The footsteps waited, then came towards the washroom. More knocking.

'Herr Obersturmführer?'

Peichl's voice sounded almost obsequious. Jäger had been right. Peichl had been so relieved when he'd told him he wasn't going to the Front that he was sure he'd have kissed Neumann's feet in gratitude if he'd asked him to. He wondered what Peichl had made of the artillery in the night. He must ask the auxiliaries if there was any news. Although, of course, it would be the usual nonsense if it was from the radio.

Neumann breathed deeply.

'I'm shaving,' he called out, and his voice disgusted him. It sounded like a weak old man's. 'What do you want?'

As if he didn't know.

'It's time, Herr Obersturmführer.'

'I must be running later than I thought. You take it, Peichl.'

'As you wish, Herr Obersturmführer.'

Peichl's footsteps walked off.

Neumann let the icy water run over his hands then leant his head underneath it and his mind went silent at the freezing shock of it. He stood it as long as he could before reaching for his towel and scrubbing the feeling back into his scalp.

That was better.

He picked up his razor. Time to decide, he thought, as he looked at the straight edge, whether to shave his throat.

Or cut it.

52

AGNETA LOOKED DOWN at her hands, pale and wrinkled, and it occurred to her that, if they hadn't been scraping, rasping, scrubbing at yet another stained linen napkin, if they'd been just lying there, flat on the counter, detached from the rest of her, then someone might easily suspect they belonged to a drowned woman. She didn't care. She'd rub her hands down to the bone if needs be. The water that was rubbing her hands away, atom by atom, was becoming warm anyway, now that Brandt had got the boiler working. She had nothing to complain about.

When there was a power cut in the morning, as there was now, the only light in the scullery came from a solitary window, high up in the wall – no more than twenty centimetres in height, while running in width to a little over a metre. The light was cold and weak. Behind her, in the main kitchen, Brandt began to move – slow step, slow step. They were alone. The others were sweeping the path outside. He had come out and asked Bobrik to give him one of them and she had been the one he'd chosen. He was walking towards her – he was hesitant. He stopped at the scullery's doorway. Was he waiting for her to do something? To turn to him? He'd be waiting a long time if he was. She continued scrubbing at the napkin, harder than ever, feeling her knuckles rubbing against each other, rubbing themselves smooth. If she ignored him, maybe he'd go away. But no – three quick steps forward.

'Eat this.'

Brandt placed bread and cheese on the counter beside her. She looked down at it, but not up at him. More food – this had been going on since he'd arrived. She couldn't risk it now.

'It's bread. And cheese.'

'I see that, Herr Brandt. Thank you – but I can't.'

'You've eaten before. I take the blame if you're caught. That's all there is to it.'

'I'd be punished, no matter how much blame you took.' She was pleased with her tone – calm, patient. Not a reflection of how she felt at all. She could feel his eyes on her, willing her to look round at him. She wouldn't. She would carry on scrubbing this damned napkin till it came apart in her hands. Why couldn't he leave her alone?

'You need strength, you all do. In order to survive. Till the end.'

Despite herself, she looked round at him. He was as nervous and frightened as the others.

'You don't trust me,' he said. 'But it's important that you do. I want to help you.'

She found herself wanting to smile, to laugh at him. For this moment at least, she sensed she had some power over him. As if they'd already been liberated and she was sitting in judgement. As if she were the one with the power to say 'Eat' or 'Starve', 'Live' or 'Die'.

'Judith,' he whispered, pushing himself forward as he did so, so that his mouth was close to her ear.

She took a step backwards, her hip sliding along the sink's wet edge. She leant down to grasp it, needing its support. She stared at him.

'You don't remember me, do you? Oskar? Do you remember me now?'

He raised his hand to his face, pulling it across the damaged skin, as if to reveal his old face. A magic trick that didn't work. And yet, it was as if she was seeing him for the first time. Each scrubbed scar, each melted edge, each burst and crooked vein in his skin was fresh to her. She wanted to reach out and touch his cheek – to draw her own hand across his face, just as he had. To try and recreate him as he'd been. Because she did remember him.

'I don't know what you're talking about.'

She heard the lie, even if he didn't seem to.

He returned her gaze, his mouth hanging open like a fresh-caught fish. She felt the urge to laugh at him, but she knew it was a false emotion, this hilarity, born from fear – because at the same time she wanted to embrace him.

'I know about your mother. You told me about her.' He lowered his voice. 'I know you're Jewish, as far as these people are concerned at least.'

She should turn away but she couldn't break his gaze. She did her best to keep her face blank.

'I've never spoken to you in my life before this place.'

She felt sharp pain as her nails tried to dig their way into the porcelain sink. It was good, this pain. She needed it. All he did was nod, as if in agreement.

'My mistake,' he said, his voice softer than it had been, his mouth developing an awkward twist. 'Anyway, it doesn't matter. I'm going to get you out of here. All of you. And soon.'

Was he joking with her? Was it some kind of a trap? She couldn't find any words.

'There's nothing to be discussed. You have no choice,' he said. 'This place will be closed also, and very soon. Think about what that means.'

She said nothing. She held his gaze, searching into his eyes for the trap, the joke, the threat. He seemed sincere. But so did men like the Commandant.

'What are you talking about?'

'The Russians are coming – they'll be here soon and the SS won't want to leave any evidence behind for them. The camp will cease to exist and the prisoners will be moved or murdered. Do you want to take your chances on which it will be? You need to get out of here, hide and wait for the Russians. It's your best chance. By far.'

She swallowed. The shock she felt at seeing a man she'd thought was dead was one thing. That he should turn out to be Brandt was another thing again. And then there was the news about the camp – his proposal for an escape.

'Where?' It was the only word she could manage.

'Close by. Hopefully tonight or tomorrow night. There's no time to lose. Well?'

She nodded her agreement. She needed to think, and if she agreed then maybe he'd leave her alone.

'Good. Don't tell the others yet. If we have to delay it, then I don't want any of them walking around with my name in their pocket. One of you is enough. Do you understand?'

She felt panic rising in her, but something else as well. She nodded again.

'I'll let you know more this afternoon. Now eat the damned cheese and bread. I'll keep watch. Tell me when you've finished.'

She heard him walk towards the staircase that led to the floor above. She reached for the bread and began to tear at it, stuffing it in her face – as if the food might force out the fear as well as her hunger. When she had finished she ran her hand over the counter, scooping up the few crumbs that were left and putting those in her mouth as well.

'I'm finished,' she said.

Brandt didn't respond but she heard him make his way to the upper floor, leaving her alone.

She turned back to her laundry, picking up another napkin, pushing it down into the soapy water. She needed to calm down, she told herself. She needed to stop the tears that were falling into the sink beneath her.

53

BRANDT STUMBLED as he climbed the stairs, reaching out for the wall to hold himself straight. He was struggling to think clearly and each movement he made seemed somehow distant from his intention. He paused, his breathing erratic. It was cold inside the hut but here he was, sweating. His body and mind were not quite connecting – either with each other or with the world around them. He needed to calm himself.

There was no turning back now, and that was just as well. He wasn't sure what kind of reaction he had expected from Agneta or, rather, sought – but it hadn't been that she would deny his existence. It didn't matter – he was committed to his course. His fate, however, was in the hands of others, and perhaps it was this realization that had left him suddenly drained and distraught. Monika and Agneta wouldn't betray him voluntarily, he didn't think, but Jäger was uncertain. Then there was Bobrik, Neumann, Peichl and even the mayor. It only needed one indiscretion or suspicion and his plan would collapse. And if the Commandant gave an order before he'd managed to get them out, then all of this would end in failure anyway.

And even if he were successful, outside the perimeter fence there were a hundred things that could go wrong in the short distance to the small barn. Perhaps he would have more courage and belief if Agneta had acknowledged him. Or perhaps this whole scheme was a self-indulgent attempt to wash away his own guilt about acts that could never be, and never should be, forgiven.

Perhaps he thought too much. But time moved slowly when each second had the potential for disaster – and what else was he to do?

He found himself standing in the men's washroom, in front of the toilet Jäger had mentioned. He took off the porcelain cover and found a small oilskin package. He unwrapped it. The pistol was small and silver. He discharged the magazine. Fully loaded.

He replaced it, uncertain whether its presence was good news or bad news.

54

NEUMANN LOOKED across the dining room. The windows were scatter-crusted with wind-driven snow while outside the trees bowed under their white winter weight. Wolf padded around the room, his nose grazing the floor. Every now and then he would look up to check on Neumann's well-being and Neumann would see the hound's tongue lolling from the side of his mouth, his eyes jolly with anticipation. Wolf didn't care about the future, or the past. He looked no further ahead than the prospect of scraps from the table.

Neumann heard the footsteps of the auxiliaries approaching and straightened in his seat. He would exude confidence.

'Good morning, ladies,' he said, standing.

Werth, the plain one, had oiled her mousy hair so that it hung over her pasty face like something dead. Beck, at least, looked pretty this morning.

'Good morning, Herr Obersturmführer.'

They spoke in unison.

'Well?' he asked, when they had sat down.

His question came out like one of Wolf's barks. He should have let them speak first – relax a little. The two auxiliaries looked at each other and he was certain something passed between them. He wondered what they'd been discussing before they came into the room. As if he didn't know.

Wolf, meanwhile, having completed his examination of the room, came over to Anna Beck and, to her embarrassment, buried his long nose in her lap, ferreting around as if he thought something might be buried there. Beck pushed at the dog's head but she was too nervous, not forceful enough. Neumann spoke sharply to the dog: 'Wolf, get over here.'

Wolf left the poor woman alone and circled the table to
take his position alongside Neumann's chair, his head
angled towards him and his eyes alert. Neumann could see
how frightened the SS woman had been. He felt some
sympathy for her.

'He's a pet, Fräulein Beck. He's not one of the other
dogs. The ones at the camp. There's no need to be nervous
of him. He's affectionate.'

Beck said nothing. Neumann pulled the napkin out of its
holder and examined it – he would have demanded
explanations for its condition not that long ago, but what
would be the point now? He'd only get the same old
excuses – the soap was shit, the napkins were old. There
was a war on.

'Say something, for God's sake,' Neumann said.

The auxiliaries looked at him with wide eyes. If he was
honest, his outburst had come as a surprise to him as well.

'We were talking about the weather, Herr
Obersturmführer,' Werth said, her gaze avoiding his. 'It
snowed last night.'

'I can see it has snowed – I've just walked the length of
the building, past window after window – all I've seen is
snow. You can barely see out the windows for snow.'

'Fräulein Werth didn't mean to be disrespectful, Herr
Obersturmführer.'

Was Beck whimpering now? He found his irritation was
increasing. He should have left Wolf to carry on.

'I didn't think she was being disrespectful. If I did think
such a thing' – he looked hard at Werth – 'there would be
consequences.'

He paused, even more irritated with them – and also
himself.

'I'm only surprised you didn't hear the guns last night. I
would have thought any sane person would have been
taking about them. About the Russian offensive which has

just begun.'

Beck's eyes were red now and she began to sniff. He found himself scowling. Why should she be crying? All Beck would have to do was pack her clothes and move to a new posting. All she had to do was as she was told.

'Have you spoken to the camp?' he asked, knowing that they would have been on to their fellow telephonists there. 'Do you have any news from the Front? Something useful to tell me?'

Werth nodded.

'The radio says that our men are repelling the invader, Herr Obersturmführer – the girls at the camp know nothing more than that. Not yet, at least.'

'I see.' A muscle was twitching in his cheek – he lifted a finger to hold it steady. Outside, four of the women prisoners were clearing the snow. He wondered what had happened to the fifth. If Peichl had murdered her, he would give him to Jäger and have done with it.

'Herr Obersturmführer, the girls at the camp . . .' Werth paused. 'They say that the prisoners are to be marched to the west. That the first columns will be leaving tomorrow.'

He must instil confidence in them – that was his duty as their superior officer.

'They are needed elsewhere.'

'They say some of the officers have left without permission,' Beck said.

Werth spoke in a voice barely above a whisper.

'They told the girls they don't want to end up with a hangman's noose around their necks, or worse.'

Neumann wondered if she was aware how her hands were twisting around her throat – as if she were making a noose for herself with her fingers.

'What about us? What will they do to us?' Beck's voice was shrill and her knuckles white around the spoon she held in her hand.

He wished he hadn't come to breakfast – he wished he'd gone straight to his office.

'The girls at the camp say they've begun to evacuate German civilians from Krakow and Katowitz. That the same will be happening here soon.'

Neumann slammed the table. The crockery and cutlery lifted as one, then crashed back down. Nothing broke. That was something.

'That is enough.'

He felt ashamed of himself. Why shouldn't they ask such questions? Except that if everyone was always asking questions, what kind of order could there be?

'I will call the Commandant. Until we have orders we proceed as always. No doubt our men will counter-attack today or tomorrow. A battle goes back and forth before the final victory is achieved. Do you understand?'

The door opened behind him as he spoke and, without looking, Neumann knew it must be Jäger. He should have cut his throat at the sink.

'Quite right, Neumann.'

They made to rise, to acknowledge his superior rank.

'No need for that on my account. Stay seated, please.'

Jäger walked around the table to sit opposite him. Wolf went and placed his head against Jäger's elbow. The SS man reached back, rubbing the dog between the ears. Wolf's eyes hooded with pleasure – the treacherous beast.

Jäger's complexion was nearly as pale as Beck's.

'Did you sleep well, Herr Hauptsturmführer?'

Jäger nodded absently before turning to face the table. 'I would like to taste real coffee again,' he said, sniffing at the coffee pot.

Anna Beck sniffed. Neumann hoped she wasn't going to cry again.

'What will happen, Herr Hauptsturmführer?' Werth asked. 'Now that the Russians have attacked?'

Neumann glared at her, but she was oblivious. She only had eyes for the tanker in his black uniform, the silver badges on his collar and shoulders and his calm, grey eyes. The Hauptsturmführer put his hands on the table and turned them palm-upwards, lifting one and then the other.

'To you? I don't know,' he said. 'But I'm not certain it will matter much. Human beings are insignificant as individuals, don't you agree?'

Fat tears rolled unwiped down Anna Beck's pretty face. Outside, in the laneway, Peichl began to shout and swear at the women – threatening them with the foulest depravities.

Neumann looked over at Jäger, who returned his gaze and smiled.

55

ALL THE COLOUR had been sucked from the world.
Everything was white. Except for the black river and the
grey-green pontoon bridge.

Polya opened the driver's hatch wide to have as good a
view as possible. Her face was numbed by the wind-driven
snow but inside her uniform she was sweating. It was hard
physical work to steer the tank – harder still at low speed –
and perhaps her nervousness wasn't helping. They were
only a few metres behind another of the battalion's tanks –
close enough to be half-poisoned by its diesel fumes. The
other side of the river was far away – when she could even
see it through the swirling snow. It was sluggish, the river,
as if it were about to ice over. And evil – she'd seen it kill
once already this morning.

Despite the roar of the engine she could hear her heart
thudding in her ears. She could taste blood in her mouth
from where she'd bitten her tongue. The thought of letting
go of one of the steering levers to wipe the snow off her
face made her sweat even more. She would have to put up
with it until the other side. She pushed Galechka forward
and asked the Virgin for her protection.

The pontoon bridge swayed as it took the tank's weight
and she felt her stomach sway with it. Behind them was a
never-ending line of tanks, trucks, carts, horses, self-
propelled guns, jeeps, wagons and the Lord knew what
else. They would have another bridge in operation within
hours, they said – but for the moment half the Red Army
was coming over this one narrow, bucking path.

If only there was a wall or something to work off – even
on one side – that would be something, at least. Instead
they advanced between two lines of soldiers who crossed
the river at a run, weighed down with weapons and kit.
Officers and NCOs yelled them on. If one of them

stumbled, he'd be gone – either into the river or under a tank. The choice was his. The man she'd seen die had chosen the river – and the river had swallowed him whole.

Lapshin had his feet on her shoulders, pressing one then the other to tell her what he wanted from her. His touch was gentle, not like in a battle. His feet almost caressed her shoulders. If they were in a fight, he'd be kicking and pushing her as if she were the tank itself. Then, likely as not, she wouldn't be able to see what was going on so she would just do what his feet told her. Now she could see as well as he could, and his guidance was unnecessary. She didn't mind it, though. In fact, as she hauled and pushed on the steering levers, trying to keep the tracks straight while keeping their place behind the T34 in front, she found Lapshin's feet comforting. They were a welcome distraction from the fear.

It was difficult to be accurate with a fifteen-tonne machine and a bridge that rolled under its weight. Not least because the most important thing was to keep moving, to be confident. Lapshin had been clear about that. She had to use her fear, not let it incapacitate her. Her sweat was pooling wherever it found a hollow or curve – she'd suffer when it cooled. A rotten cold, that's what she'd have.

The tank in front slowed and she prayed it wouldn't stop. Lapshin had told her the tank commanders had orders to push tanks out of the way if they got into difficulties – and good luck swimming to the crews inside. What if they had to do that to the fool in front? But then with a slight twitch of its tail, the forward tank picked up speed and Polya eased up behind it, breathing once again.

Thank the Lord the infantry and artillery had wiped the Germans from the hills in front of them . . . There was some German artillery fire but it was erratic. Very seldom did it come anywhere near them. Although the thought of what would happen if the pontoon bridge were cut in half by a random shell made her sweat just a little bit more.

Up ahead of her, through the snow, she caught a glimpse of the other side – tanks were speeding up the pock-marked slope, infantrymen clinging to their sides, rolling past caved-in trenches and bloodied bodies, fanning out and advancing at full speed.

And that made her smile.

They were going to Germany. To drag the fascists from their lair.

56

IT HAD BEEN two days since the Russians attacked and still Brandt had heard nothing from Hubert. Meanwhile, a doctor would be coming to see Jäger today, after which the SS man must finally leave. And once he was gone, the hut must be shut down, with all that must mean. Brandt felt the situation slipping away from him.

'Brandt? What are you doing? Dreaming?'

Peichl was standing so close that he felt the spray of his spittle on his cheek. The truth was, he'd no idea what he was doing – he looked down to find he'd been reading the cellar list, over and over again. Had Peichl been talking to him for long?

'I'm preparing an inventory for Obersturmführer Neumann.'

He croaked. As if he'd forgotten how to speak.

'Not worried about what the Ivans will do to you, then? You should be – they'll want to know how you won all your medals. How many of their comrades you killed.'

Brandt opened his mouth to speak but no words came.

'You don't look well, Brandt. Perhaps you are frightened?'

He was, But not for himself so much.

'Nothing to worry about,' Brandt said. 'Just a fever.'

'Don't pass it to me. I need my wits about me. I want to make sure I know exactly what's going on. I want to make sure I know who can be trusted and who can't.'

Brandt turned and found Peichl's malevolent eyes were only centimetres away from his. Peichl held his gaze, challenging him in some way. Brandt stared back, wondering what was happening. Eventually Peichl took a step back to look around the wider kitchen.

'Prisoners. All of you. Out here and line up.'

Rachel and Agneta came from the side rooms while the

others left off what they were doing, standing where Peichl indicated. He walked along the line, examining each of the women in turn. Brandt watched him. Could he know something? Could someone have blabbed?

'I'm taking two of the prisoners, Brandt,' he said. 'I need their company in the guardhouse for a little while. It seems we are missing a key and I'd like to know how this happened.'

There was something sly about the way Peichl spoke, as if there was a joke that only he understood. Brandt felt ice roll down his spine.

'As you wish, Herr Scharführer.'

'Aren't you going to ask me which key?' Peichl's lips curled into a smirk.

'It's none of my business,' Brandt managed to say, despite his dry mouth.

'I thought you'd made the prisoners your business, Brandt. All this nonsense about winter jackets – you think I don't know who put the Obersturmführer up to that? And now the key to their bunker goes missing. I wonder if that might not be of concern to you as well.'

The Scharführer's smile was wide now. He held up a finger and wagged it from side to side, chiding Brandt.

'You thought I wouldn't notice, dear Brandt? About your little kindnesses? More fool, you, if you did. Which one? The Pole is attractive enough, I suppose.'

The penny dropped.

'What are you suggesting?'

His surprise wasn't invented. Peichl's reaction, however, was to look still slyer.

'Or maybe the Austrian? I think it's her. Yes. That must be the case. She's the one you can't take your eyes off.'

'This is nonsense,' Brandt said, turning his fear into anger.

Peichl laughed.

'Why go out of your way for them? That's the question I asked myself. It could be pity, I suppose. But you don't strike me as a kind man, Brandt. I think you're just the same as me, underneath that burned skin. After all, you work here, same as I do. Kind men don't work in a place like this. Do they?'

Peichl went up to Agneta, whispering into her ear loud enough for Brandt to hear.

'Does he take advantage of you, Prisoner? Does he take you into that scullery where you work and bend you over the counter? Or does he visit you at night?'

'Herr Scharführer, this is unacceptable. I will go directly to the Obersturmführer.'

'You have nothing to worry about, Brandt. If you've done nothing wrong, of course. Maybe I'll ask a few questions, while these two are cleaning the guard tower. I tell you this in all honesty, Brandt, when I start asking questions of prisoners – I always get answers. I wonder what answers I'll get this time.'

Peichl laughed and jabbed a finger at Joanna and then Agneta. He pointed his thumb towards the door.

'You and you. Outside, now. And be quick about it.'

Neither of the women looked at Brandt as they left, but he could tell from their lowered heads and the way they carried themselves that they feared the worst.

And so did he.

57

BRANDT WATCHED Peichl take the women to the gatehouse through the window. He ushered them inside. Brandt imagined what was being said in there. He imagined Peichl beating them – he imagined things worse than a beating. He imagined Agneta telling him about their conversation. At least, thank God, she knew nothing about the key.

He was about to go up to Neumann to demand the release of the women back to his kitchen when he saw Anna Beck, the SS woman from upstairs, approach the guardhouse and knock. When Peichl came to the door the two top buttons of his tunic were undone. He was pleased with himself. He exchanged a few words with Beck, doing up the undone buttons as he did so. Then he closed the door behind him, leaving Joanna and Agneta inside, and followed Beck back to the main building, looking over to the window Brandt was standing at and waving. A friendly wave. What did it mean?

Brandt was conscious that the prisoners in the kitchen were watching him.

'Let's get back to work,' he said, and looked again at the cellar list. It was somewhere to look, no more than that. He listened to the sound of Beck and Peichl's footsteps on the floor above. Peichl walking to Neumann's office where his steps paused, then entered.

Had Agneta told him something? No, not possible. Agneta was tough – she'd keep her mouth shut for longer than a few minutes. He was sure of it. And Joanna knew nothing.

He occupied himself with work. It passed the time.

§

'Herr Brandt?' Katerina said. Peichl had been in Neumann's office for twenty minutes now. Katerina was preparing vegetables near the window, from where she had a view of the main gate. Brandt walked over and she nodded towards a truck that was driving in. At first he thought it must be the doctor coming for Jäger. But when it came to a halt, an Order Police officer stepped down from the driver's cabin and approached the hut's main entrance. Men with rifles began to climb out of the covered rear – standing around in their heavy coats, cigarette smoke gathering around them. They couldn't be here because of anything the women had said to Peichl. They had to have come from the town at the bottom of the valley.

Unless Peichl had called them earlier. And then there was Bobrik. And Jäger. Why hadn't he walked around the village with a placard? He might as well have called the Order Police himself.

He looked down and saw that he'd squeezed the cellar list into a tight ball without realizing. He was meant to give it to Neumann that afternoon and now he'd have to rewrite the whole thing. That was all right. He needed something to distract himself. He'd begin directly.

§

'Herr Brandt?'

When Anna Beck's voice called down the stairs for him he said nothing for a moment, carrying on with copying out the list, hearing the steps creak as she came down the steps, one by one. He was thinking. They would have sent Peichl and the Order Police down if it was serious, wouldn't they? This was good news.

'Herr Brandt?'

'Yes, Fräulein Beck. I'm here.'

He scanned her face as she told him Neumann wanted to speak with him. He followed her up the stairs, his missing hand making its presence felt. In the space beneath the empty sleeve, its ghostly echo clenched and unclenched repeatedly.

'What does he want me for?'

He asked the question out loud – it seemed reasonable to. He sounded surly, as if he were annoyed at the inconvenience which, he thought, was the right approach. He was a decorated veteran, after all – a hero of the Eastern Front. But at the same time he was trying to guess who might have betrayed him, if anyone had, and what they could have said.

'I don't know what he wants. All day long we've been waiting to be told something. But nothing.' She sounded exhausted – as if she were one of the prisoners and not one of the upstairs folk. 'He just told me to bring you upstairs. He's with Hauptsturmführer Jäger and an officer from the Order Police. And Peichl.'

'The Order Police?'

'I don't know why.'

Could Jäger have betrayed him? Had their conversation been a provocation? He wished he had the gun from the cistern in his pocket. There was laughter inside the office, then Neumann's voice called for him to enter. Brandt could hear other voices talking. Jäger sounding relaxed. Perhaps it was all right – perhaps he had nothing to fear. He twisted the door handle.

The conversation stopped as he entered. The room was full of smoke and he found himself the focus of attention of the room's silent occupants. Jäger was sitting in an armchair, one leg sloped across his knee. An Order Police Hauptmann, his greatcoat open, sat in the other armchair. Neumann leant against his desk. Peichl, standing by the filing cabinets, looking less happy than he had – was the only one who ignored Brandt – instead staring at Jäger.

Neumann pointed his cigarette at him.

'The man we need to speak to.'

'Herr Obersturmführer?'

Another pause. Were they playing with him? Neumann

looked over to the Order Police officer.

'You're part of the village's Volkssturm, aren't you?' the officer asked. 'A local?'

'I am.' Brandt nodded his agreement. It was just a Volkssturm matter. He would have been more relaxed if the Order Police Hauptmann hadn't had a face like a cell door. And why was Jäger wearing a white camouflage smock? Jäger caught his glance and gave him a smile that didn't bode well.

'Hauptmann Weiss here needs our assistance. Some British prisoners of war have escaped – they've taken to the hills near here.'

He resisted the temptation to ask what this had to do with him. At least he wasn't going to be arrested.

'When did this happen?'

'Last night, in one of the factories in the town,' the Order Police officer said. 'They attacked their guards. One of them is half-dead in hospital.'

'Well,' Jäger said, 'it's their job to attack us – and the other way round. They're soldiers, after all.'

The Hauptmann snorted.

'They're prisoners of war. Anyway, we'll do our job when we catch them – exactly the same way they did.'

Brandt didn't need to be told they were nearby – it was obvious to him. Someone must have spotted them close to the village. Jäger nodded, as if following his chain of thought.

'Feldwebel Brandt has worked out why we need him.'

The Order Police Hauptmann's glance flicked between them quickly, his expression cautious.

'The thing is, Herr Brandt,' he said, 'they were seen early this morning near a farm on the other side of the reservoir. The family's name is Dorfmann.'

'I know the place.'

The Red Farm. Where the shoot had taken place.

'Good – my men don't know the area very well. We're going after them, of course.'

'It's up to you, Brandt,' Neumann said, looking up at him. 'The mayor has given his approval, however.'

'I don't know the valley as well as I used to,' he began. 'I've been away some time.'

'The mayor said he was sure you'd do your duty,' Neumann said, and Brandt found himself nodding.

'And Ernst Mayer is to go with you as well. Do you know him?'

'He's my uncle.'

'The mayor said he was the best tracker in the valley.'

'The mayor's not too bad,' Brandt said, mainly to give himself time to think.

'He's otherwise engaged.'

'Are they officers or enlisted men – the British?' Brandt said, deciding there wasn't much point in trying to duck it.

'That's a real soldier,' Jäger said. 'Straight to the point. Few like him left. Around here, anyway.'

Weiss, unfamiliar with the Hauptsturmführer's ways, seemed to have swallowed something that disagreed with him.

'I thought you were leaving us, Herr Hauptsturmführer,' Brandt said, nodding toward the camouflage jacket. 'I heard a doctor was coming to see you.'

'The doctor isn't coming till tomorrow morning now. Another delay. Plenty of time for me to join the hunt.'

58

IT WAS A wild-goose chase. The British had covered their tracks where they could and the ones they hadn't managed to obscure, the wind and snow were taking care of. In theory they were still following them, but Ernst had lost the trail an hour before. They'd circled twice around the last place they'd seen the Britishers' tracks, spread out in a long line in the hope that someone might see something. The Order Police weren't used to this kind of work. They had been sloppy and disorganized to start with but now they carried their rifles like spades and muttered amongst themselves. Their officer, Weiss, deferred to Jäger in everything. As for Peichl and the four Ukrainians that Neumann had volunteered – in much the same way as he'd volunteered Brandt – they were at least alert. Jumpy almost. Bobrik, in particular. Peichl, on the other hand, just looked cold and miserable. But every now and then he glanced over at Brandt and nodded. As if to remind him he hadn't forgotten about the key.

It didn't help that the fresh snow was making the going difficult – particularly if you were missing an arm for balance. Brandt stumbled and Ernst, God bless him, reached out to support him, smiling. His face was red as a strawberry and the breath wheezed out of him like a steam engine. He was too old for this. So was Brandt, for that matter. It didn't seem likely that they were going to pick up the trail now, not with the shadows lengthening and the snow still falling. Brandt was happy about that.

Brandt looked along the line. The Order Police and the Ukrainians were clustering together now. They slogged on, towards the next farm, looking less and less soldierly as they went. He should say something, but it wasn't his place. He wasn't even sure why he was here. Once it had become clear that Ernst knew each tree and bush as if it were his own, neither Weiss nor Jäger had bothered speaking to him. He doubted any of them would appreciate his advice now.

The farmer at their next stop had seen nothing and heard nothing – but they searched his outbuildings anyway, just in case. They found nothing, of course. And it was just as well – the Order Police had gone about it in a stupid way. Just walking in and looking around. Sitting ducks.

When they reached the Red Farm, so called for a barn that wore the colour – faded from neglect now, of course, like everything else these last five years – Jäger stopped to let them recover their breath. It was becoming even colder as the last of the light left the valley. Brandt took off his helmet and wrapped his scarf around his head from top to bottom, tying it under his chin, covering the side of his face where the skin was rawest. He replaced the helmet and looked around at the others. They stood in a rough circle, not speaking – smoking cigarettes, if they had them. It was too dark now to see their faces clearly, except when their features appeared for a second or two in the glow of a cigarette, fading away as quickly as they'd come.

After five minutes precisely – Brandt watched Jäger check his watch more than once – the SS officer nodded to Weiss and they moved off. Brandt stayed at the rear – they'd given up looking for tracks now. Quite what they were trying to do, he wasn't sure, and he needed to relieve himself. He should have gone when he'd had the chance back at the barn but he knew where they'd stop next – they'd stopped there twice already – and it wasn't far. He could wait until then.

Brandt was cold but he felt a still deeper chill as he realized they were walking through the same long field in which the officers' shoot had taken place – that they were passing only twenty metres from the spot where the prisoners had been murdered. There was something about the place that filled him with foreboding. Ernst turned towards him, his eyes shaded by the brim of his antiquated helmet, but Brandt knew him well enough to detect his concern. His uncle stopped, inclining his ear – as if he thought he might have heard something. Brandt wondered if he should call out to Jäger. But the Hauptsturmführer was already in the forest, following the same narrow path they'd walked along twice already. The only sound now was the squeaking of the snow under their boots and the occasional crack of a frozen branch.

No one spoke, even though they'd gathered together into a tight group – no man more than an arm's length behind the one in front. After all, who would want to be left behind, alone in among the dark trees? They were doing their best to be quiet, moving slowly, testing the ground in front of them before putting their full weight on it. But the idea that they might catch the British was laughable. They could pass within metres of a British soldier in this light and they wouldn't see him. At least the kitchen would be warm when he got back; he could rest his backside on the stove and have a glass of hot milk – with something in it perhaps.

Brandt saw the pale break in the canopy up ahead that marked the spot that they were sure to halt in and decided to take his opportunity, stepping off the path and finding himself a bush. He saw the others form a shadowed circle and the splashes of orange as more cigarettes were lit. Or maybe the same ones, saved from the last stop. No one had missed him.

He reached down to open his trousers and just at the moment when he put his hand on the top button, someone placed the barrel of a gun alongside his ear.

'Stay still and silent and you might see the morning yet.'

Brandt wasn't completely certain he'd heard the words, so quietly were they whispered, but the gun was real enough. The man spoke in Polish – the accent was local. What was more, he thought he recognized the voice.

Brandt stayed still. He stayed silent. He concentrated solely on making sure he took his next breath, and then the one after that. The one thought he managed was to be grateful he hadn't opened his trousers before the gun was put to his ear. He wouldn't like to be found like that. Someone would laugh – they always did. It was a way of releasing the tension – like shaking a dead man's hand for luck. He'd like his death to be more dignified. He didn't know how long he stood like that, in limbo – it was hard to keep track of things with a bullet only a dozen centimetres from the inside of your head.

When the shooting started it was almost a relief. It was like a sudden tempest that tore through the forest, ripping bark and branches from the trees. The air around him filled with the whip-crack of flying bullets – and dull thuds when they embedded themselves into wood and flesh. Someone threw a grenade and he saw bodies lifted like rag dolls in the flash of light. The cold barrel resting against his cheek didn't budge. He heard Jäger shouting but he knew it was too late. The return fire from the clearing dwindled. Eventually, it ceased.

And then there was silence – the only sound the ringing in his ears. Every part of his body was sending him a message to run from the place. His vision was streaked and blotted with the starbursts and flame lines of the brief battle. He'd stopped breathing, he realized, and was forced to risk a shallow breath, as much to check that he was still alive as to keep it that way. He inhaled the bitter taste of cordite that filled the air around him.

Now that it was over, he replayed it in his mind. The others had followed the narrow track down to the clearing and they'd stopped. They'd lit their cigarettes, making them visible to their ambushers. The men in the trees had either heard them coming or been waiting for them – this was the third time they had come this way, which had been foolish. The Order Police and the SS, he wouldn't miss, but Ernst deserved better.

A calm voice – accented Polish, a Russian, he was sure of it – called out from over to his left: 'Anyone hurt? Speak up.' When there was no answer, the Russian spoke again: 'The big one was mine and so are his boots – the others I don't care about.'

He heard the sound of low laughter from all around. He knew what it meant – relief that you were alive while others were dead. Part of him wanted to laugh as well.

'All right, then. Let's be careful about this.'

The killers moved down through the trees, reliving the excitement as they did so. Some were serious men, others inexperienced. None of them was British. He wondered if they knew they'd killed a nice fellow called Ernst, whom no one had a bad word to say about.

Hubert would, he thought. But Hubert didn't join the others, he stayed with Brandt. His pistol still resting against Brandt's cheek.

Men moved through the clearing, and he could see the flicker of torchlight as they checked the bodies. He saw a thickset man busy himself removing Ernst's boots – first the left one, then the right – and then he heard Ernst's weak voice, distorted with pain. It was cut off by the wet rasp of a blade cutting through flesh. Brandt closed his eyes and wished he could shut his ears.

Then there was a muttered conversation and the sound of the partisans moving off.

'Isn't it time you gave up being a soldier, Paul Brandt?' Hubert's words were not much more than a breath in his ear. Brandt had no answer to that.

'Wait till we're long gone before you move. If the others see you, there's nothing I can do. Not here.'

Brandt said nothing.

Hubert hesitated as he moved past him, no more than a hint of a shadow as he passed in the darkness. He turned and leaned in close.

'Monika has the things you asked for. I did it for the women in the hut, not for you. Just so that's clear. And I spared your life tonight for Monika. No other reason than that.'

59

BRANDT FOUND himself standing alone in the darkness. The cold was creeping into his bones, deep into his body. The only noise was his own oh so tentative breathing. Eventually, the clouds that had been obscuring the moon allowed it to shine through for a moment, revealing the clearing below in its milky light and the tangle of bodies that filled it.

And then a drop fell onto the snow at his feet, then another. Blood. He pulled off his glove with his teeth and felt where the scarf he'd wrapped around his head was now torn and wet. Feeling inside it, he found his right ear had been nicked by a bullet. A few centimetres to the side and he'd have been killed.

It was painful now that he noticed it. He moved the scarf around a bit, tried to pull it tighter, and decided it would do as a bandage for the moment. He *was* alive, wasn't he? He pushed at the ear and it told him he was. It didn't seem possible. He should be dead. But the dead don't bleed and they didn't make this low keening sound. A sound he shouldn't be making. He stopped it by putting his hand over his mouth, biting into his palm.

The shock and the cold seemed to make his mind work more slowly than usual. He didn't know how long he had been standing there – it could have been a minute, or an hour. Finally, he found himself taking a step forward, beginning to make his way down to the clearing, placing each foot with care. He'd forgotten how exhausting being terrified was.

He arrived in the clearing just as the moon broke through the cloud cover once again. It looked as though the contents of a clothes shop had been strewn around it – the partisans had gone through the men's packs and pockets and stripped them of anything that might be of use to them, discarding whatever wasn't. The men's corpses – collapsed shapes on the snow, shadowed by the pale light – were almost indistinguishable from the garments and objects that surrounded them, except in size. He moved around the clearing, bending down to feel for a hand – slipping a finger inside a glove, if it hadn't been stolen, and checking for a pulse. The partisans had done the same thing, of course, with a different intent. He found himself gripping cold soft dead flesh time after time.

'Is anyone alive?' he whispered.

Someone moved. He was sure of it.

'Can anyone hear me?' he whispered.

'Brandt?'

He recognized the voice, even in a whisper.

'Peichl?'

'Where are they?'

'They've gone.'

Peichl sat up, looking around the clearing at the others, inhaling so loudly and suddenly Brandt thought he might be about to vomit.

'Thank Christ. Thank Christ. Thank Christ. I thought that was it. I thought I was gone.' He patted himself as he spoke. 'Not even a scratch. Not even a scratch.'

'You were lucky.'

'Brandt? Peichl?'

Another voice. Weaker. Jäger.

'Herr Hauptsturmführer?'

'Over here.'

Peichl didn't seem to have heard Jäger. Brandt could hear Peichl patting his body down, looking for a wound.

'Not a scratch. Thank Christ.'

'Check the bodies over there,' Brandt said. 'Maybe they missed someone else.'

Peichl, still muttering his relief, walked to the far side of the clearing. Brandt knelt down beside Jäger. The SS man was making a strange noise, like a pot just coming to the boil.

'I'm finished,' he said.

'I'll turn you on your side. We'll get help.'

'Don't worry. There's no point. Is it just you and Peichl?'

'I think so. Peichl's checking.'

'It was my fault. I was careless. A waste.'

There was silence between them for a moment – and Brandt leant down to offer him his hand. Jäger took it and pulled him down, whispering to him.

'Have you still got your weapon?'

'Yes.'

'Then you need to shoot him.'

'What did you say?'

'Kill Peichl. He suspects you. He spoke to me at one of the rest stops. He says you are planning to get the women prisoners out – that you have a key to the bunker. You can't let him live.'

Brandt said nothing. On the other side of the clearing he heard Peichl turn a body over.

'You have no choice, Brandt.'

Jäger's whisper was edged by pain. Brandt remembered the snarling rage of Peichl when he'd beaten the women. He remembered the murder of the Jewish prisoner on his first day working in the hut.

'They're all dead,' Peichl said in a low voice, walking back over.

'Hauptsturmführer Jäger is alive. He's in a bad way.'

'Can he walk?'

'I don't think so.'

'We can't stay here,' Peichl said.

'I'll go for help,' Brandt said, undoing the flap of his holster. 'I know the area best. You stay with Jäger.'

There was a silence.

'We should both go,' Peichl said, and Brandt could hear the fear in his voice. He didn't want to be left alone in the forest with partisans close by.

'Peichl,' Jäger whispered.

'Yes, Herr Hauptsturmführer.'

'Come closer.'

Brandt found that he was shaking, but it wasn't from fear. Peichl leant down over Jäger. Brandt moved to one side. He couldn't see Peichl's face but it was probably just as well. He slipped the gun from the holster, millimetre by millimetre.

'Will you stay with me?' Jäger asked.

'It's best if we get help, Herr Hauptsturmführer.'

Brandt took a step forward. Another step. He lifted the pistol.

'Stand away from Hauptmann Jäger, Peichl,' Brandt said.

'What is it, Brandt?' Peichl said, standing and stepping towards him.

Brandt shot him in the chest – the muzzle flash lighting Peichl's face orange. There was a sly smile on the SS man's face in the instant it was visible, and Brandt saw that his hands were bunched into fists.

There was silence. The sudden gunshot hadn't startled any birds or dislodged more snow. There was no echo. The only reaction was, after a moment or two, an involuntary sigh that Brandt knew came from himself.

He took two steps forward to where Peichl lay, another broken body in a clearing that was full of them, and pushed at it with his foot. Dead, heavy flesh. He leant down and placed the barrel of the gun against the side of Peichl's head, shooting him once more for good measure. Before he'd pressed the trigger he'd been uncertain – but now that he'd killed the man, he had no regrets about it at all. He'd killed men before and for less good reason.

'He deserved it,' Jäger said.

Brandt said nothing. He listened to Jäger struggle for each breath, to the quiet of the forest. It was peaceful now and snow began to fall. Little frozen splashes on his skin. They might have been refreshing if he weren't already cold.

'I'll get help.'

'It will be too late, Brandt. I'm not going to last long. I don't want to die here on my own.'

'I'll wait with you, then.'

60

JÄGER WAS RIGHT. He didn't last long. Brandt held the SS man's hand and listened to the blood bubbling in Jäger's throat each time he breathed. Jäger gave a slight cough when he finally passed, his hand going limp in Brandt's grip.

Brandt stood up, his body stiff, and whispered a prayer for the dead – not that any of them except poor Ernst deserved it. Certainly not Jäger. He was shivering with cold now and very tired. He was almost grateful for the injury to his ear – the pain from its chafing against his helmet's chinstrap was keeping him alert. He started walking, hoping it would warm him up, but by the time he made his way back along the path to the open fields, the snow was coming down thick and fast – the wind picking up so that it swirled around him. It was close to a blizzard now and there were no lights to be seen. Soon he realized he had no idea where he was. Still, if he kept heading downhill he should, with luck, reach the reservoir – and when he reached the reservoir, he'd have reached the road to the village. If he reached the road, then there was a good chance someone would find him – it wasn't even that late – dark as it was. There would still be people travelling, even in this weather.

After a certain point, he realized that the world around him had become less tangible. His legs appeared to know where they were going but he wasn't sure how. In his mind's eye, he kept seeing Peichl's face lit by the muzzle flash, the sly, malevolent expression. He wondered where Peichl had come from – what he'd done before the war. What decisions had led him to the clearing and his appointment with Brandt's bullet?

Every now and then he had to climb over a fence or a wall, but where or when he couldn't be sure. Then he found himself on an endless flat field, which in a moment of clarity he realized must be the reservoir. Beyond it, through the snow, he could see a flickering light. He climbed towards it, clambering over still more fences and walls that blocked his path. He was exhausted now and he hoped the light was real. It seemed to come in and out of focus, sometimes disappearing from sight altogether. And then, to his surprise, he was standing in front of the hut's main gate, swaying as a searchlight was pointed at him. Falling forward.

When his helmet hit the metal gatepost, it sounded like a hammer hitting a cracked bell.

61

AT FIRST IT wasn't clear what was happening. The klaxon was going off outside and one of the female auxiliaries was screaming that the Russians were attacking. Neumann shouted at her to be quiet.

'It's the search party, that's all.'

Neumann had almost given up on them, thinking that once it became dark and began to snow, they would find somewhere to hole up until the morning. All the same, when he went outside to greet them, he carried his pistol.

He had to hold his free hand over his eyes to see anything at all. Within metres his uniform was covered in a crust of wind-driven snow. He made his way down the lane that led to the main gatehouse, feeling the cold numbing his fingers. One of the guards loomed out of the white so suddenly he almost walked into him.

'It's Brandt, Herr Obersturmführer. We found him by the gate.'

Two others followed, carrying the unconscious steward between them.

'Get him inside – and turn off the damned klaxon.'

The guard ran toward the gatehouse – and a welcome silence soon followed.

They carried him through to the sitting room, where Neumann had them lay the unconscious man on a chaise longue close to the fire. The burning wood crackled and spat as they tried to make him comfortable.

'He needs a doctor,' Weber said. The mayor was wearing his Volkssturm uniform, his hand resting inside his open holster, his expression startled.

Neumann looked at him for a moment, confused, before remembering he'd come to ask if the Volkssturm could use the hut as their base once the imminent civilian evacuation began. The snow had stopped him leaving. He had a point about the doctor.

'Fräulein Beck?' Neumann said over his shoulder, 'See if you can get through to Doctor Münch in the village.'

There was no response. He turned to find Anna Beck swaying from side to side, transfixed by the blood that covered Brandt's face and coat.

'Fräulein Beck?' he repeated in a sharper tone, and she shook her head twice, as if to revive herself.

'I'll see to it. Excuse me.'

She turned and walked quickly towards the telephone room.

'You men get back to your posts. Keep your eyes peeled.'

The two guards who had brought Brandt in stood to attention and saluted. They looked reluctant to leave.

'The others?' One of them began, and Neumann remembered the four guards who had accompanied the patrol.

'As soon as I hear anything I'll let you know. For the moment, we need to be alert. Walk the perimeter – use the searchlight.'

When they'd left, Neumann reached down to feel Brandt's cheek. It was like ice, but the unconscious man moved away from his touch.

'Well, he's alive.'

'But where are the others?' Weber asked. 'The rest of the patrol.'

The other telephonist, Werth, came into the room carrying blankets – at least someone had kept their head.

'I called the police station,' she said. 'They've had reports of gunfire in the hills, a couple of hours ago.'

Some sort of battle then, Neumann decided – perhaps Brandt had become separated in the confusion. He tried to take the man's helmet off but dried blood had stuck the strap and lining to a scarf that was wound around his head –

and the steward moaned as he tried to detach it. He had better luck with the greatcoat – opening the buttons and then, with Weber's help, managing to get it off. He could find no wound apart from the one to his head. He leant down to listen to Brandt's breathing – it was ragged. He put the blankets over him and they pushed the chair closer to the fire's warmth.

'Call the Order Police Headquarters. Find out if they've heard anything from Hauptmann Weiss or his men.'

Werth nodded and left the room.

'What do you think happened?' Weber asked, but all Neumann could do was shake his head. The only thing certain was that Brandt had been wounded and that he'd somehow made his way to the hut.

'The doctor is on his way,' Beck said, coming back in. She was calmer now but she was still shaking. She wouldn't do.

'Fräulein Beck, can you fetch one of the Bible students up from the kitchen?'

'Of course, Herr Obersturmführer.'

'Also bring a sharp pair of scissors. And soap and warm water. We need to clean away this blood and get his helmet off.'

Brandt stirred once again. His eyes moved behind their closed lids and then the left one opened, looking up at the light above, turning to examine Neumann.

'Brandt?'

'Herr Obersturmführer.'

Brandt's voice was little more than a croaked whisper. His other eye opened. Weber reached past him to push at Brandt's shoulder.

'Brandt, wake up.'

Neumann pushed the mayor's hand away, irritated. The mayor looked at him in surprise.

'But we need to ask him what happened. Where the

others are.'

Weber's voice sounded higher than usual.

'Don't touch him.' Neumann felt anger rising up inside him. 'Go and stand over there and keep your mouth shut.'

'But—' Weber began, before falling silent, standing to his feet and walking to the other side of the room.

Neumann had to close his eyes for a moment, to calm himself.

'An ambush.' Brandt's voice was barely audible. 'Partisans. In the forest. To the east of the Red Farm. Near where the shoot was. The others are dead.'

'Dead?' Neumann counted them up. Peichl, the four Ukrainians, Jäger and Weiss, the Order Police Hauptmann. Was it ten Order Police? And the Volkssturm man from the village. Eighteen men. At least. 'All of them?'

'I checked the bodies.'

'Peichl? Jäger?'

'All of them.'

More footsteps – Werth coming back from the telephone room.

'The Order Police have heard nothing from Hauptmann Weiss or his men, Herr Obersturmführer.'

'How many partisans? What kind of weapons?'

'I couldn't be sure – maybe twenty. They had machine guns. Grenades. They took the weapons and ammunition our men had.'

'Which direction did they head in?'

'It was in the forest, hard to tell.'

'Could you point to the spot on a map?'

'More or less – but it was in the trees. I could find it myself, I don't know if I could direct someone else to find it.'

'You're sure they weren't the British?'

'The voices I heard were Polish, some Russians – I didn't hear any speaking English.'

Neumann relayed the information to Werth – instructing her to notify the Order Police and the Volkssturm on the dam. Half his command wiped out while he'd been sorting out papers to be burned.

'Where are you hurt?' he asked Brandt when Werth had left the room.

More footsteps. He turned to see Beck returning with the Austrian political prisoner – towels and a basin in her arms.

'I told you to bring one of the Bible students, not this one.'

'This one says she has medical training, Herr Obersturmführer.'

He turned his attention to the prisoner.

'Well?'

'I was a medical student for three years at the University of Vienna.'

'Let's see what you learned, then.'

The prisoner leant down beside Brandt.

'It's my ear,' Brandt said.

'It's best to check the rest of you, just in case.'

Her fingers had been working at Brandt's helmet as she'd spoken and somehow, where Neumann had failed, she succeeded. It came off along with the bloody scarf and she began to clean the blood away from his face and neck, Brandt's grimace of pain notwithstanding.

'The ear isn't too bad,' the prisoner said, her voice softer than Neumann expected it might be. He realized he hadn't heard her speak more than a dozen times. 'A few stitches and it will be all right. You've lost some of it, I'm afraid.'

'I'm careless with body parts.' Brandt whispered – and Neumann was surprised to see the wounded man was smiling.

Neumann looked at his watch. He had better report the situation to the Commandant. Perhaps he would send men from the camp, if they could be spared.

62

AGNETA DIDN'T LOOK UP when Neumann left the room, instead she found herself searching Brandt's eyes. He returned her gaze. She wanted to run back down to the kitchen – to change her mind. But it was too late now. When the SS woman had said it was Brandt upstairs, she'd stepped forward. There had been no time to think about it. She washed the last of the blood from Brandt's face and neck, rinsing the towel out into the bowl. Pink soap bubbles now floated on its surface. She couldn't have stayed down in the kitchen – it would have been impossible.

'If you're warm enough, I need to take off your tunic,' she said.

'You'll have to help me up.'

She gave Brandt her hand and he squeezed it as he pulled himself forward. A signal? He was lighter, more frail than she'd expected.

'Is this wise? To move him?' the mayor asked. 'Shouldn't we wait for the doctor?'

'I'm fine, Herr Weber,' Brandt said. 'Just fine.'

She peeled the jacket over his left shoulder and then down and away from his truncated arm. She found that her breath left her when her fingers brushed his stump. She remembered his arms around her. When was the last time she'd touched a man, gently, like this? Not since Vienna.

She must show no emotion.

The other side was more difficult, dried blood had melded the collar of the tunic to his hair but she used the warm water to separate them. There was no visible injury, apart from the ear itself.

'See?' Brandt said. 'I told you I was fine.'

'Would you like a brandy?' Weber asked.

'That would be good.'

Weber fetched Brandt a cognac and he drank some,

coughing.

'We'd better take your undershirt off as well,' Agneta said, and Brandt looked over to the auxiliary and Weber. 'May I have some privacy, Herr Weber? Fräulein Beck? Just for a moment or two.'

He inclined his head down toward his half arm, the look suggesting he was embarrassed by it.

'Of course, of course,' Weber said.

The mayor and the SS woman left them alone and Agneta noticed that the light from the fire had softened Brandt's face, turning it almost golden.

'What happened?' she asked, keeping her voice low.

'The patrol was ambushed. Peichl is dead. Bobrik and three of the Ukrainians as well.'

She pulled the undershirt over his head, careful to avoid the injured ear – underneath, he wore another cotton vest. Peichl dead? It was as though a weight had been removed from her shoulders.

'You're sure about Peichl?'

He shrugged, looking away from her.

'I'm sure.'

He was quiet for a moment.

'It doesn't matter if you don't remember me,' he said. 'I remember you.'

Once again she found it difficult to breathe. Or speak.

'We can't talk like this,' she managed.

She was taking off his vest now. She heard his intake of breath as she pulled it over his head, the fabric rubbing against his wound.

'But I remember you also,' she said, in little more than a whisper.

He was naked to the waist now. Scars and burn marks covered much of his chest and shoulders – aside from the rounded elbow that ended where his forearm should have begun.

'I didn't know you studied medicine,' he said.
'I didn't,' she answered. And allowed herself to smile.

63

NEUMANN WAITED FOR the Commandant to speak. He'd reported the dead, their probable location and the few details he'd had from Brandt concerning the perpetrators. But there had been no response. Neumann began to wonder if he'd been speaking to himself for the last two minutes. The phone lines were erratic these days and it wasn't hard to lose a connection.

'Four of ours, you say?'

Neumann relaxed a little. The Commandant's voice sounded brittle – but that might only be the quality of the line. 'Five guards, including Peichl, Herr Commandant.' The Commandant and he were not, Neumann suspected, on first-name terms this evening. 'And Hauptsturmführer Jäger makes it six.'

'Of course, Jäger as well,' the Commandant agreed after a slight hesitation. 'Six SS. What a mess. The Order Police are responsible, of course. They're the ones that allowed the partisans to establish themselves in the hills. They're the ones who did nothing to stop them. Now we see the consequences.'

There was another silence. A door slammed somewhere on the Commandant's end of the line. The evacuation must be well under way by now.

'This fellow Brandt, he's certain all of them are dead?'

'He says he checked each body for a pulse. The partisans finished the wounded off.'

'But he survived? I remember him. A local, isn't he?'

Neumann heard the suspicion in the Commandant's voice.

'Yes. The one-armed steward.'

'Ah. The war hero. I take your point. He's not likely to throw his lot in with the partisans.'

'No,' Neumann agreed after a moment's thought.

Although he wasn't certain, now that he thought of it.

'Is he able to be more specific about the location?'

'I don't think so. He says he could take us there, though.'

There was another pause. Neumann wondered if the Commandant was wondering, as he was, about the strange symmetry of the SS being ambushed so close to the shoot at which they'd killed the prisoners.

'The bodies will need to be recovered,' the Commandant said.

'I'll organize a search party. Weber is here – he could call out the Volkssturm but there are only four SS men left here in the hut. If we could have some men from the camp or one of the sub-camps?'

Another door slammed somewhere close to the Commandant, and Neumann could hear someone shouting orders.

'Herr Commandant?'

'Yes?'

'It sounds as though things are busy there.'

'The Russians are advancing very fast, Neumann. Which means I can't send any men from here or any of the sub-camps. Every one of them is needed. Decommissioning the camp takes precedence over everything else. The orders are from the highest authority.'

'Decommissioning?' Neumann asked. There were a number of things that stood out from the Commandant's brief outlining of the situation – but that was the first one that came to mind.

'The prisoners are being moved west.'

'And the hut, Herr Commandant?'

'Yes. It too.' The Commandant sounded as though the hut wasn't something he'd given much thought to up until this moment. 'Leave nothing behind.'

'Understood, Herr Commandant.'

'The prisoners will have to be dealt with, of course.' The

Commandant paused, sighing. 'I forgot. Peichl is dead, isn't he? But there might be an alternative. How far away are you from the mining camp? Five kilometres or so?'

'Less.'

'They'll be removing the prisoners from there the day after tomorrow – send the women to them along with your guards. They could use the extra men on the march and then they'll be someone else's responsibility. The guards and the prisoners.'

'Thank you, Herr Commandant.' Neumann felt as though the conversation were happening in another room and he was listening through a wall. 'What about the auxiliaries?' he managed to ask.

'We need them here. I'll send Schlosser to pick them up in the morning. There's too much to be done – we expected the army to put up more of a fight. We need longer.'

He wondered how long they had. He wondered if the mayor would get his chance to play at being a soldier sooner than he'd thought.

'And me?' he asked.

'You could come here once the hut is dealt with, but perhaps it's best if you make your own way to Nordhausen. I can send orders and a travel permit with Schlosser. It's up to you.'

'I . . .' Neumann began, and then couldn't think what else to say. The thought of going to the camp filled him with disgust. The thought of going to another camp – further to the west, filled him with the same emotion. Neumann heard more noise and shouting at the other end of the line.

'I'll send the papers with Schlosser,' the Commandant said eventually.

'What about the ambush?'

'Inform the Order Police. It was their patrol. See what they say. Otherwise, recover the bodies in the morning.

There's no point in going out in a blizzard if they're all dead.'

64

THE FIRST DAYS had been easy. There were no Germans to be seen – no live ones, anyway. They'd seen bodies – bloody streaks of flesh and fabric pressed into the road they travelled on, identifiable only by the scraps of grey uniform, or crumpled shapes curled along the base of a pockmarked wall. Each time they saw an enemy corpse, she thought it was a good omen. One less who might shoot back at them.

The only fighting seemed to be happening elsewhere. The gunfire they heard was always at a distance. The roads were crowded with their own men moving forward, carts, wagons, trucks, artillery and infantry from several divisions all mixed together – an army on the move, smiling as often as not. Everyone had been expecting a hard fight – so why shouldn't they be? And it wasn't as though they were fooling themselves either – everyone knew they'd be fighting soon enough.

Whenever possible, Major Raskov took to the fields. The going was quicker away from the traffic and it was perfect countryside for them – flat, but not too flat. There was plenty of cover for a good driver to manoeuvre across the open spaces. Raskov pushed them hard – and Headquarters pushed him hard in turn.

But each time they reached their latest objective, either the fighting had moved on or it had never begun. They would have kept going, but often as not they had to wait for their fuel tenders to catch up with them – their diesel tanks empty even if their ammunition racks were still untouched.

On the afternoon of the third day, however, they were given orders to move to a town to the north-west where the Germans were making a stand. No one knew whether there were really Germans there or not – but the battalion moved quickly all the same. The infantry clinging on to the turrets, bouncing as the tanks rolled and bumped over anything in their path.

When they ran into a retreating German column on the way, it was as much of a surprise to them as it was to the Germans. As they came over the top of a rise Polya saw Raskov's tank – about forty metres to their right – stop, its turret turning and then firing. Meanwhile, Lapshin was shouting.

'In the dip, on the road. Fascists. Fifty metres forward then stop.'

She pushed the tank down the slope and did as she was told, hearing the turret turning as she did so. Almost as soon as they stopped, the tank shuddered as Lapshin fired the big gun and the tank was full of the smell of cordite. Avdeyev, sitting beside her, was firing the machine gun and she still hadn't seen them.

'Forty-five degrees right. Thirty metres.'

Again she did as she was told and now she saw them – stretched out along a country lane not more than a hundred metres ahead. There were only a few trucks – an artillery unit to judge from the guns being towed behind them. Apart from the trucks, the transport was mostly horse drawn, the flatbed wagons loaded with wounded men and equipment.

There was no time for the Germans to unlimber their cannon, no room to turn in the road and no cover even if they'd been able to. The soldiers who could scattered, but it was too late. How could they not have heard them coming?

Did the battle last even a minute? It had been a blur – she remembered the screams as Galechka had rolled up onto one of the carts full of wounded men before it had folded flat beneath her weight. She didn't like to think about that. Anyway, the cart had been in the way and she knew as well as anyone that they had to catch the infantry before they reached the wood on the other side of the small valley. She remembered the faces of the soldiers running towards the trees, looking over their shoulders to see how close they were behind, eyes black with fear, mouths open as they screamed – falling as the machine guns mowed them down. If they'd taken any prisoners, she hadn't seen it.

They lost one tank to a Panzerfaust but it didn't burn and the crew made it out all right so no one complained. The victory was so quick and complete that they were moving on again almost immediately – although somehow Avdeyev found enough time to weigh down his wrist with three fine German watches.

When they reached the town they'd been sent to, it was a different story. It spanned a river and the bridge was still standing, so they were ordered to attack straight away with what infantry they had. But the Germans were dug in with anti-tank guns and Panzerfausts and the first attempt cost them four tanks – two of them in flames. After that, they kept their distance and worked alongside the infantry towards the river, house by house, street, by street through the course of the night. Each company took its turn, while the others stood back in support, catching some sleep if they could – two crews on, two off.

And just before dawn it had been their turn again and they'd broken through. Although she didn't remember much about that either – except Major Raskov's burnt-out tank on a crossroads, blackened bodies the size of children around it in the melting snow. And the blast when the Germans finally blew the bridge – not that it mattered as the river was fordable.

When they reached the other side, the battalion was down to twenty-one tanks – out of thirty-two – and Lapshin was now commanding their company, which had lost four of its own eight tanks.

65

THEY LEFT AT dawn to recover the dead from the ambush. The Order Police, it turned out, couldn't send even a single man to fetch the bodies of their comrades. A civilian evacuation of the area had been ordered from midnight, and as for tracking down the terrorists that had murdered them . . . ?

'There's nothing I'd like more, Neumann,' the Order Police Oberst had told him. 'Nothing in the world. But I've my hands full keeping the roads open for the army and getting the civilians out before the Russians come. I need ten times as many men as I have as it is. If you can bury our fellows, I'd be grateful. If the situation changes, of course, it will be a different matter. Then we'll come and hunt the terrorists down with a will.'

'Where are the Russians now?'

The Oberst had sighed.

'Their tanks are this side of Krakow. Warsaw is in their hands. Our men are everywhere in retreat.'

'Warsaw?'

'Yes.'

Neumann knew what the Soviets would find in Warsaw – a burnt-out husk of a city. Its inhabitants exiled or murdered. Another atrocity.

'And Krakow?'

'Yes,' the Oberst said. 'Krakow. That was yesterday. Who knows where they are by now.'

There was a short silence. 'As I said,' the Oberst continued eventually, 'if the situation changes, I'll send people straight away.'

The Oberst hung up without saying farewell.

Krakow wasn't far away – not at all. Far enough though, he imagined. They would be gone from the hut tomorrow. The Russians couldn't be here by then. Not even if they had passed Krakow.

Neumann and two of the Ukrainians joined the Volkssturm in the search for the bodies. In the forest, the going was slow. No one knew where the partisans were, after all. When they finally stumbled across the dead men in a small clearing, their bodies had been completely covered by the blizzard of the night before so that, at first, all they saw was a tumble of soft contours. It was only when they approached more closely that it became clear the shapes marked where dead men lay.

There was almost no conversation as they cleared each body and checked it for life – not that there was much doubt that the men were dead, given that the bodies were frozen.

No one slacked – not even the mayor. They brought the dead men out one by one to where the wagon waited. It was hard work. The boys and some of the older men struggled with the stretchers and it wasn't long before any feeling of care they might have felt towards the bodies disappeared. They piled them onto the wagon like logs of wood, throwing them in one on top of the other. Neumann was reminded of other corpses and another time. Of a train's freight wagon with bodies cascading out of its open door. The jumble of naked feet and legs was much the same.

Later, when they brought the dead back to the hut, Weber ordered the Volkssturm to dig a grave behind the hut. There were no longer as many Volkssturm as there had been. They had been slipping away all morning. By the time the mayor realized what was happening, nearly all the older men had gone.

'Herr Obersturmführer?'

Adamik, the young blonde Ukrainian guard, came to stand beside Neumann as he stood looking down the dead men, wrapped in the white bloodstained sheets that Neumann had ordered the women prisoners to sew them into. The sheets wouldn't be needed any more. Not by the officers from the camp, in any event. Neumann looked up, his fingers playing with the fistful of identity discs he'd placed in the pocket of his tunic.

'Yes?'

'We'd like to bury our comrades separately, Herr Obersturmführer. In the Catholic graveyard, down in the village.'

Neumann nodded his agreement. He didn't care one way or another.

'As you wish. You won't find a priest down there now, I don't think. The civilians are all leaving.'

'A priest?' the Ukrainian asked, shrugging. 'A priest wouldn't be much use to us, Herr Obersturmführer. It's past the time for priests.'

Neumann watched him walk away – he hadn't known the Ukrainians were Catholic. It surprised him.

Neumann walked around the hut to see what was happening down in the valley. Brandt had made his way across the frozen reservoir in the middle of a blizzard the night before. It wasn't so strange – if it weren't for the curve of the dam, you would hardly know it was there. Dark, low clouds leaned down on the valley below and a column of humanity was moving slowly along the road that ran alongside the reservoir's frozen shore. No wonder the Volkssturm were leaving – everyone else was.

There was a cough behind him. Another interruption.

'Yes?' he said.

'Herr Obersturmführer?'

He turned. It was Beck, the auxiliary. She looked pale – she had fainted when she'd seen the dead bodies in the cart. She would see much worse at the camp.

'The grave is finished but the mayor has to take his men down to supervise the evacuation – he has received orders from the Party authorities. He said he can leave two here.'

'Very good. The prisoners can fill it in. Are you and Fräulein Werth packed? Obersturmführer Schlosser will be here soon.'

'Yes. We're ready.'

'The files?'

'Everything is outside, waiting to be burned. Only the papers in your office still need attending to.'

It was time to cleanse the building of its past.

He met Brandt at the entrance, a bandage wrapped round his head. One of the prisoners must have washed his tunic, or done their best to, but it was still stained pink down one side.

'Should you be up?'

Brandt looked down at his tunic, as if checking the damage.

'I'm alive. My uncle was the Volkssturm man in the forest.'

Neumann remembered the older, portly fellow with the Volkssturm armband. He remembered the partisans had cut his throat so deeply his head was barely still attached to his body.

'I remember now.'

'My aunt will want to see to his burial. Mayor Weber has given his permission.'

'Of course,' Neumann agreed, nodding. 'If you're able to. Do you need help?'

'I fetched a horse and cart from our farm.'

Neumann looked around and saw a cart stopped inside the front gate.

'I'll report back here when we've buried him, Herr Obersturmführer.'

Neumann examined him, wondering if he could possibly be sincere.

'We can make do without you, Brandt. Most of your comrades have already left, why don't you join them?'

'I'll stay till the end,' Brandt said, his voice low.
Neumann wondered why. God knew, Brandt had already
given all that could be expected in the defence of the
Fatherland.

'That won't be long as far as the hut is concerned – the
auxiliaries will be gone before lunch. The Ukrainians leave
with the prisoners tomorrow and I won't be long behind
them. If you think Weber will stay much longer, I suspect
you're wrong. He's mayor of no one now – most of the
village are already walking to the west.'

Brandt shrugged, as if other people's actions were of no
concern to him. Neumann watched him closely and wasn't
entirely convinced.

'What time are the guards leaving tomorrow?' Brandt
asked. 'I'll make sure they have rations for the journey.
And for you, of course. For your journey.'

Neumann smiled, bemused but prepared to go along with
whatever Brandt was up to. For the moment, at least. What
difference did it make, after all?

'As you wish, then. They'll leave at five in the evening.'

'I will be as quick as I can, Herr Obersturmführer.'

'Thank you, Brandt.'

Neumann watched him walk across to where two of the
prisoners were lifting the body of his uncle into the cart.
Grey smoke billowed from the brazier on which the hut's
papers were now burning, and for a moment it obscured
Brandt. When it cleared, Neumann saw that he was in
conversation with the Austrian prisoner who had tended to
him the night before – thanking her, no doubt. As Brandt
pushed up the buckboard to obscure the corpse from
Neumann's view, he saw that there was an old army
rucksack sitting beside the body. Neumann wondered what
the rucksack contained. Perhaps that was what he was up to
– taking what he could from the hut's stores.

He didn't care – Brandt could have whatever the hut had

and be welcome to it. Rather Brandt than the Russians.

66

BRANDT KNEW it was often the smallest of moments that defined a life, or ended it. If Ernst had been elsewhere when the Order Police had called looking for him, he might still be alive – not lying in a sheet on a cart swaying its way to his funeral. And if Brandt hadn't needed to relieve himself the night before, he might be lying beside his uncle, just as dead, instead of sitting on the cart's seat. Jäger might still be alive if the doctor had been able to come the night before. Even Peichl might have survived, if he'd kept his suspicions to himself – although where that would have left Brandt was another story. Chance – that was what damned you or saved you.

Brandt found Pavel standing in the yard of his father's farm. The older man looked into the cart's flat bed at the sheet-wrapped corpse.

'Ernst?' Pavel asked, and held out his hand to help Brandt down from the seat. It was the first time Pavel had spoken to him since the summer.

'They're letting me take him to Ursula,' he said. 'So she can bury him.'

Pavel examined him carefully, nodding towards his head bandage.

'Something happened to you?'

'Nothing.'

Pavel nodded, as if agreeing with him. There was another pause. Brandt wondered if he knew that it was his son Hubert who had spared him.

'Your father says he isn't leaving,' said Pavel. 'He says he has no reason to leave.'

Brandt squinted up at the house, in case he might see his father standing at one of the windows.

'Do you think he would be safe here?'

Pavel ran a hand over his unshaven chin and thought

about it.

'I'd say go, all of you, and come back when things are more certain – we'll keep an eye on the farm for you. And anything you might leave behind. Why take the risk? We owe you that and more.'

Pavel placed a slight emphasis on 'anything' – enough for Brandt to turn and examine him. Pavel returned his gaze, his expression unreadable – so unreadable as to be suspicious. Was he talking about the prisoners? Pavel nodded, as if reading his thoughts.

'That would be – kind of you,' Brandt said. He wondered if Pavel spoke for Hubert as well. He'd said 'we' instead of 'I', after all.

'So what will you do?' Pavel asked, and inclined his head in the direction of the hut rather than the farmhouse.

He knew about the women – Brandt was certain of it now. One more person to worry about. One more life to take into account.

'I'll talk to him. Aunt Ursula and the children need to leave as well. They'll need him more than this farm will.'

'Good,' Pavel said. 'I'll feed the horse.'

§

His father sat in his usual chair. He pulled himself to his feet as Brandt approached. He'd aged since the day before. And his hand, which Brandt now held, was bone and skin and little else.

'You have him? Ernst – poor Ernst, of all people.'

'He's down in the yard. In the back of the cart.'

His father reached a hand up to Brandt's ear.

'Münch fixed it up. A stray bullet. Just a scratch.'

'He knows his business, Münch. A good doctor.'

He squeezed Brandt's hand again – hard this time, the dampness in his eyes reflecting what little light there was in the dark room.

'I thank God for preserving you.'

Brandt glanced down at the main valley road. It was lined with horse-drawn wagons and carts, women and children – all dusted with snow – moving slowly and sluggishly onwards. He was cold after the short journey from the hut; they must be frozen to the core.

'Why are they so slow, these people?' his father asked. 'I've been watching them. If one stops, everyone stops. They need to keep moving. Why don't they overtake the slow ones?'

'There are orders to keep one side of the road free for military traffic.'

'I don't see any military vehicles.'

'There are police and Volkssturm, however – and we're under martial law now.'

'Still.'

'Don't worry. They'll learn not to be polite if someone slows them down. It will be everyone for themselves once the Russians are snapping at their heels.'

'Where are they going?'

'West. To the Americans. Or the British. Anyone but the Russians. We need to go with them.'

'Ernst isn't even buried.'

'If we stay here, we'll likely be buried beside him.'

His father glanced up at him – weighing up his options.

'Why? We were born here. My father was born here, and his before him – for hundreds of years.'

'We need to go because of what those men in the hut, and men like them, have done.' Brandt took a deep breath. 'And not just that. I said I'd a good reason for being at the hut, do you remember? There are five women prisoners there who I mean to get to safety. If I'm caught, there will be consequences, and not just for me. You and Monika are all I have left in the world. I will follow as soon as I can.'

For a moment, he thought it might have had some effect – but then his father shook his head in the negative.

'You want us to leave – but are you sure Monika will go?'

Brandt thought about Hubert and Monika – their relationship that had survived five years of German occupation.

'She's staying?'

'Ask her. I don't know.'

It wasn't impossible. He would have to talk to her.

'Father?'

Brandt waited until the older man met and held his gaze. 'Ursula has to take the children to safety. The journey will be hard. The weather will be freezing. She'll be on her own. The children are our family as well as hers. And you're a doctor. You and Monika can help them reach safety. I just have to do this thing first. Once it's done, I'm not waiting around for the Russians. You can be sure of that.'

'You'll follow?'

'If I know where you're going, I'll join you. I promise it.'

Brandt looked at his watch. He had to hurry – he didn't want to leave the women without his protection for longer than he had to.

'Think about it. Anyway, let's take Ernst's body to Ursula. We'll help her bury him and then pack to go. You still have time to decide.'

67

EVERY NOW AND THEN Agneta would risk a look at
the boy with the gun. He was slight for his age. The old
army greatcoat he wore was too big for him – the material
folding in with a dimple on shoulders that were too narrow
for its width. Its hem brushed the snow when he walked
back and forth. He looked cold. Each time she glanced up
at him, she found his pale eyes waiting for her. How could
it have happened that her life had ended up in the hands of
a child? Each time she caught his eye, he smiled at her.

He terrified her. The earth had frozen, locking itself into
tight pellets. It sounded like gravel when it landed on the
sheet-wrapped bodies. It required effort to prise it out from
the mound that ran alongside the trench.

Someone – his mother? – had given the boy a scarf the
colour of a bright red apple. A thin strip of it appeared
between the Wehrmacht grey and his pale cheeks. The
scarf's colour matched the boy's red lips. If he'd been a girl
you'd think he wore lipstick.

She wondered if the other women were as frightened of
the boy as she was. Sometimes she had to stand in amongst
the dead bodies, sometimes even on them, in order to make
sure the earth was evenly spread, but she was used to dead
bodies. They didn't unnerve her the way the boy did. It was
the boy's smile that was most chilling. His clear, pale eyes
knew neither guilt nor sin. The gun, she suspected, was
heavier than he was comfortable with. He held it at an
angle, the butt underneath his armpit and the barrel pointing
at the ground in front of him. Both hands supporting its
weight.

She tried to think of something from before – of
something from the past. Something joyful. She thought
back to her last moment of freedom – of sitting down
opposite Brandt in the cafe, how he'd leant across and

taken her hand. How he'd looked into her eyes and how warm she'd felt, all of a sudden. How her stomach had felt lighter than her body, lifting her up to the ceiling. But the boy kept pushing himself into her consciousness and Vienna was a world away while the child with the gun still stood there, his finger resting on the trigger, his eyes following her every movement. She looked over at him once more, feeling her skin sing with fear when again he caught her glance and held it. She imagined him telling his friends about how he'd guarded hardened prisoners. How one of them had been a Jew. She wondered how the story ended.

The boy began to whistle.

She wondered where Brandt was. She wondered if he'd told the truth. She wondered if he would be able to do what he'd said he could.

68

NEUMANN HEARD Schlosser long before he arrived –
the noise of the car's engine reverberated along the valley.
He walked to the window and saw the Commandant's grey
Mercedes slowing for the Volkssturm checkpoint at the
dam, then after a few moments' delay, he watched it pass
the almost stationary refugees before taking the turn up
towards the hut. When he made his way outside to greet
him, he found Schlosser in conversation with one of the
young Volkssturm boys.

'Schlosser,' Neumann said by way of a greeting.

Schlosser clicked his heels and flung his arm up in the
Party salute.

'Neumann. Heil Hitler. A tragedy. Good men.'

Schlosser wasn't a tall man, by any means – the SS
wouldn't have taken him in the old days – and the salute
made him seem smaller than he was.

'Heil Hitler,' Neumann replied, conscious that his salute
was less enthusiastic. Surely it didn't matter any more.

'What steps are being taken?' Schlosser said. 'The
Commandant will want to know.'

'What steps?' He heard the brusqueness in his voice.
Schlosser's speaking in bursts had always irritated
Neumann.

'To avenge the fallen.'

Neumann looked at him in confusion.

'The Commandant informed me there are no men
available from the camp and there are only four guards left.
The Order Police have washed their hands of the affair.
What steps can I take?'

Schlosser inclined his head slightly to the side, as if
contemplating a tricky diplomatic situation.

'But you plan to take some action all the same, surely?
The local Volkssturm will assist. I spoke to Mayor Weber

at the checkpoint. He is prepared to take action.'

Neumann reached for the cigarettes in his pocket. The teenage boy who was guarding the women stood at attention, the model of preparedness. Neumann pointed a cigarette towards him. He found he was very tired all of a sudden.

'He and a few boys are all that is left of the village's Volkssturm, Schlosser. The older men have deserted their posts. I doubt Weber has more than a handful of even these boys left. Do you want to send a squad of children into the hills to hunt partisans? Or do you want them to murder some civilians in reprisal? German civilians around here, mostly, I believe. This,' Neumann's cigarette sweeping a wide circle to encompass the valley, 'has been part of Germany for some time now. And will remain so until the Russians come. Perhaps they should murder their own families?'

Schlosser said nothing at first – his mouth turning downwards. Neumann didn't understand his scowl. He must know this was nonsense. He found his fingers toying with the identity discs that he'd placed inside his pocket. More dead men. Eventually, Schlosser held out an envelope – reluctantly, it seemed to Neumann.

'Here are your orders. And your travel papers, as well.'

'Here,' Neumann said, irritated, and handed Schlosser the metal circles from his pocket. 'These are the dead men's identity discs. Someone in the camp will need them.'

He dropped them one by one onto Schlosser's outstretched hand.

69

IT WAS COLD on the cart and it had begun to snow once again. Brandt pulled his greatcoat closer around him. The farms they passed were deserted, their hearths cold, the doors and shutters closed, the life and warmth of them a thing of the past. They were slowly disappearing under the snow. Soon they would be nothing more than white hillocks in an empty landscape.

'Everyone's gone,' Brandt's father said.

That wasn't entirely accurate. There were some people in the village, although not all of them wanted to be seen. Brandt heard the sound of wood splintering down the narrow alley near the butcher's shop and caught a glimpse of a figure entering a house when he turned to look. As the German population retreated, others were coming out of the shadows. And who was to say these people didn't deserve whatever they took?

In the small square in front of the Catholic church they came across a family Brandt had known since he was a child. The old man in the group didn't see them but his daughters nodded, half a greeting and half a farewell. Both of them had lost their husbands to the war. Their father stood looking around at a village he might never see again. There was no need to say anything. They'd join the long queue of winter-bundled walkers and canvas-roofed wagons. Behind them, in the graveyard, Brandt saw the Ukrainians filling in the large hole they'd dug for their comrades – no time now for individual graves. He pulled the cart to a halt and went to join them. His conversation with Adamik and the others was short. He told them that they would be taking the prisoners to the mining camp and that from there they would be guarding a prisoner march to the west. They weren't surprised. Then he asked them what they knew about the arrangement with Bobrik.

§

When he returned to the cart, his father looked at him enquiringly. 'They are burying four of the SS guards from the hut. I went to pay my respects.'

'They were worthy of your respect?'

'My respect isn't worth much.'

His father said nothing.

The lane they took towards Ernst's farm led them alongside the column of refugees for a hundred metres or so. They stood still, like an audience waiting for a performance to begin, until somewhere up ahead a blockage must have shifted and they began to move, the jangle of harnesses and the creak and roll of wheels growing in volume as the forward march started up again. The refugees stretched along the twists in the road as far as the eye could see – a line that divided the snow blanketed fields on either side. Their faces were pale as the morning fog that still clung to the higher slopes – their shadowed eyes dark as the clouds that glowered behind them to the east. They travelled on farm carts and other horse-drawn vehicles mostly, but not all were so fortunate – some just walked in the wagons' wake, carrying what they could on their backs, or in their arms, or pulling it behind them on small wooden carts. A mother bore a rucksack from happier times – with scouting and mountaineering badges stitched to its sides – and held her daughter's hand firmly in hers. This retreating army was made up almost entirely of women and children. One of the few men, in his sixties at least, had only a blanket slung over his back, tied up to make a sack – its contents shaping it.

'Do you remember we discussed what I might have done in the east?' Brandt asked.

His father turned his head towards him by way of an answer. He had his attention.

'It was in forty-one – in that first month when we swept

everything before us. We captured an entire Soviet battalion almost without a shot. Maybe some of them got away – but there were still four or five hundred of them. I don't know where the orders came from – up until then we'd sent prisoners back to the rear. But we advanced so quickly that summer we weren't sure where the rear was some days. The company commander told us that anyone who didn't want to be involved could stand aside – that no one would think the worse of them. He had tears in his eyes. He was replaced soon afterwards – he was a good man, I think.'

Brandt's cigarette was almost finished. He stubbed it out and lit another – he didn't want to tell this story but it was important his father understood.

'We had three trucks with tarpaulin covers. We told the Ivans they were full of food and they lined up, mess tins in hand. The trucks weren't full of food – they had machine guns in them. The Hauptfeldwebel gave the command, the tarpaulin was opened and I remember the look on the Russians' faces as if it were yesterday – the ones at the front, the ones who saw the guns before they fired. I think some of them knew. But most of them were surprised.'

He looked across at his father. It was hard to work out what he might be thinking. His expression revealed nothing.

'It took no time at all. Some of them tried to run – I don't think they got more than five metres. Then the men from the company walked among them and finished off any that were still living.'

His father said nothing – Brandt was glad he couldn't see his face.

'They'd no idea – the Russians. Afterwards some of the men joked about it – "Stupid Ivans," they said. They thought they'd never be caught out like that – that they were too smart to be killed so easily. Of course, most of them were dead or wounded within the year.'

'That was in nineteen forty-one,' his father said.

'Yes. The summer.'

'Did you stand aside?'

'No one stood aside.'

'At least they were soldiers. At least you were following orders. You weren't killing civilians.'

Brandt inhaled a lungful of cigarette smoke and held it there, he let it out slowly.

'Nobody had thought what to do with the bodies – so we just left them there. It wasn't unusual that summer. An SS officer told me a similar story at the hut. About a field of dead Russians. The soil in that place was almost black and the summer was hot. It was an empty place. I imagine, in the end, they just became part of the earth they lay down on.'

His father's voice, when he spoke, sounded constrained.

'Was that the only time?'

'That I was involved in that kind of killing? Yes. Although after that summer neither side took many prisoners. It was Total War, remember. But that was the only time I was involved in a massacre like that.'

'You were ordered to kill those Russians. The choice wasn't a real choice – not when you're in a situation like that. You have to do what your comrades do. You can't stand apart from the group – no one would trust you. Once the order was given there was only one outcome.'

Brandt listened to his father and heard his own voice – trying to convince himself. Someone had to shoot them. Once the order was given, the men were dead, and what did it matter who pulled the trigger? It was the order that was to blame. But the burden didn't shift. It stayed there. A weight on him.

'It was my responsibility, that's what I think, and I have to atone for it. More than that, there's a woman in the hut who I knew in Vienna, I was arrested at the same time as her and the arrest was my fault. I have to atone for that as well. Which means you have to go with Ursula.'

His father said nothing in response.

'Once this thing is done, I'll come and find you. I promised and I meant it.'

They turned to make their way to Ursula's house, the refugees pausing to let their cart cross their path, as if they knew what it contained. No one called out or acknowledged them but Brandt felt their gaze on his back as he flicked the horse into a trot.

'Well?' Brandt said, as they left the column behind.

'If Ursula will take me, I'll go with her. But don't get yourself killed. And come to us as soon as you can. Bring Monika with you.'

The horse came to a slow halt in the small yard.

'Is that him?'

Brandt turned to see Ursula standing in the barn's open doorway, a long spade in her hand. She put it against the wall and pulled the thick coat she was wearing tight around her. She nodded, as if encouraging herself, then took a step forward to look at the contents of the wagon, her breath like smoke in the freezing air as she sighed.

'Poor Ernst,' she said. 'His body,' she began – and her words tailed off as she examined the shroud the women had sewn Ernst into.

'It's better if you don't open it.'

Her left hand moved up to her chest, its fingers splaying out.

'We'll leave him as he is, then,' she said, her voice low.

Brandt thought he saw movement at one of the windows. His cousin Horst's children.

'All dead?' she said. 'All except for you, that is. He should have avoided them when they came looking for him.'

'Paul was wounded,' his father said – as if his survival needed defending.

'I didn't mean it that way. You earned some good fortune, Paul,' she stopped and swallowed. 'I'm glad you survived.'

She was lying, of course. He didn't mind. Who in their right mind would want someone else to survive when their husband hadn't?

'We'll help you bury him.'

She looked at his empty sleeve then shifted her gaze.

'I'm still capable of digging. Don't be fooled by this.'

She opened her mouth to say something then seemed to change her mind, nodding her agreement.

'We'll bury him in the garden. He can keep an eye on the place until we can come back.'

§

He hadn't been telling the truth about the digging. He found an old entrenching tool, swinging it one handed to break up the soil, but it was hard work. He could feel the burnt skin on his back stretching and cracking and he was tired from the night before. And, all the time he was digging, he couldn't stop thinking about Agneta and the women – and wondering whether they were safe. Whether he should have left the hut.

He stopped for a moment to rest, and saw Monika standing with Pavel at the corner of the house. Pavel held his hat in his thick gloves as though it were a pet he'd killed by accident, while Monika's face was ghost-white against the black coat she wore. She looked drained. He wondered if she knew that her fiancé had been one of the men who'd ambushed the patrol. And that Hubert had been the one who spared his life.

Ursula pushed her shovel into the ground so that it stood upright, glancing over to Brandt as if seeking his approval. He nodded, not sure what she wanted from him. 'If you're here we could use a hand with the digging. I'll fetch more tools.'

Pavel pulled off his gloves and placed them beside his hat on a window ledge. He took Ursula's shovel and started digging with the fluid strength of a man who'd spent his life doing it. Monika took the entrenching tool from Brandt, pushing him after Ursula.

'They need to be ready to leave, Paul. Three is enough to dig a grave.'

'What about you?' Brandt asked.

'I'm staying.'

'She'll be safe with us,' Pavel said.

There wasn't time to argue.

'You're sure?'

Monika nodded. Brandt stepped towards her and embraced her, burying his nose in her soft hair for a moment. He felt her hand push something into his hand. The Ukrainians' papers.

'They're the best that could be done.'

He took the opportunity to look through them. Eight sets of papers.

'They'll do,' he said handing back four of them. 'But these aren't needed. In case they can be used by someone else. Thank you. And Hubert. Say that to him from me.'

He embraced his sister once more then followed Ursula around the house to the courtyard.

'They'll look after Ernst's grave, Ursula. Where's your wagon? Let's make sure you have everything you need.'

She didn't argue.

'In the barn. It's ready, I think. The horses just need to be harnessed.'

'I can manage that for you. Could you take a person with you?'

'Who?'

'Father. You could use him, I think – on the journey.'

'Of course. And Monika?'

'I think she's staying,' Brandt said.

'With Hubert?'

He wondered how much she knew.

'I haven't asked.'

When Ursula went inside to finish packing, Brandt checked over the wagon. He inspected the canvas cover that would protect them from the weather, tightening it. Ernst had placed a mattress just behind the driver's seat for the children to sleep on and blankets were neatly folded to its side. Behind it there was fodder for the horses, food, blankets, a Primus stove and two tins of fuel – stockpiled from the Lord knew when – a barrel of drinking water and two leather suitcases kept closed with buckled belts. He wondered if the contents would be worth the weight. It would be a tight squeeze, but they would be all right, he decided.

Brandt brought the wagon out into the yard and left it standing beside his own. The horses were wary, and the mare's eyes fixed on Ernst's body, her ears twisting this way and that as she tried to back away. He wondered if she knew it was Ernst. He heard footsteps and turned to find Ursula carrying out another box.

'I have some things for you.'

She put down the box and he handed her the small rucksack he'd brought with him from the hut. She opened it, her eyes widening.

'We can't take these.'

'You can. The cigarettes above all. They'll buy you food when you need it – and shelter. Just don't let my father smoke them all. I need a favour in exchange, though.'

'What?'

'If you are leaving Ernst's clothes behind, can I take some of them?'

§

When the time came to bury him, they tried to be as gentle as they could, but Ernst was an awkward shape and weight. The sheet kept slipping through their hands and Brandt prayed the stitching wouldn't split. But somehow they lowered him into the narrow grave without mishap.

'Would you like me to say something?' Brandt's father asked. The two children stood beside Ursula, their eyes fixed on the white-sheeted shape.

'Let's keep it simple,' Ursula said. 'Children say goodbye to your grandfather – we'll come back to see him very soon. We'll do things properly then.'

That was when Eva, the little girl, began to sob – and Brandt had the devil's own job not to join in with her.

70

BRANDT DIDN'T look back. He had to presume they'd be safe and there was little point in worrying when there was nothing more he could do for them. As for Monika, she'd loved Hubert since he could remember – of course she'd stay. How could he tell her to do otherwise?

A farmhouse was burning on the other side of the reservoir. The column of smoke was black and straight against the grey sky – the flames a vivid orange against a landscape otherwise stripped of colour. The horse's head flicked left and right, ears flat against his head one moment, pointing in opposite directions the next. Brandt was certain that on the forested hills human eyes watched the traffic below. Somewhere up there people were waiting to come down and take the place of the refugees. Perhaps the horse felt it too.

As he passed them Brandt couldn't help but weigh each person's chances. Yes. Yes. With Luck. No. Already some of them were having to make the choices that must be made on a march like this – precise calculations with no room for error. How much could they carry and for how long? Just how close behind them were the Russians? If they went slowly, they might carry more – but might they be caught? What, of all that they owned, was essential for their future?

The evidence of the refugees' decision-making lay littered along the road's length. A gramophone here. A mattress bent double against a wall over there. A suitcase. Pots and pans. An armchair. Another suitcase, open – its contents rifled by the owner or those who had followed after them. A box full of china, some of it broken. A crate of framed photographs from another century – a stout family, with waxed moustaches and concerned expressions, waiting for the photographer's permission to move again. And this was the first day. If it stayed this cold, tomorrow there would be bodies joining the discarded belongings along the road.

'Herr Brandt?'

The boy's voice startled him. For a moment he looked around, confused as to where the voice had come from.

'Herr Brandt?'

'Wessel.' Brandt could see him now, standing in the shadow of a barn alongside another of the Hitler Youth – Müller. He pulled the horses to a halt.

'What are you two up to?'

'Keeping the road clear for military traffic, Herr Brandt. This side of it, anyway. Mayor Weber has ordered it. The Zugführer, I mean.'

Scraps of Wessel's black fringe snuck out from underneath his helmet.

'Has there been any military traffic?' Brandt asked, looking at the empty half of the road – a contrast to the other side and its sad cavalcade.

'There was a car,' Müller said. 'It went up to the hut.'

'The hut?'

'Yes, SS. An officer and a driver.'

Brandt tightened his grip around the reins. He had been a fool.

'Where are your families?'

'They've gone. Our mothers wanted us to go with them, but the mayor sent them packing.'

Wessel seemed, on balance, pleased with this development, but Müller looked away and Brandt saw his lower lip swell downwards. How old was he? Twelve?

'You know where they've gone to, though. You'll see them soon.'

'Yes,' Wessel said. 'My mother's sister lives near Munich.'

Müller said nothing.

'Most of the older men have run for it,' Wessel went on

cheerfully. 'The mayor's not happy about that. You stayed though, Herr Brandt.'

'Of course. Keep warm and stay alert. Everything will be all right, I'm sure of it. Understood, Müller?'

Müller attempted a smile. Brandt flicked the horse into a trot and pointed the cart up one of the side streets that led, indirectly, into the village's square, the cart's wheels rumbling over the icy cobbles. Brandt was pleased to be away from the refugees.

When he came out just in front of the church, he had to pull to a sharp halt when a car, travelling at speed, turned the corner into the square. Brandt recognized it from the hut. A long-bonneted, low-slung, military grey Mercedes, its chromed furnishings covered with dull paint and its fat, frog's eye headlamps lidded with blackout covers that left only the narrowest of slits. As it drove quickly past him he caught a glimpse of Schlosser, one of the Commandant's staff, in the front passenger seat – a sub-machine gun held across his chest, while in the back the two female auxiliaries sat. Anna Beck's unnaturally round eyes meeting his for a second as the car sped past, her face pinched down to the bones beneath her skin. Then the car was gone.

Brandt forced himself to sit still for a moment. He shouldn't rush. He should allow the horse to trot, but no faster than that. That would be the sensible approach – to keep a consistent pace. But up ahead, from the direction of the hut, a thin column of smoke rose up into the sky.

Perhaps the time for caution was past.

71

NEUMANN watched the car disappear around a bend in the road. After a few moments, even the sound of its engine receded to nothing. Neumann pushed at the papers in the brazier with the brass poker he'd brought out from the dining room – they curled and crackled as the flames consumed them. The heat was melting the snow, revealing dead wet grass. It was a depressing task, burning the papers, and futile, surely. It was impossible to cover up what had been done. What other explanation could there be for the missing people, the empty houses and deserted ghettoes than that they had been murdered by men like him?

At least the auxiliaries were off his hands. He was glad he no longer had any responsibility for them. Let the Commandant worry about them.

He poked at the fire once again and, satisfied, left the flames to do their work. He climbed the steps to the hut with heavy feet. Fear was tiring. Burying bodies was tiring. Burning papers, it turned out, was tiring as well.

Inside the hut, the only sound was the slow tick of the grandfather clock in the entrance hall – that and the creak of the floorboards underneath his weight. The emptiness was profound. He parted still air when he moved.

He remembered the times when the hut had been busy and the officers – the overseers and specialists necessary to their enterprise – had sat in these chairs and stood in these rooms. They'd all had different roles. The architects and engineers who'd overseen the construction of the buildings, the accountants who'd collected the loot and balanced the budgets, the medical men who had chosen who could work and who should die, the transport officers who'd scheduled the trains and trucks that had brought people and materials to that small town further down the river where they'd built the camp. And then arranged to have the clothes, shoes, money, suitcases, spectacles and even the very hair from the heads of the murdered taken away in their turn.

It had been a production line. Perhaps the technical nature of many of their tasks had allowed those overseeing its smooth running to ignore the horror of it. Each role was insignificant in itself yet each was vital to the whole. The men who counted the foreign currency were just as guilty as the men who operated the gas chambers. And so, for that matter, was he.

He could argue, perhaps, that he was not as guilty as others. But, when it came to the crimes that had been committed, did being less guilty make a difference? He didn't think it would matter to the Russians. It didn't matter to him. And anyway, all he had to do was remember the way his bayonet had scraped against the spine of the old man. For that alone, he deserved his fate.

Neumann crossed to the window, looking out at the snow-crusted buildings, the humped back of the bunker, the guard tower, the fence. He was close enough to mist the glass, obscuring some of his reflection. Dark, tired eyes returned his gaze. He looked older than he remembered.

72

BRANDT DIDN'T have to pull on the reins to halt the horse. It stopped of its own accord, wheezing great plumes of steamy breath. He pulled the wooden brake and swung himself down from the seat. The five women were throwing the last of the earth onto the burial pit and they were alive. That was good. He walked over to Fischer, the boy who was guarding them. The boy looked cold but proud of the responsibility he'd been given.

'Show me your rifle, Fischer.'

The boy held it towards him. The safety was off and Brandt pushed it back on. He let loose some of the tension and anger he felt when he spoke. Enough to frighten the boy, he hoped.

'Your task is to guard these prisoners, Fischer. Nothing more. If you shoot one by accident, I shoot you. On purpose. Is that understood?'

The boy nodded – his face pale, his mouth open.

'Brandt?'

Neumann stood on the hut's steps, his hands deep in the pockets of a greatcoat. He looked at Fischer then back to Brandt. Had he overheard him? Brandt raised his hand to salute him.

'Herr Obersturmführer.'

'Come with me.'

Neumann turned to re-enter the hut and Brandt took the opportunity to look properly at the women. Their hands were skin-covered bones, blue against the worn wooden handles. Their fear was apparent in the stiffness of their postures, their tight-skinned faces.

'I promise it, Fischer,' he said to the boy as he passed.

It was cold inside the hut. Brandt was surprised to find it annoyed him.

'I'll see to the fires, Herr Obersturmführer. I should have

322

done it before I left.'

'Thank you,' Neumann said, making for the dining room. The long oak table glistened as Neumann walked its length – trailing a finger along its surface. At the far end, he turned.

'The mayor has asked to use the hut as a base for the Volkssturm. His . . .' Neumann hesitated, perhaps unsure how to describe the youths that made up the unit, '. . . men can sleep in the guards' dormitory. Weber can sleep in one of the officers' rooms. You too. The Volkssturm can eat in the kitchen with the guards. The mayor and I will eat here. You will join us.'

'I—' Brandt began, searching for an excuse.

'Would be honoured, surely?'

Brandt found himself shifting his weight from one foot to the other. He stopped – forcing himself to stand still and meet the SS man's gaze. He wondered if Neumann was mocking him.

'Of course.'

'We'll eat what the men eat, but search the cellar – let's drink something good. The Ukrainians as well.' Neumann paused before continuing. 'But not the mayor's men, I don't think. Certainly not the very young ones.'

'As you wish, Herr Obersturmführer.'

'And Brandt?'

Neumann paused once again and, unless Brandt was much mistaken, observed him closely.

'Be sure to prepare provisions for the women. For their journey. It is likely to be chaotic. Who knows what arrangements have been made for feeding the prisoners on the march? Perhaps none.'

Brandt was certain now that there was an edge to Neumann's instruction. As if he was looking for some kind of reaction. He did his best to give him none.

73

THE BOY STOOD to attention when Brandt came down the steps. Agneta looked up and felt hope inside her once again, warming her.

'I need some of you inside – there's work to be done. You, you and you.'

Brandt pointed to the two Bible students, Katerina and Gertrud – then at her. His tone was brusque. Exactly as it should be.

'You two,' he said to the others. 'Finish as soon as you can. It's warmer inside. Fischer, send them straight in when it's done.'

Brandt led the way to the kitchen, giving instructions as he walked.

'I need some bedrooms made up – that will be your job, Gruber. As for you two,' Brandt turned his attention to the two Bible students. 'You have cooking to do – but, first let's light the fires and put some heat back into this place. Quickly now. Gruber, follow me.'

Agneta followed him into the dining room, where Brandt turned the key in a heavy oak cabinet. The inside sparkled with silver.

'I need you to set the table for three. Get to work,' he said, perhaps a little too loudly. Neumann must be in his office.

She watched him leave before walking over to the cabinet. As she reached towards the pile of linen tablecloths, she saw he had left the cutlery canteen open and there, twinkling up at her, lay a small, sharp kitchen knife. She picked it up and then placed it back down immediately – Brandt had come back into the room. She turned, and saw his gaze fall from hers to the knife.

'The plan is that the guards will leave tomorrow evening – to go to the mine camp,' he said in a low voice. 'They are to take you with them. All of you. From there, they are to march to another camp to the west – I don't know where. I'm not sure Neumann does either.'

She felt her hope sink slowly down through her body, down her thighs, her calves, until it reached her feet.

'I have a plan of my own,' he said. His gaze pointed to the knife. 'But if things change suddenly, you might need that. The situation is chaotic, as you know.'

She picked up the knife. She knew she wouldn't last more than a day or two on a march in this weather. Maybe she should use the knife on herself.

74

'WELL?' ADAMIK, the blonde Ukrainian, turned when Brandt entered the dormitory. Sixteen beds – eight facing eight. A muddle of blankets on some of the beds, clothing and equipment strewn on the floor.

'This place is a mess,' Brandt said.

'It's not as if Peichl is around to tell us what to do, and Neumann doesn't come down here. Anyway, what concern is it of yours?'

'The boy soldiers are sleeping here tonight.'

'More fool them.'

He spoke quietly now, his gaze having shifted to the ceiling. Brandt could hear footsteps in the room above. Neumann's bedroom. And if Brandt could hear the creak of his leather boots each time Neumann turned, then Neumann could probably hear their conversation down here just as easily.

'The prisoners will prepare food for your journey. How much can you carry, do you think?' Brandt asked. He spoke carefully, measuring each word.

'As much as we can get in our rucksacks,' Adamik said.

Neumann walked back and forth, stopping always at a point about two metres from the window. Where his bed was. Perhaps he was also packing.

'It will be a cold march – to the west.'

'And a long one. But we'll manage, I think.'

Brandt held Adamik's gaze.

'I think I have everything you'll need for your journey. In terms of rations, certainly.'

He wanted to be certain he understood and, after a moment, the Ukrainian gave the smallest of nods.

'That's kind of you. Good luck for the future, Brandt. Don't get caught by the Bolsheviks – or anyone else.'

Adamik closed the small bag he had been filling with

possessions, nodded once again and left the room.

Brandt stood for a moment, thinking – then began stripping the dead guards' beds, as quickly as he could.

§

Upstairs, Neumann changed his mind. He picked up the pack and emptied its contents back onto the bed. He placed the photograph of his wife and children on the bedside table, angling it so that it caught the light. Then he began to return the clothes to the wardrobe.

He wasn't leaving just yet.

75

AT DINNER, Brandt drank sparingly. He was tired and he was angry and he didn't want to show it inadvertently. The mayor had arrested six men during the course of the day as suspected deserters and locked them in the barn outside with a guard keeping watch over them. Now he was talking about holding a court martial. Then there was the anxiety. He thought of his father and Katerina, Monika and the women.

'Brandt?'

He turned to find Neumann examining him.

'Are you all right? You seem quiet.'

Brandt wondered how to respond. What did he expect from him? If the SS man wanted livelier company, he should dig up Peichl.

'I apologize, Herr Obersturmführer. A long day and a long night before it.'

'Of course. How is your wound?'

'I find wine helps,' he said, drinking from the glass he held in his hand. Perhaps it was his exhaustion but the SS runes on Neumann's collar, shimmering in the candlelight, writhed like small silver snakes. Brandt reminded himself, again, to be careful.

'You are an example to us all, Brandt,' the mayor said, 'I knew you wouldn't desert the men. Not in their moment of destiny.'

The mayor was delighted with his new uniform. Rachel, the Jewish prisoner, had made it up for him and it fitted snugly – too snugly. Weber's neck bulged over his collar, so that he looked as if he were being throttled by a silver-piped noose. Brandt wondered if Rachel had made it too tight on purpose. The mayor hadn't been happy when Brandt had asked him to call in all the checkpoints except for the four boys guarding the dam. He'd agreed with the decision when Brandt had explained they were down to fourteen, including Brandt and the mayor, and the remaining boys would need sleep. But still, it seemed, he felt his authority had been questioned. He had been truculent all evening.

'What is their destiny, Herr Zugführer?'

The irony in Neumann's question wasn't lost on Brandt. The mayor gave no immediate answer. He turned his attention to his plate, the sheen of sweat on his round forehead flickering in the firelight as he did so. He'd been drinking steadily since he'd sat down.

'To do whatever our Führer demands of them,' he said eventually. 'They are soldiers now. They will defend the village and the dam until the last man.'

'The last man?' Neumann's smiled appeared lopsided. The slight emphasis on 'man' wasn't lost on Brandt.

'If needs be,' the mayor said. He leant forward, making a fist of his hand and placing it on the table. His expression was so grave as to be ridiculous. 'We must be prepared for the ultimate sacrifice.'

There was a moment's silence. Then Neumann began to laugh. At first it sounded more like a strangled bark than a laugh. There was no joy in the sound but there was no doubt whatsoever that the SS man was amused at the mayor's expense. Brandt kept his eyes fixed on the mayor, seeing his confusion turn to anger.

'I don't understand why you are behaving this way, Herr Obersturmführer,' the mayor said when Neumann paused for breath.

Neumann sat back, wiping his eyes with a napkin. His lopsided smile was back in place.

'You're correct. It wasn't a very funny joke.'

The brittle ringing of the phone broke the silence. Neumann waited for a few moments before pushing back his chair.

'Excuse me, gentlemen, I'd better see who it is. Who knows, Weber? Perhaps the Russians have heard about your men and surrendered.'

The mayor waited until the SS man had left the room before he turned his attention to Brandt. His mouth was pursed.

'I'm disappointed. It's shocking to hear an SS man talk that way. I should call the Commandant and report him. It is precisely this kind of defeatism that has led us to this point. It was the same in the last war. People lost their will.'

Brandt watched Weber wind himself into a stiff coil of righteous rage – and all he saw was the fear. He kept silent. He would wait his time.

'Was the meal all right?' he asked. Only for something to say.

'Yes,' Weber said, pleased to change the subject. 'Very good. And the wine as well.'

As if to underline the point, the mayor drank from his glass. A red drop rolled from the side of his mouth.

'It is the best there was in the cellar. The Obersturmführer picked it out. "Rather us than the Russians," he said.'

'Typical of him.'

'He said we may all be dead in a few days' time. Just scraps of flesh under a tank's tracks.'

The mayor's glass paused in mid air. He didn't say anything for a moment, but then he moved the glass a little higher, holding it so he could look at the colour against the candlelight.

'French?'

'Yes.'

'They lost their will – in nineteen forty. Look where they ended up.'

'Quite so,' Brandt said, listening to Neumann returning.

'It's for you, Weber. In my office. Party Headquarters.'
The mayor lifted himself from his seat, avoiding
Neumann's gaze.
'Have I offended him, do you think?' Neumann asked
when the mayor had left.
'I'm afraid so.'
'A shame.'
Neumann didn't sound particularly concerned. Brandt
tried to rub some of the tiredness from his eyes.
'Why don't you like him?' Brandt asked.
'Weber? I'm not even sure I do dislike him. He's like all
of us, a willing fool for the last ten years and where did it
get us? We all have reason to fear the end of this war. He
won't admit it, of course.'
'Do you think he'll stay to the end?'
'I'm not certain. I think he thinks he will. What about
you, Brandt? Will you stay? What holds you here now,
even?'
Brandt shrugged. 'Duty.'
'To whom?'
Brandt avoided Neumann's gaze, grateful when Weber
reappeared at the doorway. The mayor stood for a moment,
his eyes downcast and his expression difficult to read in the
candlelight.
'New orders, Herr Zugführer?'
The mayor looked up and shook his head.
'No. It was Schneider from Regional Headquarters. He
said the Gauleiter and the Party hierarchy are pulling back
towards Breslau.'
'And us?'
The mayor considered the question.
'Our orders are unchanged. We continue to defend the
dam and keep the roads open.'
He didn't appear pleased at the prospect, or displeased. It
was more like resignation. Brandt rose from the table.

'If you'll excuse me, I must go to the toilet.'

It was time, he decided, to retrieve Jäger's pistol from the cistern. It was small and snug and would fit in his pocket.

76

'EAT.'

'I'm not hungry.'

She wasn't. The smell of burning flesh and diesel still filled her mouth. Her throat was raw from it. Each time she swallowed she felt as though she were swallowing the dead.

'Eat, Polya. Eat, or I'll be upset.'

She looked up at Lapshin. He was sitting on the other side of the table in the cottage's kitchen, with only a candle to light his face. She could see the concern in his eyes, even in the way he held the chocolate out to her. American chocolate. It looked small in his large hand.

'Sometimes you need to have something to take your mind off unpleasant things, Polya,' Lapshin said. He peeled off the paper wrapper and broke the bar in two. He handed her the larger piece.

'I'm fine,' she said, taking the chocolate all the same. She took it to please him. For the same reason she broke off a square and placed it in her mouth. He was watching her, waiting for her to eat some of it. She chewed.

'It tastes good,' she said.

She wasn't telling a lie.

'Do you want something to wash it down?'

He held up a German canteen and shook it from side to side. It was half full.

'Water?'

'Schnapps. German schnapps. Buryakov gave it to us in exchange for a watch.'

'You gave Buryakov your watch?'

'No,' Lapshin said, smiling and pulling back the cuff of his jacket to show his watch safely where it should be. 'Avdeyev did.'

'Avdeyev's watch?'

She found she was frowning. Why would Avdeyev swap his watch for schnapps?

'Not Avdeyev's own watch, Little Polya. Some German's watch. He doesn't want you to feel bad about that thing. None of us do. These things happen. War isn't a tidy business where only soldiers get hurt.'

'I should have seen them.'

'They shouldn't have been there. What were they thinking? If it hadn't been us, it would have been someone else. One of ours or the Germans. There were bullets and shells flying all over the place. What could we have done anyway? The road was narrow and that German gunner knew his business.'

Polya reached across for the canteen and unscrewed the cap. If Avdeyev had given up a watch for it, she had no choice.

'Thank you.'

'Anyway,' Lapshin said, 'I gave the order. So it was my fault, if anyone's.'

'I was the one driving.'

'Under my direction.'

She hesitated, not wanting to say aloud what he must already know. That sometimes she ignored his feet on her shoulders. She saw his slow smile.

'So you admit you don't always obey my orders,' he said. 'At last, I have an admission. I should have you sent to a penal unit.'

They'd stopped for the night in a small village – she didn't know where they were. All she knew was that once again they had to wait for supplies to catch up with them. They'd been in and out of action for most of the last forty-eight hours and Galechka's white paint was chipped and scraped all over, her fuel tank nearly empty, and they'd fired off nearly all of their ammunition in one action or another. There were only fourteen tanks left out of the thirty-two that had crossed the Vistula and Lapshin was now second in command of the whole battalion. He'd many other things to be doing – and yet he was making time to talk to her. A silly little girl.

'I'm sorry,' she said. 'I'm better now. I was just tired.' And cold. And filthy. She looked down at her overalls. They were almost black with dirt. That was the problem with tanks. There was the oil, the grease the ammunition came in and the fact you could never take them off, even when you slept. It was unpleasant but everyone was the same. She couldn't expect to be different just because she was a woman. Especially as none of the men had burst into tears at the blood that was sprayed all over Galechka's front armour.

'It wasn't the cart that upset me.'

She stopped herself, considering the statement. Of course the cart had upset her. They'd rolled right over it – they'd come to a crossroads and a German cannon had blasted a shell at them from less than fifty metres, so close they heard it scrape along the side of the turret. Lapshin had told her to get the hell out of there – down the road to the left. The only problem was the family of refugees that was in the road ahead of them, a huddle on their cart. For an instant she'd been face to face with the mother. She'd been looking straight into her hatch – a blonde woman. It was hard to tell what she had looked like because she'd been screaming, turning to try and shield two children, wrapped up in scarves and hats so that only their eyes were visible. Polya could have reached out and touched them if she'd wanted to. And then they were gone – all of them, and the wagon as well. Galechka just rolled over them.

'It was Yermakov,' she said in a quiet voice.

In the same village as they'd killed the woman and her children, Yermakov's tank had gone up like a match. And they'd been stuck behind it, twisting back and forth and from side to side while Yermakov and his boys roasted, their ammunition exploding inside until it blew the turret off. She'd been sure they were going to be hit next, the heat of the flames had made Galechka's metal hot to the touch, but she'd managed to ram them through some carriage gates and into a courtyard that had led to safety.

Lapshin took a drink from the canteen.

'Here's to Yermakov.'

She nodded and reached across to take another sip, feeling it burn her throat – but in a good way. Not like – well, she didn't like to think about Yermakov and his flaming tank. She would put all those thoughts away now. She'd faltered, that was true. But no one, not even Lapshin, hadn't shown themselves to be human at one time or another. Her moment of weakness was behind her – she was stronger for it, she was certain.

'Back to work, then, Little Polya. The supply vehicles will be here in an hour. We need to be ready to move in two.'

He reached across the table and took her hand. It felt tiny in his – which wasn't really the case. But it felt that way. And when he squeezed it tight and held it for longer than was necessary, it was as though he squeezed all the breath out of her as well.

She sniffed and dried her eyes and smiled and – whether it was the schnapps, or the chocolate, or Lapshin's fingers wrapped around her own – she found she felt much better.

77

IN THE MORNING, Brandt rose when it was still dark and rousted out the relief watch and took them down to the dam. The sky, when they walked out the gate, was that chocolate grey that comes before the dawn, the few stars still visible slowly fading into the lightening sky. The first refugees were already on the road and Brandt wondered where they were coming from. There couldn't be many more left up in the hills and surely, if you were on the Czech side, you'd stay there rather than come over in this direction.

There was no sentry guiding traffic at the dam, although wagons and pedestrians were crossing it. And when they looked in the bunker they found no one there, and no sign that anyone would be coming back. The power station was also empty, although the generating wheels still turned. Everyone was gone.

'Do you think the partisans got them?' Fischer asked.

Brandt shrugged.

'What then, Herr Brandt?'

Brandt shrugged again.

'The power station workers may have run. Maybe the others decided it was a good idea to join them.'

The four boys said nothing, and he saw the way their gazes fell away from his. Except for Wessel's.

'They're cowards if they ran.'

Brandt shook his head slowly.

'Who was here? Frick and Jünger? Kurtz? Frick's only twelve. I can't blame them if they went to join their families. Most probably it's where they belong – where you all do, for that matter.'

He could see Wessel's irritation building and reminded himself to be careful.

'What about you, Herr Brandt?' Müller asked. 'Will you

stay?'

'I'll stay until I've done what I have to do, Müller. Of that you can be certain.'

The beeping of a motor vehicle's horn came from towards the village. A military truck was decanting a handful of men and boxes beside the bridge. An officer peered over the parapet, pointing down at the arches. The men moved quickly to follow his instructions and, seemingly satisfied, he climbed back into the truck which was soon speeding up towards the dam. They seemed in a rush.

'Engineers,' he said. The Russians must be close.

§

Brandt pulled wide the curtains in the mayor's bedroom. The room smelled of stale alcohol and the kind of sweat that went with fear. He opened the window to let the air in.

'What time is it, Brandt?' The mayor sounded as though he might be still drunk.

'Nearly seven, Herr Zugführer.'

As he finished speaking, three aeroplanes roared across the hills that overlooked the hut, banking right as they did so – red stars and bombs visible on the undersides of their wings. The sound of their engines rattled the windows. The guardhouse machine gun threw up a line of tracer after them – someone trying to get them all killed. He turned to find the mayor standing in his bare feet, his face a match for the yellowing long johns he was wearing. He had lifted a hand to his chest, placing it on his heart.

'What was that?'

'Ivan fighter-bombers,' Brandt said. 'Maybe they're after the railway station in the town. Or one of our positions.'

The crump, crump, crump of exploding bombs echoed up the valley a few moments later, along with the sound of anti-aircraft fire. Weber's legs, Brandt noticed, were shorter than he'd thought. His gut was wide-hipped and heavy – as if he were six months pregnant.

'Fighter-bombers? Here?'

'They're past Katowitz now. The army is in full retreat. They must have overrun one of our airfields.'

'That can't be. Not Katowitz. Not so soon.'

'I'm afraid there's a Leutnant of engineers down at the dam with orders that say differently.'

As if to make Brandt's point, there came the sound of a massive explosion from the village. It wasn't just the windows that rattled this time – the whole building shook.

'What the hell is going on?' Neumann appeared in the doorway, a towel around his waist.

'The village bridge, Herr Obersturmführer. I was just telling the Zugführer – the Russians are past Katowitz.'

The bridge had stood for over five hundred years. Gone, just like that.

'And those aeroplanes?'

'Theirs.'

Neumann considered this for a moment before nodding.

'Will they blow the dam, as well?'

'Not until the last moment.'

'Very good.'

Brandt noticed the white scarring of ancient shrapnel wounds on Neumann's shoulders as he left the room. From the first war, it must be.

'Christ,' the mayor said. Brandt had almost forgotten him.

'Also, I'm afraid we lost the guard on the dam last night, Herr Zugführer.'

'Lost?'

'Well, they aren't there this morning. The power station staff are gone as well. Maybe they deserted or maybe the partisans took them.'

The mayor's thinking was almost visible – a silent film played across the rounded screen of his face. He wasn't so keen on the war when it wasn't all talk. Or when people were likely to shoot back at him. Or take him up into the hills to make him answer for his crimes.

'I'd better get dressed as well,' he said, but Brandt saw none of the enthusiasm for the Volkssturm uniform he'd shown the night before. The Soviet fighters roared overhead once again and the mayor dropped to his knees. Brandt counted the planes as they returned the way they'd come. No losses.

'I've organized some breakfast in the kitchen.'

'Get out, Brandt.'

The mayor's annoyance was understandable. It wasn't an ideal way to start the day.

78

NEUMANN TRIED calling the camp but the local exchange was no longer answering. He would have liked to speak to the mining camp as well, but short of getting on his bicycle and cycling over there, or sending one of the Ukrainians with a message, there was no easy way of communicating with them. With the situation changing so fast, he wondered if the march might have left already. He looked out the window at the guardhouse. A silhouette appeared, moving across to the machine gun. It looked like Adamik. If he were in the guards' shoes, he'd want to leave sooner than five o'clock this evening. Neumann tried the phone one more time. Nothing. In some ways, it was almost liberating. The last of the hut's papers had been burned and all he had to do now was leave. He could just go. He could tell the Ukrainians that they should make their way to the mining camp and then just leave.

But if he left, he would end up in another camp, and who knew what the arrangement would be there? The Commandant had promised to take him with him, but in the end he'd left him to make his own way there. The Commandant, his old friend, was no longer looking after him in quite the way he had – perhaps the promises he'd made after the horrors of the train no longer applied. Perhaps the Commandant would require Neumann to take a more active role when he reached the Nordhausen camp. The situation was difficult – perhaps an exception for him could no longer be made. The chill made him reach out to hold the wall for support.

But what did it matter anyway? Once you had killed even one innocent person, then the number became irrelevant. Look at the Commandant. No one would ever know for certain how many deaths he had been responsible for in his role – and would it make him any more guilty if they did?

They were both of them guilty past the point of any form of redemption – on any scale. Neumann helped himself to a brandy from the drinks cabinet. He drank it down straight. He whistled for Wolf and made his way outside. When he reached the gatehouse he called up to Adamik.

'All in order?'

'Yes, Herr Obersturmführer. Nothing to report.'

He turned at the sound of the shouting. The mayor, white-faced, was pushing the men out of the barn.

'Line up, line up, line up.'

He shot the first one before Neumann realized what was happening. And by the time he had reached him, there were six dead men lying beside the barn and blood on the snow. The victims hadn't even tried to run.

'You shot them.'

'I should have hanged them. They were traitors.'

He heard Brandt's footsteps coming along the gravel path and turned to see the steward stop and reach in his pocket.

'Herr Zugführer?'

'What do you want to say, Brandt? This is martial law. These men were traitors and they had been dealt with. Do you object?'

Behind Brandt, in the distance, Neumann saw three dots in the sky. Aeroplanes that were coming low along the valley. There must be anti-aircraft guns up there now as the puffs of exploding shells bloomed behind them. They were flying so fast that by the time Neumann pointed them out, the planes were only a few hundred metres away and the roar of their engines was shaking snow from the roof of the hut. Neumann watched the mayor trying to fire his empty pistol at the Soviet fighters as they flew past. The mayor looked at his pistol, screamed then threw it at the planes, which were no longer visible.

'Have the women bury them,' Neumann said when the mayor had walked off, swearing and waving his fist after the disappeared fighters.

He watched one of the boys pick up the mayor's empty pistol from the snow.

79

THE MAYOR appeared smaller now – as if his rage had
reduced him. He appeared bewildered by the things he was
seeing – the abandoned village, the column of refugees and
all the other signs that the world he'd taken for granted was
being washed away. He was surprisingly calm about the
situation. They had been patrolling the road for an hour
now and the mayor hadn't arrested anyone, or shot them –
as yet.

'Brandt?' The mayor's voice was soft. Ahead of them
the bridge, which had stood for hundreds of years, was
missing two of its arches.

'Herr Zugführer.'

'Look what they've done to the bridge.'

'We knew it must go.'

'But no one asked me. Wouldn't it be correct to ask the
mayor if you're going to destroy a village's only bridge?'

'They're going to blow up the dam as well, Herr
Zugführer.'

'They should have asked. It would have been correct.'

And when they did blow the dam, it would likely sweep
half the village away. The town below would be flooded
and God help any refugees still on the road beside it. And
for what? It might slow the Russian tanks for a day or two
on their way. But perhaps that would be time enough for
his father and Ursula to get away.

'There will be no retreat,' the mayor said quietly,
gesturing at the refugees. 'What is needed here is order.
Look at these people.'

'Herr Zugführer.' Brandt couldn't help it if giving the
mayor his military title always sounded ironic. 'Would you
like me to go to the top of the valley and find out what the
situation is? If a stand is being made there, then perhaps the
senior officer will have new orders for us.'

The mayor looked at him for a moment, before nodding. 'Yes,' he said eventually. 'Do that.'

80

NEUMANN walked down to the dam to see if they had news. The valley was silent – almost. No more planes had come, although he couldn't help but scan the sky in case they returned. Wolf nudged him yet again.

'All right. Find one, then.'

Wolf bounded off into a clump of trees, returning with a snow-crusted stick held in his mouth. Neumann threw it and watched as the dog leapt over the low wall that separated the lane from the field that ran alongside it. Sprays of snow fountained up behind him as he hunted for it, his brown chest deep in white.

It wasn't until they were closer to the main road that he noticed the refugees had changed direction.

'Which way are you going?' he asked a mother and daughter whose cart came to a halt as he passed. They looked at his greatcoat and he could see their gaze take in the SS insignia. The mother looked away but Neumann thought he caught a glimpse of a bitter smile before she did so. The civilians were laughing at them now. Or were they smiling at the thought that justice was coming for them.

'We were going to Breslau,' the daughter said, looking over her shoulder. 'But now they say we'll be safest going over the pass to the Czech side.'

The column started up again and the mother flicked the reins at the horse. An infant's cry came from underneath the wagon's tarpaulin. He felt the insistent nudging at his knee once again and looked down to see Wolf's kindly eyes looking up at him.

At the dam, there was no sign of Brandt or the mayor. Instead a platoon of grenadiers had arrived with two anti-tank guns. They were barring the crossing to the never-ending column of refugees, sending them up the valley road instead.

'Why can't they cross?' he asked.

The grenadier Leutnant shrugged his shoulders. He looked exhausted.

'Orders. They can go across the reservoir if they want but the dam is for military traffic only. I don't know why. Maybe reinforcements are coming up? If we have any reinforcements left, that is.'

'But why are they coming up this road in the first place – I thought we were retreating towards Breslau.'

'Breslau?' The Leutnant shook his head. 'I wouldn't go towards Breslau. It's tank country down there. We can hold them here along these hills but everything down that way will be overrun.'

'Where are they now?'

The Leutnant shook his head.

'I don't know – but we've been told to dig in, so they must be close.'

'Did you see the village Volkssturm?'

The Leutnant shrugged, and Neumann wondered what he meant by the gesture.

'I sent them away. They're no use to us. I don't want the blood of children on my hands.'

As he walked back towards the hut, Neumann wondered if Russians had already reached the camp. There had been no time to destroy it, of course. Nausea threatened to overwhelm him. He looked down across the valley and saw scattered figures walking across the reservoir – some of them dragging small carts.

One of the walkers suddenly disappeared through the ice. No one went to help them, or even seemed to notice.

81

AGNETA examined Brandt. He was facing the women, a line of small brown canvas bags – five of them – rested on the long kitchen table standing between them. It was as if some of the colour had been washed out of him – leaving him greyer and less substantial. He looked exhausted. The bags were worn and well used, each fastened at the top with cord. He pushed at one of them with his hand, lifting his gaze to meet Agneta's.

'Obersturmführer Neumann has asked me to prepare provisions for a journey,' he said. 'Your journey. To another camp. In the west.'

Someone began to sob. Agneta didn't look to see who it was. It didn't matter. Brandt's gaze had fallen back down to the canvas bags. All that mattered was that he'd failed them – failed her. She could see it in his pale, battered face. And now he thought he could make up for his failure with scraps of food? She'd been a fool to trust him.

'There's bread, some cheese, oat biscuits, carrots and cooked potatoes.'

Agneta took a step forward, impatient, but Brandt held up a hand.

'The guards will take you to the mining camp in one hour. From there you walk to the west. I don't know where to or for how long but this food may have to last you for some time. Conserve it.' His eyes met Agneta's once again. 'The war is nearly over. Don't lose hope. Things can change in an instant for the better.'

He took a step backwards. The women hesitated, until Agneta stepped forward and reached for the bag that looked as though it had the most in it. She would not lose hope. She had lasted this long – she planned to last longer still.

Brandt went to each of them, taking their hands, wishing them well. She saw their gratitude and it angered her.

Soon it was Agneta's turn.

'I'll see you soon, I hope,' he said.

She felt calm, in control of her emotions. She nodded politely, as if saying farewell to an acquaintance she'd met by chance, and when he took her hand she let it lie limp in his. As he turned away, she saw him wipe his hand on his tunic, as if to wipe away her anger. He'd understood her.

And yet, when he left the room, she felt her mouth curling downward, her eyes filling. She tried to overcome the emotion, angry with herself now. She wouldn't cry over this half man. She placed the bag of food on the counter beside the sink and poured herself a glass of water to wash her mouth clean of the taste of despair. She looked around at the others. They'd known since the SS women's departure the day before that the hut must be closing – but, even so, they appeared stunned.

'So we'll have a long walk,' she said. 'It's not so bad. We'll stick together. We'll look after each other. We've made it this far.'

She hadn't meant to say anything – but it was true, they would be stronger together. And if they were going with the prisoners from the mining camp, they might be the only women on the march. If they wanted to hold on to their food, they'd need to protect it.

'We have an hour,' Katerina said. 'And we have things we need to do – there's no point in looking for trouble.'

No one said anything – they got back to work. It was easier not to think about the future when you had something to do. When the guards came for them they put on the winter jackets that would mark them out among the other prisoners, but which might also save them from freezing.

'Stand in line.' The young blonde, Adamik, was the one giving the orders now that Bobrik was dead. The afternoon was coming to an end – it was almost dark now and the long shadows were beginning to merge into each other. Somewhere, overhead, aeroplanes flew and the guards looked up, squinting their eyes as if they might see them. Many aeroplanes.

Brandt was standing by his wagon, and raised a hand in farewell – to whom it wasn't clear but Adamik lifted his in return. A look passed between the two men, she was sure of it – but it was dark and she could make nothing of it. Did Brandt know their fate? She tried to decipher the way he turned away, the way he held himself. If they were safe until the mining camp, there was no point in risking anything. But if they wouldn't reach the mining camp – then even the smallest chance was worth taking. She watched as Brandt released the wagon's brake and set off towards the open gate – guarded now by two Volkssturm boys. As he went down the lane, the horses broke into a trot. Why was he in such a rush? Did he want to be far away when the guards took them into the forest?

'Here comes Neumann,' one of the guards said.

'Look at him,' Adamik said. There was contempt in their voices.

Neumann came down the steps – a slow descent, his boots seeking out a firm footing on each step's surface.

'Well, gentlemen?' he said, pausing to draw on his cigarette. 'Form a line, pretend you were once soldiers. Come to attention if you can summon the energy.'

The guards did as they were told – reluctantly. Neumann walked in front of them, examining each man in turn before circling behind them and coming to a halt – the guards to one side, the prisoners to the other. The guards wore scarves under their helmets and under their greatcoats, thick woollen gloves on their hands. They looked irritated at the delay. Neumann, on the other hand, looked relaxed. If he was aware of the prisoners' anxiety or the guards' anger he showed no sign of it. He looked up at the blue-black sky, at the last trace of light as it moved down below the horizon. He smoked his cigarette. The resentment from the guards at being made to wait in the cold was palpable.

'Time to go, gentlemen,' he said, when it was finished. 'I wish you luck.' He glanced towards the prisoners. 'All of you.'

The guards gave a half-hearted salute and turned towards the gate, Adamik gesturing the women to lead the way. The two Volkssturm boys standing beside the guardhouse stepped back to make way for them. Agneta wanted to look back to see if Neumann was still standing where they'd left him, watching them as they marched down the snow-packed lane, but she didn't.

She kept her eyes on the road ahead.

82

THE MINING CAMP was further up the valley and so they followed the main road that led along the side of the reservoir, walking away from the dam. The guards soon fell back and began to talk in low voices amongst themselves.

'What do you think?'

Joanna's question was barely a whisper, but Agneta heard it clearly enough. It was the same question she was asking herself.

'I don't know.'

'They gave us food.'

'That could mean nothing. A trick.'

'Who wastes food? It must mean something.'

'Brandt might have been responsible for it. Maybe he persuaded the SS. I don't know.'

'Quiet,' one of the SS men said loudly from almost next to them. Had he overheard their conversation? Joanna moved slowly in one direction and Agneta moved in the other until they were soon a couple of metres apart and no longer capable of discussion. It had been foolish. She should have ignored Joanna.

'Don't worry,' the SS man said in a quiet voice. 'You're going to be taken care of.'

He spoke in German, but his accent was thick and she couldn't be certain if the ambiguity was deliberate. She risked a sideways glance – but she couldn't see his face clearly in the evening gloom.

They were walking alongside German refugees – mostly women, like them. She felt their eyes on them – the five prisoners walking in front of the SS men – their striped prison caps, the dirty quilted jackets, the striped prison trousers and their battered wooden clogs, the rags that bound their feet inside them already wet and cold. She couldn't help herself – she couldn't stop the hatred she felt for them almost overwhelming her. She had nothing to be ashamed of, no matter what they might think. It was them, the fat women in the wagons, the plump children who sat beside them – they were the ones who should feel shame. Their silence had brought them to this. Nothing she had done.

Somewhere up ahead there was the sound of a pistol shot followed a few moments later by another. The guard who was walking beside them unslung his rifle. Another SS man came forward and joined the one who now carried his rifle under his arm, his gloved finger inside the trigger guard. They lifted themselves onto the toes of their boots, straining to look over the refugees towards where the sound of gunfire had come from. Soon they were fifty metres ahead and extending their lead.

'Close together, close together,' a guard said from behind them. 'Don't do anything stupid.'

There was a shout from ahead. A man's voice. The two SS guards who had gone on ahead had stopped, their rifles held at the ready. There was a commotion of some sort and Agneta heard the sound of a woman screaming – not in fear, but in grief. The SS men seemed to relax and waved them forward.

They found a group of men standing beside a bonfire, their hands held up in the air. A youngster, his narrow face poking out from his greatcoat collar, watched over them. The boy's expression was hard to read in the flickering firelight, but she'd the sense that he was on the point of tears. The men stood still, their mouths open as if about to speak – their faces red in the fire's glow, their cheeks hollow and their eyes black.

A body lay on the ground behind the boy with the rifle – a dead man lying on his side as if asleep, blood turning the snow around him a wet pink. A woman in a black overcoat knelt beside him, cradling his head in her hands, her face wet with tears. The mayor stood above her, replacing his pistol into its holster. His expression as he looked down at the body suggested that things had taken an unexpected turn which he couldn't quite explain.

If the mayor saw the prisoners and their SS guards he didn't acknowledge them, and they kept on walking. Agneta saw the silver edge of an Iron Cross on the dead man's chest – perhaps he had thought it would protect him. On the other side of the road, the refugees avoided looking at the woman or the dead man in her arms, or the mayor, or the men beside the bonfire. As for the SS and the prisoners, they might have been ghosts. The guards spoke amongst themselves in their own language. Their dark, dry laughter sounded like a commentary.

'Will we spend the night at the mining camp?' Rachel whispered when they had passed through the checkpoint. 'Or will they march us out straight away?'

'I don't know.'

'Here,' the guard who'd told them not to worry called from up ahead. He stood where a narrow lane led off to the left.

'Two hundred metres in,' Adamik spoke in a low voice, in German, as if quoting someone. Agneta could hear the tension in his voice. When the guards reached the lane they stood for a moment in a half circle.

'Well,' Adamik said, unslinging his rifle from his shoulder – the other SS following suit. 'Let's be careful how we do this.'

Agneta caught the sympathetic gaze of a pretty girl – about fifteen years old – on a passing wagon. She discounted it. If it wasn't false, it was futile. The girl could do nothing. She would only watch while the SS took them into the trees. She might cry if she heard shots but she would do – could do – nothing to help them. Agneta held the girl's gaze until one of the guards pushed her towards the laneway with his rifle. She wanted her to remember the moment, at least.

The wooden clogs on her feet had never felt so heavy – each step like walking through mud. The snow seemed to be sucking at her, pulling her down into the earth. She knew she must run, that the SS would shoot them now, but whatever waited for them along the narrow lane was like a magnet that couldn't be resisted. She was cold and tired. Beside her Joanna was whispering. She tried to hear her but the thud, thud, thud of her heart was all that filled her ears. It was hard to breathe – the cold air was thick in her mouth.

Milky moonlight broke through the trees and she saw that the Bible students, three paces in front of her, were holding each other's hands. Without thinking, she reached out for Joanna, finding her elbow and following her forearm down until their fingers interlinked – taking solace from the fierce strength of her grip. She reached out for Rachel on her other side and clasped her narrow hand tight. They walked along the lane, the three of them, like little girls afraid of the dark – the only noise the sound of their clogs squeaking into fresh snow.

Adamik stopped, holding up his hand for them to stay where they were. He walked on, slowly – a hunter's considered advance – careful how he placed his feet. He stopped again, listening for a moment, before motioning them to follow. Now they could see how the road widened and how the forest had been cleared around a weathered shrine, its wooden-tiled peaked roof, sagging with age, carrying a cross. Perhaps there was a graveyard there. Perhaps their grave was already dug.

'There it is,' one of the Ukrainians said.

Adamik turned, gesturing them to follow him. He was more confident now.

'Quickly,' a guard said, so close behind Agneta that she braced herself for a blow. She shuffled forward, still holding on to the others' hands, her mind too full to think. No blow fell.

She could hear Katerina reciting a prayer. 'Into the Valley of Death,' Katerina was whispering and Agneta wanted to stop and shout at everyone. The whole situation was beyond ridiculous. Why couldn't they all just go home? Why did any of this have to happen?

'Can you see it?'

A guard's voice – anxious.

'Behind the chapel, he said. It's quiet here, he chose well.'

Agneta felt as if someone else walked the short distance towards the clearing. As though she watched the women from a distance, like they were actors in a play – their movements delicate, considered, full of meaning. The sensation was so real that she began to doubt herself. Perhaps this was all a dream. Perhaps she could wake up from it.

They turned the chapel's corner. There was no graveyard. No half-dug trench. There was only a wagon and a horse, its head bowed. It snorted.

A cough, from the darkness. 'You're late.'

There was the flash of a match that illuminated a man's face and the cigarette that hung from his thin, twisted mouth.

Brandt.

83

BRANDT LIT one of the storm lanterns he'd brought with
him – then the other. The yellow glow it produced was just
enough to light the gaunt, terrified faces of the women.
Behind them the guards stood, fingers on the triggers of
their rifles, their wary eyes hooded by darkness. Adamik
stepped forward, allowing the muzzle of the rifle to drop
away as he did so. Brandt was pleased it was no longer
pointing at his stomach.

'Neumann kept us waiting,' Adamik said.

'Well, you're here now.'

'Have you got everything?'

'The clothing is in the chapel. You can change in there.
Here are your papers. I've lifted some floorboards – put the
uniforms under and I'll nail them down later. Best not to
leave them lying around. The army are digging in further
up the valley but the ice on the reservoir will bear your
weight.'

One of the Ukrainians laughed quietly. A sound of
delight – joy, almost. As if he thought he could just take off
the green-grey tunic, put on some old clothes and all would
be well with the world – as if the past were something a
man could choose to forget or to invent as it suited him.

'And?'

'Here.'

Brandt handed the envelopes over. The SS man made a
show of counting the money. Then weighing the teeth in
his hand. He smiled.

'What about our rifles?'

'They can go with the uniforms. Leave them against the
wall.'

The women were staring at him as though they didn't
believe he existed.

'Didn't I tell you things would take a turn for the better?'

Brandt said.

The women said nothing and he didn't expect them to, not in front of the guards. But when he led them into the trees, using the lantern to show the way, they were still silent, and it bothered him. He wasn't sure what he expected from them – there wasn't time for conversation – but still.

'Here it is,' he said, and showed them the low wooden building, not much taller than he was. It was hidden in the trees. Even now, the roof was sound and it was as good a place as any to hide five women. He had made sure of it over the summer, fixing the windows and replacing rotten planks. He pushed open the door.

'It's not warm, but it's dry – more or less – and we have plenty of blankets for you. Some mattresses to lie on as well. You can't start a fire, of course, or have light – but, well, it's safe enough, I should think. There's no one left to come looking for you, after all.'

As if to give the lie to this, a branch cracked outside and they all turned at once. A figure appeared in the doorway, too small to be a soldier.

'Paul?'

Monika. She must have been waiting in the trees, ready to make a quick escape if his plans had gone awry.

'This is my sister, Monika. She'll do what she can for you.'

The women still hadn't spoken. They seemed incapable of speech.

'Paul,' Monika said again, her voice sounding distorted, as if something were holding her mouth in a strange shape. He turned to examine her. She appeared frightened, more so than she should be.

'What's wrong?'

'It's Hubert. He's been detained by Weber.'

He took hold of her arm, reassuring her, he hoped.

'Where?'

'Near home. We were on our way here.'

'Did Weber see you?'

'I don't think so.'

'But he knew who Hubert was.'

'He must do.'

Brandt handed her the lantern, then turned to the women.

'I have to go. One of us will check on you as soon as we can. Monika, if you see Pavel, tell him to stay away from the roads until this is over.'

He caught Agneta's eye and did his best to smile.

'I have to go, but I hope we'll have a cup of real coffee again one day. Perhaps in Austria? In front of the Hotel Imperial.'

Agneta nodded, but said nothing. And, anyway, there wasn't time for talk.

§

The Ukrainians were waiting for Brandt when he reached the wagon – dressed, he could see by the weak lantern light, in the clothing of various members of the Brandt family. He put his hand in his pocket, Jäger's automatic warm in his hand.

'Well?' he said as he neared them. 'Shouldn't you be off?'

'We're going. We just wanted to thank you.'

Brandt stopped in his tracks, considering Adamik's outstretched hand. If he took it, and it was held, he'd be defenceless. He hesitated.

'Don't worry, Brandt. We mean you no harm.'

'I'm not worried,' Brandt lied.

Adamik's grip was firm, and Brandt got his hand back. The others offered theirs in turn. Afterwards they stood in an awkward semicircle, facing him.

'Well, then,' Adamik said. 'We have plenty of distance to cover by morning.'

He watched them until they were out of sight. He was glad they carried with them the small clots of gold mined from the teeth of the dead and the money that hadn't belonged to him. They had left their rifles leaning against the wall of the chapel and he took them inside, pushing them in with the uniforms and then hammering the floorboards back into place. When he was finished, he pressed his foot down – no creak, no movement. They might never be found.

Outside, he pulled himself up to the wagon's seat and with a click of his tongue and a flick of the traces, he pointed the horse in the direction of the hut. More than once he expected to see armed men coming out of the trees, so strong was the impression that he was being watched. But there was no one.

He had done it.

84

IT WAS COLD – but they were warm. They'd placed one
mattress against the wall and the other on the floor. They
sat in a row, hip to bony hip, elbow to elbow, clean soft
blankets that had belonged to free, living people covering
them – their noses poking over the top. They had warm
soup in their stomachs and the smell of it lingered. Chicken
soup. It smelled like somewhere safe and far away.

It was dark in the shed. She could see nothing. She could
hear the others, their breathing, the rustle of clothing when
one of them moved. Sometimes there were sounds from
outside. Planes occasionally flew overhead – she followed
their trajectory in her mind's eye. She imagined the pilots
sitting in their glass bubbles. Perhaps this one was looking
for Germans to bomb – she wished him well. She imagined
him looking down on the fighting far below. Orange
explosions lighting up snowfields, yellow fire where whole
towns burned. She imagined the long line of these signs of
war, stretching from north to south – advancing, kilometre
by kilometre, towards the west. Towards them. 'He must
have planned it for months,' Katerina said.

'He did,' Agneta agreed, her fondness for Brandt
colouring her voice. 'But when we were walking up that
lane. In the dark . . .'

'I thought the same,' Joanna said.

'We should thank God.'

Gertrud's voice strained for breath. It must be tiring,
believing in God in the middle of all this. Agneta wanted to
ask how she could still do it, after all she'd seen in the
camp. How could a God, a supreme being, have allowed
such things to happen? But let her thank her God if she
wanted to.

'He was right not to warn us,' Agneta said. 'Brandt, that
is.'

'Do you really think we're safe?' Rachel asked. 'Really?'

'Safer than we were, that's certain.'

'We should get some sleep,' Joanna said.

'I don't want to sleep,' Agneta said. 'I want to stay awake.'

And she did. When the dawn came, she wanted to watch the sky above them through the small window. Perhaps the sun might even shine.

But, even as she began to imagine the light changing, she could feel her eyes closing.

85

THE ROAD WAS emptier now. Most of the refugees had stopped for the night and, in a field down by the frozen reservoir, he could see a circle of wagons and carts that had gathered around a bonfire. Shadow figures moving in its light seemed to be engaged in some kind of dance at first, but when he came closer he realized they were throwing their belongings into the flames rather than leave them for the Russians.

'Halt.'

He must be tired – the checkpoint was signalled by three lanterns and a fire and he had almost crashed into it. The young voice that called out was confident, accustomed to being obeyed. He looked to see who it was. Wessel – the crow-haired boy from the other side of the valley, his rifle now pointed squarely at Brandt's head. Again. Brandt lifted his hand slowly, as if to shield his eyes from the lantern light.

'It's me, Wessel. Brandt.'

Müller stood beside Wessel, carrying his rifle under his arm. Three men, all far older than the boys, sat on the snow at the side of the road, their hands on their heads, their sideways gaze fixed on Brandt. Further along from them, illuminated by the fire, a body slumped against a low wall, a placard fixed to his front.

'Herr Brandt,' Wessel said. 'I thought you might be another deserter.'

He lowered his rifle slowly, as if reluctant to believe he wasn't, even now.

'What deserters?'

'That one for a start.' Wessel pointed to the dead man. 'And these three are French workers.'

'What does the sign on the dead man say?'

'A traitor to his people and his Führer.'

The dead man looked to be about the same age as Brandt's father. There was an iron cross on his chest and a dark red crust had formed around the collar of his shirt, underneath his silver hair. Without the blood, and the scrawled message, you might believe the dead man had simply sat down for a rest.

'The mayor did this?' Brandt asked, knowing the answer.

'This one kicked up. The others have been taken up to the hut. These three just arrived. I thought we'd better hold them and wait and see what the mayor said.'

Müller spoke up, looking uncertainly at the dead man.

'He said he was too old for the Volkssturm. The mayor didn't believe him.'

Brandt wondered how many men like the mayor were between his father and safety. He wondered also how he was going to put a stop to this madness.

'I don't think these men are dangerous,' Brandt said. 'Do you?'

They returned his gaze, their faces grave – coming to a decision. Wessel exchanged a glance with Müller.

'No,' Müller said in a firm voice.

Wessel nodded reluctantly. Brandt nodded to the prisoners.

'You can go.'

The men looked at him in surprise before backing slowly away. Once they were away from the circle of light around the bonfire he heard them break into a run. 'Jump up. There's no need for this checkpoint this late. We'll need you fresh tomorrow. Come on.'

Müller smiled as he climbed up beside him, but Wessel looked more reserved. Brandt looked down at the dead man and wished he could have seen him buried, but they had no spades and the ground was still frozen hard.

And there wasn't any time.

86

ONE OF THE BOYS, Jünger, was on duty at the
gatehouse. He waved as they approached.

'Herr Brandt,' he said – Brandt could hear a breathless
relief. 'We were worried something had happened to you.'

'Nothing's going to happen to me anytime soon.' Brandt
spoke with a confidence he didn't feel. 'I hear we have
taken some more prisoners.'

'They're in the bunker.'

'How many?'

'Seven.'

'Seven traitors.' Wessel's voice reminded Brandt of an
angry wasp. 'And it should be ten.'

Brandt turned to look at the boy, holding his gaze until
Wessel had the good sense to look away.

'You think I'm a traitor too, Wessel?'

Wessel said nothing.

'Take over from Jünger. Maybe you need a few hours
out here to clear your head.'

'I wish to speak to the Zugführer,' Wessel said. Brandt
reached out and grabbed the back of the boy's helmet,
pushing him forwards until his head was between his legs.
He rapped the helmet twice to make his point.

'Wessel. You are a soldier now. Not a child. Behave like
one. Any more disrespect to your superiors and you will
also be seeing the inside of the bunker. Understood?'

The boy looked up at him, his eyes wet. Brandt could see
anger in the thin mouth but he could live with that.

'Understood?'

'Of course, Herr Brandt.'

'Good. You others, see to the horse and then go inside
for food. There is stew in the oven. Jünger, once you've
had yours come out here and send Wessel in.'

Wessel couldn't help but look relieved.

'Everyone needs hot food, Wessel. You as well.'

Seven men in the bunker. One of them Hubert. And the bunker's key sitting in his pocket.

'Obersturmführer Neumann asked to see you when you came in,' Jünger told him as they led the horse towards the barn. Brandt nodded his acknowledgement.

It was warm inside the entrance hall but the electricity was off. It came as no surprise. The only light came from the embers in the fireplace. He put on some kindling and more logs. There were voices coming from the dining room. Neumann. Brandt wondered why he hadn't left and how that might affect whatever the situation might be with the mayor. He would soon find out.

'Well, Brandt?' the mayor said when he entered the dining room. 'You have things to tell us, don't you?'

The mayor's cheeks were red in the candlelight. They appeared to have only recently finished eating. Three bottles – two empty and one half full – stood on the table between them and the mayor's voice was slurred. Neumann, in contrast, appeared quite sober. He waved Brandt towards them.

'Join us, Brandt.'

Neumann smiled a welcome then glanced toward the mayor before raising an eyebrow to Brandt. It felt like a warning.

'Thank you, Herr Obersturmführer,' Brandt said, sitting down. He took his time, settling himself in the chair.

'You visited the positions at the top of the valley?' the mayor asked.

He wasn't quite drunk, Brandt decided, but he was close enough as made no difference.

'Just now. They're well dug in with artillery and some tanks. I explained our situation to an army Hauptmann. He gave me written orders for you, Herr Zugführer.'

'Can he order me about, do you think? An army

Hauptmann?' Weber asked, his words slurring once again. 'Where does a Hauptmann stand in relation to a Zugführer? What do you think, Brandt? You who know everything?'

The wine seemed to have given the mayor back some of his confidence. There was a belligerence to him that didn't bode well.

'Higher, Herr Zugführer. On top of which he's Oberst Wenke's adjutant.'

'If you say so.' Weber nodded. He began to read the note aloud. 'I am instructed to keep the main road open and clear for military traffic until the enemy enters the valley. At which point I am to withdraw immediately to the established positions either at the pass or on the western side of the valley, at my discretion. It seems we are now part of Fighting Group Wenke. Who is this Wenke?'

'An army Oberst, he is gathering together whatever men and units are available as well as those which have been assigned to him. It's standard in fluid situations like this.'

'Fluid situations?'

'When we are in retreat and there is chaos.'

Weber opened his mouth to say something, then hesitated. 'I see,' he said.

'I brought back the two boys from the furthest checkpoint. Oberst Wenke's men have another not much further along the road. I thought they'd be more use here.'

The Wenke checkpoint wasn't true but the mayor couldn't know that. A silence fell in which Neumann and the mayor exchanged a look. Brandt found his mouth was dry. Neumann lifted his glass and swirled the wine to catch the candlelight.

'Did you see the Ukrainian guards on your travels this evening?'

Brandt paused before speaking, conscious that there was no breath left in his lungs. He shrugged.

'Not since I left here.'

'Strange, you must have been on the road at the same time. Weber here saw them at his checkpoint.'

'Not that strange. They probably passed me while I was talking to Hauptmann Bohm.'

'The Zugführer arrested some more men this evening, Brandt.' Neumann didn't look up from the glass of wine he held in his hand.

'So I understand. Is it necessary at this stage, Herr Zugführer? Our priority has to be to keep the road open. We shouldn't divert our efforts.'

The mayor shook his head slowly.

'These weren't ordinary prisoners, Brandt. One of them is known to me. And to you. Well known. And a partisan, I'm certain of it.'

The sweat that had gathered between Brandt's shoulder blades turned cold. Hubert. Had he told them anything?

'Who, Herr Zugführer?'

'Hubert Lensky. You look surprised. He's an old friend of Brandt's, Neumann. The fellow nearly married Brandt's sister before the war. A lucky escape for her. And Lensky's father, as it happens, works on Brandt's father's farm. The families are close. Very close indeed.'

'I haven't seen Hubert in eight years – but he never struck me as the type to end up as a partisan, Herr Zugführer.'

Brandt heard the lie in his voice. What else could he be, after all? Everything had been taken from him by men like Weber. But he needed to say something.

'That's not all, Brandt. When we brought him back here, we searched a bag he had with him. We found these.'

Weber reached inside his top pocket and pulled out four civilian identity papers. He placed them on the table like a black-jack dealer laying down a winning hand. Bobrik's black-and-white face stared up at the ceiling. Brandt said nothing.

'He must have got them from the bodies, Brandt – don't you think? Which means he must have been involved in the ambush. What other explanation could there be? Of course, you were also present at the ambush.'

Brandt's confusion wasn't feigned.

'You think I set up the ambush? Did Hubert say this?'

Neumann shook his head in the negative.

'The Pole has said nothing – even though Weber here roughed him up a bit. No, I don't think the mayor really thinks you were responsible for the ambush, Brandt. Although how the Ukrainians managed to get their hands on false civilian papers is a concern.' Neumann appeared relaxed about the situation, even while Brandt could see Weber's face was turning darker.

'And I'd like to know whether the four I've just sent off had them as well. Of course, if you had bothered to search the Pole at the checkpoint, Weber, you might have found these then and been able to ask the guards about them when they came through. They've probably deserted, of course.'

'Who is to say they have deserted?'

Brandt took advantage of the mayor's moment of confusion to reach across for Bobrik's identity card. He held it close to the candle. The quality of the forgery was poor – even a rudimentary check would pick it out as suspicious. The paper felt wrong.

'When did you arrest Hubert?' Brandt said, letting his hand drop to his side. 'Was it before or after the guards went through?'

'You're asking the questions now? Don't you think I see what you're up to? There was only one survivor from the ambush. You. And then your childhood friend shows up with papers from the dead men.' The mayor picked up the letter Brandt had brought back down the valley. 'For all we know this letter is another trap. He probably wants to lead us into another ambush.'

Neumann reached out to take the orders from Weber.

'They look genuine enough to me. Anyway, all you have to do is walk across the dam. You'll be doing that soon enough. As I recall, Brandt was reluctant to go with the Order Police – and couldn't have known about the search in advance. So I think the idea that he set up the ambush is ruled out.'

Brandt held up Bobrik's identity card.

'I have to ask again, Herr Zugführer. When did the guards pass through the checkpoint and when did you arrest Hubert?'

The mayor banged the table with the flat of his hand, knocking over his wineglass, which was fortunately empty. It rolled across the table towards Neumann.

'I'm asking the questions here,' the mayor growled. 'Me.'

Neumann righted the glass.

'Except I'd like to know the answer as well, Weber. If you don't mind?'

Neumann leaned back in his chair and linked his fingers across his chest, his gaze moving between Brandt and the mayor. He seemed to be enjoying himself now.

'They came through a few minutes after we arrested him.'

'Going in the same direction?'

'Not that it makes any difference. But yes.'

Brandt placed Bobrik's papers back on the table.

'I heard a rumour that Lensky was involved in criminal activities. Black marketing, that sort of thing. My guess is he sold these papers to them. They must have met along the road to make the exchange. These papers were unwanted.'

Neumann clapped his hands.

'There you are. I told you, Weber. A simple coincidence and a misunderstanding.'

Brandt touched the bandage that covered the side of his

head.

'I wouldn't shoot my own ear off for anyone, Herr Zugführer. And Bobrik was a friend of mine, if you remember. My own uncle died in the ambush. I helped my aunt bury him yesterday. And, as for my loyalty, in case you haven't noticed, I've already given half my body to the Fatherland. Now, do you mind if I go and get my dinner, Herr Zugführer?'

'He has a point, Weber. More than one point, as it happens.'

The mayor looked confused.

'It doesn't make sense.'

Neumann patted him on the shoulder.

'Very little makes sense when you think about it, that's what I've discovered. Bring up some more wine while you're down there. And Weber, admit you're wrong about him.'

The mayor squeezed his eyes shut, as if concentrating. He put his hands on either side of his head, squeezing hard.

'Maybe I'm wrong. Maybe I'm wrong.'

Neumann looked across to Brandt and shrugged his shoulders.

'It's a difficult time, Weber. We're all under great pressure.'

'All the same,' Weber said, placing his hands on the table, 'Lensky will be executed in the morning.' There was a stubborn jut to the mayor's chin that suggested further discussion was pointless. Not while he was in this state, anyway. Brandt pushed back his chair.

'If those are your orders, Herr Zugführer – they will be followed.'

'That's decided, then,' Neumann said. 'Now, let's get more wine and talk about happier things.'

'May I go and see him?' Brandt asked. 'Lensky? He was a friend of mine.'

The mayor seemed not to have heard, staring instead at
his splayed fingers that radiated out on the table's surface
like two puffy stars. Neumann smiled.

'I don't think that would be appropriate, Brandt,'
Neumann said. 'Do you?'

Brandt shrugged his shoulders, as if to say he couldn't
care less.

'After all,' Neumann continued, 'visiting a condemned
man will be depressing. We should be joyful this evening.'

Neumann's amusement seemed false to Brandt.

'As you say, Herr Obersturmführer.'

'Make sure you bring up the good wine, Brandt.'

Brandt nodded his agreement.

The kitchen was empty – the boys had left their bowls
and cutlery piled beside the scullery sink, still streaked with
the remnants of their meal. It looked untidy but Brandt no
longer cared. He lifted the cover from the pot and sniffed at
the stew. It smelled good and he needed to eat something.
He would sit with them upstairs and he would drink with
them and, later, when they were asleep, he would see what
could be done about Hubert. He could feel the weight of the
key to the bunker in his pocket.

In the cellar, Brandt filled a wicker basket with bottles of
wine. He didn't understand it. How could Hubert have been
so stupid as to get himself caught? Especially now, so close
to the end. He found he was breathing hard, like an athlete
who had run a race. He leant against the cellar wall for a
moment to recover. He was tired, that was all. He picked up
the basket of bottles, forcing his legs to carry his weight,
feeling how heavy his feet were.

'Herr Brandt?' Wessel was sitting at the long kitchen
table, a bowl in front of him – a spoon in his mittened
fingers.

'Yes, Wessel?'

'I thought you'd want to know. The mayor has ordered

that anyone approaching the bunker should be shot. Jünger asked him what that meant and he explained that meant anyone. Any of us. The SS Obersturmführer. And, most especially, you.'

87

IT WAS IN THE early hours of the morning that they reached the village. The place looked deserted from a distance – snow had piled up against doorways and obscured paths – but they had learned hard lessons in other villages and towns that had appeared to be uninhabited. The infantry scouts dismounted and made their way forward. They would reconnoitre before the tanks exposed themselves to narrow streets and overhanging windows.

They found no Germans – although it was as though the inhabitants had just gone out to fetch something, and might be back at any moment. In some houses the tables were set for a meal. In others the fireplaces were filled with wood and kindling, needing only a match to flame into life. The sense of calm didn't extend to every house, however. Some had been broken into, the contents ransacked. Lapshin had them park their tanks in front of the steepled church and posted sentries on the village outskirts while they waited for Headquarters to tell them what to do next.

'We'll be here for a while, with luck. So take the chance to warm up. Make some food. Have a wash, if you're so inclined.' Lapshin smiled, his teeth white in his smudged face. 'But leave the engines running – just in case. One man from each crew stays on watch with their tank. Understood?'

The house they chose hadn't even been locked – the owners had left the key in the door. They found a ham in the larder and a sack half full of potatoes. Polya lit the stove and put water on to boil. She stretched. Then scratched. They could all do with a wash.

Upstairs she could hear Avdeyev moving from room to room, looking for his souvenirs. All she wanted to do was lie down in a bed and sleep – she could barely keep her eyes open, she was so tired. But she was hungry too.

There was water in the tap and so she washed her face and hands with a piece of American soap Lapshin had found for her at Headquarters, surprised to see her own pink skin coming through the grime.

'Well, Polya?'

She turned to see Lapshin leaning against the doorway, and though he smiled at her, even in the candlelight she could see that he was just the same as she was – exhausted.

'Will we have time to sleep?' she asked.

'They may ask us to push on.' He ran his hands up and down his grime-shiny tunic. 'I thought I had some cigarettes.'

'I have some,' she said, offering him the cigarette case in her pocket as though it were her heart.

'Good girl. Thanks.'

When Avdeyev came back down he had two summer dresses slung across his arm and a pair of women's shoes.

'For Katya,' he said, smiling. 'Unless you want them, Polya?'

She imagined herself wearing the dress after the war, walking beside a riverbank – a towel under her arm – going for a swim. It was a foolish thought. She shook her head.

'Not for me, brother. Parcel them up for Katya – there's paper in the sitting room. I saw it on the desk.'

She turned away to tend to the food, rubbing a hand over her eyes to take the moistness out of them. She was just tired, that was all. Her arms ached and her back ached and her head was out of sorts. There was a comfortable chair in the corner but if she sat down in it, she'd never get up.

'You look the worse for wear, Little Polya.'

Lapshin had come to stand beside her, washing his hands in the sink then dipping down to wet his face.

'You don't look the best yourself, Comrade Senior Lieutenant.'

Lapshin scrubbed at his cheeks and chin – but he was

just moving the dirt around. She passed him the soap.

'The men won't recognize me.'

She smiled and he took it from her.

'Only a short time now, Polya, I think,' he said as he began to wash his face once more.

'Till when?'

'Till the end. All we have to do is last a little while longer. Then we can go back home – pat ourselves on the back for a job well done and forget all about it.'

'That would be nice.'

She tried to smile, but her lower lip had a mind of its own, and she could feel it curling over on itself.

The shame – a tear rolled down her cheek.

Lapshin reached over and smudged it away, his thumb gently pushing her mouth up into a smile as he did so. His brown eyes, so kind and true, looked into hers. Right down into her soul.

'We'll see this war out together, Little Polya,' he said in a low voice. 'You and me. And then we'll talk. Maybe we'll see out more than just this war? What do you say?'

She could say nothing. Except that her hand had reached up, of its own accord, and taken his. Now his fingers were wrapped around hers. She sucked at her teeth, getting some air into her chest – because if she didn't she might pass out.

'Well?'

'We'll see,' she said. She wanted to say more, a lot more – but her chest was too tight. There was no air in her for words. All she could do was try to smile – and even that not very well.

'Is there any string?' Avdeyev said, coming back into the kitchen. He stood there as they turned to look at him, their hands still entwined. He looked from one to the other and smiled – a big, hearty smile.

'Don't mind me, Comrades. I'm sure the string is out here. Somewhere.'

§

Later, a motorbike roared into the village, just as they put the food on the table, and someone began to call out for the battalion commander. Lapshin went out to see what it was about. Polya shared a glance with Avdeyev – there was no need for discussion. They began to eat as quickly as they could. Sure enough, when Lapshin came back in, his expression was grave.

'Let's eat as we go, Comrades. There's a dam that Division wants secured first thing. We're going over the hills. We have a Polish guide to show us the way.'

88

THE HAND THAT shook Brandt's shoulder was tentative. As if it expected to be punished for its transgression. He looked at his watch. Five o'clock.

'Herr Brandt?'

'What is it?'

He was awake, although he was reluctant to leave the warmth of his bed. Aside from anything else, his mouth tasted of stale red wine and his stomach felt none too good. He had stayed up until late with the mayor and Neumann, drinking, the mayor veering between melancholy and bonhomie and Neumann smirking all the while. He needed to go to the toilet. Then there was the small matter of his ear, which, it seemed, he had been lying on.

'Herr Brandt?' The young boy's voice was close to despair.

'Yes.'

'There's something you should see, Herr Brandt. Outside.'

Brandt resigned himself to his fate and opened his eyes. Fischer. His face close enough that he could feel the boy's breath on his hand. Brandt looked across the dark room to the window – it was just before dawn, a faint light marking where the curtains had been pulled closed.

'What is this something?'

'There are some men. In the lane. Four of them.'

'What are they doing?'

Brandt was sitting now – he swallowed, disorientated for a moment by the shift in position. He handed Fischer his trousers.

'It will be quicker if you hold these.'

Fischer looked at the trousers, then at Brandt's stump. He blinked, his mouth opening with surprise.

'So I can step into them.'

'Of course,' the boy said after a moment. 'I don't know who they are – the men. We didn't see them come up the lane and we were vigilant, I swear it. No one fell asleep on duty. But Jünger and I found them lying on the side of the lane just now, in the bushes.'

'Dead?'

'It looks like it. We thought we should get you before we checked.'

Which was sensible. Brandt walked over to the window, pulling back the curtain. 'What about the mayor?'

'We thought we wouldn't disturb him just yet.'

Because, after all, the mayor shot old men for nothing – who knew what he'd do to children who fell asleep on guard?

'All right, then. Hold my tunic.'

He wriggled into the jacket Fischer held open for him, bending his knees so that the boy could hold it up as high as his shoulders. He turned to examine the youngster. He seemed less frightened now – probably relieved that he hadn't been questioned more closely. Brandt smiled. Not that there was anything amusing about dead bodies lying in the lane, but the boy needed reassurance.

'Well, you might as well give me a hand tying my bootlaces, seeing as you're here.'

§

The men were lying under the low-hanging branches of a tree – their feet pointing towards the guardhouse so that it was possible to see the holes in their socks. Eight legs. Four pairs of feet. Their upper halves were hidden by the lower branches.

'Perhaps they're asleep?' Fischer asked.

Jünger nodded his agreement. The elderly trench helmet Jünger wore shadowed his eyes while most of his face was hidden by a scarf. It was as though he were staring out of a pillbox.

Brandt shrugged in response. Men didn't take their boots off to fall asleep in the snow. He was about to lean down to take a closer look when he was distracted by the sound of a beeping horn. He looked down towards the dam and saw an open truck in Wehrmacht grey, filled with what looked like wounded men, wrapped up as best they could be against the cold, passing along the road. It wasn't only the truck, there were soldiers on the road as well – marching, heads down, their field packs rounding their backs – in amongst refugees.

'They've been passing for the last three hours,' Jünger said.

Brandt wanted to ask why no one had bothered to come and tell him. If soldiers were retreating up the valley, that meant the Russians were likely close behind.

'Go down and ask them where the Russians are, will you? Find out anything you can. Quickly.'

He watched Jünger trot off before turning to Fischer, looking at his watch.

'Let's have a look at these men. Stay back here and keep me covered, just in case.'

Brandt unclipped the flap of his holster and pulled out his Volkssturm pistol – a captured Soviet revolver. It was reliable, though.

'Hello,' he said when he was close. His voice sounded uncertain, even to him. As he expected, there was no response. He wondered how many other men had woken up dead this morning, stiff in their trenches, their hands frozen tight around their rifles.

He took another three steps and, now that he was close enough and the sun was beginning to shine on the very top of the other side of the valley, he saw why they weren't answering. They weren't asleep, that was for certain, but what was worse – he recognized them.

'Go and fetch Obersturmführer Neumann, Fischer.'

§

Neumann leant down to look in at the bodies. Brandt could make out his father's beige waistcoat – stained dark red in places, thanks to Adamik's blood. Neumann's skin was pale, almost blue – his cheeks unshaven.

'What is that? On their chests? Can you see?'

Brandt pushed a branch sideways to get a better look. It was for show, however. He knew what the small nuggets that were, scattered over the men, glinting in the weak light.

'They're teeth. Gold teeth. And fillings.'

He heard Neumann swallow. A loud noise. Neumann stunk of last night's alcohol and Brandt wondered if he might be sick. It took Neumann a little while to gather himself.

'I don't remember them having gold teeth,' he said eventually. 'Not that many, anyway.'

'I think the guards must have collected them . . .' Brandt paused, choosing his next words carefully. 'From elsewhere. Perhaps that's why they were killed.'

He thought about this, wondering if he'd been responsible. Then he discounted the possibility. They were SS. The partisans would have killed them anyway.

'A message, then? Is that why they were left on the body, do you think? Is this something to do with your friend Lensky?'

'I don't know.'

It seemed the safest answer. What was more, it was true. He had no idea why the killers had gone to this effort. What purpose could it serve? Neumann grunted as he stood to his feet. He ran a hand back through his hair, then picked up a long branch, poking at the twinkling teeth scattered on the dead men's chests.

'What do you think happened to the prisoners they were escorting?'

Brandt could almost hear Neumann's mind working it through.

'I don't know, Herr Obersturmführer. With the partisans who did this, I should think. Does it matter? They're either dead or alive – there's not much we can do about either.'

Neumann stood and looked up into the forest that rose above the hut, squinting his eyes even though the sun hadn't managed to crest the hill as yet. Perhaps he was looking for partisans.

'I wonder how the bodies got here,' he said. 'The boys in the gatehouse saw nothing, you say?'

'No, but they are children, not sentries. The partisans would have been quiet.'

'Weber saw the guards at the checkpoint – the one at the far end of the reservoir – he mentioned it last night. The one you closed down. The killers must have brought them from at least that far away, if not further.'

'I don't understand it, Herr Obersturmführer.'

'Do you think they might be up there, watching us?'

'The partisans? Perhaps. They won't come down – our men are on the reservoir road now.'

Brandt pointed down the laneways at the ragged column of soldiers and civilians that was making its way as quickly as it could towards the pass. Scores of people were taking their chances and crossing the frozen reservoir. The soldiers on the dam were allowing wagons to cross now but movement was slow. There was nowhere for the wagons to go – the road on the other side was solid with traffic.

'The Russians are on the outskirts of the town. It won't be long before they break through.'

'And the dam?'

'Our engineers will blow it soon enough. When they do the water will slow the Russians down, if not send them a different way.'

'What about across the ice?'

'If the dam goes, the reservoir will go, ice and all. That's what they told me yesterday, anyway.'

Neumann shrugged, as if he'd expected nothing less.

'Best not to get caught on this side of the dam, then, I should think.' He nudged one of the dead men's legs with his foot – drawing attention to the worn trousers the corpse was wearing.

'Where do you think they got the civilian clothes, Brandt?'

There was a note of false innocence to Neumann's question. Brandt pretended to examine them, leaning down to avoid Neumann's gaze while he worked out what to say. He reached forward to touch the fabric. It was stiff with cold.

'Would you have any suggestions?'

Brandt stood up and shrugged.

'They must have broken into one of the houses. There's been looting in the village – perhaps they broke in when they went down to bury Bobrik and the others.'

They gazed at each other – Brandt determined not to blink. After what felt like half a lifetime, Neumann gave him a slow smile. There was something complicit it in and Brandt wondered what the SS man meant by it.

'That must be it. There's no other possibility, I'm sure. I'm going inside.'

'And the bodies?'

'We shouldn't leave them here – bring them in.'

Neumann turned to walk back up the lane but then he stopped and turned.

'You'd better wake the mayor. He's likely to react badly to this, I should imagine, and that may have consequences for you and your childhood friend in the bunker.'

Brandt wondered if he should reply and decided it was best not to. Instead, he kneeled down and pulled at one of the legs. It was hard to shift the dead weight of a body across the icy ground but he managed to get the first of them out from under the tree without too much difficulty. As it slid away from the others, Adamik's head fell to one side, revealing his open mouth. His angelic smile was no more. All his teeth had been broken, down to their roots, the chipped remnants a gory half circle – white splinters embedded in the dead man's blackened tongue.

They would bring the Ukrainians in but someone else could bury them. The most important thing was getting the boys ready to go. And getting the remaining prisoners out of the bunker.

89

SHE THOUGHT she was awake – but it was only in her dream that she sat looking up at the pale square of blue sky. The window that she saw there was cracked, and streaked with rain-crusted dirt. Yet despite this the blue of the sky was clean and pure. High up above her, dissecting the square, a white vapour trail disintegrated slowly. She watched, fascinated. She couldn't understand why Rachel was asking her to wake up, pushing at her shoulder.

'Good morning.'

A man's voice, speaking Polish. A rush of consciousness. The cold air on her face, the muggy smell of the other women's bodies from under the shared blankets. The stiffness in her neck from where her head had fallen forwards. She opened her eyes. Two men were standing inside the room, looking down at them.

She couldn't see the taller one's face. The window was behind him so his features were in shadow – but she could see the machine gun he carried, its stock nestling under his armpit, the barrel pointing at the ground. It must have been him who had spoken. He was the leader between the two of them. They wore red arm-bands.

'You have nothing to fear,' Joanna said, in German. She must be translating.

'Is German preferable?' the Pole said.

'More of us speak German,' Agneta answered carefully. She thought about standing up, but she felt safer here, under the blanket, the other women's warmth close around her.

'You're from the SS hut. Prisoners, yes?'

It wasn't a question – the man knew. Perhaps he understood that she couldn't see him because he moved to one side, turning his head slightly so that some of the light fell on his face. He was younger than she'd thought.

'Don't worry. You're safe with us. We'll look after you.'

Agneta realized that she, in his eyes, was a German. Even though she might have spent the last five years behind barbed-wire fences, she and the others still bore some burden for the crimes committed by their countrymen.

'I'm not German,' she said in a quiet voice. 'They took my country from me.'

He looked down at her, unsmiling.

'If you say so.'

'What do you want with us?' she asked.

'We need to move you. One of our men was captured last night. He knows you are here. He may talk.'

He must have taken her blank look as some kind of misunderstanding.

'He may be forced to talk.'

90

NEUMANN STOOD in his office. The table was bare, the filing cabinets were empty. The phone wasn't working. There was no electricity. And now the valley echoed with gunfire.

Neumann considered Brandt. Had he helped the women prisoners escape? Maybe. He didn't think he'd been behind the ambush or the death of the Ukrainians – but perhaps he had helped them plan their desertion. Lensky might have provided the papers. If he were to make a guess, Brandt had bargained with them for the prisoners. All his little kindnesses. Peichl must have been right about him, after all. He must have some decency left in him.

Wolf paced back and forth, his ears flat against his head. Every now and then the dog made a sound somewhere between a bark and a moan and looked at Neumann with pleading eyes. Neumann tried to reassure him with a smile but when he moved to stroke him, the dog padded away to a far corner and curled up there – watching him.

Anyway, what did it matter if Brandt had helped the women escape? It certainly didn't matter to Neumann. It was as Brandt had said; those that were dead now were dead and those that lived, lived – there was not much he could do about either. Perhaps, Neumann considered, everything had been predestined – the world and history one enormous machine that had whirred onwards towards this moment. Each person who had lived up until this point had been an infinitesimal, fated cog running in its settled pattern until it was time for it to be replaced by another. All part of the machine, all destined to their fate. He, certainly, had always followed the path set out for him, without much thought. And it had led him here. If Brandt had chosen to find himself a different path, wasn't that to be admired?

Over at the dam, he could see soldiers carrying more

wooden boxes from an army truck, taking them down inside the structure. He imagined the ice and water from the frozen reservoir cascading down the valley. It would be a sight to see, he thought with some regret.

He took the record from the bookcase where he'd kept it. He walked through to the drinks cabinet in the entrance hall and helped himself to a brandy. Then he wound the gramophone player up. He placed Jäger's record on the turntable. Mendelssohn.

He stood for a moment and closed his eyes, listening to the music and remembering, as if it were yesterday, that summer afternoon from long ago. How things had been in his father's house – before the first war, before Verdun, before all of this. He could hear Clara's laughter and the scent of dead roses filled his nostrils. He could feel the summer heat pushing its way in through the open doorway. So many lives had been open to him then – so many paths and opportunities that he'd spurned – all to end up here. He remembered Marguerite, the first time he'd met her. How she had smiled down at their oldest boy when he had been born. The happiness he'd felt. He drank down the brandy. It was early in the day, but this was not an ordinary day. He picked up the half-empty bottle.

He left the door to his office open so he could hear the music, removed his pistol from its holster and placed it on the table's surface. He could hear the sporadic rumble and popping of the fighting as it moved closer. It had come so quickly, in the end. He had thought there would be more time.

Neumann looked at the pistol – such a small thing, really. If you didn't know what it was for – if you came from the past – you might have no idea. You might admire it as an object, if you didn't know what it could do. He ran his finger over the rough texture of its grip, along the straight smoothness of its barrel.

He remembered a drunken dinner over the summer – in the very early hours of the morning, sitting with two of the doctors, away from the more general conversation. Poison, they'd agreed, was a dirty business and hanging took too long and wasn't certain. Shooting was best. The side of the head was unreliable, the doctor with the gapped teeth and the dark complexion had said – his blue eyes moist. The danger came from a reflexive turning away from the bullet – survival became a distinct possibility. The tall doctor with the thinning blonde hair and the cherubic cheeks had agreed – the mouth was far more reliable. The barrel placed right inside, so that the sight pushed against the top of your mouth and the barrel lay along your tongue. Infallible, the doctors had agreed, and once the trigger was pressed – there could be no pain. Death would be instantaneous. The cleanest method, beyond doubt, from a clinical point of view, was a bullet fired into the mouth.

He'd known then, when the doctors had taken to discussing methods of inflicting death upon themselves instead of others, that events had come full circle. He'd known long before, of course, that things must come to this – but here was the final confirmation. And he had listened to them, and agreed – and determined to do as they advised.

He filled his glass once more and drank it down in one go, coughing as the alcohol burned. He picked up the gun and pushed the muzzle inside his mouth – it tasted of gun oil and metal.

Outside, in the hut, underneath the sound of the music, he heard the front door opening – a long squeal. He didn't want to be interrupted – but he had some time. He closed his eyes. The memories that came to him now, as he'd known they would, were from the train. He remembered the old man. He could smell the blood, the rot and excrement from the wagons. He could hear the screams. He knew if he opened his eyes once again he would see the man standing there in front of his desk, regarding him expectantly. He mustn't disappoint him.

He listened to the music, breathed in the scent of dead roses once again, heard Clara's laughter and the scream of bayoneted children – and pressed the trigger.

91

THE VALLEY, usually so quiet, now reverberated with the sounds of artillery. A young partisan, a red armband pinching the sleeve of his worn brown overcoat, led them along a path through the forest. They had been given similar armbands and Agneta didn't like them – she felt they marked them out. But then so did their prison uniforms and their short-cropped hair.

'Where are you taking us?' Joanna asked him.

The boy turned to them – he looked as though he were going to a football match. He carried a large revolver that he switched from hand to hand as he walked. Agneta wondered if it was heavy for him.

'One of the higher meadows – not far now. You'll be out of the way of things there.'

A flight of aeroplanes flew overhead so low they could feel the wind from their passing. The sounds of explosions and cannon fire followed soon afterwards from the direction they had flown in. The boy stopped to look up at the sky, as if he could tell from the empty space the planes had left behind what was happening elsewhere.

'They're giving the Germans hell,' he said. 'It will all be over soon.'

He laughed and Agneta understood. It was terrifying – yes – but after years of terror, that didn't seem to matter so much. The prospect of change was the exhilarating thing.

And they, the women, had survived – even if the fear she had suppressed for so long made her want to lie down and never get up again. But their survival had been due to Brandt and he was down in the valley. Yet she hadn't even thanked him, and she had things she had yet to say to him.

When they reached the edge of the forest, the boy motioned them to stay back while he went ahead. They stood in a rough circle, looking at the ground rather than each other. She noticed they were all leaning forward, almost crouching. The noise of the guns, even though not close, was unsettling. It was instinctive to want to make oneself smaller – less of a target. None of them spoke.

'Come, come.' The boy was back. 'Quickly,' he said as he led them out of the trees, towards a small farmhouse that stood some forty metres distant. Their clogs dragged through the snow and she felt herself out of breath and not from the running. It was the thought that Brandt might, even now, be dead. And she hadn't spoken to him.

Just as they reached the house there came the sound of crashing trees and rolling metal. A white tank, bedecked with infantry in camouflage overalls, poked its nose out of the forest on the other side of the field. There was Cyrillic writing on its turret – 'To Berlin'.

'The Russians,' the boy said, laughing. 'They came through the forest.'

The infantry spilled off the tank and out onto the long field, and when the tank rolled forward others followed, lining up on either side of it, disgorging more soldiers who raced ahead, as if creating a protective screen around the tanks. It was only moments before a group approached them, shouting in Russian at the boy – who called back, pointing to his armband and then to the women, explaining them perhaps. One of the soldiers ran back to the tanks and returned with a tank officer, his uniform shining with ingrained dirt but his face pink as a pig's bottom. A good-looking man, who smiled at them. Another tanker followed and she had to look twice – a woman – and there was another man in civilian clothing, also with a red armband.

The first tanker carried a map, which he showed to the boy, who began to talk quickly – the older Pole who had accompanied the tankers joining in.

Agneta turned to the others and found that they were sitting on the low wall in front of the house, their heads in their hands. She could hear the sounds of their sobbing. Yet, while the other women had been overwhelmed by emotion, she felt nothing – no relief, no exultation, only concern for the things she hadn't said to Brandt. The female tanker came towards her, pointing at Agneta's shaved head, then at the other women.

'Camp?' she asked.

'Camp,' she answered.

She was surprised to be folded in the woman's arms, the earthy ripe smell of her filling her nostrils, their cheeks were pushed tight together and the tanker's tears made Agneta's skin wet. But still Agneta felt numb – as if the tears and the embrace and the joy were being experienced by someone else.

She pushed the woman away as politely as she could and stood back.

'Polya,' the woman said, pointing at her chest. 'Polya.'

'Agneta,' she said and pointed at herself.

Over the woman's shoulder she caught sight of the tall man who had come into the shed where they'd been hiding. He was standing beside Paul Brandt's sister, who met her gaze and nodded. Agneta smiled at the Russian woman and walked towards Brandt's sister – who walked towards her in turn.

92

BRANDT STOOD looking down at Neumann. The SS man's body was lying on the floor behind the desk. One of the window panes behind the chair he'd fallen from was broken and blood had spattered the intact glass around the hole the bullet had left. Neumann's dog lay across his master's corpse, whimpering. Brandt picked up the open bottle of brandy and took a swig, the alcohol raw enough to scrape his mind clear for a moment. Another problem. Another corpse. The dead bodies were piling up at the hut and he wondered when it would end.

'I heard a gunshot.'

The mayor, wearing a wrinkled collarless shirt – his trousers suspended from braces that accentuated his gut and cut into his shoulder fat, stood in the doorway. His unwashed, sleepy hair sloped to the right, turbulent and stiff. A pistol hung from one hand, while the other rubbed the hangover from his eyes.

'Neumann shot himself.'

'Neumann?'

Brandt offered him the bottle of brandy but the mayor shook his head. Brandt glanced out of the window. Soldiers and civilians were moving quickly across the dam now and, as he watched, a cart that had become stuck was heaved over the side onto the ice, horse and all – leaving only a ragged hole to mark where it had fallen.

'The Russians are in the town. Which must mean they will be coming up this side of the valley soon. If they aren't already. I've told the boys to be ready in five minutes.'

'I give the orders here,' the mayor said, his eyes still fixed on Neumann's lifeless body.

'The Ukrainian guards showed up an hour ago,' Brandt said, deciding on a different tack.

'They did? Where?'

'Outside the front gate. Dead. Whoever killed them smashed their teeth then cut their throats.'

'My God.' The mayor's mouth, Brandt was pleased to see, hung open. His teeth uneven and, so far, intact.

'They were carrying gold fillings and teeth – from the camp. We found them scattered over the bodies.'

'God in Heaven,' the mayor whispered.

'We have orders, Herr Zugführer. Retreat across the dam. Join Oberst Wenke's force.'

The mayor said nothing in response.

'Or stay here and have your teeth broken in and your throat slit. I'm taking the boys across in five minutes.'

Brandt pushed past the mayor, who offered him no resistance.

93

'HERR BRANDT?' A breathless voice was calling for him
outside. Wessel. He'd sent him down to the dam with
orders to alert them to any change in the army's plans. And
to keep him out of the way.

'In here,' he called out, and the boy duly appeared
framed in the kitchen's doorway.

'They're going to blow it up,' he said, as if Christmas
had unexpectedly come around for a second time.

'Who says and when?'

'The army Leutnant.' Wessel paused for breath; he must
have run the whole way.

'Half an hour; quicker if the Russians come.'

'We leave in two minutes. Go and get your pack.'

Wessel hesitated, as if about to ask a question.

'Immediately, Wessel. This isn't an exercise.'

Wessel ran out, shouting to the others. Brandt put his
own rucksack on and followed him. As he crossed the yard
he passed the Ukrainians lying in a row beside the barn,
covered with tarpaulin. There wasn't time to do anything
more for them. He took the key to the bunker from his
pocket and inserted in the lock. It needed all his strength to
turn it but eventually the bunker door squealed open.
Brandt swallowed and stepped in. Frightened faces
surrounded him. He nodded to Hubert.

'The Russians will be here soon – the dam will be blown
in half an hour. If you want to avoid them, best to be on the
other side. Or you can stay here, if you want,' he said to the
men. 'The door's open. Wait until we've gone.'

Hubert looked at him blankly. Brandt reached inside his
pocket and handed him Jäger's pistol.

'Weber may still be around. Shoot first if he comes in.
Look after Monika and tell Agneta I mean to have that cup
of coffee with her when all of this is over.'

Outside, he pushed the door so it would seem as though it were closed, then trotted towards the front gate. The boys were gathered with their packs and weapons. Brandt counted them – one missing. Wessel.

He turned to see Wessel sprinting towards them.

'Right, gentlemen. We are ordered to the other side of the dam. We'll see Zugführer Weber there, no doubt.'

He saw Wessel's sly glance towards the bunker, his mouth half open. He caught his gaze and held it.

'Wessel.'

'Herr Brandt?'

'There will be plenty of Russians to kill today. But not if you're on this side of the reservoir.'

94

SHE COULDN'T see the path ahead of them, it was so steep, but Lapshin's feet on her shoulder pushed her, and the tank, forward. At one stage, Galechka's nose dropped with a lurch and Polya had to brace with her legs to stop herself tumbling onto the levers. The tank slid down the frozen soil and loose snow until her tracks bit and Polya managed to slow the descent – pulling at the levers, this way and that – avoiding the larger trees when she could, rolling them down when she couldn't. Still upright, still moving.

The path hadn't been designed for a column of tanks, that was for certain – it was little more than a narrow track – and Galechka's progress was winding and sporadic. At times Polya had to turn Galechka through forty-five degrees, the tank's tracks spinning sideways on the slope and Polya imagining the tank rolling sideways through the forest, the turret crushing flat as her momentum grew. Lapshin was sitting in the turret. He would die, almost certainly, as would the partisans and scouts that clung to the tank's sides.

'I'd rather charge a battery of 88s than come down here again.' Avdeyev's voice sounded tinny and distant in her helmet's headphones, although he was leaning across to help her with the levers and his shoulder rested against hers.

'We're close, Comrades – and we'll catch the fascists napping when we get there. Mark my words.'

Even with Avdeyev's help, Polya could feel every sinew in her arms and shoulders burning. She could smell her own fear.

'The worst is over,' Lapshin's voice reassured them.

She hoped so – and remembering the warmth of Lapshin's rough fingers wrapped around hers gave her strength. She imagined what his stubble would feel like under her lips. The pain in her shoulders receded – her arms no longer trembled with the strain.

And he was right, the path was no longer as steep and had even widened. She nudged Avdeyev and he went back to his machine gun. There was a clearing ahead. A crucifix stood to its right, the bearded Christ covered by a snow-capped wooden roof. He looked straight at her, his eyes full of pity.

No Germans to be seen.

'Straight through, Polya. Let's pick up some speed now. The guide says it's only a hundred metres further, then hard left and fast, fast, fast along the road. Keep your eyes peeled, gunners.'

She could hear the scouts and the Poles repositioning themselves on the tank's hull above her – they must have been tucked in behind the turret on the descent, being whipped and torn at by the trees and bushes. It sounded as though they were stamping their feet with approval at Galechka's achievement. Polya felt happiness swelling her like a balloon. She would float up to the roof, if she wasn't careful.

And up ahead she could see the white expanse of the valley's floor.

And the frozen reservoir.

95

BRANDT HADN'T run like this since before his injury, and it was hard. He was holding the boys back. They ducked as planes flew overhead, but the Soviets were intent on whatever was happening further down the valley and didn't bother them.

Brandt looked ahead to the dam. It was only a few hundred metres away – people, like them, were running towards it, except for one soldier who was walking backwards towards the far side, carrying a drum of wire which he played out. The detonation cable. It wouldn't be long now.

'Brandt. Stop.'

He turned to see the mayor running after them, a pistol in his hand – wearing that ridiculous uniform. It turned out Weber was a faster runner than he was. The mayor would catch him. Brandt stopped and the boys slid to a halt around him. Confused. In the moment of silence, he heard them. He couldn't see the T34s, but he knew they were there. The memory of that noise, their crunching, clattering tracks and the deep roar of their diesel engines, had woken him up more than once in the middle of the night, his sheets twisted and damp with sweat, his heart racing.

'Tanks. Run to the dam, all of you. As quick as you can.'

The boys hesitated for an instant.

'If you're still here in two seconds, I'll shoot you myself.'

They ran. A tumble of grey helmets and greatcoats sprinting towards safety.

'Tell them the Russians are right behind you,' he called after them, then turned to face the mayor.

Weber slowed, lifting his pistol to aim at him. His chest was heaving – his grey eyes bleary with dull anger.

'Brandt,' he said, and paused to take another breath.

Behind the mayor, Brandt saw the familiar shape of a T34 come down out of the forest, turning towards them – accelerating. Soldiers clinging to its side, seeing the two Germans on the road ahead and pointing their weapons. Brandt dived into the trees at the side of the road as bullets cracked above his head. He lay perfectly still where he fell, his face in the snow.

Cannon fire now. From the German side. Explosions all around him. The tank had been hit, the only soldiers that clung to its side now were dead. He pushed himself to his feet, saw the mayor lying motionless in the road and ran for his life towards the dam.

96

'COME ON, come on.'

He could hear the soldiers shouting encouragement. The first of the boys were on the dam, their heads and shoulders bobbing above the parapet as they ran towards the other side. Behind him there was a burst of machine-gun fire and the sound of more tanks breaking their way through the forest. He didn't stop running. He was past the Volkssturm's homemade pillbox now and the snow-filled tank traps, and onto the dam itself, his nailed boots rattling on the concrete walkway. Alongside him others were running but his vision had tunnelled so that all he could see was the army officer, his eyes willing him on. Behind him the Russian tanks were louder than ever. He heard the boom of a cannon – saw the shell send up a geyser of snow and ice out on the reservoir – and then the ripping noise of machine guns and the pitter-patter of the bullets as they impacted. But he was nearly there now. Another few metres. The flash and roar of cannons and machine guns on the German side of the dam – bullets and shells whistling and cracking past him from every direction.

And then he was flying, accelerating towards the cluster of soldiers waiting in the woods, his gaze meeting that of a round-eyed soldier, his hands on the depressed plunger of a black detonator – a huge force pushing Brandt through the air until he landed on the snow, the breath knocked out of him, dazed by the blast.

They'd blown the dam.

But he was on the other side. He was alive.

97

SHE WAS LYING in a ditch – her tank helmet forward over her eyes. She pushed it back, taking stock of her surroundings. How she had managed to get out of the tank, she didn't know. She looked along the road to where Galechka stood, smoke pouring from her open hatches and turret. Lapshin. Lapshin had dragged her out.

'Is everyone all right?' Lapshin asked, shouting because there was so much noise.

Polya lifted her hand, which was all she could do. She couldn't speak.

'Polya?'

Lapshin crawled along the ditch towards her on his elbows. She could see a dead man hanging from a branch above her, his clothes on fire, swaying as if being pushed by a breeze. She thought it might be the guide.

'I don't think I can walk,' she managed to say. Her foot was angled strangely, although it didn't hurt. Lapshin's left cheek was red and blistered and he'd lost most of the hair on his head – but he was alive. He checked her over, opening her tunic, looking for a wound. She could hear swearing close by and glanced over to see Avdeyev putting a tourniquet on Vitsin's mangled leg.

'She's going to go at any moment,' Avdeyev said. 'We need to move back.'

At first Polya thought he must be talking about her. She was conscious now that there were other men lying along the shallow ditch, their blood staining the snow that filled it red. The scouts that had been on top of the tank – some dead, some alive. She felt something hit her face, small and sharp. A splinter from where bullets were hitting the trees around them. The burning corpse was knocked off his branch by one and fell onto the snow a few metres away.

'Let's take Polya first. Quick now.'

She felt Avdeyev take her under her shoulders and Lapshin took her legs, smiling down at her reassuringly. They stumbled and slipped their way up into the forest until they found a fallen tree. They placed her gently behind it, the solid trunk protecting her. It seemed far quieter in here. She looked around for them but she was on her own.

She waited. She wondered what would happen if they couldn't come back. What if they were killed? What would she do then?

But here they were. Vitsin and his mangled leg swaying between them. Other men were coming up through the trees now – she recognized a man from one of the other tanks and an infantry sergeant.

'We're safe here,' Lapshin said.

And then the explosion came, the force blowing through the forest like a storm.

'I'm afraid Galechka is gone,' Lapshin said. 'Don't take it hard, Little Polya.'

'Poor Galechka,' she said, feeling dazed. She had built Galechka, driven her and named her. For her mother. 'She always did her best for me. And when they took her away from me, she set me on a path to you.'

Lapshin squeezed her shoulder gently.

'We'll get you another one. Although, who knows, maybe we've done enough. Maybe they'll let us spend some time in hospital. And maybe, by the time we get out, it will all be over and we can all go home.'

Polya smiled – amused that Lapshin thought she'd been talking about the tank.

98

FISCHER AND MÜLLER ran forward to pick him up, dragging him with them into the trees. He was conscious of bullets whipping around them but they made it – the boys pulling him until they came to a stop behind a pile of logs, collapsing into the snow.

At first he thought the roaring in his ears must have been caused by the explosion – but then he realized it was the dam. He peeked over the logs and saw water pouring out of a wide crack in its curved wall and watched the concrete crumble away from the flow, ever larger boulders being pushed out by ever more water.

With a tremendous crash, half of the dam's rim collapsed forward, a wall of water and ice cascading after it. The noise was incredible. On the other side of the valley he saw the T34s retreating – anti-tank shells exploding around them. Bodies were scattered in the snow on the road and in the fields. He couldn't tell whether they were Russian or German.

Brandt stood – conscious that the Leutnant was shouting something to him, a smile on his face. But even though the officer was standing no more than a matter of centimetres away from him – he could hear nothing. The noise was like the end of the world.

He imagined the water surging down through the valley, along the river's course – until it reached the camp. He imagined the water cleansing the valley of the last five years, stripping the earth back to the rock beneath.

'Time to go,' he said – but no one could hear him. He had to push the boys into movement.

There was a flash of orange as a tank went up in flames on the other side of the dam. He pushed the youngsters up the slope, deeper into the forest. Away from the bullets and the shells and mess they left behind them. After a hundred metres or so he gathered the boys together, counted them off and checked them over. All accounted for. All in one piece.

The sound of the battle receded as they walked up through the trees.

99

THE WAITER saw him coming across the square, the folded sleeve of his jacket carried like a shield against the military traffic that sped along the Ringstrasse. It was quiet in the cafe – Tuesdays were always quiet. In fact, the only thing of note that ever happened on a Tuesday was the arrival, so punctually you could set your watch by him, of the one-armed man.

At a quarter to four he would sit down at the same table in the back room – the waiter made sure it was free, it was the least he could do. The waiter would let him look at the coffee list on the table for a minute or two and then approach. They had a routine now – after six months of this.

'Good afternoon, sir,' the waiter said.

'Any message for me?'

'None, I'm sorry.'

And he was. He didn't know who the man was waiting for but it must be someone for whom he cared deeply. And everyone had lost someone in the chaos. It wasn't as bad here as elsewhere, of course. But still.

'It's not your fault. A coffee, please.'

'Of course. Straight away.'

Perhaps the man smiled, it was difficult to tell, and a party of American officers were calling loudly for him, so the waiter had to turn away and make sure they were happy. It was best for everyone if the Americans were kept happy. And the British. And the French. And the Russians. There might be trouble if they weren't – and no one wanted trouble these days. Everyone had had enough of trouble.

When the waiter brought him his coffee the one-armed man accepted it with a nod. He would sit and watch it until four. Then he would drink it. And then, at four fifteen he would leave. It was always the same.

He was serving the Americans when a woman entered the room. Her hair was short, and completely white – even though she seemed too young for that. She was thin, her cheekbones sharp. She was almost beautiful but it was hard to be sure. Perhaps her sadness made her seem so.

She stood for a moment, looking around the cafe. She ignored the Americans – and then her gaze fell on the one-armed man. The sight of him seemed to fix her to the spot, as though, if she even breathed, she would lose a moment that shouldn't be lost. Even the Americans stopped talking and watched her. The one-armed man hadn't seen her, his head was bent forward looking at the table in front of him. The waiter watched the white-haired woman approach the one-armed man. She took the empty seat beside him and reached for the man's hand. She squeezed it. The man didn't move – nothing about him changed – and so she leant forward to put herself in his line of sight.

Then she kissed him.

The waiter walked straight through to the kitchen, ignoring the Americans. They could wait one minute. He stood inside the doorway and, when one of the other waiters asked him what was wrong – why he was crying – he could say nothing in response.

He was still soft, that was all. Even after everything. And that was good.

Author's Note

Sometime in 1945 an SS officer called Karl Höcker put together an album of photographs documenting his service in what was then the German Reichsgau, or province, of Upper Silesia. For sixty years the photographs disappeared until, in 2005, they were acquired by the United States Holocaust Memorial Museum.

At first glance the images the album contains might be considered innocuous – groups of ordinary people, albeit many in SS uniforms, enjoying themselves. There are photographs of men and women picking berries in the woods, relaxing on sun loungers, having dinner together and even lighting the candles on a Christmas tree. But these aren't innocent images – Karl Höcker was adjutant to the last Commandant of Auschwitz, Richard Baer, from May 1944 until the Russians liberated the camp in January 1945, and these photographs were taken during a period when Auschwitz was at its most lethal. Many of the people in the photographs, happy and smiling, are among the worst mass murderers in history – including Josef Mengele, Rudolf Höss and, of course, Richard Baer.

Perhaps the photographs' ordinariness derives from the fact that few of them are taken in the environs of Auschwitz – or not the Auschwitz we know. Many of the pictures seem to have been taken at a rest hut near a small village called Porabka, about twenty kilometres away, where Höcker must have gone quite often. It was staffed by a handful of female prisoners who never appear in the photographs, which instead concentrate on the hut's idyllic location and the apparently pleasant atmosphere. The hut itself was demolished a few years ago – but a house apparently once owned by Rudolf Höss, the first Commandant of Auschwitz, still stands not far away. This novel is set in a fictional version of that rest hut – in fact, none of the characters or places in this novel existed as they are described, although, of course, they often echo real people and real history.

I found two of Höcker's photographs particularly interesting – one of Höcker lighting the candles on a Christmas tree in

December 1944, and another of him, looking cold and unhappy, at a game shoot in early January 1945. Both images are replicated in scenes in the novel. The images are interesting because the Red Army crossed the Vistula River on 12 January, a few days later. The Soviet attack overwhelmed the German defenders, advancing hundreds of kilometres in a few days and reaching Auschwitz and the rest hut on 27 January. The photographs suggest, to me anyway, that Höcker was aware of the imminent Soviet advance. It also seems likely that Höcker, a bank clerk before the war, was probably considering the consequences of his involvement in the administration of several of the most notorious concentration camps, culminating in Auschwitz itself.

It wasn't only Höcker who was aware that the end of the war would result in a terrible reckoning. The part of Upper Silesia where Auschwitz and the Porabka rest hut are located had been part of the Austro-Hungarian Empire, Poland and then Nazi Germany within a period of not much more than twenty years. Before 1939, the area contained a mixed population of mainly Poles and Germans, although other substantial ethnic minorities existed, including Jews. German, and Jewish, settlement in the area stretched back to the early Middle Ages and beyond. After

1939, the region was incorporated into the Reich and Aryanized – with much of the non-German population forcibly removed and the Jews being sent, eventually, to Auschwitz. After the war, the German population was in turn evicted, and by 1949 very few remained, ending a history of German settlement that stretched back at least seven hundred years.

After the war. Karl Höcker was arrested and spent eighteen months in a prisoner of war camp before being released. He returned to his old job with the same bank he'd been employed by before the war. In 1952 he turned himself in for denazification and was sentenced to nine months in prison for membership of the SS, but, because of a 1954 amnesty law, didn't serve a single day. In the 1960s, however, Höcker was sentenced to seven years for aiding and abetting the murder of one thousand people. On his release he was, yet again, given his old job back, at the same bank, working there until his retirement.

These are some of the most useful and thought provoking of the many works of non-fiction I read while researching *The Constant Soldier*:

Hannah Arendt. *Eichmann in Jerusalem: A Report on the Banality of Evil. Faber, 1963.*

Christopher Browning. *Ordinary Men: Reserve Police Battalion 101 and the Final Solution in Poland. Harper Collins, 1992.*

Artem Drabkin and Oleg Sheremet. *The T34 in Action.* Leo Cooper Ltd, 2006.

Mary Fulbrook. *A Small Town Near Auschwitz: Ordinary Nazis and the Holocaust. Oxford University Press, 2012.*

Karl Hoess. *Commandant of Auschwitz: The Autobiography of Karl Hoess. Weidenfeld and Nicolson, 1959.*

Ian Kershaw. *The End: Germany, 1944 – 45.* Penguin, 2011.

Keith Lowe. *Savage Continent: Europe in the Aftermath of World War II. Viking, 2012.*

Sönke Neitzel and Harald Welzer. Soldaten – On Fighting, Killing and Dying: The Secret Second World War Tapes of German POWs. Simon and Schuster, 2012.

Alexandra Richie. Warsaw 1944: Hitler, Himmler and the Crushing of a City. William Collins, 2014.

Duncan Rogers and Sarah Williams. On the Bloody Road to Berlin: Frontline Accounts from North-West Europe & the Eastern Front, 1944–45. Helion, 2005.

Gitta Sereny. Into that Darkness: From Mercy Killing to Mass Murder.

André Deutsch Ltd, 1974.

Robert Jan Van Pelt and Debórah Dwork. *Auschwitz – 1270 to the Present*. W. W. Norton & Co., 1996.

I would like to thank John Delaney of the Imperial War Museum for clarifying some key points about T34s, and the United States Holocaust Memorial Museum for allowing me to use some of the photographs from the Höcker album – in this book and elsewhere – as well as pointing me in the right direction when researching this novel. Ed Murray and Peter Ride were careful and helpful readers of early drafts of *The Constant Soldier* – their enthusiasm was generous and reassuring.

About the author

William Ryan's Moscow Noir series – *The Holy Thief*, *The Bloody Meadow* and *The Twelfth Department* – set in 1930s Stalinist Russia, has been shortlisted for the Theakston's Crime Novel of the Year Award, the CWA New Blood Dagger, the Irish Fiction Award, the Ireland AM Irish Crime Novel of the Year Award and the CWA Ellis Peters Historical Dagger Award. His standalone novel, *The Constant Soldier*, was shortlisted for The Irish Crime Novel of the Year, The CWA Steel Dagger and the HWA Historical Fiction Gold Crown. As W.C. Ryan *A House of Ghosts* was shortlisted for the Irish Crime Novel of the Year. *The Winter Guest* was published in January 2022.

Discover more at
facebook.com/WilliamRyanAuthor
www.william-ryan.com
@WilliamRyan_

Also by William Ryan

The Moscow Noir Series
THE HOLY THIEF
THE BLOODY MEADOW
THE TWELFTH DEPARTMENT

As W.C. Ryan
A HOUSE OF GHOSTS
THE WINTER GUEST

Printed in Great Britain
by Amazon

22491716R00239